STILL WATERS

STILL WATERS

A Quin and Morgan Mystery

John Moss

A Castle Street Mystery

DUNDURN PRESS
TORONTO

Editor: Michael Carroll
Design: Jennifer Scott
Printer: Webcom

Library and Archives Canada Cataloguing in Publication

Moss, John, 1940-
    Still waters / John Moss.

ISBN 978-1-55002-790-7

    I. TITLE.

PS8576.O7863S84 2008   C813'.6   C2008-900691-7

1   2   3   4   5   12   11   10   09   08

ONTARIO ARTS COUNCIL
CONSEIL DES ARTS DE L'ONTARIO

We acknowledge the support of **The Canada Council for the Arts** and the **Ontario Arts Council** for our publishing program. We also acknowledge the financial support of the **Government of Canada** through the **Book Publishing Industry Development Program** and **The Association for the Export of Canadian Books**, and the **Government of Ontario** through the **Ontario Book Publishers Tax Credit** program, and the **Ontario Media Development Corporation**.

Care has been taken to trace the ownership of copyright material used in this book. The author and the publisher welcome any information enabling them to rectify any references or credits in subsequent editions.

J. Kirk Howard, President

Printed and bound in Canada.
www.dundurn.com

Dundurn Press
3 Church Street, Suite 500
Toronto, Ontario, Canada
M5E 1M2

Gazelle Book Services Limited
White Cross Mills
High Town, Lancaster, England
LA1 4XS

Dundurn Press
2250 Military Road
Tonawanda, NY
U.S.A. 14150

For Bev, as always,

For Tobi Kozakewich,

For Bea and Julie and Laura,

For Margaret Atwood,
whose wicked candour was taken to heart,

And for Morgan and Miranda,
who are real, as only fiction can be.

1

Water Weavers

The dead man with comb-over hair fanning away from his skull was floating face down in the fish pond. Although still unidentified, he was appropriately dressed for a Rosedale garden. Another pond, closer to the ravine, settled into the landscape as if a ground depression had been filled with primordial sludge. Windows in the large house looming over the scene were empty, the curtains half-drawn. Aside from the police, there was no one around, not a gardener, no family, no maid. Most houses in this part of Toronto's Rosedale had domestic help. At 7:15 each weekday morning women of colour spread out from the subway station, through the tree-lined streets, along the red brick sidewalks, and into the private worlds of the gentry by blood and by money. An hour later pickups arrived with Dutch names on the sides, carrying men wielding rakes and mowers, and in winter, shovels and buckets of sand and salt. By now the workers had gone home, the owners had returned, children had changed out of school uniforms and were doing homework, and prepared dinners had been taken from refrigerators. It was quiet in Rosedale in the early evening in Indian summer. But it was preternaturally quiet in this garden, even with all the police activity. In the unseasonable heat, among dappled shadows, it was like being underwater.

Miranda Quin knelt against the limestone parapet. As the body swung by, she reached out to draw it closer.

"Don't touch him!" David Morgan, Miranda's partner, said.

"I wasn't. I can't see his face."

She prodded the dead man's shoulder until his profile lolled into view, washed pale and streaked with light. There was nothing about his bland features to connect with, but death made his face seem familiar. As he drifted across her reflection, Miranda flinched. It wasn't the intimation of her own mortality — she had a working relationship with death — but something inexplicable, like vertigo, seemed to rise inside her. A mixture of horror and panic, strangely tempered by a flutter of relief, all held in check by the need to sort out her feelings before revealing them.

Morgan stared into the depths of the pool. He was captivated by the fish weaving the water with eerie striations of light. The body on the surface was a minor distraction — not to the fish playing in the dead man's shadow — but to Morgan, whose current enthusiasm was imported koi. "Japanese," he murmured. "From Niigata."

"Caucasian," Miranda responded. "From Rosedale."

"Ochiba Shigura," said Morgan. "The big one near his ear."

Perhaps it was, she thought.

"Ochiba Shigura," he repeated. He had never before said these words out loud. "It means 'Autumn leaves falling on still water, I am sad.'" He paused. "They know this guy. That one's a Utsuri. What about you?"

"What? Know him? Why would I?" She surprised them both that she found his question invasive.

Morgan shrugged. "It's a folly." He took in the entire garden with a sweeping glance. "This guy spared no expense to make it look natural."

"There's nothing natural about gardens," Miranda declared. Were she not preoccupied by the gnawing within, they might have wandered into a discussion about the vanities of landscape architecture. Instead, she forced herself to focus on the corpse. She bent closer and felt a surge of revulsion.

There were no visible wounds.

She looked back at Morgan through a veil of shoulder-length hair. "You've been studying fish?"

"Koi," he clarified. "I've been reading."

"Good timing."

His personality and looks coincided, she thought. Unkempt, tousled. Features bold enough to cast shadows. Dark eyes, highlights when he smiled, sometimes exposing, more often concealing. Good body, tall, lean but not lanky. Good hair, all there. Fiercely intelligent.

They had made love once but preferred to be friends.

"Look at them," he said. "They're disturbingly beautiful ..."

"To us or each other? They're carp. Genetically manipulated scavengers." She rocked back onto her feet, grasping his arm to pull herself upright.

"Expensive carp."

She envied his esoteric diversions. Persian tribal carpets, Ontario country furniture, vintage Bordeaux, now Japanese fish. She suspected he could evade himself endlessly. After more than a decade working murders together, she wasn't sure why.

He hadn't noticed her suppressed anxiety. That pleased her. It also annoyed her. She tried to imagine her bathtub. She usually had showers. "Morgan," she announced as if it were a point of contention, "water moves counter-clockwise."

"Not in Australia."

She extended an open hand toward the corpse. As he moved slowly around the pool, the dead man seemed to rotate on an unseen axis.

"He's turning the wrong way," said Morgan.

"Exactly. And he's floating."

"Yes he is. Very postmodern — he's part of the garden design."

"He's dead."

"Dead's easy, dying is hard."

She couldn't tell from the sun glinting in his eyes whether he was being thoughtful or quoting Oscar Wilde. Or Dashiell Hammett.

"Not that hard," she said. "He was probably unconscious when he entered the water. Otherwise he'd be on the bottom."

"I knew a kid in grade one. He used to scare hell out of Miss Moore by holding his breath till he fainted."

"You remember your teacher's name?"

"And the kid's — Billy DeBrusk. He died in Kingston."

"Maximum Security or Collins Bay?"

"He was an accountant. Secondary drowning in a triathlon. His lungs flooded a day after the race, filled with bodily fluids in his sleep. He got kicked in the swim."

"I didn't know you could drown in bed." She paused. "Did he win?"

Morgan loved the way her mind worked, convinced it was in complementary opposition to his own, which needed channels to contain the discursive energy. He thought a lot about his own mind. It was a place to visit and explore. It wasn't where he lived.

"Virginia Woolf filled her pockets with stones before she walked into the Thames," said Miranda. "That way, it was out of her hands. Like diving from the Bloor Street Viaduct. You commit, then you wait. Death happens. It's not your fault."

"She drowned in the River Ouse in Sussex, not the Thames. She left a note to her husband, saying, 'You have given me the greatest possible happiness.' Do you think you could drown yourself?"

This bleak sense of dread inside her, was that what it felt like? But there was also the unsettling sensation of release. Release tinged oddly with guilt. *No, I could not.*

"Whoever called it in —" Morgan began.

"Left him floating. Must have known he was already dead."

"How?"

"Perhaps patience."

There was something bothering her, he thought. Macabre humour was either a mask or a masquerade. His own humour ran more to wordplay and irony.

"You sure you don't know him," he said. Stolid silence. "It could have been called in by the person who killed him."

"That's an idea," she said, indicating by her tone she didn't consider it likely.

They contemplated the pool; the sun was low in the sky, so there was little reflection. It was difficult to separate the surface from the depths, except close to the floating corpse, and out near the centre where twin columns of fine bubbles mushroomed from the darkness below.

"There has to be a pump somewhere processing the water through a filter system," Morgan said. "Pushing clockwise."

Morgan looked around, but there were no outbuildings in the yard. He glanced up at the neighbouring house. Only its upper storeys were visible above the high stone wall separating the properties. Someone looking across would have to be in the attic to get a decent view of the ponds. The windowpanes in the attic gable glistened in the early-evening light.

Spotlessly clean, he thought.

"It must be in the basement," said Miranda. "The filter. I doubt the other pond has one — it looks like pea soup. Soylent green."

"Charlton Heston." He affirmed her allusion. "Nutrition from human remains."

A uniformed officer approached and asked if the body could be moved.

"Wait for the coroner," said Morgan. "No, take him out. Make sure they've got pictures. Be careful with the fish."

The uniformed officer wandered away to get help.

Miranda contemplated the dead man, wondering if his secret lives somehow intersected with her own, long before death had brought them together. "They'll go deep. It must be nine or ten feet."

"Three metres, think metric" said Morgan conscientiously. "Even if it's heated, they need the volume to stabilize against temperature fluctuations."

Metric came in when Miranda was a child; Morgan was five years older. He insisted that Fahrenheit generated a skin response, and Celsius was only numerical.

"We'll need to drain it," she said.

"No."

"We'll send in a diver then. Do you think there's a difference between a pool and a pond?"

"I'd say a pool is hard-edged and clear." He looked down toward the ravine. "The soylent pea-souper, I'd call that a pond."

"You're okay with a diver?"

"Yeah, it's better for the fish. There's a fortune in there." *Detective sergeants.*

She smiled at the presumption of authority. He had seniority by several years, but they were both detective sergeants. Usually, she was in command. He preferred it that way.

Miranda strolled off toward the house, then circled around and walked out past the murky green pool into a narrow grove of silver maples that soared defiantly against the urban sky, their foliage blocking out the banks of office buildings and the CN Tower. From a vantage by the sudden slope of a ravine, the city reappeared at close quarters. This was how the rich lived. In Toronto at least. Miranda didn't know rich people anywhere else, and in Rosedale only when they were murdered, or as happened more often than people might think, when they did the murdering.

A police crew worked beneath her, combing among the overgrown rubble below the property line for anything out of place: a gum wrapper but not a Dom Perignon cork; a footprint, freshly broken twigs but not cut branches; evidence of urgency, not the residue of a carelessly cultivated life.

She gazed up into the leaves of the maple trees, vaguely expecting a revelation. That was how it occasionally happened, and she would walk out and surprise Morgan with an accounting that seemed to come from nowhere.

This time all she saw were blue-green edges shifting softly in the freshening breeze of early evening.

Generally, Morgan was the more intuitive one. He gathered random particulars until everything fell into place, while she extrapolated an entire narrative from singular details. She was deductive. Like Holmes, though Morgan wasn't Watson. More like Moriarity, she thought, but one of the good guys.

Morgan remained by the pool. He knew almost every fish by its generic name. He recognized a young Budo Goromo with markings the size of a cluster of grapes, Cabernet Sauvignon with the bloom still on. Its other name might have been Bacchus, he thought, or maybe Lafite or Latour. Morgan got sidetracked for a moment, rifling through the files in his mind for the names of First Growth Bordeaux. This would be the garden of a Bordeaux drinker. *Premier grand crus.* Not Burgundy. These fish had been too carefully selected. Burgundy was always a risk.

And its third name is known only to God.

He shuddered. Morgan wasn't a believer, but the familiar phrase, whether as an epitaph for the Unknown Soldier or casually applied to fish in a Rosedale garden, sent a chill of loneliness through him.

"Have we heard who he is yet?" Miranda asked. She had been standing close for several minutes, watching him think.

Morgan shrugged. Neither of them carried a cell phone. Access meant control. Sometimes she compromised. Self-reliance wasn't always enough.

"Margaux," said Morgan, apparently addressing the Budo Goromo. He was pleased. He had retrieved the name of another Bordeaux *grand cru.*

Miranda couldn't remember which Hemingway granddaughter hadn't committed suicide, Muriel or Margaux. One of them starred in a Woody Allen film.

Side by side they stared into the pond, intent on their separate reflections, while a surreal tableau was enacted around them. In a flurry of quiet activity the investigating team searched out myriad anomalies that would make the immediate past comprehensible. The grounds, a luxuriant green, though summer was gone, had been cultivated by generations long dead. The more distant past made the crime scene merely a passing disturbance.

The Ochiba Shigura disappeared into the depths and then returned, swimming slowly against the dead man's face, back and forth in a kind of caress or secret language. A powerfully proportioned Showa the size of a platter nibbled at the fingers of his left hand, which draped low in the water, though the body itself rested stolidly on the surface as if buoyed from below.

Miranda settled on the retaining wall with her back to the pond. She looked at the huge brick house that opened onto a portico one storey below street level across the back, embracing the garden with an intimacy that belied its grand proportions. Miranda tried to penetrate the architectural layers of the house, finding clean Georgian lines nearly obscured by unseemly Victorian flourishes and superfluous Edwardian columns and porticos. She decided the house had remained in the same family over the years, the changes accruing as each generation imposed its own taste on the last, and the next.

She twisted around as the dead man swung by and gently tugged at his jacket collar. The corpse shifted, brushed against the edge of the pool, and slumped over onto its side. In a rush of water it settled on its back, floating face up, open eyes limpid, opaque.

Miranda flinched, her breath caught in her throat.

Again she was struck by the sickening familiarity of death. Something happened to human features in extremity. The very obese, the emaciated, faces contorted in pain or by fear, and faces in absolute stillness, bore similarities in kind. Fat men looked alike; corpses resembled one another like kin.

Morgan bent close to examine the dead man's face, then leaned away as if coming to a dissenting judgment about a celebrated portrait after evaluating the brush strokes. They watched while the body drifted away from the wall and slowly rolled over again.

"That's better," said Morgan when the face was no longer visible. "His name is Robert Griffin. He's a lawyer."

"Really?" said Miranda. "And you know that because?"

"He was news about a year ago."

"Good or bad?"

"Rich. There was a piece in the *Globe and Mail* buried beside the obituaries." He chuckled at the pun. "It wasn't a big enough story to make television."

"But you recognized him wet?"

"Yeah. They used a file photo. He looked sort of dead already. He spent a fortune at Christie's in London for an artifact from the South Pacific."

"And that was newsworthy?"

"Something called Rongorongo, a wooden plaque from Easter Island about the size of a small paddle blade with writing on it."

"Rongorongo?"

"It's filled with opposing rows of hieroglyphs. It's the writing that's Rongorongo, not the board, and the people from Easter Island can't read it now. No one can read it. They still carve replicas, and no one knows what they say."

Miranda had studied semiotics in university. She wondered if this accounted for the poignancy she felt for a language indecipherably encoded. She tried to imagine not being able to read your own writing.

Morgan continued. "The islanders, they call themselves Rapanui, the island is Rapa Nui, two words, they used to have joke tournaments. Koro 'ei." He savoured the words. "Jest fests, the losers laughed, and had to throw a feast, a weird form of potlatch —"

"Morgan —"

"I think there are fewer than twenty authentic Rongorongo tablets around, pretty well all in museums. He paid half a million."

"Well, Mr. Griffin!"

It pleased them to have arrived at the victim's identity without resorting to actual research. They watched him drift by as if he might reveal more of himself if they waited.

"No shoes. He wandered out from the house in socks," said Morgan, dispelling any doubt that this was the dead man's home. "Where did Yosserian go? I thought they were hauling him out of there."

"Mr. Griffin seems a little soft around the edges," said Miranda, who didn't work out but was trim. "Not in very good condition." ↳ annoying

"He's dead," said Morgan, who occasionally worked out but mostly skipped meals. ↳ annoying

"I doubt if he even played golf. Too pallid to belong to a yacht club. Clothes not sufficiently stylish to suggest peer influence. I'd say he's a loner. But don't you think it's peculiar, a high-priced lawyer, and I've never heard of him?"

CHOPPY BANTERING B/W MORGAN and QUIN - NOT IMPRESSED YET.

"Cops and the law don't always connect. Sometimes it's a matter of luck."

"You'd think he'd have some sort of a public presence, Morgan. Look at the house."

"I'm not sure he had much of a presence at all. He looks exceptionally ordinary."

"As you say, he's floating in a fish pond. Let's get him out before the family comes home." Miranda turned to see that Yosserian was standing by with another officer, apparently not wanting to disturb their forensic deliberations. She caught his eye, and they moved forward.

"There's no family coming home," said Morgan. "They'd be here already. It's too late in the season for Muskoka, everyone's down from the cottage by now. The yard's too orderly. No bikes, no barbecue. The big Showa wants food, he's nibbled those fingers before. Look at that. The Ochiba — look at him nuzzling. They're closer than family. These fish are Griffin's familiars."

"Familiars." Miranda often repeated Morgan's key words, sometimes to mock him but sometimes intrigued. "That's creepy. With scales."

"They don't all have scales. Some of them are Doitsu."

Miranda was equivocating about whether or not to give him the satisfaction of asking for an explanation when a stunning young woman emerged from the shadows of the walkway along the side of the house. She moved toward them with an air of belonging.

"Maybe I'm wrong," said Morgan.

"She's not family."

The woman stood to one side and gazed at Robert Griffin as he was hauled over the pool edge and spread out on a groundsheet. While the officers manoeuvred the bag, she seemed to focus on the rasping of the zipper and the squishing liquid sounds as the body settled into its plastic receptacle. Then she spoke with deliberate calm. "You're quite right, Detective. I'm not family."

"Really," Miranda said, realizing her disparaging comment had been overheard. The striking young woman was one of those people defined by style. Someone you had trouble imagining with a home life or childhood memories. A prosperous self-reliant urban adult of purposefully indeterminate age.

Somewhere between twenty-six and thirty-two.

She had the subdued flare of a woman who read *Vogue* to check for mistakes, Miranda thought. She probably subscribed to *Architectural Digest*, never travelled by bus, and arrived early at the dentist's so she could read *Cosmopolitan*.

Miranda brushed imaginary creases from her skirt and straightened her shoulders inside her jacket. She glanced at Morgan. He shrugged almost imperceptibly.

"I take it you knew the deceased," Miranda declared too formally as she gazed into the woman's eyes, searching for personality.

"Yes, I did," said the woman. Then, as if she were ordering a martini, she added, "I was his mistress. I still am, I suppose." The woman smiled. "Wives become widows. There's no past tense for a mistress."

Mattress, thought Morgan, but said nothing. She was an interesting anomaly, not because she was the mistress of a flaccid man with a comb-over but because she obviously didn't need to be. She was addressing Miranda. He turned away. There was a jousting so subtle neither woman seemed aware of it, and it didn't include him.

"Griffin didn't like *mistress*," the woman said. "I rather like it myself. *Lover* is just too depressing."

"Was he depressed?" Miranda asked with a hint of aggression.

"Why, because he killed himself? He wasn't a man to die from excessive emotion." She paused. "From business perhaps. He never talked about business."

She made it sound like suicide could have been a tactical ploy.

"It's unexpected, if that's what you mean," she continued. "But not surprising. Robert was a very secretive man, but he could be quite impulsive."

The woman studied the black plastic bag, tracing the zipper line as if it were a wound. Her features softened, then she glanced up directly into Miranda's eyes, her dispassionate aplomb instantly restored. For a moment Miranda felt an unnerving bond between them.

"With some people, you know, you can't really tell," said the woman.

"What?" Morgan asked. "If they're dead?"

"Whether they're depressed," she said. "I suppose he might have been." She smiled as if forgiving herself for a minor oversight.

Miranda looked at her quizzically. The woman didn't seem concerned about a display of grief. Perhaps that would come later. Perhaps, more ominously, she had dealt with it already. Or sadly, thought Miranda, she felt nothing at all.

"Do you have access to the house?" Miranda asked.

"Do you mean, have I keys? Yes, of course."

"Then perhaps we could look inside," said Morgan.

"Of course," said the woman. Touching Miranda on the arm, she casually amended her assessment of the victim's mental stability. "He sometimes took Valium."

"Sometimes?" said Miranda. "It's not an occasional drug."

"He said he had trouble sleeping."

"And did he?"

"We didn't sleep together, Detective. I'm not his widow." She seemed vaguely amused by her own witticism. "My name is Eleanor Drummond." She held her hand out to Miranda, then Morgan.

The woman was gracious without warmth, as if they were Jehovah's Witnesses and she a lapsed Catholic. Some people offered their names as an invitation, but with her it seemed more like a shield or a disguise.

They introduced themselves in turn, both fully aware Robert Griffin's mistress had taken the initiative.

Together the three of them walked beneath the trellised portico to a set of large French doors, which Eleanor Drummond unlocked. "Did you need permission to enter?"

They stepped into a room busy with artifacts.

"No," said Miranda.

"But if it was suicide?"

"This was murder," said Morgan.

Eleanor Drummond's eyes narrowed for a moment, but she said nothing.

The room was large and cluttered, with massive doors leading away on either side and into the interior depths of the house. It seemed cramped; it was the room of a man who needed to see what he thought, piled on shelves. Morgan felt vaguely embarrassed, the way he did gazing at an open cadaver.

Windows flanked the French doors along the outer wall. There was a fireplace, there were shelves against the other walls packed with hardcover books, with the occasional oversize volume stored horizontally on top of the rows. Books with pictures of koi lay open on the sofa and floor in cross-referencing piles. There was a small pile of books beside a wingback chair that faced out with a view of the garden. A slender Waterford vase sat poised on one of the bookshelves with three wilted long-stemmed roses. The walls were adorned with antique guns, animal heads and old maps, aboriginal masks and photographs of blurred shadows, likenesses of nightmares. There was a bar to one side littered with koi paraphernalia, water-testing potions, gauges for testing salinity, ammonia, oxygen quotients.

"Odd that it was locked," said Morgan.

"Maybe he went out another door and walked around," suggested Miranda.

"In his socks?"

A pair of dress shoes sat neatly on the floor, facing away from the sofa. The shoes had been removed by a man at rest, not parked there on his way outside.

"He usually used the wingback," said Eleanor Drummond as if they were piecing together the same puzzle.

Morgan motioned for her to sit, then took a seat opposite. Miranda drifted away and, despite the forensic specialists coming in through the French doors, the woman focused on Morgan as if there was no one else in the room.

Miranda usually found books comforting. At first she had thought the room was a sanctuary, but as she wandered around she found it unsettling. What she had initially taken to be evidence of personality was actually its absence.

The shelved books were arranged by subject matter. She arranged her own books by colour and size. There was a cluster of postcards tacked to a bulletin board. On the obverse side they were blank. Sometimes the most telling story was no story at all. The opulent vulgarity of the Waterford vase attracted her eye. It was Victorian and still had a Birks label affixed to the base. There was no radio, no outlet for music. There were no paintings, only a pair of diplomas, a couple of studio graduation portraits. On a shelf an unlikely sequence of ornamental porcelain ducks was arranged next to some antique etchings in whale ivory.

"Scrimshaw," said Morgan, glancing in the direction of her gaze.

She nodded. Looking down at the colourful runner beneath her feet, the coarse wool blunt with age, she wondered if it was good. Morgan would know. Must be antique, she thought. Not much resilience. And no underpad.

Close by the fireplace was a ceramic bin, out of which an array of walking sticks protruded at odd angles. She noticed a flat wooden blade leaning against the bin which, on closer examination, appeared to have hieroglyphs etched into its surface. My God, she thought, gently tracing her fingers along the rows of figures running its length, this was half a million dollars. She held it aslant to the light, trying to capture the inscrutable shadows.

It saddened Miranda to realize that Easter Islanders couldn't possibly afford to repatriate their heritage. How could they compete with museums or with a wealthy collector from Rosedale who was too feckless to put it on display?

Did Rongorongo have any meaning if its meaning was lost?

Morgan watched her scrutinizing the hieroglyphs. Her auburn hair and slightly aquiline nose, lips poised in concentration rather than pursed, hazel eyes squinting to make out the writing, as if by peering more carefully she could understand what it said, all made her appear like an actor playing the role of detective: detached but absorbed, quietly confident, attractive but not distracting, hints of a strong personality bringing the scene into focus.

He returned his attention to the dead man's mistress. She was both subtle and flash. Maybe Griffin preferred the word *lover* to make them seem equal; she preferred *mistress* to affirm the divide.

Morgan fidgeted while they talked. He watched more than listened. Eleanor Drummond seemed not to know she was being interrogated, and yet revealed virtually nothing.

Miranda tried several doors before finding a staircase that was surprisingly steep and narrow, leading up to the main part of the house. She ascended the stairs and rambled from room to room, turning on lights as she went.

"Personally, I think it was suicide," Eleanor Drummond repeated to Morgan as if the possibility had just crossed her mind.

"Everything suggests he wasn't anticipating the end," Morgan said. "Books laid out to be read, shoes by the sofa — it all gives the impression of a man who had no intention of dying."

"Perhaps that's what he wanted us to think."

"And why would he want *us* to think that?"

"So you'd think it was murder."

"Which I do."

"Drowning in a pond doesn't seem like murder, Detective."

"Dead men don't drown. He probably died in this room."

She looked away, out to the garden. She shared the habit of all beautiful people, inviting him to assess her without seeming to stare.

There was no way she would have been able to manoeuvre a man to the pond, dead or alive, without leaving skid marks on the grass and bruises on the body from hefting him over the retaining wall. Morgan was certain there would be no bruises. Griffin's clothes weren't twisted on his limbs, his body seemed inordinately relaxed. The fish weren't spooked.

She didn't strike him as a person who would work with an accomplice. Eleanor Drummond might have the capacity for murder, he thought, but judging from her disinclination to express appropriate emotion, probably not the desire.

Morgan thought of the koi. They weaved the shadows, wefts of colour sliding through warps of dark clear water. He lapsed into wordlessness, his mind occupied with images.

Awkwardly, the woman withdrew a cigarette, then glanced around. Seeing no ashtrays, she slipped it back into the package and set the pack down on the coffee table. She settled back on the green sofa as composed but on edge as if she were in an oncologist's waiting room.

Miranda reappeared, stepping through the massive doorway back into Griffin's retreat. She had been uneasy, almost anxious, in the rest of the house. It felt unnaturally empty, as if the ancestral ghosts haunting its spaces and furnishings hadn't yet embraced their newest arrival. In the den, perhaps because the dead man's predilections appeared on display, the ghosts seemed more accommodating.

"Would you excuse me?" said Morgan abruptly, addressing Eleanor Drummond while gesturing to his partner for help. "Detective Quin will have some questions. I'm needed outside ..." His voice trailed off as he closed the French doors behind him. He took a deep breath of the evening air, annoyed with himself for having offered an explanation to account for his exit.

Activity in the garden had faded with the evening light. He walked over to where the body bag lay on the ground sheet, with a solitary attendant standing vigil. Morgan nodded.

"Waiting for the Black Mariah," explained the corpse's companion. "The ME ran out of gas. It didn't seem I should leave the guy here on his own."

Morgan was taken by the man's innate courtesy. "It's okay. See what you can do inside." As the officer was about to disappear under the shadows of the portico, Morgan changed his mind. "Yosserian, go on out front. Show the medical examiner where to come when he gets here. Where did you get the body wrap?"

"Left over from the multiple last week in Cabbage-town."

"You're not supposed to be driving around with those."

"Yeah," said Yosserian.

Morgan knelt beside the remains of Robert Griffin and unzipped the bag to the shoulders, peeling the synthetic material back in dark folds. The pallor of death, highlighted by the lights from the house, gave the visible remains an appearance of antique marble, like the toppled bust of a Roman senator. Morgan stood and contemplated the nature of human flesh. He thought of the bust of Homer in a poem he imagined he had forgotten.

Strange, this had happened and nothing had changed. A man was mysteriously dead and it made no difference. Usually by now Morgan's mind was teeming with intimations, possibilities, connections. But here was a death for which no crowd gathered.

The medical examiner came around through the walkway, led by Yosserian, the body's self-appointed keeper. "Is that you, Morgan?" she asked, trying to penetrate the gloom.

"You ran out of gas?" said Morgan. He moved close enough so that Ellen Ravenscroft could see it was him, then shrugged agreeably and turned away.

She squatted by the body. "All right then, love, I've got work to do."

Morgan gazed into the closest pool, the fish now indistinct wraiths deep below the surface. The low green pond down by the ravine appeared brackish in the dying light. He walked over to it. It smelled fresh. Why no water flowers, no grasses around the shoreline?

He tried to block out the banal chatter between Yosserian and the ME. They were arguing about the body bag. He listened to the water and thought he could hear the hush of its limpid surface as it settled against the earth. His mind seemed both empty and filled until in the distance he heard a siren and returned to himself in the garden.

When a diver appeared by the lower pond, Morgan watched for a while. Her light, as she submerged, transformed from a shimmering cone to a glowing green corsage, then a vague flicker, until it extinguished in the opaque depths, only to reappear again here and there as she groped her way to the edges. It made him queasy, watching her hand reach up through the murk to signal her assistant the direction of her quest.

"She won't see anything in there," said the assistant, standing tall as if the higher perspective would let him see deeper. "This kind of thing is by touch alone."

Morgan felt claustrophobic. He nodded and retreated to the upper pool. The diver had already checked this one thoroughly, moving gently among the fish, and come up with nothing.

By the time Miranda joined him, Ellen Ravenscroft had left with the body, the diver was gone, and the night sky was flushed with the lights of the city. The water in front of them was black, like anthracite sheared from its motherlode. Morgan remained motionless, staring into the impenetrable depths. Miranda moved close enough that they could feel the body heat between them, but they didn't touch. They were comfortable with silence.

Eventually, she said, "It's strange, that huge house, it's creepy. Except for the den the place could have been decorated by committee."

"Or successive generations of Rosedale matrons."

"A committee of ghosts." She reflected on the secrets implied by the water's dark surface, then returned to her previous theme. "There's no evidence anywhere of his so-called mistress, no lingerie under the bed, no scented shampoo in the shower."

"Has she gone?"

"Yeah. We'll connect in the morning." She paused. "Why mistress, not girlfriend?" She paused again. "You know, he wouldn't walk across the yard in socks."

"No. He wasn't wearing a tie."

"So?"

"Well, his top button was done up. So he's the kind of guy who prepares for death by taking off his shoes and tie but forgets to unbutton his shirt?"

"Do you own a tie?"

"One, utilitarian black."

Morgan looked at her in the evening light. She had seen him wear his tie at funerals. Her hazel eyes gleamed silver and bronze from the surface reflection of light from the city. He pushed his hair back from his forehead, a habit from twenty years earlier, when it was longer and obstructed his view.

"Eleanor Drummond figured that Griffin wanted us to think it was murder," Morgan said. "He locked himself out, then drowned himself, expiring among friends. She *wants* it to be suicide. Strange, most people would rather a loved one was murdered. Then they can grieve guilt-free."

"She was trying to smoke in there! She seems an unlikely smoker."

"Yeah, she tried with me, too."

"I was out of the room for a minute and she lit up," Miranda said. "Someone told her to put it out. She made quite a production of going down the hall to the bathroom."

"She flushed the toilet?"

"I know, but they said they'd finished with it."

"*Mistress* is a way of distancing herself, making sure we don't think they were friends."

"Or of convincing herself of the same."

"Funny," Morgan said. "The door being locked." He paused. "There's no Chagoi."

"No what?"

"No Chagoi. I've read that every koi pond should have a Chagoi. It's big and affable, wrinkled like gold foil."

"Maybe it's lying low."

"A furtive Chagoi. No, it's a personality fish. It mediates between species. It's got the mind of a mammal. Extravagantly subtle. Billy Crystal wearing Armani." He seemed pleased with the allusion.

Miranda glanced at his rumpled clothes and smiled. He would look good in Armani. She hadn't noticed before, but he had a day's growth of beard. Was it stylish, or had he forgotten to shave? Probably the latter.

"She didn't know there were no ashtrays. She doesn't look like a smoker," he repeated.

"She doesn't smell like a smoker. You ever kiss a smoker, Morgan? Like sucking garbage through a straw."

"You used to smoke."

"That's how I know."

"I never did."

She wanted to kiss him right then and there. It wasn't a sexual impulse, at least not directly, not rising out of the hollow inside. It was the need to connect, by touching someone intimately who actually gave a damn about her after the lights were out. Maybe a little sexual, she thought, and thinking so made it sexual.

"Hey, Morgan." Maybe she should reveal her anxiety, the horror and panic and strange sense of relief.

"Yeah?"

"Did you notice the books?"

"The koi books? Or the others?"

"Not many people these days buy hardcover books except lawyers and scholars with grants," said Miranda. "Did you see the degree?"

"Linguistics."

"Semiotics."

"Same thing."

"Not."

Miranda had been holding an envelope in her hand that she had picked up from the floor near the wingback chair. It was a piece of unopened junk mail with some writing scrawled on the back. She handed it to Morgan.

He walked over to read it in light streaming through the French doors that wavered as the forensic people inside moved about, finishing their work. "'Language is immanent but has no material existence.' Good opening. That's how I feel most of the time. Here but not here." He continued to read, mouthing the words with just enough volume that the hyphens were audible. "'Language is imm-in-ent, preceding our being in the world; imm-an-ent, providing the dimensions of knowledge and experience. Language is consciousness, whatever the case.' I doubt if he was much for small talk."

"It's interesting, though, isn't it?"

"Doesn't exactly solve the mystery."

"Which one? About language and consciousness, or about death?" She smiled slyly as if she had been caught in a thought-crime. "Did you see the Rongorongo?"

"I saw you admiring it. You've got to wonder what's locked up in a language that no one can read."

"Precisely," she said. "But it's not the language that's indecipherable. It's the script. You can understand why a guy with a doctorate in semiotics might want to own it if he had the money."

"And then he stores it beside a brolly stand with a clutch of old canes!"

"Strange guy, our lawyer-philosopher."

"Yeah," said Morgan. "So why would someone kill a philosopher. I mean, lawyers, even Shakespeare said 'kill all the lawyers,' but a semiotician?"

"Morgan, this note? It contradicts its own declaration." She wanted to go on. Words shaped thoughts in Miranda's mind; she wanted to let them out. But Morgan was back with the fish. She wanted to talk about language and writing, about Rongorongo, about speaking with the dead.

Morgan was bent over, peering through reflections of the night sky into the obsidian depths, but all he could see was an illimitable absence of light.

"You want something to eat?" she asked. "Come on. The koi aren't going anywhere. Tomorrow they'll tell us their secrets. Tonight they're in mourning, draped in black."

"Fish and chips or sushi?"

Over dessert Morgan offered a discourse on carpets. The Kurdish runner in the den: antique, its pile worn, a tribal rug, coarse wool, natural dyes. The indigo blue a desert lake; abrash, the hue variations, like water under the desert sky. Persian. He didn't say from Iran. Carpets had more longevity than nation-states.

He went on to describe the Qashqa'i hanging as a wall piece behind the wingback chair.

She interrupted. "The runner! Why would a valuable carpet on a slate floor not have an underpad?"

Morgan smiled. He had read about rugs, subscribed for a couple of years to *Hali*, the opulent trade journal from England, had learned about designs and dying, weaving on hand looms by nomads, on village looms for the rich, about symbols and patterns, trading and auctions. But it hadn't occurred to him that there should be an underpad beneath the Kurdish runner.

"So we have a carpet problem," he said. "Mystery upon mystery. Do you think she did it?"

"Eleanor Drummond? She had access, possibly motive — all mistresses have motives for murder. I doubt she did it."

"No," he agreed.

"She delivers herself, or a version of herself, as someone too self-possessed, too emotionally self-sufficient, to bother killing her lover. It was a business arrangement."

"The murder?"

"No, her life." Miranda tinkered with her cutlery.

"So who do we think did it?"

"*We* don't know, do we?"

"I think the koi are the answer," he said. "Maybe we should have drained the ponds."

Miranda ordered coffee, black, for both of them. He usually took double-double.

"You should have seen the diver in the lower pond," said Morgan. "She virtually disappeared. For goodness' sake, it swallowed her whole. Twenty thousand gallons of pea soup."

When he said "for goodness' sake" and "my gosh" and "holy smoke," she liked him best. "How do you know that?" she asked.

"I saw her. She had to feel her way, like being submerged in soylent green."

"The gallonage, how do you know that? Nobody knows twenty thousand gallons."

"Grade ten geometry," he said. "It's easy to calculate."

"Geometry was in grade eleven."

"I know about what interests me — or maybe I'm interested in what I know about. Koi interest me. Carpets interest me. A good carpet on slate, that interests me. Wine interests me. Really good wine, *premier grand cru, brunello di montalcino, trockenbeerenauslese*." Each designation he enunciated with an appropriate accent — French, Italian, stage German. "I read about the stuff. I don't drink it."

"Who came from the Coroner's? Was it Ellen Ravenscroft? She seems to turn up whenever you're on a case."

"Uncanny coincidence. I'm a homicide cop, she's a coroner."

"Come on …"

"She's earthy. I like her. What did you think about Eleanor Drummond?"

"Definitely not earthy. I can't imagine that woman in 'snuggle' mode even on a rental basis."

"She's stunningly beautiful."

"Yeah, like a magazine layout—she looks airbrushed. Seriously, you found her attractive?"

"Yes and no. More yes than no."

"It's time to go home," she said, shifting in her chair.

As he rose to his feet, Morgan reached over and gave her shoulder a companionable squeeze. She flinched. He didn't seem to notice, but she was surprised. It wasn't him; it had something to do with the dead man in the pond. She couldn't see the connection. She settled back.

"Think I'll stay for a bit. No, really. Good night, Morgan." She watched him walk away. "You can stay, too, if you want," she added softly as he wandered away through the tables.

He waved backward with a small hand gesture, then she heard, trailing off in the ambient din as he approached the exit, "There's got to be a Chagoi."

And he was gone.

2

Parrotfish and Barracuda

Miranda's condo on Isabella Street was Gothic by neglect, not design. The fountain in the courtyard hadn't seen water since the Great Flood. The fascia drooped behind gingerbread swirls; acid-worn gargoyles leered over downspouts that leaned precariously away from the eaves.

In the lobby she paused to pick up her mail and press her own buzzer before letting herself in. Years ago whimsy had turned into ritual; she felt reassured, knowing the sound was filling her empty apartment. She carried a scaled-down 9 mm Glock semi-automatic in a shoulder holster or holstered against the small of her back, or in her bag when it was too hot to wear a jacket, but she had no desire to use it. The buzzing would scare away burglars; and sometimes she could sense the reverberations still lingering to welcome her home.

Miranda was fond of the old place. The stair treads were worn marble, the wood trim was walnut, darkened by age, the fixtures were bronze. There was an air of decadent longevity rare in the centre of the city. She had lived here as a student when the building was still apartments. It was seedy enough to seem subversive but structurally sound and aggressively urban.

When she returned to Toronto after three years away, she had raised a down payment, retrieved her furniture from storage, and moved back in. It was as if she had never been away. She felt toward her apartment the kind of myopic affection usually reserved for an appallingly inappropriate lover — of whom there had been several, she thought as she paused at the foot of the stairs to jettison flyers into the trash bin.

The bin was overflowing. It, and having the walkway shovelled in the winter, were the only perceptible services for the condo fee. There was no lawn to speak of, no gardening to be done beyond the annual trimming of a few stunted spirea bushes in the courtyard and a couple of grotesque forsythia against the sidewalk out front. The lobby was cleaned just enough to maintain an aura of genteel dinginess.

Almost lost among duplicate Victoria's Secret catalogues and an alumni magazine from the University of Toronto was a manila envelope with no return address. Miranda might have thrown it out but for the spidery handwriting. Grasping her mail, she started up the stairs, then stopped and pulled away the cellotape holding down the manila flap. There was a one-page letter, a fragile newspaper cutting, and a legal document of some sort, folded in the middle. The letter was dated yesterday. She looked at the postmark on the envelope. It was obscure but genuine. Yesterday, as well. The letter, which began rather quaintly, "My Dear Miranda," was signed by a dead man.

Miranda shuddered, and with her mail held tentatively in hand like a urine specimen, she hurried upward to the relative security of her third-floor home.

Once inside, with the lights on and everything familiar, she set the mail down, deliberately unread, and went into her bedroom, which doubled as a study, where she methodically eased out of her clothes. In the shower she let the pulsing flow of hot water work away the tension of the day that as usual had settled into her neck and shoulders. She put on cotton pajamas imprinted with grazing moose. She flipped on her computer and walked out into the cramped kitchen, where she was momentarily surprised to see the mysterious contents of the manila envelope still on the counter.

"Why don't you get a decent apartment," Morgan had asked after their one brief tryst.

"Was that your problem?"

"We were good," he had said, neither amused nor taking offence. "I thought we were very good. Did you have a problem?"

"Screw you."

"Miranda ..."

Sometimes he used her last name. Usually, the first. Tone could make it mean anything. Then it had conveyed good-natured wariness.

She always called him Morgan; she liked the sound. Soft and abrupt, a controlled expletive, like swearing at someone you loved. Yet she had found herself repeating his first name during sex. *David, David*. She almost never called him David to his face.

Ellen Ravenscroft had once challenged her about "the name thing."

"His last and your first — what's with that?"

"It's not about power," Miranda had responded.

"Of course it is, love. It's always about power."

Not always, she now thought. Sometimes words were just words.

When Morgan and she undressed that time and had faced each other, she had felt uncomfortably discon-nected. She was thinking about Ellen, about how much Ellen would like to be in her place. But the moment to stop things had passed. It had seemed more intimate to resist or explain. And then she had abandoned herself, and it was as good as Morgan had suggested.

During their prolonged coital embrace — that was the term, inept as it was, that had come to her mind — she had luxuriated in the indulgent pace. Morgan was physically uninhibited — strange for a man — and yet emotionally shy. He was a lovely lover and that had frightened her. She had never been married, never lived with a man, not because she didn't have needs, but because she needed too much.

"I like this apartment," she had told him. "I've been here from day one. Second year university, after first year in residence. I shared it with a roommate. She had this room, the boudoir, and I had a fold-out in the living room. I lost the toss of a coin. Then she started having layovers — guys laid her and stayed over. Alphabetically, she was working through the student directory. I don't think she even liked it much. I lived in her vestibule. My love life, of course, was zero. She tried buying me off, but I didn't want leftovers. We tossed another coin and I won. She left, she became a lawyer. I practised celibacy. Turned out it didn't take practice."

"You must have saved a fortune by now. And no car."

"Nor you."

"Bad driver."

"Bad driver, poor lover, no sense of humour. Most men won't acknowledge their failings."

"Miranda, I —" he had begun, stifling his protest, then touching her gently.

"It's a clean well-lighted place."

"Yeah, and it smells good. There's nothing, nothing, as erotic as the smell of a single woman's apartment."

"Go home, Morgan."

And he had gone.

Miranda wasn't prepared yet to read the letter. She picked up the newspaper cutting and smoothed it on the counter. It was actually an entire tabloid page, torn along one edge and tattered as if someone had repeatedly handled it. Top, centre, a photograph. Standing third from the right, a little distorted by the glare of a flash, an earlier version of herself. She didn't remember posing for the picture or its publication.

Beside her was Victor Sandhu, Ph.D., professor of semiotics, or semiology, as he preferred. He had arranged a major fellowship that would have enabled Miranda to pursue graduate studies in the Department of Linguistics at a level just above poverty. That was a significant accolade, considering the fact that she was graduating in honours anthropology and had only taken semiotics courses as electives.

The small cluster of faculty and students in the photograph was parsed, left to right, each identified either by discipline and credentials or by award. The caption ran to several hundred words, longer than some of *The Varsity* articles. The last words in the caption read: "Absent, co-winner of the Sandhu Semiology Fellowship: Robert Griffin."

"No way!" she exclaimed. "No bloody way!"

Her words echoed as if the walls, though accustomed to her voice, now refused to absorb her incipient panic. She looked around, then back at *The Varsity,* page six.

Robert Griffin. Indisputably: co-winner ... Robert Griffin.

Miranda poured herself a tumbler of red wine from an open bottle on the counter, took a sip, then reached for a wineglass from the cupboard above the sink and transferred most of the contents into the tulip crystal. She drained the dregs from the tumbler, held the bottle up to examine the label, set it down, gazed off into the middle distance, and surprised herself to find the world was blurred and that her eyes had filled with tears.

"I don't remember Robert Griffin." Miranda spoke out loud with a zealot's conviction. She put her fingers to her mouth as if to stifle her own voice.

I saw his face, dead, through a veil of water, she thought. *A stranger. I saw photographs of him in legal regalia and robed for his doctorate. My presence in the newspaper picture authenticates only myself. My God, we shared a prize. I didn't collect. The rich man took it all.*

The tightness of tears drying on her cheeks made her realize she had stopped crying. She was angry. She felt violated. She was appalled at her own anxiety and confused by her fear.

Miranda settled back on the sofa, resolved to penetrate the shadows that made her past seem a thronging of separate events. She assumed most people lived inside continuous narratives under occasional revision. Searching, unexpectedly, she encountered her boyfriend from their last year in high school. She smiled to herself, turned the stem of her glass between her fingers, and remembered.

She and Danny Webster had kissed a lot but had always kept their intimacies from the neck up. They talked to each other in funny voices. They played cryptic word games.

"Do you want to go to a movie?" he might ask.

Someone else would have responded with a tired aphorism like, "Does a bear poop in the woods?" But not Miranda.

"Did Sandy Koufax pitch on Yom Kippur?" she would answer with a world-weary shrug, and they would both groan and go to see a replay of *Cool Hand Luke*.

Or she might ask, about classmates, "Do you think they're doing it?"

And he would answer, "Is Dr. Ramsay Catholic?"

That one was tricky. Miranda's family was Anglican, so the archbishop of Canterbury was indeed a primate of the "holy catholic church." However, Danny was Baptist and insisted the Church of England was a breakaway Protestant sect. Yes and no. And to increase their pleasure, they both knew that Ramses were condoms. Were their friends "doing it?" They had no idea.

They were both attractive, so behaving like geeks was an ironic disguise.

At the end of the school year they hugged passionately. Miranda didn't attend her graduation and never saw him again. She thought they had restricted themselves to kissing because that was what she wanted, and because he was a Baptist, but it turned out Baptists like sex. He was gay. According to her mother, who refused to believe the rumour, he came out at Bible College, where he was surrounded by people eager to forgive.

They had played on the margins of adult experience and had parted as innocents. She wondered if Danny Webster had discovered sex without love. Or was he happy?

Miranda walked into the bedroom and was startled by flickering shadows emanating from her screen saver. Having descended through real barracuda and drifted

among parrotfish and somnolent groupers in the Cay-
mans the previous winter, she found the underwater fantasy on her computer reassuring, in the same way a tacky
souvenir was, brought back from a genuine adventure.
Within the virtual perfection on the screen she caught
sight of her face in reflection. She was drifting against
the receding depths, and a prolonged shiver made her
gasp for air.

She had never felt so secure, she thought, as being
enfolded by the warm waters of the Caribbean, hovering
beyond gravity at sixty feet down. It had seemed almost
pre-conscious bliss among the mounds and tentacles of
coral, breathing in a soft rhythm through an umbilicus
of gear. And now visual Muzak on her computer screen
was the disingenuous reminder of a stranger's cadaver,
someone misplaced in the drowned caverns of her mind.

Miranda set the Griffin papers down by the computer,
switched on the gooseneck lamp, and twisted it around
to shine into a closet jammed with boxes and files. She
withdrew a cardboard container labelled "U of T," and
sitting on the floor, dumped the contents between her
splayed legs.

Shifting the pile around with her hand, she came up
with the snapshot she had been expecting. It showed an
oval table surrounded by a dozen faces leaning in for the
camera. On the table were books and a couple of screw-
top wine bottles, along with an array of plastic cups
and open potato chip bags. This was the end-of-term
celebration, hosted and catered by Professor Sandhu for
his semiology seminar.

Miranda had to scan for a moment to establish which
indistinct features were her own, at the farthest end of the
table. Standing behind her, looming over to get in the shot,
was a face she had never seen before except on a corpse.

She didn't remember him, she didn't remember him being in the picture, this man who was older than the rest, perhaps in his forties, who aligned himself for the camera to appear connected, somehow, to the young woman in front of him. She would have sworn he wasn't in the picture the last time she had looked. Of course, that was a decade ago. She wasn't nostalgic about her student days.

Ten years back her ex-roommate in an act of apparent contrition for unfettered sex had come over to welcome Miranda back to Toronto. The two of them had gone through the old pictures, embarrassed they couldn't restore identity to faces etched into memory from across seminar tables, cafeteria tables and, most of all, across tables topped with endless draft beer in the pubs around campus. Miranda could have named every kid in a class photograph from the village public school she had attended in antediluvian times, but university seemed farther away, less accessible.

Griffin had worked his way into a photograph. He had even cast a shadow like the rest of them. How real was the past, she wondered, if someone could slip into it who was never there? More to the point, how real was it if someone who was actually there could be erased?

For some reason she thought of Jason Rodriguez. He seemed like a character she had read about in a novel, an actor in a nearly forgotten movie, far less real than Robert Griffin, the proof of whose being lay on a slab in the morgue.

During the three years she had spent in Ottawa, Jason Rodriguez was Miranda's lover. They had met at work. He was her boss, he was married, they were both outsiders. He was considerate to a fault.

Miranda had met him her first day on the job. He had kind eyes, a soft voice, and a preternatural understanding of her loneliness, something she seldom acknowledged even to herself. The first time they made love she was surprised. It happened as a sort of mutual consolation for the unfairness of life.

Their early courtship was in Spanish, which put her at a disadvantage since his parents had been in the diplomatic service before settling in Canada and that was the language of his childhood, while she had taken a first-year undergraduate course in Spanish, which she dropped to protect her grade-point average. Still, Spanish made everything tentative, as if they were kids trying to figure things out for the first time.

After they became lovers, they gradually switched to English. They talked about problems, confiding with each other in an urgent rhythm of revelation and tenderness. Two years passed. Jason's wife was in a car accident and she died. He was vague on the details of his grief.

After that Miranda ruminated, arranging and rearranging the details of their affair in her mind, spending long hours by herself trying to recover the past. When she quit her job, he seemed disappointed, but he didn't try to dissuade her. She explained that all she had revealed about herself was a way of concealing. Now that he chose to withhold his own secrets, this gave him power that frightened her.

He had touched her lightly on the cheek as if he were whisking away tears. "Frightens you? I don't think you're afraid of anything."

She had laughed. She wasn't going to cry.

Now Miranda dropped the photograph of Professor Sandhu's seminar onto the debris from her past; she would clean up in the morning. She fingered the letter, then unaccountably put it down. She would read that, too, in the light of day.

~ ~ ~

About an hour into sleep she became aware she was dreaming. Photographs displaced one another in random sequence. In each the image of Robert Griffin leered over the scene. Sometimes she was in the picture herself, and sometimes she was an observer. Sometimes Griffin was there as soon as it clarified, and sometimes he emerged after everything else had resolved into a static emblem of strong but elusive emotion. Sometimes he was blurred from the light, and sometimes he was blurred because water was sheeting over his features like a fluid shroud.

Then she was making love with Morgan, surrounded by a flurry of photographs. She was leaning over him; she liked the weight of her breasts pressing against her own skin from the inside as she brushed them across his face in slow, pendulous motion, though actually she had small breasts that were firm and high and she knew this was a dream, and suddenly she became frightened because she also knew that if she arched back to look at him in the os-cillating waves of light emanating from their pleasure, she knew he would have Griffin's face. It would be Morgan, but he would have the drowned features of a stranger.

Refusing the power of her dream, Miranda thrust away from the deadening embrace of her lover and sur-faced into wakefulness. She turned on the light, got up, and took the letter and legal document from her desk. Walking into the kitchen, she made herself a hot choc-olate, even though the night was warm and she had awakened in a sweat. She sat down to read, stood up, changed her pajama top for a dry T-shirt from a pile of folded laundry on the counter, felt to see that her breasts were small and firm, checked her hips with the flat of her hands, checked her bottom. Everything was there as it should be. She sat down, got up, dumped the hot chocolate in the sink, opened the fridge, got out a cider, opened it, drank from the bottle, held it for a moment to her temple, enjoying the cool glass against her skin, sat down, and began to read.

Miranda Quin, spelled correctly. Address. Yesterday's date, now the day before. She squinted at the postmark on the envelope: definitely dated the day before yesterday. "My Dear Miranda." The text was terse yet florid.

> Due to circumstances beyond my control, it seems prudent to make final preparations for my death.
>
> As you may or may not be aware, I am under an obligation to you beyond recompense. We might both find consolation, however, should you agree to act as the executrix of my estate.
>
> You will be neither swayed nor compromised by the modest honorarium attached for your kindness. However, there may be satisfaction in the sum to be administered at your discretion for the benefit of others.
>
> Should you decline, these bequests shall be subsumed residual to my estate and distributed as the court deems appropriate.
>
> I hope your placement within the line of largess will allow you to find in your heart the generosity to forgive me.
>
> The enclosed document has been signed and witnessed. The notarized ap-

plication of your signature will make it
legal and binding.

Yours truly,
(Signed) Robert Griffin, LL.B, Ph.D.

All this for accepting her share of a scholarship! A
macabre joke? Or had a dead man given her the power
of absolution for unspecified wrongs?

Unfolding the legal document, she skimmed through.
It seemed authentic. She was named sole executor, and
her name was repeated throughout. Griffin's signature
was witnessed by Eleanor Drummond and dated the day
before yesterday. The full will would be made accessible
to her upon signing. Contingent to her acceptance, respective parcels of ten and twenty-five million dollars (Canadian) were designated for the Policemen's Benevolent
Fund and to establish the Mary Bingham Carter-Griffin
Institute of Semiology.

Nothing for a koi sanctuary!

She picked up the Bakelite telephone receiver from its
antique cradle, the first rotary-dial phone to be installed
in her mother's family home. It still bore a label with the
original number: OLive 3, 4231. This was from a time apparently before people had the mnemonic capacity to remember seven digits. *We push buttons now,* she thought,
and still say "dial." She remembered her father's number
from when he was a child: 557-J. He had once asked the
operator to speak to his grandmother — no other information than that — and she had put him through. Every
call with this phone, its innards updated, invoked a rich
fluttering of images and thoughts. It was like a talisman of
ancestral memories.

"Morgan," she said when he answered.

"What?" His voice was thick with sleep.

"I've got to talk —"

"Are you all right?"

"Yes, but —"

He hung up.

She called back. "Morgan, listen —"

"You're not hurt, not in danger?"

"No, but —"

He hung up again.

She had once called him in the small hours of the night after wakening from a nightmare; she was weeping and residual images of violence were still flooding her mind, refusing to coalesce into the shattered narrative from which she had emerged, refusing to fade. "Morgan," she had said into the phone beside her bed, into the darkness. "Help me."

"Turn on the lights," he had told her. How had he known? She was afraid the walls might be drenched in blood; she was afraid of the light.

"It's okay," he said. "Turn on the lights, Miranda. You've been dreaming."

She tried to tell him about the nightmare. Her voice was tremulous. She could only remember shrieking, and terrible silence, fragments of horror, images of shattered flesh.

"I've been there," he said. "We see too much. You can't suppress horror forever, Miranda. Are you in bed? You relax and just listen. Did you ever consider, during surgery maybe you feel the scalpel at work? Anaesthetic isn't a painkiller. It just snuffs out the memories of what you've been through. Dreams are like that — they absorb the pain. It isn't the nightmare. It's waking up in the middle. Doctors have nightmares about patients on the operating table becoming suddenly conscious.

Ambulance drivers and firemen ..."

He let his voice drone, reassuring her with empathy and morbid detachment, and then he told her to lie back with the phone on the pillow beside her and try to empty her mind.

After a while she wasn't sure whether the sounds of breathing were her own. "Are you still there, Morgan?"

"Yeah, you go to sleep."

And she did. And when the natural light of morning filled the room, she awoke with no recollection of further violence. She mumbled into the phone beside her, "You still there?"

"Yeah. You have morning breath."

"Thanks, Morgan. It's okay now. See you at work."

"G'night," he said, and a dial tone displaced the open line.

"Good morning," she had said into the room. "Good morning, David."

Now she grabbed the black receiver again and dialled his number. It rang for a long time, then he picked up.

"Sorry," he said. "I was taking a pee. So what's the crisis?"

Morgan listened, envisioning his partner in bed. It made him feel lonely. He was sitting on the blue sofa in his living room in boxers and a T-shirt. The city through open blinds loomed under a canopy of dismal light that erased the stars.

"He doesn't say who's going to do it? He doesn't say why?"

"No," she said.

"He doesn't say how he knows?"

"No."

"The mistress, Eleanor Drummond, she said nothing?"

"No."

"She witnessed a bizarre codicil to her lover's will. He dies. She says nothing?"

"Yes."

"He couldn't anticipate you'd be on the case, Miranda."

"I wonder if he knew how he would die?"

"Surrounded by koi?"

"He seems almost to welcome it."

"He accepts — there's a difference."

"He doesn't say why he's picked me or how we connect."

"You don't remember him? Nothing?"

"Complete blank. When I heard his name today — I mean, WASP names are always familiar, you know what I mean? There are only so many to go around. But I never saw him before. His face in the class photo is indistinct. It was a grad course and I was an undergraduate. Everyone was older. He must have been in his forties if he's the guy in the pond. Morgan, I was the only undergraduate in linguistics to receive a graduate award. I noticed everything, everything."

"I got a philosophy scholarship in my last year. I didn't use it, either."

"But this is not about you." She waited for a response, then decided to override his silence in case he was sulking. "Griffin wants the Institute to be Semiology not Semiotics — in deference to Sandhu's Continental bent, I assume."

"It's extortion, you know."

"If I'm not onside, the Benevolent Fund loses big and the Canadian future of signifiers and signs is in peril. Morgan, maybe he didn't want to save himself."

"Or maybe that's what this is all about — saving

himself." They both considered the implications; the quiet of their shared breathing held them together. "Chateau Mouton Rothschild came out with a Balthus line drawing on the label of its 1993 vintage — a naked prepubescent vixen, and a threat to neo-puritan propriety. Outside of Europe the vintage was marketed with a blank label. And that's the one collectors want. Not the Balthus. They covet the empty label."

"Which only has meaning if you know the story."

"Exactly. You have to know what isn't there."

"That doesn't help," said Miranda. "Everything about this guy escapes me. What if we were friends or lovers and it's all gone away?"

"Unlikely!"

"But what if?"

"Then it will come back."

"Do you think you could have a real relationship with someone you don't know?"

"I saw a woman on the subway once when I was a kid, and she looked like I thought my mother could have looked if the world was different. I think of that woman sometimes, even now. She stayed the same age while I've grown old and cranky and my mother grew old and cranky and died. That woman I never knew has been a shaping influence in my life, and I just saw her once standing on the Rosedale platform, not even on the train. I was the one passing through."

"You wanted to become a Rosedale matron?"

"Good night, Miranda. We'll sort this out in the morning."

He didn't wait for her to respond but hung up gently. She wandered into the bedroom and turned out the lights.

The screen saver was still on. She sat in front of the

computer, stared into the vacuity of a virtual undersea world, and let the computerized parrotfish transform in her mind to real fish swimming beside her in crystal-clear water, butting their beaks against coral to free up nutrients, sliding lazily between dimensions like colourful ideas drifting at random, hovering asleep against boulder outcroppings, darting toward her bubbles, and swinging away in disdain from their urgent ascent.

Breaking from the sensual languor that was closing around her, withdrawing her hands from between her thighs where they had settled palms out, afraid the soporific of sex with herself might bring on nightmares, she punched up her email account. She dragged the entire bundle of new messages into the delete folder. As they flicked from view, a return address caught her eye. Retrieving the message, she slotted it back to the in box. The vaguely obscene Anglo-Saxon resonance of *kumonryu. ca* was overridden by the hint of something mysterious, and the message opened on the screen, confirming her instincts. It was a note from Robert Griffin.

Enough for one night, she thought. After skimming Griffin's detailed instructions on the care of his prize fish, which struck her as a not very odd directive, given their current relationship, she opened her Web browser and wandered from site to site, looking at koi, looking at fashion design websites, coming back to koi, looking at travel destinations, and more koi, until her personality was soothingly extinguished among worlds of pure information. Leaving the monitor on, she lay down and faded into a sleepless torpor that lasted until dawn broke open the day and she fell into herself once again.

3

Chagoi

The 911 call was from an elderly woman who had a clear view of the Griffin garden from her attic. She admitted it readily to the officers who came to her door early the next morning, and she ignored their query about why she hadn't given her name. The woman made it clear it would be an impertinence to ask why she had been in the attic. She enjoyed being interviewed. She didn't know Robert Griffin, she said, though her house had once belonged to his family.

As neighbours, they had exchanged occasional pleasantries, and when her husband died, Griffin delivered flowers in person. It was several years since they had last spoken. He employed cleaning and gardening services that came every week. And he had a *friend*.

His *friend* visited on a regular basis, usually midweek, late afternoon, and never stayed over.

Mrs. Jorge de Cuchilleros had observed nothing unusual on the day of Griffin's murder. She referred to "he" and "him" when he was alive as if that were his name, finding in the pronouns an appropriate distance from the sordid events and their tantalizing details. She couldn't imagine how the "remains" — said with the relish of an habitual Agatha Christie reader — how "it," as she thereafter referred to the body, depriving Griffin in death even of gender, got into the pond. She just glanced out, and he was dead. She felt it was her civic duty to inform the police. The uniformed officers assured her she had been very neighbourly and that real detectives would call by if there were any more questions.

When Miranda arrived at the Griffin place with two black coffees and cinnamon-raisin bagels, toasted, with light cream cheese, Morgan was beside the upper pond, talking to the officers who had interviewed the woman next door.

She handed Morgan his coffee and bagel. Information at this point was sparse. She had checked on the way over with Ellen Ravenscroft. A preliminary examination confirmed no evidence of significant wounds or bruises. A superficial cut on the forehead, nothing more.

Miranda sat on the limestone parapet. After a while, Morgan joined her. They consumed their breakfast without talking. Why would someone practise law on his own? she wondered. Why semiotics? It wasn't a middle-aged hobby. She couldn't get a grasp on Griffin as a living person, only as a corpse. Why would someone want to work homicide? Things like that just occurred — here they were, Morgan and her, hovering on either side of forty, with murder in common. At the moment, with the chimerical Robert Griffin in common. No, not a chimera; he was real. Yet she connected with him only in death.

Sometimes it happened that way. Both of them felt tremulations on occasion, returning to a crime scene where they had seen a locket around the neck of a derelict beaten to death, emptiness clutched in the dead hand of a rape victim. This was different. It wasn't empathy she felt, but a strange anxiety. Despite the lack of emotional hooks, Griffin's murder had taken on an eerie life of its own.

Was he the architect of a plot gone awry, or a victim of malevolence beyond his control? There was a lot of money involved, there was his stunning asexual mistress, there was Miranda's connection, there were the koi.

Miranda had absorbed more than she had thought the previous night, reading about koi on the Net. She had checked out Chagoi and wasn't convinced that every good pond would have one. She thought she could tell a Sanke from a Showa, a new-style Showa from an old. The intensity of black pigmentation against slashes of red on vibrant white was more intricate on the actual fish, and as they carved elusive patterns through the water she faltered, not sure she could tell one from another.

"We'd better feed them," she said.

"I did."

"How did you get into the house? I have the keys."

"There's food in the bin by the door."

"And you knew how much, of course. Nice Sanke, that one."

"Which one?"

"The big one."

"Which big one?"

So, she thought, those two were Sanke. The other big guy, the length of her arm with black on its head, had to be a Showa.

"I like the Showa best," she said. "Old-style. Lots of black."

"Sumi," he said. "Black is sumi, red is hi."

"What got you going on koi, Morgan? It's unusual even for you."

"A magazine cover in one of the big box stores. I was grazing through the magazine section, looking at gardening journals —"

"You don't garden."

"I know, but it was spring."

"Right."

"I saw the word *koi* in bright orange letters across the top of a magazine for the English country gardener, and I didn't know what koi meant —"

"You would hate that."

"So I've been reading. Good thing, too."

"For sure — if this is a crime about fish."

"Exactly."

"I was on the Net last night," said Miranda. "Emailed an old friend of mine, a marine biologist in Halifax. I asked her about the water swirling in the wrong direction. She's one hour ahead of us, so I got my answer this morning before I left home."

"We figured it was the filter."

"Yeah, but do you know why? It returns perpendicular to the wall to create a current, so the fish are always swimming. To keep them in shape. It can probably be reversed, so they swim both ways."

He chewed his bagel and sipped his coffee, resisting what to him seemed an obvious quip about swimming both ways. "Have I ever met her?"

"No, you don't know everyone I know, you know."

"I know."

They walked over to the lower pond. It was skirted by rocks placed with casual artifice as if by the hand of a thoughtful god. Set off against shrubbery, grasses, moss, and well-placed Japanese maples, close under the towering silver maples, there was a lovely decadence about it, haunting, like a Southern mansion from Faulkner drifting toward ruin.

"Must be a spring down there," said Miranda. "And enough seepage through the embankment to keep it fresh."

"Must be," said Morgan. She was right, of course. There had to be considerable flow if there were no filters or even an aerator.

"It's lined with bentonite clay." She settled down on her heels to scoop a handful of muck from below the waterline.

Of course, he thought.

"I'll bet there are fish in there," she said. "The diver missed them."

Of course: still water, the clay, freshness, the opacity.

"Have you ever tried to catch hold of a fish when you're underwater? You wouldn't even see it in here. A perfect growing environment for prize koi." She scraped the clay off her hand, rinsing in the opaque water.

"There's apparently a grate of some sort along the fence side," said Morgan. "The diver didn't think it went anywhere, part of an old drainage system. She said there was no current. Maybe fish were hiding behind the grate."

They walked back toward the house, agreeing the best fish might be hidden in the lower pond.

Like diamonds in a vault, a mink in cold storage, a stolen painting kept under the bed. Like a bottle of 1967 Chateau D'Yquem buried in the deepest recesses of a wine cellar, too valuable for an honest cop to consider drinking.

"'Fallen rain on autumn leaves,'" said Miranda as they stopped by the formal pond. "That's what Ochiba Shigura means. There's nothing about 'I am sad.' I checked it out."

He repeated the phrase. Then he added, "Nice, what you can do with words when you don't know their meaning. It's the most beautiful, the Ochiba Shigura."

"A little austere for me. You're very Presbyterian in your fish taste."

"Lapsed," he shot back, "and you're fallen. We lapse, Anglicans fall. It's all predetermined."

"The weird thing, the money — we haven't talked about that."

"Have you told Legal Affairs?"

"They'll pull me off the case."

"So don't tell."

"I have to. I'm just stalling."

"How come?"

"It's not much of a murder as murders go. A dead guy in a fish pond. And the world goes on."

"Yeah, except —"

"I'm the guy's executor."

"Executrix."

"Even if I turn him down, I'm compromised."

"Not so, unless you did it."

"What?"

"Killed him."

"I didn't even know him."

"And that's the real mystery."

"Morgan, I swear to God I don't remember the guy."

"He knew you."

"Or thinks he did."

"Could he have possibly known you'd be investigating his death?"

"I don't see how."

"Neither do I."

"Clairvoyance? Conspiracy? Coincidence?"

"Concupiscence!" she added to his list. "I'm not sure what that means, but it alliterates." She didn't know if *alliterate* was a verb.

He looked at her and thought about Freud. "Concupiscence means sexual desire."

"Yuck."

"Listen, I checked him out on the Web last night. Couldn't find much on Griffin personally — a rich lawyer, no record of ever pleading a case in court, not listed in the current *Who's Who,* no club memberships. I found more about the property than him, and the family. He was called to the bar in 1966, so he was a lawyer before he got into linguistics. He received a Ph.D. in 1987 from the University of Toronto. 'Language Acquisition and the Descent of Man.' Two copies of his dissertation are in the Library and Archives Canada, one copy registered with the Library of Congress in Washington, two copies in the Robarts Library at U of T. Published privately in a limited edition of fifty. No ISBN. You'll be handling a sizable estate. This house is older than you'd think. The family were in the mill business. They owned a feed mill and a carding mill in the Don Valley — paved over now. Woollen mills at one time and even a shingle mill. And farmland. They owned a good chunk of prime nineteenth century Rosedale, and several more grist mills in southwestern Ontario — your part of the world. I checked out the architectural drawings for this place. Do you know there's even a registered plan for the fish garden? A son and heir, probably Griffin's grandfather, built the Tudor monstrosity next door, made it bigger than the old man's, built a stone wall between them, then put in a gate, which looks as if it hasn't been opened in a century. He even drew up plans for a sheltered passageway, a tunnel affair, to get back and forth in inclement weather."

"*Inclement?*"

"Inclement weather."

"You know," she paused, looking at the Ochiba, trying to see what he saw, "someday the words that swirl inside your skull are going to explode."

"Implode."

"You know what you know, Morgan, and then you die."

"That's Presbyterian. Which I am not, by the way, not practising."

"You don't need practice to be a Presbyterian. There's no point. Isn't that the whole point — there is no point?"

He smiled. John Calvin in a nutshell, and from an Anglican.

"What's a Kumonryu?" she asked.

"Spell it. Your Japanese is terrible."

Miranda spelled it. She hadn't mentioned Griffin's email about caring for the koi.

"Known also, I think, as the dragon fish," said Morgan. "The Kumonryu changes colour as it grows, becomes dark and furtive, dissembling behind a progression from silver to platinum to pewter. You can never be sure with a dragon fish that it is what it seems."

"Sounds like people I've known."

"The dark side eventually takes over. A bland little fish becomes a creature of the shadows — the darkness is offset by radiant flashes of white, reminders of lost innocence."

"Dragons can be complex," she said. She couldn't always tell when he was quoting some esoteric text and when he was constructing his own modest parallel universe.

He didn't pursue her Kumonryu query. Sometimes the suppression of curiosity was strategy, sometimes carelessness or indifference.

Inside the house, in the den, they examined bins of chemicals behind the bar — sodium thiosulphate, salt, a canister of potassium permanganate. It had all been catalogued by the forensic squad.

"It's like a medieval alchemist's place," Morgan observed.

"More like a drug lab."

"I don't think so. This is how lawyers with fish fetishes live."

She reached down to open the door of a refrigerator under the bar. It was stocked with diet ginger ale and plastic bottles of something which, as Miranda read aloud from the label, turned out to be an aquaculture management product containing non-hazardous and non-pathogenic naturally occurring microbes, enzymes, and micro-nutrients. "If they're naturally occurring, why are they in plastic bottles?" There was a side-by-side freezer. She opened it. "Shrimp, and space for more shrimp. Ice cubes."

"Shrimp?"

"Treats for the fish." She looked down at the carpet. "Morgan, you knew this was antique and Kurdish from Iran. Persia. And I knew that you wouldn't keep a rug like this on a slate floor without an underpad. The other carpets in the house — he has a beautiful collection — are on wood floors, all of them on pads. Or displayed on the walls. So, what's happening here?"

"Damned if I know."

"And damned if you don't."

"Now that's Presbyterian," he said. "Let's go find the Chagoi."

"First, let's talk carpets."

After a tour of the house to show him the carpet collection, which was even better, according to Morgan, than she had imagined, they wandered back out to the garden, chatting about carpets and fish and dead lawyers. Here was a dead lawyer who worked on his own, who lived on his own, the last heir apparently of an old family fortune, truly to the manor born, in spite of his elderly neighbour's reported intimations to the contrary. Morgan had also checked out Mrs. Jorge de Cuchilleros during the night, guessing that it was the neighbour in the attic who had called 911. She was old-world money, her family was a "name" with Lloyd's; she was an only child from the other Rosedale, by the other ravine, where estates had gatehouses and the help lived in. She had married into impecunious European aristocracy.

As Morgan and Miranda talked by the formal pond, they watched a great shadow emerge from the depths, slowly rise, and take on colour that resolved in the sunlight into muted bronze, like crinkled foil. As the nostrils appeared above the surface and then the sad limpid eyes looked up at him, Morgan knew he had his Chagoi.

"Hand me the net," he said without breaking eye contact with the sad fish. "The big black one under the trellis. And the plastic tub."

When he slid the tub into the water beside the Chagoi, before he got the net into position to guide it, the big fish glided with a slight flutter of its pectoral fins into the container. Together Morgan and Miranda lifted the tub onto the low wall of the pool, then Morgan picked it up himself, carried it over to the pea-green pond, and gently lowered it into the water. After a few minutes to adjust while pond water flooded the container, the Chagoi flicked its tail and disappeared into the murky deep.

Morgan and Miranda waited so close that their clothing touched like the rustling of dry grass on a still day or the sound between calm water and the shore of a northern lake. They both knew northern lakes from working as students in the summers. They both loved summer, and the heart of winter. And the suddenness of spring, the slow advent of autumn. They agreed that March and November were the dismal months.

After a while, the big Chagoi surfaced and mouthed the air to express a healthy appetite, then faded back into opacity until Morgan returned with food. The fish rose to feed from his hand, and as it did, softly shifting patterns of red and white slowly came into focus in the water behind it. Heartened by the Chagoi, a myriad fish hovered randomly below the surface. Then, gradually, as the Chagoi swam away and back, taking food and releasing pellets into the surrounding water, they all began to eat.

"Okay," said Miranda. "We were right. These are fabulous Kohaku. There must be a fortune tied up in this pool. People pay astounding sums for fish like these."

"Yesterday you thought koi were pond ornaments. Miranda, the woman next door is watching us from her attic. Don't turn around! I saw her glasses, maybe binoculars. Okay, let's both look at once."

Miranda wheeled, and they both gazed at the attic window. There was the briefest flash, then the window emptied of even that much of Mrs. Jorge de Cucherillos.

"Who talked to her?" asked Miranda. "Don't you love the name? I knew someone called Snot once."

"You did not."

"I knew Finks and Risks and Underhills and Over-dales, and I went to school with Juliet Smellie —" She stopped suddenly, her banter overtaken by an observation. "Someone was here last night."

"How so?"

"There are no leaves on the ponds. There's a skimmer thing sucking most of them away on the upper pool, but not this one."

"It wasn't the pond maintenance people," said Morgan. "They checked out as water mechanics. They don't know much about the fish themselves. There was a guy here this morning when I arrived, just after sunrise. He seemed more concerned about lost business than murder."

"You were here at sunrise?"

"Got a call from a friend in the night, couldn't sleep for worrying. So, anyway, Griffin must have brought the fish directly from Japan. We can check customs, though maybe they're smuggled."

"A fish-smuggling lawyer with a language obsession!"

"Who he could sell to is an open question."

"Whom," Miranda corrected. "What about Mrs. Jorge de Cuchilleros?"

"She's housebound, apparently. Let's go and talk to her."

"My great-grandmother and her friends used to call each other by their last names. 'Mrs. Nisbell came to tea,' she'd say. 'And Mrs. Purvis and Mrs. Frank Pattinson, and so on.'"

"A bygone era when —"

"Women were women."

"When life was gracious."

"For the rich," said Miranda. "We weren't rich. Maybe village rich — we had indoor plumbing."

"I want to see inside the house."

"You weren't rich, either."

"I remember." He touched her on the arm as if to hold her back, though she was standing still. "I don't recall my father ever being called mister. My mother got Mrs., but only from people above her talking down."

"My parents were Mom and Dad even to each other."

"Mine were Darlene and Fred. And we lived in Cabbagetown when it was still Cabbagetown."

"The largest Anglo-Saxon slum outside England — I've heard it before, Morgan. And now there's no room there for the poor."

"I grew up on the cusp of transition, one neighbour's house derelict and the next a designer showpiece."

"I know — if you had owned and not rented from a slumlord, and if you had waited long enough, you would have made a killing. And your mother had a Scottish accent after eight generations in Canada."

"Yeah," he said, pleased and irritated by her familiarity with his life. "Let's amble over and visit our voyeur."

"*Amble,*" she said. "Okay, let's amble."

As they walked, she ruminated about what Morgan called "her part of the world." She still owned her mother's house in Waterloo County. She thought of it that way, as her mother's, though her parents had lived there together until the summer she had turned fourteen, when her father died. Her mother passed away four years ago. She and her sister in Vancouver were orphans. You were still an orphan even in your thirties when both parents were dead.

Miranda's sister had her own life and seldom came east. She had signed her share of the house over to Miranda. She and her husband were professionals, and Miranda's welfare, according to them, was more precarious. That was a judgment on her marital and not her financial status. Single

John Moss

women of a certain age inspired righteous condescension. Miranda didn't argue. It was satisfying to have the old house, though she didn't rent it out and only visited occasionally. She hadn't slept over since her mother's funeral. The village of Waldron was changing. When she walked to the general store, she sometimes recognized a familiar face but went unrecognized herself. Mostly, there were strangers now living in the old houses clustered around the crossroads, down the hill, and along the river.

Morgan and Miranda were greeted at the door by a Filipino woman who showed them into a formal receiving room that was dark and excessive, with numerous old photographs in sterling frames propped in strategic formation, a genealogical gallery that seemed to have reached its terminus about the time of the Great War and before the Great Depression. Everything was "Great" back then until the age of irony set in. There were heavy velvet drapes pulled back and ferns in the window, a perfect camouflage for someone observing the street without being seen.

When Mrs. Jorge de Cuchilleros entered the room, it was with a sense of occasion, as if her presence gave the encounter significance in excess of what a dead lawyer might conjure, especially one found in a fish pond. Yet she was herself neither stately nor ancient, and while she may have preferred to avoid crowds since Toronto had become so cosmopolitan — as she would describe it, her tolerance for ethnic diversity implicit — she wasn't bound to stay in by virtue of any crippling condition. She simply enjoyed the role of reclusive widow, which she did with relish for Mormons, meter readers, and homicide detectives, even for policemen in uniform. Since the Georgian Room at Eaton's had closed a generation ago, she hadn't been south of Bloor Street.

On the floor was a magnificent carpet. Morgan recognized the stylized peacocks of an antique Akstafa from the southern Caucasus. In spite of that the room made him uncomfortable. While the women talked, he assessed the furnishings. Apart from the carpet, it all seemed in opulent bad taste, a sad relic of Victorian imperialism. He asked for the bathroom and was surprised when the Filipino maid answered the ring of a small crystal bell to show him the way.

There was a convenience on the same floor at the back, he was told. He was led through a panelled dining room and caught a glimpse of the garden. When the maid seemed about to wait for him outside the lavatory door, he motioned her away a bit awkwardly, trying in the gesture of his hand for casual civility, neither excessively familiar nor imperious. It was the first time in his life that he had encountered someone in the role of servant who answered to a bell. Instinctively, he wanted to call after her that he was from Cabbagetown, at least as alien from all this as Manila.

Back in the dining room, he examined the huge Heriz carpet spread almost wall to wall, then gazed outside. The garden was rather dismal, compared to its neighbour, but to his surprise there was a large green pond.

When he returned to the receiving room, he asked Mrs. de Cuchilleros if she kept koi. No, she explained. Not really. A few, nothing to speak of. She wasn't sure. Thirty years ago, when they bought the property, Robert Griffin had asked if he could keep a few fish in her pond, and on several occasions, she didn't know how often, she had looked out very early in the morning and seen him by the pond as if standing vigil. He would stare into the water like an Inuk hunter — which meant Eskimo, she explained — and then without coming to the door he would leave. There was no upkeep; it was a natural system. Sometimes in the autumn he came over and skimmed leaves off the surface. It never froze over completely in winter. She had seen movement in the murky water but couldn't say if it was fish, flesh, or foul. She spelled out the last word for the sake of the pun.

"Does it smell?" asked Miranda. "The pond next door is fresh."

"No," said Mrs. de Cuchilleros, annoyed that her jest had provoked a literal response. "Not at all. It is as fresh as his." She summoned her maid and said something to her in apparently fluent Spanish. A colonial habit, Miranda thought. Spanish is the old language of the Philippines, supplanted by English and Tagalog, but both women would regard it as the appropriate language of servitude — the maid speaking it out of deference and Mrs. de Cuchilleros, because she could.

The maid responded with a brief expletive and left.

"No," Mrs. de Cuchilleros repeated. "I asked Dolores if she ever noticed a smell — I hardly ever go out there — and she said no. So there you are, my freshwater oasis. If there are fish in it now, I expect they'll stay for the duration. No one feeds them, they get enough wild insects, as opposed to the tame ones, and they live longer than people. I have a gardener come in most days, but he just mows to the edge of the pond. It's clay, you know, brought in by the Griffins generations ago, the one who built this place. It's a nice old pond. My first husband loved it."

"Mrs. Cuchilleros, were you married before?" asked Miranda in surprise.

"*De* Cuchilleros, *my dear*. Jorge de Cuchilleros was my only husband, my first and last."

"Oh," said Miranda.

When they said goodbye and were outside, Miranda

took Morgan by the arm and led him around through the walkway into the lawyer's garden, talking all the way. "*My first husband*. How quaint. *De*, and *my dear*. Her little jokes. She's a caricature. What she said to the maid, besides asking about the smell, was 'Do not serve tea.' Did you notice she called her Dolores, almost the same as your mother's name?"

"Darlene."

"Who?"

"My mother."

"Sorry. I thought it was Delores. Did you find anything when you went to the bathroom? She gave me the creeps. We should have asked to see the attic. Reminds me of *Psycho,* Anthony Perkins rocking in the window. I wonder if she had children."

Morgan said nothing.

"She killed him!" Miranda blurted.

"Anthony Perkins?"

"She killed Robert Griffin."

Morgan smiled. He liked when she held his arm. He knew he wasn't supposed to, but he could feel the curve of her breast as they strolled through the garden.

"I'd better check in with Legal Affairs," she said, pulling away from him. "See you about five."

He watched as she walked away. She should always wear skirts. How did a woman decide if it was a skirt or pant day? He never understood the subliminal conspiracy in the way women dressed, how one day it was décolletage and another short skirts. One short skirt in the morning, and he knew it would be legs and short skirts for the day. He thought of a joke: would a community of nuns aspiring to sainthood all experience stigmata at the same time of the month? It was a woman's joke. To him it was more of a mystery.

4

Kumonryu

Miranda left with the keys. Morgan could still feel the weight of her hand on the inside of his arm. Walking around to the front of the house, he descended the ramp from street level to the garage where the door was still open from the night before. He ducked under the yellow tape marking it a crime scene and entered a large vault with enough space for three or four cars. Only a classic Jaguar two-seater was parked there at the moment. He didn't know the model; he had never developed an interest in cars. Growing up where buses, the subway, and trolleys were the alternatives to pedestrian transit, he had never known anyone who actually owned a car until university. Even then he wasn't much interested in students who insinuated cars into the sanctuary of a campus with gardens and manicured lawns in the heart of the city. He didn't learn to drive until after his degree, teaching himself on a rental automatic, using fake ID, graduating to standard shift a few weeks later.

Morgan had never worked traffic. His university specialization in the sociology of deviance got him into investigations from the start, so he didn't work his way up from the streets. He liked to present himself as an academic bumbler, but as Miranda surmised, he had been a stellar student and might have pursued an academic career except he had an undisciplined imagination and too many enthusiasms. Though he majored in the human sciences, he preferred philosophy. Morgan was a Heideggerian, as he recalled, no longer sure what that meant.

He would have to learn about cars. There was a certain perversity in his sustained ignorance, however, that gave him the same kind of pleasure as not knowing about hockey. Only a fact junky can appreciate the pleasures of purposely not knowing. He could name complete rosters from the old National Hockey League before 1967 when there were only six teams and every player was a star. He had no idea what teams out of Tampa and Pittsburgh were called. He could name every player on the women's Olympic team that won in Nagano. He was the only person in Canada who had never played hockey, according to Miranda, who used to play shinny on the Ice Pond outside Waldron — called that because ice had been harvested there long before she was born.

There were two doors from the heated garage into the house. Both were locked. The one he tried opened easily enough with a little persuasion. From an efficiently rectilinear space that smelled of machine oil, he stepped into a musty confusion of brick work and stone, muffled odours of other times, shadows converging, the air ominously still.

As he made his way among the convoluted inner foundations, he had the sense of walking outside the boundaries of history. The original structure of the house was virtually intact, though on the exterior it had been tarted up with Victorian turrets and verandahs and gingerbread trim. He knew he must be on the same level as the garden out back and the den, but this was a world apart.

Morgan stopped beside a great oak door with huge hand-forged hinges. He sat on a makeshift bench in the bleak light of bulbs strung sparingly between hand-hewn beams, their illumination barely extending through the darkness from one pool of light to the next. Here were remnants of a Toronto beyond his experience.

This city was his place of origin, his genetic source, not Ireland or Wales, as his name would suggest, or Scotland, where his mother's people originated. He came from nowhere else. In the motley assemblage of clay brick, rough plaster, and stonework over a cobbled floor, in the adze marks gouged into the squared oak beams, the hammered ironwork on the door, he saw the residue of a past that was strangely familiar. Like discovering a fingerprint embedded in the surface of an ancient relic; it wasn't someone else's history he sensed, but his own.

His ancestors had built these walls, or maybe they had owned them. Class and money had a way of sideslipping in Canada every few generations. He was at home here, connected to cobwebs and dust, though there were surprisingly little of either. The echoes of dead artisans' dreams resounded around him, and he rose to go about his silent business, moving by stealth, it would seem to a ghostly observer, to take in the emanations that might be clues to the mystery of their lives.

He returned to the oak door. Beside it was a control panel with a thermostat and humidistat, the keyboard to an alarm system, and a light switch. There was a small window in the door. When he peered through the glass, which was two layers thick with a space between, he realized the oak, despite its mighty appearance, was a facade for a thermal door. He flicked the switch, but the room remained dark. He could make out rows of bottle ends in a rack opposite the door, which was securely locked, though the alarm, oddly enough, was disarmed. This was what a real wine cellar was like.

Wandering through the subterranean maze, Morgan was surprised at the images that popped into his mind, some of them curiously macabre, some strangely erotic. He thought of his first encounter with sex, with Francine Cardarelli in the janitor's closet near the end of grade eleven at Jarvis Collegiate. He thought of a severed head in a garbage container under a sink. Frankie married Vittorio Ciccone. They sent him a wedding present, but he was working homicide by then and returned it despite Lucy's objection. Nothing was proven; the Ciccone family might not have been involved.

A strange underground concatenation of opposites, he thought — it was warm but cool on the skin, bone dry and musty, darkness striated with light, sounds reverberating in the hushed air, closed in and endless … endless. It was like walking through the inside of somebody's brain, maybe Griffin's, maybe his own, or the collective mind where disparates converged.

Approaching what he estimated to be the back corner of the house closest to the garden wall, he came to another oak door. It, too, appeared to be elaborately bolted and locked. Backtracking to the near side of the labyrinth, he discovered two more massive doors. One had to lead into the den, perhaps through the hall where the bathroom was. It seemed to be bolted from the inside. The other was at the bottom of a further descent into the depths of the earth and, to his surprise, it swung open with a tentative touch.

Walking through he found himself in what looked like the inner workings of a submarine. There were pumps and pipes and tanks in profusion. A symphony of small motors and the muffled gurgle of water moving against smooth surfaces filled the room with the aura of inspired efficiency, like listening to Rimsky-Korsakov at low volume.

Morgan slid back the cover of one of the cylindrical chambers that narrowed to a cone at the bottom and observed a vortex of water with a pump-like contraption at the centre that seemed to filter particulates from the flow. He had read about filter systems when he took up virtual koi, but since he had no experience with real fish, he generally glossed over the details of polishing water to absolute purity.

Moving methodically about the room, he traced the flow from a series of three converging intake pipes coming through the outer wall below the frost line — these would be from the bottom drains in the formal pond — into the self-cleaning filter in the first vortex chamber and the other chambers, through a two-speed pump into a huge bead filter where little nubules devoured nitrites and ammonia from fish waste and released harmless nitrates back into the water, past a sequence of three ultraviolet lights enclosed in chrome tubes the size of torpedoes, and finally to an outtake pipe leading underground back to the pond.

There were various configurations of short pipes and shut-off valves whose purpose he couldn't quite divine, a couple of tanks that looked like hot water heaters that were on a bypass, a completely separate smaller system to activate and flush out the skimmer, and an outlet accessed from the main line by a series of valves that led in the direction of the lower pond, perhaps to top it up if the natural system broke down.

Against the wall beside the door he had come through there was a computerized control console, and beneath the raised window that looked out through shrubs at ground level across the garden there was an old-fashioned concrete laundry tub. Draped over the brass waterspout, inconspicuous in its everyday utility, was a rag that on close examination might once have been lingerie.

A door leading to outside steps up into the garden was sealed. He had noticed the low window partially obscured by shrubbery the previous night but had assumed it accessed a closed-in crawl space. The cellar stairway outside must have been filled in. One could only get to this plumber's fantasy through the den or the garage, which seemed a little inconvenient, though with everything run by computer and insulated from the winter cold, there would be no need to spend much time here. He expected the computer could be monitored from somewhere else in the house, probably the study on the second floor where he had noticed a daunting array of electronic paraphernalia that stood out from the shelves of books like zircons on a platinum ring.

Turning to leave the way he had come in, Morgan noticed a scrap of yellow notepaper pinned against the edge of a shelf above a workbench. He leaned over the small array of power tools and read slowly, finding it difficult to decipher the smudged script:

> Jacques Lacan suggests language is an essential precondition to the development of the unconscious mind, without which there could be no consciousness, and therefore no sense of the self.

There were a couple of lines he couldn't make out. He pulled the note from the pin and took it to the window, holding it slantwise into the light. Several sentences were intentionally obliterated, as if half-formed thoughts had been deleted, then it continued with a certain obstinate obscurity that Morgan found pompous and provocative:

> It seems reasonable to suggest that in the evolution of the species it was the emergence of language that led to consciousness, and not the reverse. Signifieds in the environment had to separate from signifiers before signs became possible —

The text stopped abruptly, but the writer had found his ruminations worth keeping, if only impaled on a cellar shelf. Morgan folded the note neatly and stuffed it in his pocket to show Miranda.

As he turned back into the subterranean labyrinth he had come through, made somehow macabre by light bulbs dangling against shadows, the notion of this as a mausoleum for his anonymous forebears gave way to images of the catacombs beneath poppy fields outside the walls of Rome. He half expected burial niches in the walls, an illusion the play of light and shadow on the rough foundation reinforced.

Morgan remembered how eerie it was that, for all the desiccated corpses and piled bones he had seen in the crypts of Europe, he had felt a stronger presence of death from the absence of human remains in the catacombs. Meandering at the back of a guided tour, past gaping small tombs cut into the lava rock, he had been struck by their emptiness as a mockery of resurrection, their occupants dust inhaled by cadres of tourists. He had felt the cold impress of mortality then, despite the relative warmth of the place. And he felt it now, the familiar chill, yet given the nature of his work and why he was here, morbidity seemed appropriate.

He stopped again at the wine cellar and peered through the double glass window, regretting not having a flashlight. Only in movies did flashlights appear from nowhere as the plot demanded. If he were in a movie, he would be a younger Gene Hackman. When the credits appeared, his name wouldn't be there. He would still be inside the story. Closure was only for actors and authors.

It was in Europe that he had decided against graduate school, though he had tried it briefly when he came back. He went over for two and a half years, crossing both ways on the *Stefan Batory*, one of the last passenger ships not flaunting itself for the carriage trade. He hadn't taken out student loans, having been on a scholarship and working in the north each summer, one year building a spur line into a mine, two years on road crew, and one year, the toughest and most lucrative, planting trees. Unlike his middle-class contemporaries, he finished university with money in the bank.

Trees paid his way through Europe. He was a high-baller, sometimes planting three thousand trees a day, and his savings, subsidized by illegal bar-tending jobs in London and for a while on Ibiza, meant he came home broke but debt-free.

In graduate school he felt distant from other students who had gone directly into their programs, and had little in common with the older students who were making meaningful career changes. He hadn't picked up his graduate fellowship cheque by the end of the first week, so he just walked away. At the end of the next week he was enrolled in criminology at George Brown College. It had never occurred to him to join the police; it just happened.

His first autumn in London he met the woman he should have married. Susan. He married Lucy.

From the beginning, when Susan answered the door next to his, after he moved into a shabbily genteel bedsitter in Beaufort Gardens on the fifth floor of one of the last unreclaimed buildings in Knightsbridge, he called her Sue.

"Very Canadian," she told him. "In England it's with two syllables."

She was amused, however, and agreed to join him for a Guinness at The Bunch of Grapes on Brompton Road.

He had never before had a friend like her, someone so emotionally complete. Through the long, wet autumn, winter, and spring, when he wasn't working, they spent weeknight evenings in his room, which was smaller than hers and easier to heat. They were relatively impoverished — London was expensive and wages were low — but they talked their way through the seasons and hardly noticed. He realized, more than two decades later, he must have done most of the talking, while Sue listened with cheerful forbearance, filling gaps in his rambling narrative with self-deprecating anecdotes and funny explanations about the fine points of being English.

On the weekends she went home and Morgan wandered London. Some Saturday evenings he returned to his garret so exhausted by the miles he had walked that he fell asleep across the top of his lumpy single bed without undressing, pulling his thick Canadian coat around him, shoes still on for warmth. He slept until dawn, got up, peed in the rickety sink, splashed water on his face from the single faucet, brewed a quick cup of tea on his hot plate, and ventured out into the pale green spaces of Hyde

Park to watch early arrivals, even in the dreariest weather, taking their morning constitutionals. Then he wandered for the rest of the day, and by afternoon began to anticipate Sue's return so he could tell her about London.

They didn't have a storybook romance; they didn't fall in love with each other at the same time. He was in love with her now, though his memories of her had merged with Miranda. Sue was patiently in love for at least part of that year before he took off to the Continent. With her coppery red hair and refined complexion, gentle good humour, and patiently inquiring intelligence, she had been remarkably lovely. But Morgan had constructed his personality as someone astonished by the adventures that lay before him, desperately self-reliant and determinedly unattainable. He wanted to explode at the centre of the universe, while Susan remained generous and serene.

On and off, Morgan worked behind a bar most of the time he was in London, and Susan, as he now thought of her, held a demanding secretarial position with a boss called Nigel and a friend called Fiona, names that seemed eerily exotic. Class, the English pestilence, was never an issue between them. He was educated; Susan was elegant. Neither could place the other in a social hierarchy that made any sense. They had never been good lovers; both of them were relative novices. He was selfish and she was gracious, a bad combination. Their time together was defined more by warmth than by passion. He encouraged her to visit Canada, and she invited him to meet her parents. When Morgan was engaged to be married, he had dreamed Susan would turn up in Toronto. She did, briefly, but the timing was off. He had known even she couldn't rescue him then.

Morgan became aware that he was comfortably ensconced on the bench opposite the wine cellar. He didn't remember sitting down, but he was absorbed in the atmosphere of the place and it didn't bother him that he had lost track of time. He forgot about Susan and London. They faded from consciousness like the particles of a dream.

"What is it, Morgan?" Miranda would say. "Where have you been?"

But he seldom answered. It didn't seem important to sort out recollections from the swarming of information careening through the sometimes unfamiliar places in his mind. He wasn't unstable, but wary of being too much himself.

The oak door leading toward the den opened this time when he gave it a vigorous shove, and he found himself in a short hallway with the small bathroom to one side. The door at the far end of the corridor leading into the den stood ajar. It was an exterior door made of steel, painted and panelled to look like wood. He had noticed the night before that it had a large lock with a dead bolt, which didn't strike him as unusual, given that it probably led in from the garage. There was a patina of dents and scratches on the corridor side that advertised its serviceability.

Availing himself of the bathroom convenience, Morgan admired the absolute simplicity of the room. It was like being inside a tiled box — even the ceiling was tiled — and the toilet and sink were built in. The shower head draped like a pewter sunflower from high on a wall, and the shower stall area was defined only by a standing drain and a ridge in the tile on the floor. There was no mirror, there were no shelves, no pictures, nothing to intrude on the mind or distract the eye, and yet the overall effect was pleasing. Still, it didn't encourage lingering. Maybe that was the point — a small architectural joke by Robert Griffin, perhaps not shared by anyone else.

The thought of Griffin made Morgan uncomfortable. This was the first point of connection he had felt with the victim. The passion for koi, he understood, and the books and the carpets, but comprehending the facts of a person's existence was different from recognition of their secret whims. What other secrets were in this place hidden by the obvious? He stood and pressed a plunger panel that was flush to the wall over the toilet and walked away from the swirling noise, washing his hands and leaving the room without glancing back.

Morgan settled down in the den on what, from the comforting way the cushion met the weight of his body, he was sure would have been the favourite chair of the dearly departed, sustaining him through long hours of contemplation about koi and linguistics. Gazing out across the garden and lawn, Morgan could see, beyond the trunks of the giant silver maples, intimations of the city he loved like an old family home. This made him feel closer to the house surrounding him, as if it were the mantle of what might have been. Here, but for the grace of God and a lot of money, and the random perversity of genetic progression … his thoughts were outpaced by emotion.

There was something very sensual and vaguely distressing about letting his feelings run free. Morgan was used to the effects of an unbridled intellect, but sensibility, open and indiscriminate, took him by surprise. It was knowing about wine, not tasting, that enthralled him.

He shut his eyes and tried to envision Susan as she might be now. She looked like Miranda. He tried to focus, and the name Donna came to mind, preceding an image of someone he had forgotten he had known.

Susan was his first love. But his first "affair" was Donna. Not *with* Donna, but Donna herself. She *was* the affair. Donna didn't haunt him the way Susan did. She didn't remind him of Miranda. But Donna had helped shaped who he was.

She had worked as a waitress in a Jarvis Street diner on the edge of Cabbagetown in a nondescript building squeezed between two former mansions. He had wandered in one night on the way back to his room near the university after one of his rare visits with Fred and Darlene. He and his dad had been sitting on the stoop all evening, drinking beer. His mom was out with her friends. She had been drinking, too. When she came back, they had a raucous three-way quarrel. He couldn't remember why. The important part of his recollection wasn't the fight, but meeting Donna.

"Coffee?" she had asked in the diner.

"Please," he answered in a slurred voice, leaning over his elbows on the grey Formica table, head in his hands.

She brought him the coffee. "You okay?"

He remembered looking up with tears in his eyes, even though he couldn't remember why he was crying. Maybe it was something his mother had said, and suddenly he was confronted with childhood's end. Maybe his father had made a crack about the effete life of a student. Or it might have been the fight itself — being drawn into domestic squalor that he wanted desperately to put behind him.

The waitress placed her hand over his. "This one's on me."

Instead of saying "what" or "thank you," he asked, "Why?"

"Because you're drunk, you're not a drinker, you need coffee."

"Must be lots of drunks come in here."

"Yeah."

She smiled as he stared at her face, bringing her eyes into focus. They were bright blue, sparkling in the fluorescent light. Her lipstick was a thick red, and her dark roots made her hair radiate like a platinum halo around her head. In spite of her garish makeup, she was young. They were about the same age.

He smiled back. "Thanks. He glanced around and realized he was the only customer, then announced in a significant tone, "I'm a virgin."

"Good. I'm glad there's one left."

"One what?"

"Virgin."

"I'm a virgin. Technically. You know what I mean."

"I can imagine. You're drunk. But very pretty."

Morgan was bewildered. No one had called him pretty before. He didn't know whether to be flattered or insulted. He decided flattery was preferable. "You're very pretty, too. Do you want to take me home?"

She did, and that was the beginning of Morgan's first affair, which after ten days burned out because they had nothing to say to each other. She taught him about a woman's body as if she were much older, and he felt secure enough that he learned with awkward enthusiasm more than he could have imagined and far less than he needed to be a good lover. It didn't occur to him to resent her experience.

Their last night together, after she finished the late shift and before he went to his morning class, they both knew their relationship had run its course. In a gesture to make the finality of their parting less certain, he invited her to a lecture he would be giving in two months.

"What are you talking about?" she asked him.

"It's by invitation. My philosophy prof asked me to speak at a graduate seminar. It's a big deal. They don't usually let undergraduates speak."

"What's it gonna be about?"

"Heidegger ..."

She smiled benignly, drawing him to her. "You really are sweet."

A couple of months later he stepped up to the podium in a lecture hall at the university before anyone else was in the room. His topic had aroused considerable interest, and Father Harris, his professor, had asked if he would mind opening his presentation to a larger audience. Morgan was thrilled. He looked out across the rows of empty seats. He wasn't at all nervous. He was sure of his material and confident of his ability to deliver. This was a prelude, he thought, to a career in the professorial ranks.

Father Harris came in and chatted with him. A few students entered and gathered in clusters toward the back of the room.

"It's always this way," Father Harris assured him. "Lecture halls fill up from the back." Father Harris was enough to make Morgan want to be Catholic, even though he was already agnostic.

Morgan glanced up the aisle as a flash of brilliant red appeared at the back of the hall. He looked away, then back again. It was Donna, and she was dressed for a party. She waved and manoeuvred precariously on stiletto heels down the incline to where he was standing with the lectern between them. He stared at her with his mouth open, completely thrown. Father Harris reached out his hand and introduced himself. Donna smiled a huge red smile and curtsied slightly. She had never before talked to a priest.

Struggling to regain his composure, Morgan was too flustered to say anything. Donna leaned around the lectern and kissed him on the cheek. The scoop neck of her dress gaped open. He could feel the smudge of her lipstick like a scarlet letter glowing on his skin as she moved slightly away, being uncertain of the protocol such an occasion demanded.

"I'm proud of you," she said.

Father Harris took her arm in a proprietorial way, bowing slightly. He smiled at her as if she were an old friend of the family. She gazed up at him and smiled her red smile, and turned and smiled at Morgan. Her eyes dazzled blue in the lights of the hall.

"Won't you join me, Donna?" asked Father Harris. "We'll just give David a few moments. Even the most experienced of us gets a little anxious before giving an important lecture." He led her to a seat beside his own, making a clear and subtle show to the audience who had understood in the last few minutes that she was his guest.

The presentation was well received and led indirectly to the offer of a scholarship to do graduate work. At the informal reception following his lecture, Father Harris kept Donna by his side, and when the evening began to subside, he called her a taxi and paid the driver in advance. As she was going out the door, she turned to catch Morgan's eye and mouthed the words "Thank you" with her full red lips as if it were the best day of her life.

Morgan was ashamed of himself for weeks afterward and went off to plant trees, then on to his adventure in Europe, without picking up his degree.

Donna, he thought now, *whatever happened to you?* As he stirred uneasily in the embrace of the wingback chair in Griffin's house, he imagined Donna's big red lips and blue eyes and blond mane of hair with its dark roots surrounding her oval face, and he felt wistful, knowing she would never have thought he had done anything wrong.

Abruptly, Morgan rose to his feet, breaking the bond between himself and the residual personality of Robert Griffin, leaving memories of Donna behind.

Morgan leaned over the ceramic box to examine an old board with worn edges, placed alongside it with casual artifice as if the owner were trying to subvert its value. He ran his hand lightly over the etched surface, feeling the hieroglyphs with his fingers.

So that was what half a million felt like, what words felt like when their meaning wasn't known.

Morgan sat down again, feeling queasy. What was he doing here? he thought in Miranda's voice. He hated when the words in his head seemed to come from her. Morgan got up and puttered around the room. He needed to know this man if he was to understand his death. He needed to distance himself.

Feelings of ambivalence toward Griffin bothered Morgan. He was better with ambiguity. Ambivalence demanded choice, and he preferred hovering between.

That was how Miranda understood him, how she explained his mind. He suspected this was a projection of how she saw herself. It didn't cross his mind that he saw himself reflected in her.

They had been together for more than a decade. They fitted together like long-time lovers who were afraid if they ever got married the vital uncertainty between them would dissipate and they would lose their separate identities.

Both of them had a poor view of marriage, Morgan from limited experience and Miranda by extrapolation from all the constrictions she thought she could see in the lives of friends and in the smug, dreary life of her sister in Vancouver. Morgan feared what he knew and Miranda what she knew nothing about.

Their first case working together had been a grisly execution. When he saw her walk through the door at the crime scene, an unconventionally pretty young woman with a steely look in her eyes, he had been surprised. He was never quite sure why.

"Where did you come from?" he had said.

"I just finished doing federal time." Since that got no reaction, she added, "RCMP, Ottawa."

"I don't need a personal history. Do you ride?"

"Horses? Had to learn."

"Did you like it?" he asked.

"Being mounted?"

They exchanged glances, and that was the last time in her life Miranda tried to be one of the boys.

"Do you like horses?" he asked, not because he was interested but to get them over the hump.

"I didn't try out for the Musical Ride if that's what you're thinking." She surveyed the ghastly scene surrounding them.

"How long?"

"In the Mounties? Three years."

"Posing for pictures with the governor general?"

"And once with the queen. I'm photogenic. The scarlet doesn't bleed out my natural colouring."

"You might have been good in the Musical Ride."

"Not very."

"You would have ended up working traffic detail."

"Or crowd control," she said. "I decided murder would be preferable."

"You're in the right place."

"They sent me up from the shop."

He had never heard police headquarters described as the shop.

"Superintendent Rufalo said I'll be working with you."

"Morgan."

"Yeah, I know. Miranda Quin. With one *n*."

"Didn't know you could spell it with two."

"Quin?"

"Miranda."

"You can't. Oh ..." She smiled, feeling relaxed.

Beside them on the floor were four bodies, hands bound with duct tape, three with tape over their mouths, their throats slit, rigid in grotesque postures of death, having squirmed in their own pooling blood until each had expired. The fourth had been decapitated and was lying separately as if the others had been forced to witness his death before submitting to their own. An object lesson of short duration.

"It's a Chinese name," Morgan said.

"It's Ontario Irish."

"China's first emperor was Qin. With one *n*."

"I doubt he spelled it phonetically."

"Second century BC."

"How do you know that?"

"Six thousand terra-cotta warriors guard his tomb."

"Oh, him," she said. "Where's the guy's head?"

"Over there in the garbage bucket under the sink, with coffee grounds and eggshells dumped over it. Whoever did this stayed for breakfast. I told forensics not to touch it until you got here. Welcome to the city of love and adventure."

"Good to be here," she had told him. "It's like I've never been away."

Morgan walked around Griffin's den and sat again

in what was beginning to take on the familiarity of a habitual posture, in what felt like his own chair, and pondered. That was his way: the resolution of the most recalcitrant mystery could usually be found in the life of the victim, especially in cases of first-degree murder. Let the observations accumulate, bits of information gleaned from the way the deceased got by in the world, and eventually, unforced, they would fall into place and the killer would be revealed in their pattern. That was how he liked to think of the process, and it worked often enough to reinforce his assumption.

Why, he wondered, was this guy writing notes to himself about language? They were obviously part of a larger discourse. He looked around for a likely repository and reached for a coffee table book called *Koi Kichi* on the floor beside the chair. The title translated as *Crazy for Koi*, the koi keeper's compleat companion. He knew the book well. Anyone interested in koi knew Peter Waddington's book. He opened it seemingly at random, but as he anticipated the pages parted where another piece of yellow notepaper lay awaiting revelation:

> Dogs can be trained to obey simple commands such as "sit" and "stay." Yet if the command giver is lying in front of the television and gives the command to sit, the dog ignores it. Why? Because the dog has been taught by a person who normally stands while giving the command. It responds not to words but to a complex gestalt of sound, gesture, posture, circumstance, after considerable training. If any one factor is significantly altered, the dog is baffled.

Exceptional dogs may in their desire to please or avoid the commander's displeasure adapt an appropriate response to what is perceived as a new gestalt after a certain amount of trial and error. Then, as likely as not, they will sit directly in front of the television. This is probably not an expression of innate perversity.

What does this tell us? Perhaps not much about dogs, beyond the fact that they are neither as smart nor as perverse as we think.

To apply the word *learning* to the behavioural modification of dogs is no more appropriate than to suggest a computer thinks or an equation resolves. The language of mathematics, of digital machines, and of dogs, is not language at all, but we have no other word to describe their function in response to human volition.

Morgan was dismayed by the revelation of an engaged personality, by the casual wit. He was intrigued with how he had known there would be a note in *Koi Kichi*. He picked up another koi book from the table beside him and flipped it open, but there was nothing inside.

Restless, he wandered back into the subterranean labyrinth. Complex patterns of shadows playing against walls weathered rough by age re-created in his mind something of the sinister melodrama in Madame Tussauds Chamber of Horrors, where he had last seen Susan in London before he returned to Canada. Morgan had spent the preceding year and a half tramping through Europe. He lived on Formentera for a couple of months, just across from Ibiza, ensconced in the ruins of a Martello tower, writing. For a brief time he thought he would be a writer. He worked in an Ibizan taverna for the entire summer, seldom letting the travelling students who were doing soft drugs in the courtyard know he spoke English. He liked the power of linguistic invisibility. He ran with the bulls in Pamplona and felt foolish for doing so; he didn't even like Hemingway very much. He travelled to Turkey where he spent a month hanging out in the bazaar and learned about carpets, especially about Anatolian kilims from across the Bosphorus.

"I have a baby," Susan told him in Madame Tussauds.

He felt a stab of betrayal. "Congratulations."

"Congratulations," she echoed.

There was a long silence. They both looked at the grotesque effigy of a Jack the Ripper victim, her blood glinting in the directed light. Susan was smiling.

"Congratulations," he said again tentatively.

"He's a lovely boy, David." She smiled up at him, her auburn hair falling away from her face. "I call him Nigel."

"Oh," said Morgan with unseemly relief. "I'm sorry."

"What, that he isn't yours, or that I call him Nigel?"

He wanted to marry her, he wanted to take her to Australia, he wanted her to meet Darlene and Fred.

"You just needed to know," she said.

"Can I see him?"

"He's with my parents in Kent. I have a picture, fairly recent."

She showed him the picture without releasing her grip, bending with him into a light beam shining on the macabre tableau so that he could make out the ambiguous features of a baby.

They hugged a long goodbye outside Madame Tussauds. After walking down Baker Street a bit, he turned and called to her, "What's his name again?"

She walked back to him. "Nigel."

"What's his real name?"

"It doesn't matter, David. Names are just names." Susan glanced to the side. "I love you, David. Do take good care." Then she had touched her finger to his lips, turned, and walked away.

Tears now unaccountably clouded his vision as he approached the great oak door at the end of the passage leading to the farthest corner of the foundation. Morgan had tried it before, and it had been locked. He was at an impasse. The door led to Mrs. de Cuchilleros's place if it led anywhere. The projected walkway between the houses hadn't been abandoned, just moved underground. It would have to come out in her carriage house or connect to her basement or go up into her garden. Was that how Griffin had crossed over in those early mornings when Mrs. de Cuchilleros said she had found him beside her pond, standing vigil — a memorable description? And then she had said he would simply disappear.

The elaborate array of iron bolts and flanges on the door was held in place by a single padlock. He hadn't noticed that before. One good knock would open it. He ran his fingers over the padlock, then turned and trudged back through the stone and shadow passageways. He wanted to surface into the light, to walk in the garden.

5

Doitsu Showa

Miranda returned to find Morgan contemplative under the trellised portico, perched on a feed barrel. As they ambled through the garden, she handed him a sandwich, assuming he had forgotten to eat lunch.

"Thanks," he said. "I forgot to eat lunch."

"I'm off the case," she said, looking at him with odd satisfaction. "And guess what, Eleanor Drummond doesn't exist."

"She's a very convincing illusion."

"Do you think so?"

"She was Griffin's witness. Does that mean you're not his executrix?"

"Executor. I had my signature notarized downtown. I'm it. You can call yourself anything you want as long as there's no attempt to defraud. It isn't illegal to be Eleanor Drummond. Just strange. She's alive for a few hours a week, then what becomes of her?"

"Vampire?"

"She has no past."

"Or too much. What about a driver's licence?"

"Dead end." Miranda wondered for a moment if irony was innate, then continued. "She listed this as her address. Her credit cards are paid up and use this address. Griffin is her guarantor. But she's never lived here, Morgan. It's like she's Griffin's creation. There were no birth records, no health insurance card. She must have one in another name …"

"Or never gets sick."

"Maybe she's Jekyll and Hyde — one self doesn't know the other."

"Dr. Jekyll knew about Mr. Hyde," Morgan said. "Is this the good side or the bad, the woman we know? Which face of Eve?"

They weren't going to resolve the mystery of Eleanor Drummond's elusive identity, whether it offered her refuge or power, by talking about it. He was anxious to show Miranda the cellar but taunted her, suggesting her status on the scene was open to question.

"Look, Morgan, I've got more access than the police. You need me just to get into the place."

"You have the only set of keys?"

"Griffin wasn't carrying keys, you realize. Maybe it was his version of leaping from a bridge — lock yourself out of your house, wearing no shoes. It's the fish pond or nothing."

"Except he was murdered," said Morgan.

"There were keys up in his study. They're at the lab."

"What about the cellar? Some of the doors in the dungeon are locked."

"We'll have to bring in the locksmith."

"Or batter them down."

"Not in front of me. I'm the executor. I'm on compassionate leave."

"Compassionate! You didn't even know the guy."

"It makes grieving easier. Do you realize I'm in charge of the dearly departed's remains? I'm thinking cremation. Burial's too claustrophobic."

"For whom, not the dead?"

"You don't know that for sure. Ashes are easier — mixed with crushed shrimp for the delectation of his familiars. Consumed by his passion, so to speak."

"He'd like it that way," he said. "Is the coroner's report in?"

"Yeah, they confirmed he didn't drown. I've been trying to check him out, but he's almost as elusive as Eleanor Drummond. He really is rich, like you said, and you can always find money. He's old money and new money and moneyed enough to blur the distinction. Legitimate credentials, but close to anonymous in legal and financial circles — a solitary wanderer in academe. Has money in a gallery in Yorkville, probably a hobby or a tax writeoff for collectibles. Listed with the Law Society. That's about it. His investment manager never met him in person. He kept an office downtown with a skeleton staff — two clerks and a legal secretary who said he was hardly there. He never had mail forwarded, they didn't know where he lived, except it was Rosedale. I mean, where else? This guy wasn't a commuter."

"He's got a nice car."

"Yeah, Jag XK 150, 1959. I saw it last night. Do you know his secretary was blown away that I was technically her boss? It made her nervous."

"Because you're a woman?"

"Because I'm a cop."

"You think she's the killer?"

"She knew when I walked in who I was."

"We're famous."

"Contain yourself, Morgan. Someone called from headquarters, looking for next of kin. The secretary had no idea how to reach Eleanor Drummond."

While they talked, they wandered around to the front and went in by the main entrance. Miranda needed to go through papers in Griffin's desk, and Morgan wanted to explore. The stairs and hallway were filled with the hush of an empty old house after someone's death. The hush spread ahead of them as they walked to the study and pushed open the door.

There was an audible explosion of surprise as they looked down into Eleanor Drummond's glazed-over eyes, staring past them at nothing.

"Oh, my goodness," said Morgan.

Miranda sighed.

Eleanor Drummond lay on the floor in a pool of congealing blood, face up but with her legs bent awkwardly to the side. Her grey pants were soiled from waist to knee, and her loose-fitting white blouse was drenched in blood so that it was hard to tell where the material bunching around her abdomen ended and her brutalized flesh began. The woman's suit jacket lay crumpled and stained just beyond reach of her outstretched hand. Her head was cocked to the side and her lips were open, as if her final voice had fallen into silence as the door was closed, her eyes fixed in the direction of her assailant's departure.

Miranda strode over to the telephone, stepping carefully past the blood and what seemed like a spreading sheet of water on the hardwood floor. She called in, then turned to Morgan, who was crouched beside the body, trying to avoid the seepage while he groped at her neck for a pulse.

"Not likely," said Miranda. He twisted around. Catching the direction of his quizzical stare in her direction, she challenged, "What are you looking at?"

"There's something moving under the desk."

In spite of herself, Miranda flinched, then bent low and peered into the shadows at a mass of gristle and red throbbing against the wet floor. For a moment she could taste her own heart.

On her knees, careful to avoid blood and shards of broken glass, she crept forward, scooped her hand around a fish about the size of a large salmon fillet, and slid it forward into the light. It had leathery skin and the eyes were dull, but its mouth grasped at the air and its gills opened and closed in a deliberate rhythm. Whatever energy it might have had to thrash about was spent, but it was far from dead.

"It's a Showa, Doitsu. No scales."

"Good, Morgan. Here, put it in the bathroom sink or the toilet or somewhere."

He took the red-and-white fish from her as if he were someone not used to holding a baby, resting its weight against his palm and forearm, while his other hand hovered, prepared to grasp firmly if his charge slid off to the side. "I'll put it in the pond," he said.

She rose to her feet. "No, not yet. It might be important here. Isn't this a tidy mess? Literally. Blood all over, but neatly contained — carnage arranged with precision."

"Miranda, I was downstairs when this happened! I should save the fish." He glanced at the koi, which lay very still, resigned to its fate.

"No one thinks you did it, Morgan."

"I was down in the cellar, I was in the den —"

"I'll be a character witness if you need one."

"I didn't hear anything. Look at her. The woman was alive an hour ago." He gazed at the fish lying listlessly in his hands. "It was eerie, how empty and quiet it was —"

"It's not your fault, Morgan. "You're not the guardian of the world. Do something with the damn fish before it dies on you, too."

"My goodness," he said as if his responsibility for the Showa's mortality had only now sunk in. "Here." He held the fish out to Miranda. "I'll get a tub of pond water. Tap water would kill it. Chlorine and all that chemical stuff."

"You look after it." She surveyed the room for something to remove the slime from the Showa on her hands, which was more imagined than real since the fish had been virtually dry when she picked it up. She reached over and wiped her hands on Morgan's shirt sleeve, over his bicep.

Morgan tightened his grip on the fish. Holding it directly in front of him, he backed out the study door and descended to the den, strode out the French doors, and found a blue plastic tub in the portico. He edged it with his feet over to the pond, set the Showa down on the grass, and filled one-third of the tub with pond water, then picked up the fish and gently deposited it in the tub. It seemed to revive immediately, indicating its revitalized condition by hovering perfectly still in the lucent water, moving only its pectoral fins in a slow, fanning motion, almost imperceptibly passing water in and out through its gills.

He carried the tub back into the den and placed it on the floor by the wingback chair, then sat in the chair so he could keep an eye on the fish and waited for activities to commence upstairs. He would listen, see what he heard.

After a few minutes, he realized he should be doing something. He could check the front door for forcible entry — no, he and Miranda had come in that way. He could check other rooms for signs of violence, but it was clear that the murder had occurred in the study. He walked back up the stairs with the Showa held out in front of him. How could a woman die such a grisly death two storeys above him? He looked up, he looked down. Maybe the old ceilings and floors were so thick that the drum rolls of hell would be muffled.

When he returned to the crime scene, Miranda was sitting comfortably in a leather desk chair, contemplating her surroundings.

Apart from a broken aquarium, everything in the room seemed in place. Morgan figured the fish must have been there, away from the pond, for observation. Maybe it was sick. If so, it was lucky they hadn't put it back in the pond. Or maybe it was a bonding thing, and Griffin kept it in the study for company.

Morgan stared at the dead woman's eyes, wishing he could capture what they had last seen, that he imagined was burned into her retinas, seared into the dead flesh of her brain. Despite the violence of the tableau presented by her seeping corpse, he thought she looked remarkably composed.

"What do you make of it?" he asked.

Miranda, too, was staring at the corpse. There wasn't much either of them could do until the forensic team and the coroner arrived. A siren wailed in the distance. When Miranda called in, she had said the woman was dead, but there were sirens and flashing lights, anyway — the full regalia of murder.

There was no rug on the floor. Miranda remembered there had been a small rug between the desk and the door. She found it rolled neatly with its pad in the closet. When she spread it out in the hall, half expecting a clue of some sort, there was nothing.

Returning to the study, she squatted close to the corpse. She peered at Eleanor Drummond's garish midriff. Taking a pen from the desk, she leaned over and drew soaked linen a little away from the torso. There was angry bruising around what she recognized as a sucking wound — deep, gaping, inflicted with considerable force, yet the blouse wasn't torn, as if it had been carefully pulled aside.

"What do I make of it? Don't know," she answered at last.

Morgan asked Miranda for the keys to the car out front and walked away so abruptly, holding the blue tub with the Showa in front of him, that she didn't think to inquire about where he was going.

Left alone with the dead woman, Miranda shifted in her ruminations to consider what she felt about Eleanor Drummond. Yesterday Griffin's mistress had appeared so in control, entering a murder scene as if it existed to offset her own subtle elegance. She seemed as shallow as invisible makeup. Now, as a corpse, she was infinitely more complex.

Gazing at her, sprawled awkwardly with her legs twisted under as if she had been kneeling, with the wound in her gut leaking viscera and blood, Miranda was struck by the absurd poise the woman projected. Her hair wasn't in the least dishevelled, her face was a tight mask of what could almost be taken for serenity, her hands from having clutched at her wound were smeared with blood, but her nails were perfectly manicured, not a cuticle askew. Miranda felt herself warming to Eleanor Drummond.

She looked around. There was a Tod's purse on the desk, there were shoes, Jimmy Choo, placed neatly by the closet door. Apart from the mess on the floor there was no evidence of a struggle.

There was no murder weapon. The assailant would have wiped it clean before leaving; but there was no evidence of blood beyond the victim's reach. This was a carefully managed and brutal crime.

Nearly two hours later Morgan returned and picked up their conversation as if he had just stepped out of the room. "The expert said she was a beauty, one of the better koi he'd seen outside Japan. I took her up to that fish place in North York. He said she isn't sick and offered to look after her, but I said I'd bring her back and put her in with the others. He said he couldn't believe there were more. He thought he knew all the collectors in the Toronto area, in the country, for that matter. This one's a female. Plump and ripe, he said. I told him that was sexist, and he got flustered because I'm a cop."

"Welcome back."

"Thanks."

As they walked downstairs, trying to stay out of the way of forensic investigators intent on doing their job, and the coroner's people, doing theirs, Morgan told Miranda he had to show her the pump room. Since the koi were in her charge, he said, she should get to know the system. She said she didn't need to, that she would make arrangements for them. But Morgan wanted her to see the subterranean maze, wanted to show her the wine cellar and find out if they could get into the tunnel if indeed that was what lay beyond the other locked door.

"All in good time," said Miranda. "We've got work to do."

"You don't want to go in there, do you?"

"Implying what?"

"Nothing. It's part of the crime scene. It's spooky. I kept running into myself, things I'd forgotten, ancestral memories, love and sex. Mostly love and sex. But you'll be okay. I'll be in there with you."

She glanced at him with exasperation and affection. "Morgan, I'm not afraid of Kafkaesque cellars, and whatever's buried inside me is too deep to rise on a ramble down memory lane. Love and sex can wait. And speaking of secrets exposed, look what I found in her bag." She slipped a worn photograph from an envelope and handed it to him. "It looks like her, doesn't it? I've never seen a purse so organized. Everything else is connected to this address. Her secret identity must be exceptionally self-contained except for this — a carry-over from one life to the other."

"But not this life to the next."

"At least we know she had a life."

"Maybe Eleanor Drummond was her secret identity. You know, not the other way around."

Miranda slid the photograph back into the envelope. Somehow she felt closer to Eleanor Drummond now than when the woman was alive.

When they reached the den, Morgan puttered around the room, reading titles on book spines, running his hands over the miniature laboratory on the bar top, fingering a kit that measured chlorine and chloramines in water, observing his reflection in the window, gazing out at the ponds in the garden.

Miranda noticed that the roses were gone from the Waterford vase. She found their dried-out remains in a waste container under the bar beside the freezer and refrigerator. A conscientious floral enthusiast on the forensic team must have thrown them out.

They browsed. Forensics and the coroner had finished here while Morgan had been off with the fish in his charge. They had gravitated to this room because it was the only place in the house that suggested the presence, or absence, of a defined personality. Morgan found the living quarters as eerie as a deserted museum — everything arranged by design, institutionally antiseptic. Miranda ascribed the soulless quality to Griffin's solitary occupation of his ancestral heritage. The house was a mausoleum where bodies had turned to dust and been vacuumed and polished into oblivion.

Miranda was aware that Morgan's eyes were following her. As she sauntered about, she sensed the languid feeling of her skin against the inside of her clothes. She didn't like it when men watched her without being implicitly invited, but Morgan was an exception. When she caught him looking at her that way, he was never embarrassed. He would smile with his eyes and say something distracting or just glance away.

Not wanting to confront his gaze, she walked down the hall to the bathroom. While she was there she thought she might as well pee. Her own brief rush of water startled her by the images it evoked of being in an undersea grotto. This was a very strange room — a combination of sensory deprivation chamber and comforting womb. She sat there, in no hurry, and recalled the thrill in diving deep among the banks of coral in the Cayman Islands, how sensual it was with the warm salt water enfolding. Her dive partners had varied through the week, but they hadn't mattered, really. They were a presence off to the side as she had moved in gentle undulations of her body against the water's caress.

Still sitting, she swung slowly on her pedestal, searching for a focal hook in the room, something to give her assurance that she hadn't slipped into a different reality. The bathroom seemed so unconnected to anything else in the house. The tiles were green stone, not ceramic. Beneath the dull lustre a patina of crevasses and gouges betrayed their sedimentary origins. The floor tiles were a complementary grey and possibly a simulation of rock dust and glue, with a sheer surface to allow water from the open shower to slide into the drain.

By the drain, caught against the silicone gap between the lip of the metal and the surrounding stone, was a dried smudge the familiar colour of blood. She stood up quickly, arranged her clothes, and bent over to retrieve the bit of detritus, whatever it was, scraping it carefully into a small plastic envelope.

"Lovely," Morgan said through the door that she hadn't bothered to close, observing her, bottom uppermost. "Today it's Calvin Klein, is it?"

She knew he was bluffing. She was wearing a sky-blue thong. It made her feel sexy to be a little outrageous under the tailored couture she affected for work. "Bad guess. Look at this."

"Blood?"

"How could Forensics have missed it?" she asked.

"It happens."

"Maybe you had to be sitting on the toilet …"

"Contaminating the crime scene?"

"Could have cut himself shaving," she mused as she folded over the plastic pouch.

"A man? In the shower? I doubt it. There's not even a mirror."

"Do you want to put this in your Filofax? It's your case."

"I left it at home. Here …" He reached for the envelope.

"I'll keep it for now," she said, implying it might be safer with her. "Must have been Eleanor Drummond. I can't imagine why she'd shower down here, though. She doesn't strike me as the type to shave her legs at her lover's. Or anywhere else ..."

"No?"

"She'd wax. So, are you ready to go spelunking?" Miranda led the way to the cellar door but stood back and waited for Morgan to open it. Then together they entered the Gothic gloominess — as if, she thought, they had passed over into another dimension.

They went through a confusion of passageways down to the pump room. She looked around, listening to his guided tour, amused at his having worked it all out. As long as the fish were all right until she could figure out what to do with them, she wasn't very interested.

They had once gone together to see a renowned magician at the Royal Alexandra Theatre. She had revelled in the illusion of an elephant disappearing from the stage. Morgan had wanted to know where it had gone, how it had been done.

"That's not the point," she had said. "It's magic."

But he had talked about the machinery behind the illusion for the rest of the evening over drinks and on the walk home. He was always fascinated by his own understanding. It wasn't the system but how he worked it out that excited him.

"What's this?" she said now, unravelling the fragment of lingerie from around the base of a brass spigot over the sink.

"Yeah, I noticed that. What do you think?"

"Well, it's not his. I'd say it's a gusset." She had said that just to annoy him. He wouldn't know what a gusset was. "A crotch panel, Morgan. From an old pair of nylon panties. Maybe a rag from the cleaning service — not something Eleanor Drummond would wear."

"It could be Darlene's. She had stuff like that."

"Your mother's?" Miranda always found it disconcerting when he referred to his mother by her first name. His father was Pop, or Fred, and his mother was Darlene. Her own mother had always been Mom, not Mummy or Mum, and certainly not Margaret. Her father had died before graduating to "Dad." She would think of him until her own end as Daddy. Her mother called him Daddy, too, in the old-fashioned way. His first name was Herbert, though. She knew that.

"You seem distracted," Morgan said. "What are you thinking about?"

"My mom. Underwear. Dying. You know, the usual."

"C'mon, I want to show you the wine cellar. Have you got a flashlight?"

Of course, she did — a small penlight. She would be Sigourney Weaver. Not as tall, but intelligent, beautiful. Younger, of course. When the movie was over, her name wouldn't be in the credits, either. She would still be inside the story with him.

Miranda shone her light through the double glass panes in the door, which the glare turned nearly opaque, then she laughed. "I thought you said it was filled with wine. That's a curtain — a plastic shower curtain with a wine bottle motif!"

"Let's see. My gosh! Isn't that bizarre?"

"That I'm right?"

"The guy had a sense of humour."

"Do you think there's actually wine in there?"

"I hope you're not part of the joke."

"That's a sinister thought."

"We're in a sinister business," he said. "We've got

two bodies on our hands — one who slipped effortlessly away and the other impaled. And you're in the middle of it all, connections unknown."

"Some joke. Let's pray it stays out of the press. Did you see the death notice in the *Globe*?"

"This morning? The guy's barely dried out at the morgue."

"It said, 'died suddenly, at home.' That's obituary code for suicide. I'd say Eleanor Drummond put it in."

"Her death is more likely to draw attention."

"She didn't die naked."

"No, but this has all the tabloid ingredients — big house, dead lawyer, mystery mistress, handsome detective, attractive detectives. And a really weird arrangement in estate management."

"Give it a rest," she said.

"Yeah, there must be wine in there," he said as if they had been talking about nothing else.

"The door looks formidable."

"Under the facade it's a thermal vault. The wood in the frame is so dry that the bolts would pull out by hand, but it's virtually impregnable. There has to be great wine in there, or why bother? You need to do an inventory, right? Let's check it out." He started feeling around along the overhead beams. "There must be a key…"

"If there's wine, it'll wait. Delayed gratification, Morgan."

Mildly irritated by her chirpy forbearance, he went back to the pump room to get a hammer to whack open the padlock on the farthest door leading to the adjoining property.

Miranda peered through the mottled light as she walked along on her own, imagining the orientation of the world outside. She felt the chill she had anticipated.

It was being afraid that bothered her, not anything she feared. She couldn't hear Morgan; she could see nothing to be alarmed about. The walls closed ambiguously around her like the setting of an ancient memory or a dream on the edge of nightmare.

She heard Morgan shuffling along, catching up from behind. His wavering shadow crept by her as she slowed, then loomed over her, rendered headless in the niche of illumination surrounding the light bulb in front. She was unnerved for a moment by what wasn't there.

Something wasn't right, evaded perception. In this Faustian maze of rough-cut stone reinforced with brick patchwork and horsehair plaster that had crumbled away from its lath, of supporting beams that were solid after generations entombed in the darkness, with great gaps where the grain had split open, there were innumerable habitations for spiders. But there were no spiderwebs. She doubted that anyone had actually cleaned here in a hundred years, but clearly there had been traffic through these passageways.

Morgan was determined to see what lay beyond the remaining unexplained door. He was curious about the wine cellar, but he displayed the ingenuous enthusiasm of a small boy bent on great tasks, insofar as the possibility of a tunnel was concerned. Miranda didn't buy much of what Freud had to say, but certainly it was amazing how grown men revealed such a childish predilection for exploring secret corridors.

He seemed genuinely excited, poking away in the musty nether regions. She couldn't think of a female alternative that would command a comparable response. She would rather be upstairs where natural materials were transformed by artifice into furniture and fireplaces, but these weren't phallic — well, possibly the candlesticks and the bedposts, she thought, mocking the essentializing contructs of the sad little doctor from Vienna. She had never been to Austria's capital, or anywhere in Europe for that matter.

When Morgan drew alongside, she turned on him and blurted, "It's all about sex."

"What?"

"Nothing. Freud. What are you talking about? Do you know I've never been to Europe?"

Morgan tried to get a focus on her in the mottled light. He was a little confused, and he shrugged. "I think you have to explore the foundation before you can understand the edifice." He thought that was suitably ambiguous — applicable to psychoanalysis, travel abroad, or their present location.

"There's Freud again — you with your edifice complex." She smiled as if she knew things beyond his grasp.

"This is a good place to think," he observed. "Not necessarily out loud."

"Okay. Let's think. Eleanor Drummond wouldn't have known you were down here. There was no car outside. She came in with someone she knew, there were no signs of forced entry or a struggle, they went up to the study ... No, she came in first, went up to the study, took off her shoes and jacket, went down, let someone in, and brought him back upstairs. Why? What were they doing? There doesn't seem to be anything in progress, no papers spread out on the desk. The computer wasn't turned on. She wouldn't have taken off her shoes if he had come in with her in the first place. Too casual. It had to be someone she knew really well."

"Why was the carpet in the closet? Why do you think the assailant was a man?"

"Could have been a woman, but there was a lot of force. What would he have used? It was a blunt instrument, which is an oxymoron. And isn't it strange that there seemed to be only one point of entry. Like he thrust it in, working his weapon inside her without withdrawing, tearing her apart —"

"We're talking about murder, Miranda. You make it sound like rape."

"Yeah, well, it must have been a miserable way to die. The assailant would have been a mess. But there's no evidence of someone cleaning up, no trail of blood when he left."

"Unless he came prepared. Maybe the killer was wearing one of those painter's jumpsuits. She'd be a bit suspicious. I think —"

"Seriously, Morgan. There's not a print, not a smudge, not a smeared footprint on the floor. I'm surprised you didn't hear the aquarium fall. Maybe he broke it on purpose after he killed her, used the water to dilute the blood so it would flow over marks of a scuffle and leave us with nothing. Is the penis a blunt instrument?"

"Speaking generically?"

She shrugged, her gesture muted in the converging shadows, the stifling gloom.

When they reached the oak door, Morgan took her penlight and checked the padlock. Instead of handing the penlight back, he clasped it in his teeth and struck the lock a glancing blow with the hammer, calculated to set its innards askew, with his free hand held ready for whatever might spring forth.

"One hit," he proclaimed as he pulled the sprung lock to the side and pushed on the door. It refused to give way.

"Morgan, the padlock wasn't holding anything. This whole system is a Foucauldian model."

"Where did *he* come from? What about Freud?" Morgan was more comfortable with Freudian allusions. Michel Foucault was just coming into vogue in North American academic circles about the time Morgan absconded to Europe. About the time Miranda was beginning her studies in language and thought.

"Look," she said, "the original lock is a Victorian antique. We have dead bolts, an Edwardian refinement. The padlock was obviously a transitional device, say, from the 1930s. Then someone installed a standard key lock around the time I was born." Trying not to look smug, she retrieved the penlight gingerly from his mouth and squatted to look at the keyhole. "You should be able to manage this."

A little sheepish, he reached into his back pocket and took out his wallet from which he withdrew a stiff length of wire. Then he bent to the task while she held the light to illuminate his progress. "There," he said finally. "Am I redeemed?"

She was about to make a religious quip when he swung the door away from them into the darkness.

"Voila, a tunnel!" he said. But he didn't go in. The intense ray of the penlight was easily swallowed by the shadowy void. "I'll bring a better light tomorrow, but for sure this connects the estates."

"There's nothing sinister about that. They used to belong to the same family. This might have been a servants' passage. They probably shared kitchen facilities. These aren't mansions, Morgan, just really big houses. I wouldn't call them estates."

"From Cabbagetown, they're estates."

"Let's go check the morgue. We might find out more about Griffin, and Eleanor Drummond will be settled in by now."

"We've got to feed the fish."

"How many times a day?"

"Three or four. I've fed them twice already."

"Let us withdraw from this foul place," she said as if quoting Shakespeare.

He wasn't quite sure if she was.

6

Shiro Utsuri

Morgues were emergency rooms for the dead. Their clients were admitted, processed by triage, and released. Morgues didn't use architectural illusions to dissemble. They opened directly onto side street pavement; they seldom had waiting rooms apart from a makeshift cluster of chairs. There was no casual traffic through a morgue. It was a place always of profound mystery, where forensic resources were brought to bear on the expiration of human beings, to capture their untoward moments of death.

When Morgan and Miranda arrived, they passed a teenage girl standing by the soft drink machine who turned away from them in a sort of innocuous slouch. As they walked through a glass door and down a brightly lit hallway in the direction of muffled voices and the sounds of small whirring motors, the girl's reflection suggested resignation, as if she had been waiting for hours.

The medical examiner was Ellen Ravenscroft. The coroner was just about to start work on Eleanor

Drummond. She dismissed an assistant and conferred briefly with Miranda and Morgan, directing them to some items on top of a stainless-steel cabinet and papers on a desk, then she drew the cover away from Eleanor Drummond's body and folded it neatly for reuse.

Miranda stood back a little so that her head and shoulders were out of the illumination cast by the low-slung lights. She was sure no one enjoyed an autopsy, but Morgan and the ME seemed to regard the body about to be splayed open with clinical detachment. The worst was when it was a child. Miranda found it easiest when the body was so badly mangled that it didn't resemble a person.

She had never before been acquainted with the victim in a murder investigation. Robert Griffin, who was filed somewhere in the bank of drawers along one side of the crypt, she knew only as a corpse, despite her intimate connection with his private affairs.

Miranda moved so that she could see past the obstruction of her colleagues. She shuddered. Despite the gaping hole in the woman's abdomen, for an absurd moment she was struck by how very lovely Eleanor Drummond appeared. Here was a woman who knew how to be naked — and dead. Miranda half suspected she had prepared, with the art of a ghoulish courtesan, for the intimate examination now underway.

Her body was groomed to perfection, her makeup was done with finesse, and her physique was toned and lotioned with loving care. There were no tan lines, she knew enough to stay out of the sun, her legs were entirely clean of hair, her pubic triangle was neatly trimmed, and the down on her belly and arms was soft in the harsh light like a fine mist sprayed on freshly cut flowers.

How could someone be more vulnerable, Miranda

thought, than lying naked on a stainless-steel tray, examined only as human remains? Even if the body didn't know it was happening, it *was* happening. Miranda wanted to cover the woman. She related to her now — while alive there had been an impossible distance between them. Miranda had only had a bikini wax once in her life, and that was before she had gone to Grand Cayman. She felt sad and oddly exhilarated by the strangeness of a woman who seemed to be so much in control despite the circumstances.

As the ME leaned into her job, the illusion collapsed in soulless procedures of cutting and probing.

"Was she a smoker?" Miranda asked the ME.

"Never."

"Then why did —"

"Stage business," said Morgan. "The worse the script, the more smoking there is."

"Playing out her role as mistress?"

"Was she?" asked the ME.

"His mistress?' said Miranda. "Apparently. Did she ever have a baby?"

"Yes, not recently, but yes."

The medical examiner described the superficial appearance of the body in detail, speaking into an overhead microphone and to them at the same time. Miranda turned to the items on the cabinet. She picked up a nail file with a tortoiseshell handle. "Anything unusual about this?"

"Yes," said the ME. "There was blood and tissue adhering to the tip."

"It was lying in the pool of blood when we found her," said Miranda.

"This was more than watery blood. It was as if the nail file had been used as a weapon except —"

"Maybe defence?"

"No, the tissue is hers, and there's enough to suggest it penetrated more than skin-deep. If it had gone right in, though, the roughness of the file would be rich with details. It's relatively clean. And there's no separate wound."

Miranda put the nail file back and approached the cadaver again to observe the procedure.

"Look at this," said Ellen, holding the flesh open. "I've never seen anything like it. The damage pattern suggests a deliberate separation of organ from organ, mutilating each in a prescribed sequence. Meticulous but brutal. It doesn't make sense."

"An exercise in methodical torture?" suggested Morgan.

"Jack the Ripper?" the ME said. "Punishment and pain? I don't know. More like cruel efficiency. Almost as if she were helping him along."

"You assume it was a male?"

"It's a generic thing, Morgan." The ME winked. "Like women are ships."

"Is that open to argument?"

"Accept it, Morgan," said Miranda. "Informed opinion, linguistic convention — men do the killing unless otherwise noted. Is there a readout on the water and blood samples?"

"Yes, love, over there on the desk."

Yes, love, Miranda said to herself, and smiled with something approaching affection. No matter how long they were here, she thought, something of the language stayed with them. Miranda nearly apologized for the gauche condescension, except that it was only a thought. Sometimes inflections from elsewhere lasted for generations; it was as if they were genetic.

They knew each other off duty and were almost friends — two professional women married to their jobs.

When Ellen Ravenscroft went home on vacation, she came back with rollicking tales of trekking through Heathcliff country alongside strapping country gentlemen, her Yorkshire accent thickened almost back to the original. For Miranda a trip home at the most exciting meant soaking up a bit of illicit sun along the mill race out past the old grist mill, something, in fact, she wasn't sure she had done since her teens.

She scanned the lab report until she found the anomaly she was looking for. "So there are traces of sodium thiosulphate in the water and not much chlorine."

"That's what you'd expect," said Morgan. "Fish people use sodium thiosulphate to dechlorinate city water, which would have killed the Showa."

"The what?" asked the ME.

"The Japanese fish we found beside the ... deceased. It was still alive, a Doitsu Showa, and a genuine beauty."

"I'm sure."

"But there are variations," said Miranda. "Some of these samples, ones taken directly from the body, contain chlorine and chloramines."

"Tap water," said Morgan.

Miranda circled around the perimeter of the room as if she were taking a stroll, lost in thought. Morgan turned his attention to the autopsy. He knew when to leave his partner alone.

"Have either of you talked to the girl outside?" asked the ME.

"What girl?" said Miranda from the shadows. "The teenager in faded jeans, Birkenstocks, and a lavender silk shirt?"

"That would be the one," said the ME. "She said she was supposed to meet someone called Molly Bray. There's no Molly Bray here, living or otherwise. She said her

mother left a note. Asked me if she could wait. She was
flicking a lighter. I'd have shown her a smoker's lungs if I
had any lying about. I don't relate well to young people.
I was there once myself, but I grew out of it. If she's still
hanging around, could you guys deal with her? Maybe
she's just a death junkie."

"You go talk to her, Miranda. You're better with
kids."

"Yeah, okay. But I think you should know …"
Miranda remained silent for a few moments until she
had their interest, then declared, "Eleanor Drummond
died by suicide."

"No way," the ME shot back.

Morgan was more circumspect in his response.
"What makes you think that?"

"Elementary, dear Holmes. Have you ever read
Yukio Mishima, the Japanese author?"

"Possibly."

"You'd remember if you'd read 'Patriotism.' It's a
short story. I'll bet she read it." Miranda nodded at the
body lying open in front of them. "Morgan, with Griffin
we have a murder that pretends to be suicide. And now
we have a suicide meant to look like murder."

He waited.

"Yukio Mishima disembowelled himself in the same
grisly ritual he described in his fiction. He knew exactly
what he was doing. Seppuku. He had already been through
it in words. Of course, he describes ritual suicide as an
honourable thing. Yet somehow the fiction deconstructs
in spite of the author. The warrior's actions as he kneels
and slides the sword into his belly and moves it through
his pain in a prescribed pattern, severing his guts organ
by organ, he and the author regard as ennobling, and
eventually Mishima emulated his astonishing story.

"There is a woman, though—the warrior's wife. She's meant to be his necessary witness to affirm his nobility. After he dies, she methodically prepares the house for their discovery and then without fanfare takes her own life. A reader sharing Mishima's fanaticism might find her role trivial. But to me her apparent passivity subverts the whole idea of seppuku. It's just a game boys play when they come to the end of things."

Morgan was fascinated by her leisurely exegesis, and baffled by its relevance to her bizarre revelation about the death of Eleanor Drummond. The ME was listening but proceeded with her work. They waited.

Miranda touched the arm of the corpse with the back of her hand as if the contact would somehow confirm her account. "Eleanor Drummond was both the warrior and the wife. She had to have read Mishima. I guarantee it. She understood the warrior's unwavering commitment and she understood the humility needed for the ignominious death of the wife, leaving no explanation."

"Even if it was suicide, why like this?"

"I don't know, Morgan. Eleanor Drummond displayed utter conviction about the necessity of death. I don't think the brutality was collateral damage. She needed to do it the way she did."

Ellen put down the instruments she was using for the autopsy, turned, and leaned against the stainless-steel table. "What about the wound? This wasn't done by Excalibur. Take a look inside, love. She was battered not sliced. And there was no warrior's sword at the scene, not even a blunt one. How could she hide it? I can't conceive of suppressing the agony. There was no evidence of drugs. Why in the world make suicide so bloody complicated?"

"Don't know," said Miranda with a trace of smugness that let Morgan know she was confident and probably right.

"Okay, shoot," he said.

"I have no idea *why* she did it. That may be our real mystery. But her desperation must have been absolute. She wasn't herself. We know that, literally. This was the ultimate act after years of ferocious dissembling. Ellen, did you notice her blouse wasn't torn? That was the first thing that struck me. Maybe she was in control of her entire death scene."

"You're right," said the ME. "Like it was lifted aside before the weapon went in."

"She was fastidious," said Miranda. "She rolled up the carpet. She could have just moved it aside, but she rolled it up and put it in the closet. She put her shoes neatly out of the way —"

"But not her jacket?" the ME interjected.

"She needed her jacket."

"She did?"

Morgan found something deeply sensual in Miranda when she was totally caught up in extravagant thought; the raw intellectual energy released pheromones or something. He listened with benign, almost indulgent concentration. They were, all three, excited by where she was going.

"Okay," Miranda continued, "she knows precisely what needs to be done. Everything is prepared. She lifts the aquarium down onto the chair. She kneels beside it. This isn't so you won't hear when it breaks, Morgan. It's because she knows once she starts she won't have the strength to pull it down from the shelf. She doesn't know you're there. She takes her nail file and jabs a hole in her abdomen to get things started. She puts down the file and pulls the aquarium over so that it breaks in front of her and spills water over her legs and lap. Then using her jacket to get a good grip — that's why her jacket is scrunched up and bloody — she takes hold of a large shard of ice she's made for the purpose. It's about the size of a small sword. She inserts the end of the ice into the gut wound, but it won't go in as easily as she anticipated. It takes all her strength to drive it through. There's your bruising. Then she leans forward against the ice and works it in a predetermined trajectory among her lower organs. Her heart and lungs are still going strong, pumping the blood through her guts. The blood spreads in a sheet across her lap. With less blood in her head the pain eases and she slips into a kind of euphoria, gouges away as much as she can, falls to the side, and dies."

The three of them stood close to Eleanor Drummond's splayed cadaver, pressed together by the intimacy of a shared secret. Then, a little embarrassed, they separated emotionally, but stayed close, not wanting to lose what they had.

"Was it the tap water?" Morgan asked. "Is that what tipped you? I've heard of icicles as weapons before, or at least it's out there in the realm of urban myth, but the meltwater always gives them away. The spilled aquarium was meant to cover it up. A bit cruel, though. She was willing to sacrifice that beautiful fish."

"I don't think she shared all of Griffin's passions," Miranda said.

"What about the ice sword? Where did that come from? You said 'prepared for the purpose.' How so?"

"Remember the vase with the long-stemmed roses?"

"The dying flowers, yeah, in Waterford crystal."

"After we found her, when we went down to the den, the flowers had been thrown out. She used the vase.

Dumped the flowers — they were dead, anyway — filled it with water, and popped it into the freezer alongside the shrimp. It's the right shape — tall and slender, tapered toward the base. In a matter of hours she had her weapon. She could have made it while we were still there, Morgan. Between talking to you and talking to me, she began the procedures of her own demise. Chilling, isn't it?"

He decided not to pick up on the ice motif.

"Why the need to inflict such terrible pain on herself?" Miranda asked rhetorically. "Why ritual suicide? It had to be more than simply an attempt to mislead. Surely, it wasn't for honour or for ritual obligation. How far can we push the Japanese connection?"

"Maybe it all has something to do with the koi," Morgan suggested.

"I don't know Mazda from Toyota, Hyundai from seppuku," said Ellen.

"Subaru," said Miranda, then conceded, "yeah, seppuku."

"Hyundai is Korean," added Morgan.

They both stared self-consciously at the medical examiner. This was her realm, the kingdom of the dead, and morbid good humour was an affirmation of primacy. She was neither stupid nor malicious, just territorial, they decided. And Miranda, while not threatening, was the one in control.

Miranda continued her rhetorical inquiry. "Could anyone need to suffer so much? How terrible or beatific to embrace absolute pain." Caught up in her own words, she lapsed into silence for a moment, then said, "Martyrs welcome arrows and flames. Yearning for release, purification, absolution, redemption, yearning for heaven? If what she was trying to resolve was bad enough — yearning for hell."

"Or oblivion," Morgan suggested.

Miranda frowned. "Oblivion? There would be easier ways, don't you think? It may have to do with koi, or maybe not."

"It does make sense," said the medical examiner. "The deliberate pattern of violence inside her gut, the bruising, the lack of resistance, no weapon, the focused brutality. I think you're absolutely on, love. Absolutely on. I still don't know about controlling the pain, though."

"I was reading a while back about operations in the early nineteenth century," said Morgan. "A witness in London described a woman being led out into an operating theatre and curtsying to the medical observers before climbing onto the surgical table and lying back while aides held her arms and legs. She had a large tumor excised from her breast without anaesthetic. According to the diarist, she didn't cry out. When her breast was sewn back up, she was helped from the table. As soon as she got on her feet, she turned and curtseyed again to the audience before being led back to the ward."

"The point being?" prompted Miranda.

"The point being, since there were no alternatives available, she controlled her nervous response. It surely isn't that she didn't feel pain. Her mind and her body conspired to deal with it by wilful quiescence, just as another person might by screaming bloody murder."

"And you agree that Eleanor Drummond could have had that kind of will?" asked Miranda.

By way of confirmation, the ME observed that she had seen women in childbirth go through absolute misery, their bodies tearing open and wracked with agony, yet they barely cried out beyond an involuntary whimper, while others, through easy births, had howled enough to wake the dead. After she told them that, she surveyed the crypt, the wall of stainless-steel drawers marked with ID labels, and the tables with sheets pulled up over their occupants. Then she looked at the body of Eleanor Drummond. "Well, maybe not wake them up, but to scare hell out of them, anyway. And look at those fakirs in India. We don't know how they control blood flow to self-inflicted wounds, but they do. And apparently pain, as well."

"There was a woman in Mexico," Morgan said, "who went into labour and was alone. When the baby wouldn't come, she knew something was wrong. She took a carving knife and delivered the baby by Caesarean. Both mother and baby survived."

"So we're agreed?" asked Miranda. "She was a very determined woman whose options had narrowed to zero. That leaves us with a bigger mystery than ever, I suppose. The big question is *why*? And how does all this connect with the death of Robert Griffin?" She took a deep breath. "Is her suicide an implicit confession that she killed the old boy? Or that she couldn't live without him? I mean, it's got to connect, but I'm at a loss." She smiled. "I've had enough for one night. Triumph is tiring. I'm going home."

"You'd better talk to the girl out there," Ellen reminded.

"Sure, on my way. Good night, Ellen. Night, Morgan." Miranda slipped out into the brightly lit corridor. The lights were kept high, she observed, even in the dead of night.

The girl was sitting on a bench by the soft drink machine, legs outstretched, staring at the floor.

"Hi," said Miranda. "Are you here with someone?" She noticed the girl was playing with a lighter, but there were no butts on the floor and her fingers weren't stained.

"My mom said to wait for her."

"Here?"

"She left a note."

"What's your mom's name?"

"Molly Bray."

"There's no Molly Bray here."

"Maybe there is," said the girl.

"What's your name?"

"Jill."

"Well, Jill, this is no place for you. You'd better go home. I'll give you a lift. I'm a police detective."

A tremor of apprehension passed over the girl's face, which resolved into a mask of studied composure. "No, thank you. I'll wait. She said I should come here."

"To the morgue? Jill, do you know what this place is?"

"Yeah, I think so. It's for dead people."

"Do you think your mother's dead?"

There was a long pause.

"Yes."

The girl regarded her with astonishing self-possession. At the same time there was vulnerability in her eyes, as if she might suddenly collapse but didn't know quite how to do it. This girl was used to self-restraint — and self-reliance. But she was so young, and underneath the bravado she must be incredibly frightened.

"Is there anyone I can call?" Miranda asked.

"No. Thank you."

"What's that pin you're wearing? It's very beautiful."

"A fish."

"Is it silver?"

"It's black and white. The silver's where the white parts are and the black is empty. So it's whatever colour you're wearing. I mostly wear black. My mother gave it to me."

"Do you know what kind of fish it is?"

"Shiro Utsuri."

Miranda shuddered. "Jill, does the name Eleanor Drummond mean anything to you?"

"No."

Miranda reached into her purse and retrieved the envelope with the photograph. She examined the picture, then held it out to the girl.

"That was me when I was nine."

"I think you'd better come with me, Jill." Miranda preceded the girl into the autopsy area of the crypt and asked Ellen to cover the body of Eleanor Drummond, except for the head.

Miranda held the girl by the arm and drew her close to the table. Gazing at the composed features of the dead woman's face, the haunting pallor giving her skin the translucent quality of a Lalique sculpture, Jill seemed mesmerized. No one said anything. Jill reached out tentatively and touched the back of her hand to the woman's cheek. She didn't flinch when contact was made with the cool flesh, as Miranda had expected. Jill related to the brutality of death in ways Miranda did not at the same age, or even now.

The girl turned and walked out of the room, and Miranda followed her, with Morgan close behind. Jill sat by the soft drink machine, staring at the floor, uncertain what to do next. Miranda wanted to comfort her, but the girl apparently needed distance.

Morgan tried for clarification, speaking in a quiet voice to Miranda. "It seems out of character. She wouldn't just leave a message saying, 'Pick up my body at the morgue.'"

"Jill, do you have your mother's note?" Miranda

asked. "Could we see it?"

The girl handed her a folded sheet of pale blue vellum. On it were clear instructions to meet her at this address. Miranda expected a spidery script, but the writing was slanted all to one side.

"Your mother didn't write this, did she?" Miranda asked.

"No."

"Did you write it?"

"Yes."

"Why? I don't understand how you knew to come here."

She gazed into Miranda's eyes with the bewildered look of a bird plucked from the air.

Miranda resisted taking the girl in her arms. They had to sort this out. "How did you know to come here, Jill?"

The girl seemed to be searching inside for an answer.

"When did you last see your mother?" asked Morgan, sitting beside her. Miranda was sitting on the other side; between the two of them they were shoring her up without touching her.

"This morning ... when she drove me to school. She said not to worry and I wasn't worried until she said that. Like, of course, I worried. She sometimes does strange things. She told me Victoria, our housekeeper, would look after me. She said you, the woman cop, would look after me. I asked her why would I need anyone to look after me. I asked her what cop. She said you'd find me. So I went into school, worried sick. When I got home, she wasn't there and she didn't come home for supper. Victoria had no idea what was going on, so I phoned all the hospitals. When I phoned here, they said there was a woman here, a murder victim, who fit my mom's description. So I came over. I was waiting for you."

She looked into Miranda's eyes, her own eyes plead-ing for release from the emotional confusion. Miranda recognized the familiar fear of a brutalized child. She had been the same age when her father died.

Almost immediately Jill rallied and spoke in an even tone. "You know it when someone says goodbye to you and what they mean is forever. I knew this morning that I'd never see her again. But it was like being inside a movie. The more scary it was the more unreal it all seemed. Now it seems real. That's my mom in there on the table. Isn't she beautiful?"

"Yes," said Miranda, "she's very beautiful. Why the note, Jill?"

"I'm a kid. Kids can't hang around places like this without permission."

"Permission?"

"Like school, a note from my mom." Miranda winced, and Jill smiled at her sweetly. "That's irony, isn't it?"

"Yes, Jill, that's irony. Come on now. Let's get you home. Is anyone there?"

"Victoria."

"Your father?"

"My father is deceased," the girl said with incongru-ous formality.

"I'm sorry, Jill."

"It's okay." She gazed plaintively at Miranda and then away. "I don't want my mom to be dead."

"I know. Come on. Let's go home."

"Call me first thing in the morning, Miranda," said Morgan. "Good night, Jill." He remained seated while Miranda and Jill walked out through the front entrance, Miranda's arm draped lightly across the girl's shoulder, the girl leaning slightly into Miranda's body, almost as if they were comforting each other.

When they were gone, Morgan picked up a chrome-plated Zippo lighter from the bench and fiddled with the unfamiliar mechanism until it flared into an orange-blue flame that burnt his finger. With a rapid flick of his hand he let the lighter drop to the floor. Then he leaned over, retrieved it, and slipped it into his pocket, where he could feel its residual warmth.

After the time it would have taken him to have a cigarette, Morgan went back into the autopsy room. "The big question is why?" he mumbled as he moved close to Ellen to follow her progress. He was thinking about smokers, not the corpse on the table.

"I can't tell you that, Morgan. I never know why. No matter how much I cut and probe, I can't get there. I can slice and dice the brain, but the mind is something else. I know that's trite, but it's true. I've never seen a soul, either."

"Maybe you'll surprise yourself someday and find a cavity the size of a walnut near the hypothalamus, but it's empty and the occupant has fled. There's a whole galaxy of souls out there, billions of walnuts rattling along the corridors of heaven. And I don't even know what you mean by the mind."

"The potential inherent in the functioning brain for awareness ..." She paused and leaned low with a bright light to peer into the depths of the body. "I don't know, Morgan. You tell me. What is the mind?"

"Maybe it's like a grasp, something shaped in the air with your hands, the way your fingers move to catch water. It's not the hand or the water but what they can do. More like the content in a computer, not the hard drive or a memory stick, but the content itself. And it can be erased. Look at her, just like that, and all you're left with is machinery."

"Late night at the morgue — the chatter never stops! Can you pour us some coffee? I don't know how much more I'm going to get out of her tonight."

Morgan got two cups of coffee and came back. "What about him?" He nodded in the direction of the stainless-steel drawers. "Robert Griffin. What's the last word?"

"Died from asphyxiation. No trauma to speak of apart from death. His lungs were rosy and plump. Seems to have died without protesting." She walked to a drawer, pulled it open, and peeled back a white cloth so that Griffin's face gleamed in the phosphorescent light. "There was a fair dose of Valium in his system. Maybe that explains it. Apart from a little water damage he looks quite passable. Death becomes him, I think."

"More so than life. He seems to have had an impoverished existence despite his wealth. No family, no friends, an indifferent lover, an obsession with fish. There was no water in his lungs, right?"

"Right."

"No sign of a struggle?"

"Right. A small cut on his left temple, nothing much."

"Would there have been blood?"

"I doubt it. It happened, as far as I can tell, virtually at the point of death. There would hardly be any to speak of."

"Unless someone cleaned it up."

"Who? He was busy expiring."

"The killer."

"I don't think there was anything much, not if his heart had stopped pumping."

"But it must have bled a little. I can see veins."

"His face was underwater."

"He didn't drown?"

"Right."

"But he was asphyxiated?"

"Right."

"So it was almost as if he co-operated in his own murder, let someone smother him."

"Possibly."

"Then maybe he had a burst of air pumped into him, say, from an aerator used for an aquarium. Just to make sure he would float."

"He was gassy. It must have gone into his gut. Why bother?"

"The killer wanted it to look like suicide but didn't want him to sink, to remain undiscovered. Or didn't want us draining the pools."

"Surely a killer would know we'd find his lungs dry."

"The killer didn't expect an autopsy. The killer thought we'd find him, write him off as an accidental drowning or suicide, and that would be that. She could bury him and get on with her life."

"You think Eleanor Drummond did it?"

"Yeah, that's what I think. And then killed herself in a sort of Grand Guignol fit of housekeeping."

"So it's all wrapped up then?"

"I think the fun has just begun," said Morgan. "How do we tell victim from villain? What about the daughter? Why the double life of Eleanor Drummond? There'll be a registered birth for Molly Bray. And what about the fortune in fish? There's Miranda's connection —"

"Miranda's connection?"

Morgan explained.

"And Eleanor Drummond witnessed the document naming Miranda executrix?"

"Executor. Yeah, and since Griffin knew he was

going to die, he must have known Eleanor would be his executioner. That's strange enough. But why bring Miranda into it? And why wouldn't Eleanor intercept the request? What could she gain from Miranda's involvement? That's as much a mystery as why Griffin would ask in the first place."

"And bribe her with bequests she could hardly refuse ..."

"She's not his beneficiary."

"Well, whoever is, is in for a lot of money, I guess. I'm going to clean up here. It's getting late."

"Sure," he said, prodding at Griffin's effects lying inside a plastic bag near his head. He took a wallet out, opened it, and removed a folded piece of yellow paper. "I knew there would be one of these here. The guy left notes all over the place."

He read aloud, his voice sepulchral in the sterile chamber. "'A farmer in Waterloo County once showed me a peculiar phenomenon. We were standing in his barn-yard near a cow and her newborn calf. He walked over and stood between them, edging the calf away from its mother. The cow became visibly anxious as the distance increased, and in spite of being wary she came trudging forward in her calf's direction. The farmer then lifted the calf off the ground, cradling it with one arm under its rump and the other under its neck. He lifted it maybe six inches. The cow suddenly stopped and gazed around in bewilderment. She could no longer recognize her own calf; she had lost it. As soon as the farmer set the calf's feet on the ground, the cow saw it again, even though it was still in the farmer's embrace. Several times he lifted it a few inches off the ground and each time the mother became confused by its disappearance. The point is, the cow had no concept of her calf. Her maternal instinct was directed toward a particular set of stimuli. When one of these was removed, namely that her calf was connected to the ground, the set collapsed. She could not extrapolate from the remaining stimuli.'

"I can't get any sense who he's addressing. *Whom*. He owned a bunch of feed mills. I suppose he knew farmers. I guess he even owned a couple of farms up near where Miranda's from. Can't see him in a barnyard, though. He strikes me as urban to the core. Anyway, there's more.

"'Bees are remarkable navigators. They travel far afield in random flight and yet like most foragers they return home by the most direct route possible. This in itself suggests mental activity no less astonishing than the migration of monarch butterflies to the place of their ancestral origins in Mexico. The bee flies home from three miles away with unerring efficiency. Within the hive she conducts a sound and motion seminar, instructing fellow workers on the distance and direction to a particular nectar trove. They travel there directly, following the path of the explorer's return flight. Communication precipitates action. In fact, it is only by their action that we know communication has taken place. Now, if the returning bee were to be cleaned of pollen and nectar when she re-enters the hive, or lost her load along the way, the same patterns of sound and motion would elicit no response from her peers. When one of the key factors is missing from the seminar, worker attention is absent. They cannot extrapolate from those factors remaining that it is in their interest to respond. Despite reinforcement for previous response to similar stimuli, conceptualization necessary for them to take action, even if their survival is dependent upon that action, is beyond them.'

"The folksiness is almost attractive. It's as if he's trying to create a speaking voice with a personality that maybe he can co-opt as his own. This is less about thinking than about inventing a personality for himself as a thinker."

"Morgan," Ellen said.

"Yeah?"

"It's time to go home, love."

"Yeah."

"You want a lift?"

"Thanks."

"To my place?"

"Yeah."

"My place?"

"Sure."

7

Rainbow Trout

Miranda dropped the girl off at a well-appointed house in Wychwood Park, the most exclusive but not the most expensive residential enclave in the city, a gathering of interesting houses nestled in a small ravine west of Rosedale that was originally conceived as a refuge for successful artists and their wealthy patrons. She made arrangements with the housekeeper to call back in the morning and gave the girl a warm hug in acknowledgement of the dark secrets they shared, then drove home. Somehow she would find provision for the girl in the will. In her mother's lover's estate there were convolutions where the welfare of a young girl could be sustained if the executor was sufficiently canny. Miranda knew that, and she suspected Eleanor Drummond knew it, as well. She felt quite certain, in fact, that she had been declared, by the curious deployment of circumstances, the girl's unofficial guardian.

When Miranda got to Isabella Street, it was almost midnight. It was too late to check the car in at headquarters. She parked in front of her building. Since it was a police vehicle, she didn't anticipate a ticket, even though overnight parking was prohibited. It didn't really matter; it had been a long day.

Miranda closed the door of her apartment behind her and felt a sense of relief. She had left the computer on all day, and she cranked it up, half expecting to find another message from *kumonryu.ca*, but there was only junk. Miranda deleted everything from the in box except Robert Griffin's directive. Tomorrow she would have the tech people check it out, and she would call the fish man in North York, and get him on the case. She could delegate responsibilities; she had the authority and she had the funds.

She couldn't remember whether she had eaten dinner or not. It was a hot evening, the last of Indian summer, and before she was completely undressed she wandered back into the kitchen, took a yogourt container out of the fridge, and scooped a few big spoonfuls into her mouth. Then she decided she wasn't hungry anymore, resealed the plastic container, and put it back. Feeling the moral necessity for proper nutrition, she reached into a cupboard, lifted out a large jar of peanut butter, and ladled some into her mouth with a tablespoon. After she replaced the jar in the cupboard, she meandered back into the bathroom, pleased with her slovenly rebellion. Looking at herself in the mirror, with her mouth clacking from the peanut butter, she grinned. "I know better. I really do."

With the ambient light of the city on a hot night washing through her apartment, Miranda left the bathroom, lay down naked on her bed, and covered herself with a sheet. She felt as if she were in an undersea grotto. On her back, with her head low on a pillow, her body fully extended, arms at her sides, hands folded in repose across her abdomen, she let her eyes wander through the depths of the bedroom, the walls wavering and indistinct, details obscure. Then, quite unafraid, she grasped the sheet and drew it aside so that she could lie in exact emulation of the body of the woman at the morgue. Eyes no longer moving, she lay perfectly still except for the tidal motion of her chest, rising and falling, perfectly quiet apart from the muffled throb of her heart.

Miranda was aware of what she was doing. It didn't seem morbid but strangely comforting, as if she were connecting to another human being in an authentic way. She was naked and vulnerable, but there was no dread, only a sense of relief, as if she had discovered something about herself that couldn't be expressed in words or images but was captured in a feeling that seemed to flood over her from outside, that wasn't mystical and was vaguely erotic, that seemed to come from her memory of the dead woman in control of her own presence even in death. Miranda alive felt the immanence of death as a release and, smiling sweetly to herself, drifted into memory — dreams of when she was younger and the world was innocent.

The figure of a rampant gryphon resolved in her field of vision into the graphic design on sacks of feed. They were piled on the loading ramp at the side of the mill, and Miranda and her friend Celia were slipping by, out of sight of workers in the background who were filling bags at a chute. She could glimpse herself from a vantage overhead, and it seemed at the same time she could see through the eyes of the seventeen-year-old version of herself she observed.

The mill was up and over the hill from the village on a millrace diverted from a stream with a year-round flow. They had walked from the village. It was summer. The mill was among the oldest in Waterloo County; it had been there before the village spread along the banks of the Grand River above its confluence with the Speed River.

They were going to a special retreat, open and private, where the race and the stream diverged. There was a small head pond, a grassy meadow kept in trim by the folds of the land and the flow of the water. The remains of the original mill were close to a small falls and sluiceway — not much more than a two-storey shed of weathered boards and broken windows, with a rusting sheet metal roof and a dilapidated Gothic tower at one end looming over the dam.

Miranda was very much aware of herself in her bedroom lying perfectly still, and she was aware of the sun beating down and of Celia chattering beside her, hunched on one elbow, talking about school things and boys. Their last year in high school was coming up — dumb Ontario with its extra year. Celia was going into the nurse's aide course at Conestoga College and didn't really need the extra year. She was going to take it in case she ever wanted to go on to university or to be a registered nurse if Donny didn't work out ... It seemed to the dreaming Miranda as if all the girls in Waldron had a boyfriend called Donny. Anyway, Celia was telling her, she might as well do the extra year. She was the same age as Miranda and was in no hurry, so why not enjoy being one of the big kids at last? A senior, only they weren't called seniors unless they were self-consciously imitating Americans. It was just called "last year" or Grade Thirteen, with capital letters implied by the way it was said.

Celia finally ran out of steam and lay back on the grass beside Miranda. They had stripped to their panties when they got there. They had been doing this for years, coming to this secret place, playing and sunbathing, just the two of them, and sun damage wasn't yet an issue. On a verbal cue they both rolled to the right, giggled, and drifted off into separate dream worlds. After about ten minutes, on cue, they both rolled to the left, giggled, and settled back into their constructed reveries. And so on through the remembered afternoon.

All the times they had done that, over the summers of their youth, seemed to meld together in Miranda's mind, and she nearly wept for the lost innocence while she lay still as a corpse in the heart of the city, knowing the world had never been innocent, fearing the illusion would collapse if she peered at it too closely, yet wanting to look closer and closer, to remember how it was. She couldn't sleep, didn't want to sleep, wished the images to return of the last time she and Celia went to their place by the old mill.

"Roll over, roll over," Celia chanted, and they rolled onto their backs, glancing up into the bright cloudless sky of midsummer, listening to the cicadas sing, the hot grass singing.

After a while, Celia stood and walked to the water's edge beside the small dam. Turning toward the pool at the bottom of the dam, she called to Miranda, "I used to fish here." She walked back to continue her story. "Russell Livingston and I, can you imagine? When I was seven and eight years old, he'd come and get me the first day of trout season before sunrise. He'd just be standing out by the road in front of the house, waiting. I guess we would have arranged it. He knew I'd wake up. We'd come here and catch rainbow trout, one or two each, and he'd clean them and we'd cook them on sticks over the fire. Sometimes we'd catch a few shiners, but there's nothing to a shiner but glitter, and he'd throw them back. Sometimes Russell would bring a can of beans and we'd eat from the can with a cedar spoon he'd split from the stump there, and we'd smell all of smoke and cooked fish and cedar, and he'd take me home. I wore a green sweater with diamonds one year. It was his sweater and I was cold and he let me wear it the whole morning, and when he took me home, he took it back …"

"What happened to Russell?" asked Miranda as if she had never heard the story before.

"He just moved away. Nothing happened to him."

"I never had a brother," said Miranda as if they didn't know everything about each other.

"Neither did I," said Celia, "unless you count Russell. Do you remember how poor he was?"

"Sometimes he came to school with rat bites from sleeping with his hands outside the covers. He said it was his own fault. There was no floor. Somebody tore their house down after they moved."

"Condemned," said Celia, thrilled by the word. "The place was condemned."

Miranda watched as her friend waded into the pond. Celia had a grown-up body, not like Miranda's, which still seemed new, like something she was wearing. Celia had filled out early — by the summer they were twelve, she was well on her way to being a woman, as if childhood had just been a gathering place to get the requisite parts in order, a prelude before real life began. For Miranda, who that earlier summer had revelled in her girlishness, striding and skipping and running and dancing everywhere that forward motion was possible, being nearly naked beside Celia then was an exhilarating revelation, for she had never seen a woman's body. Her mother and sister were obsessively private, and this … this was what she would become, this would be her. She and Celia had always been alike, and she fell in love the summer she was twelve with her friend's body, which she would fill one day with her whole irrepressible being.

Miranda stirred in the mottled light seeping in from the city. She couldn't remember loving her body, just that she had. Miranda had long lived in a world where her body and mind seemed related only by common experience, not birth. The face of Jason Rodriguez intruded without words and swirled away. What had she needed from him, what couldn't he give? He was a mirror that swallowed up images. When he came to mind, she couldn't remember herself, her RCMP history, nothing of romance. Celia leered from the water's edge and turned away.

From the perspective of seventeen, she recalled the girl she was that summer with fond regret, and as she watched Celia stepping gingerly about in the shallows, she felt a strong affection for this young woman whose life, Miranda now realized, would be so very different from her own. She lay back, and after a while, Celia joined her, flicking water from her hair across Miranda's outstretched body, then reclining beside her.

After a few minutes, she whispered, "Miranda."

"What?"

"There's somebody watching us."

Miranda sat bolt upright, drawing her knees tightly against her chest, wrapping herself around what she called her private parts, between her legs and breasts.

"It's okay," said Celia. "It's nothing. I just had a feeling. There's no one around. Anyway, who cares? There's still plenty of sun."

They both scanned the horizon, their gaze coming to rest on the ruins of the old mill not forty feet away on the other side of the dam.

"That's the only place anyone could be," said Miranda. Then she got up and purposely without retrieving her clothes, wearing only her panties, she walked over to the base of the mill. "Anyone there? Hey, pervert, you there? You, there, pervert!" There was no sound, nothing stirred. "The hell with you!"

As she walked back to where Celia was still sitting on the ground, she let her hips swing and thrust back her shoulders to lift her breasts, each step delivering her entire frame into the next exaggerated motion and the next, a woman, she felt, and she experienced an unfamiliar and vaguely embarrassing sense of empowerment.

They agreed that if it had been boys from the village, the boys would have whooped in triumph and run off, allowing the girls to giggle and fuss. If it had been mill workers, who were older, it would have been more awkward; they would have whistled to give themselves away and then stood boldly watching while the girls covered their nakedness and fled. But Celia had only sensed an intruder, and Miranda had spontaneously concurred. They had seen no one, heard no one — both thought of it as a single person, which was more sinister.

They stretched out in the sun again, self-consciously languid, their nakedness now an act of defiance. They talked with a certain urgency about private things, as if they could cover themselves from prying eyes under a mantle of intimacy. They were reasonably certain no one was watching but shared a vague apprehension that their first instincts had been right. They talked about sex — Celia and Donny were lovers; Miranda was technically a virgin. At that point in her life Miranda delighted in her mother's massager and liked boys better as friends. They both agreed that nothing beat a long lingering gentle mouth-watering bodice-busting kiss. They would be friends forever, but it would be these last moments that they would carry with them. They both knew that.

When they got dressed, they were a little self-conscious. And when they parted at the top of the hill, they hugged as if they were each going on such a long journey that they had no idea when it would end.

Celia spent the rest of August with Donny, and in October she dropped out of school and got married. Miranda was a bridesmaid. "I'm not pregnant, Miranda," she said. "I just want to get married. When you know you're going to do something sooner or later, you might just as well do it now."

Miranda thought that argument would be a logical justification for suicide, but said nothing. She was disappointed when the baby came, mostly because Celia had lied to her. She went to the baby shower, but the only ones there were Donny's sisters and their friends, and she left early.

Twitching and withdrawing uneasily from her funereal pose on the bed, Miranda raised herself and went into the kitchen. She took a cold cider from the fridge. Celia was a grandmother now, she thought. They were both only in their thirties, and yet Celia was two generations older than Miranda. Celia had looked happy at the funeral for Miranda's mother. Her friend had never really known her mom; she had come to the funeral to see her. Celia had looked good, so had Donny — Donald, he had corrected, giving her his card in front of her mother's casket. Insurance.

Miranda guzzled half the cider and walked back into the bedroom. Placing the unfinished bottle on her night table, she stretched out again in state and waited for the memories to return.

It wasn't until that night, twenty years ago, when she was lying in bed much as she was now, so that the two times merged and she could feel the chill of recognition as if it were happening for the first time, that she realized what she and Celia had sensed earlier in the day was an absence.

In her mind now she saw a flurry of grey feathers swirling about the eaves of the tower as pigeons darted about, swooping and squabbling, but there was no sound, only quietness reinforced by the soft, liquid hush of water sheeting over the dam and sliding down the flume into the trout pool. There was always the sound of birds, and today there was none. They would have heard someone in the tower unless he had been there first, unless he had been waiting. And the birds stayed away. The power she had felt that afternoon dissipated, and she fell asleep in the arms of her older self, who recognized the feelings clutching at their insides as the feeling of violation. The waking Miranda was afraid. She had to go back there, to finish the summer out, to remember what had happened.

She got up and put on pajamas. She poured back the rest of the cider in a couple of swallows, then went to the fridge and got another. Taking it with her, she curled up in the comfy armchair she had brought from her mother's. It had been her father's chair, and she sometimes sat in it for security. She missed him more than her mother. It was as if his not being there through her teens was just beginning to catch up with her, as if she were grieving retroactively. But that, of course, didn't make sense; there was no time limit on grief. Maybe she was only ready now to deal with it. Back then it just seemed as if he had let them all down, especially her. Her sister and her mother had each other; she was his special person. It scared her that she couldn't remember him clearly — more the emotions he invoked than the man himself. He must have been her age about now when he died. She had never worked out the equation.

"I went back," she said suddenly, then looked around as if embarrassed that she might have been overheard. "Damn," she declared to the room, "I'll talk out loud if I want."

But she had nothing more to say and sank back into the cushions. Almost immediately she was engulfed in a silent fluttering of pigeons, and then through the billowing grey, the crisp orange image of a rampant gryphon loomed forward, divided, and swooped by on either side of her. Still at some level awake, she recognized the Waldron Feed Mill logo, as familiar to everyone in the village as their own names.

Again she was perceiving the world from multiple perspectives. Her primary vision was through the eyes of a seventeen-year-old, but she could recognize herself from a distance, as well, walking along the millrace on her own, a day or two after last being there with Celia. And she was also aware of being in her chair, caught up in dream memory, feeling the urgency to commit, to follow the young woman who had once been her.

When she reached the grassy spot by the dam, she put down her bag and laid out a towel, books, and a bottle of lotion. She and Celia always lay down in the grass, usually on top of their clothes, and they never used lotion. Still standing, she could observe herself from the vantage of the tower, looking up in her direction. She could see herself walk deliberately toward the tower. Then her vision shifted and she watched her hand reach out and push open the door.

Inside, the light was sliced by the sun's rays streaking between the wallboards. There were great wooden cogs lying askew and a large wheel hanging from an axle at floor level into a watery trough. A narrow wooden stairway was outlined in shadow against the back wall.

Carefully making her way through the accumulated detritus from ages of neglect, she reached the bottom of the stairs.

"Is there anyone there?" she called into the shadows of the ancient rafters. "Are you there?" She took a few tentative steps. "I'm coming up. It's just me. I'm coming up."

She ascended slowly into the gloom of the second floor, intuitively chilled by the absence of cobwebs, then edged over to the base of the ladder steps suspended from the floor overhead, leading up into the tower itself.

"If you're there, it's okay," she said. There was a sudden rush, and she screamed. But it was only a loose tread slipping out, and she regained her poise. She clambered up the last two steps into a small, empty space no bigger than a tool shed. There would hardly have been room for both of them if their voyeuristic secret lover had been there.

"Gone," she said. "Nancy Drew wins again."

A single grey pigeon fluttered against the eaves and disappeared.

There was clear evidence someone had been there and left. What looked like a pile of rags turned out to be a down-filled sleeping bag, and it wasn't the least bit musty. As far as Miranda could tell without actually pushing her face into the material, it was more or less unused. She stretched out on it to see what she could glimpse of their sunbathing spot, knowing she would have a perfect view. Still, when she lined up the appropriate chink, she was shocked at how close she was — practically looming over where she and Celia had disported themselves like wood nymphs. She started to giggle at the notion of wood nymphs.

It all seemed so perverse and so innocent. Miranda hunched over in the slanted light and prepared to write a note with the pen and paper she had brought, but she couldn't think of anything to say. She sniffed the air. If he was a masturbator, he was tidy. The only thing she could smell was the dry, dusty scent of aged pine. She searched for words adequate to the occasion, a quotation, an astonishing turn of phrase, a searing double entendre. Finally, she wrote down "Words are never enough," folded the paper, and left it where his head would be, near the gap in the boards that revealed her world.

From the tower she watched herself walk back across the dam, spread out her towel all over again, remove her clothes with thoughtful deliberation, and lie down in the open sunlight.

Why did she do that? Miranda wondered now, squirming in her father's chair in her apartment. She had forgotten that, but how could she have forgotten? She had gone back by herself almost every day for the rest of the summer. Somehow she had let it all merge together — summertime and Celia and sunbathing and swimming. She remembered swimming by herself, she remembered the feeling of being watched, and she remembered lying in the sun. Celia hadn't been there, and sometimes she was sure she was being watched and would lie very still for hours or roll over onto her stomach and read until she had to go home, not sure if anyone was there, knowing he wouldn't be able to leave until she did. How could she have forgotten? Where did she lose the memory of that summer? How could she lose all of that?

Miranda got up from the chair and went to the bathroom. When she returned to the bedroom, she crawled back across the top of her bed and curled around herself like a small child. It was the next summer, she thought. Something happened out there. Not that summer.

She recalled the last time she had gone out to the pond. It was the end of August, and the mill was working overtime, farmers were lined up with their tractors and wagons, and one elderly man, the only one not wearing a hat, had a pair of Clydesdales the others admired. There was a sports car they all liked, too, and she had walked by them and gone along the millrace. She must have climbed the tower — the sleeping bag was gone. There was a note: "Sometimes that's all we have." Not too cryptic, given what she had written. Then what? She had never gone out to the pond again.

The next summer? No, she had never gone back.

Danny Webster? After Danny Webster, the summer she was eighteen … Miranda hovered between the suppressed knowledge that she had returned to the pond and a gaping abyss in her recollections of how she had spent her final months before leaving for university.

She had gone to the formal dance with a friend of Danny's who was going off to the United States on a track scholarship. Danny was away or didn't want to go. He started Bible College in July. That summer she attended a few nostalgia parties in Preston, where she had travelled by bus each day to attend high school for the preceding five years, but she was never really part of a crowd. She got her course list from the University of Toronto and bought some of her books. Her sister was home for the summer, so the three of them, her sister and her mother and herself, spent a lot of time watching television. She remembered great bouts of reading as the high-school experience petered out … and watching television reruns. That was about it.

How had she endured it? Miranda knew herself well enough to know she must have sneaked off from time to time just to be on her own. She remembered walking down along the Grand River on the way to Galt and clambering up into the Devil's Cave in a long skirt hiked around her waist, her peasant blouse covered in grime. Once there, she cracked open a pack of cigarettes she had stolen from her sister's purse. By evening she was sick with a vile nausea that lasted three days, and was addicted to a habit she wouldn't break for a decade.

She had been alone a lot that summer. Flashes came back to her of long walks on back country roads and along the river, images of walking and smoking. The summer began to reconstruct in her mind with surprising clarity. But there was nothing about the millrace, the tower, or the dam.

The whole summer took shape in her mind as an idyllic interlude before she left home. Once she got to university, she threw herself into a new world of study and essays and earnest discussions and raucous parties without partners. When she went back to visit, Waldron had quickly become a foreign place, and her mother was someone she had known long ago. They were on cordial terms, but there was no intimacy in their relationship, and Miranda realized there never had been. They had just played the roles of mother and daughter, and now the roles had changed. When she moved into her apartment, after a year in residence, this was her home.

She absolutely didn't trust the notion of an idyllic last summer. It had all been so vague in her mind until now; she assumed she had shuffled it into the back of her memory precisely because it had been unmemorable.

Miranda stretched out across the bed, rolled over onto her back, and thought immediately of Molly Bray. She decided Eleanor Drummond was the persona; the real woman was Molly. Eleanor Drummond was an elegant corpse, human remains on a slab in the morgue.

Molly Bray was a person. She had peered out at Miranda through the mask of Eleanor Drummond, watched her through Eleanor Drummond's eyes.

What did she see? What did she think Miranda could do for her daughter? There were connections between Molly Bray and Miranda that the dead woman counted on being revealed.

Tomorrow, first thing, after she arranged for the koi, she would track down Molly Bray, find out who Jill's mother was, where the woman had come from. As executrix? As a detective? For Jill or herself? Why should Jill be the concern of the executor of her mother's employer's estate? Why should a policewoman be responsible for the survivor of a suicide-murder? Jill would become a ward of the court — that was how these things normally worked. There were people to look after the details.

The problem, Miranda realized, was that she was one of those people. God, she thought, she needed sleep. She needed to sit down with Morgan and talk the whole thing out. *She* was part of the problem.

Summoning Morgan into the scene made her feel better, gave her a feeling of solidity, as if she weren't adrift in a slow-motion maelstrom, as if she were no longer swirling underwater, rushing through a flume into the darkness of some strange satanic mill. Morgan was real. He was someone she could count on, and she folded herself over onto her side and went to sleep with him stretched behind her, the warmth of his imagined breath on the back of her neck.

At five-thirty Miranda awoke with a start, responding to a click in her alarm clock that wasn't set to go off for another two hours. She woke up with Sigmund Freud on her mind.

As an anthropology major, she held Freud so far down her list of significant theorists that she usually thought of him with derision, condescension, or anger. Claude Lévi-Strauss didn't like Freud. Jacques Lacan murdered him and made a monster of the dismembered parts. None of her professors had a kind word for the simplistic, neurotic projections of the Doctor from Vienna.

Yet there he was in early morning in late September in Toronto crowding into her bed. *Go bother Americans,* she thought. *You should be in New York, not Toronto. They love you in New York.* She was with Ferdinand de Saussure. She was a structuralist, a post-structuralist, a post-structural deconstructionist. Saussure begat Martin Heidegger begat Jacques Derrida. She was a post-deconstructionist! The terms rattled through her mind, nearly emptied of meaning. The only lord of the dark-side she loved less than Freud was Carl Jung. She would take Freud over Jung, Mephistopheles over his insufferable messenger. *What do I do now?* she asked herself. *Go away!*

Then there was a flurry of feelings and images. The tower. The dam. That summer she had lost her virginity.

Miranda began to cry. She didn't remember losing her virginity. She recalled the pool, the trout catching edges of light. The dam. She remembered the dam. She wept blood. She recalled the tower and it falling, being under it falling. But she didn't remember losing her virginity.

She saw herself walking up over the hill. She saw the feed mill. It was midsummer, her last in Waldron. The heat rose in waves from the steel roof. There was no one around. Close by the mill, she heard cool water running underneath. She reached out and touched the side of a sports car parked by the loading dock with its top down, ran her fingers along the edge of the cockpit, read the insignia, XK 150, Jaguar. It was British racing green. She touched the back of the worn leather seats. She heard a door slam on its spring, heard voices. She moved on past the mill and up the incline where she disappeared into the dark tunnel of cedars that had been planted a hundred and fifty years before to shore up the mounded banks of the race. She saw herself walking, saw through her own eyes as she walked step by step under the canopy of trees, the depths of shadow opening in front of her, myriad bits of light falling through the foliage to illuminate the path in the still, hot air. She heard twigs snap under her feet and heard the dry grasses brush against her legs. She heard the sound of her blouse rushing against her skin as she walked, and she heard the hush of her own breath through her nostrils. She felt sweat slide down her legs and the inside of her arms. She inhaled the deep metal smell of water slipping along the race to the mill, and the lovely dry sweet smell of the withering cedar. Then she caught the scent of the shallows at the edge of the pond and the resinous odour of pines by the dam, and the dark tunnel opened into the glittering meadow.

Miranda watched herself carefully spread a towel on the grass beside the dam. Then, without looking at the ruined mill, consciously ignoring the tower, she slipped off her blouse and shorts and spread lotion on her arms and legs. Standing, she unhooked her bra and stepped out of her panties, dropped them into the small pile of her clothes, bent to pick up the lotion again, began to sit down, changed her mind, straightened and walked over to the shallows, moved along to the dam where it was deeper, stood tall, addressing the sun, dived into the pond, swam to the shallows, and waded to the shore where she walked back to her towel, sat down, picked up the lotion, tossed it aside, and without drying herself, lay back with her eyes closed in the beating sunlight.

Back in her bedroom, Miranda felt the rising light of day against her skin and twisted in bed to shield her eyes. She wasn't awake and she wasn't asleep. She didn't want to leave the pond. She knew she had to stay, and some mechanism inside her, the impulse for survival that had expunged this episode from her memory, now insisted she see it through. She waited, the city stayed distant in her mind, the sun beat down on her, and perhaps she slept in its heat. When the sun suddenly disappeared, she opened her eyes and a dark figure loomed over her, outlined in fire. At first she thought it was Celia; they often scared each other or shook water across each other. She didn't move; it wasn't Celia. It was a male, his outline, a man, not a boy. He was naked, but she couldn't see his penis, not with the blinding sun behind him. She tried to see it — that seemed to be the centre of the unfolding drama. He was moving slowly, his face in shadow. He leaned down. His hands grasped hers and held her against the ground. She didn't struggle. He seemed to be manoeuvring between her legs.

"Don't," she said. "Please don't hurt me."

He settled back on his knees between her legs, watching her carefully, releasing her arms which lay dead at her sides. He reached out and touched her breasts, first with his fingertips, and when she lay perfectly still, he cupped them against his palms.

"Please," she said again, "don't hurt me."

He responded to her voice, kneading her breasts as if he expected her to respond, but he wasn't passionate. He was methodical. He ran his hands down the sides of her body and drew one hand across her pubic hair, letting his fingers play in the curls at the top. She shuddered, for the first time beginning to shake, and whimpered. She lay as rigidly as she could. His fingers feigned innocence and toyed with the soft curly hairs, fluffing them out in the sunlight, gradually dropping down into the cleft of her vagina. She froze, but he seemed not to notice.

He reached under her hips and lifted her pelvis toward his own kneeling body. She felt the earth press through the towel against her back, her arms at her sides, powerless through fear and wonder. He dropped her bottom against the towel and leaned forward. With one hand he guided himself and spread the lips of her vagina with his other hand. Then, after a brief pause, he thrust deep inside her. She howled — one low deep-throated bewildered utterance that trailed off into a sob and finally silence.

The pain was intensely focused for a moment, then spread in waves through her entire body. He kept thrusting and thrusting, driving her against the ground. She felt the towel abrading her skin, the pebbles in the grass. She felt him large inside her, and it was strangely familiar, like the feeling after orgasms with her mother's massager, though she had never put anything inside herself. Suddenly, a tremendous shuddering of the man's weight ran panic into her like a weapon, and for the first time she pushed up against him, trying to throw him off, to escape.

He raised himself on his arms, crushing against her pelvis. He seemed to be smiling, but she couldn't make out his features. Then he began again, grinding into her, and she couldn't move, couldn't shrink away. Pressed from underneath by the solid earth, she could only adjust her body to his so that his pelvic bones didn't grind against hers, his rib cage didn't crush her chest. Several times he stopped, slid down so that he could mouth her breasts without his penis slipping out, sucked at her, nibbled, trying to give her pleasure, she thought, and felt no pleasure but didn't feel disgust, only fear. When he came this time, he lifted her as if he were trying to bring her along with him, and when he was spent, he lowered himself gently against her.

Time passed, and he leaned back on his knees. "Turn over," he said, lifting one of her legs awkwardly in front of him, across his body, pivoting her around.

She felt horribly exposed. "Don't hurt me," she said. On her stomach she clenched her buttocks and whispered hoarsely into the earth. "Don't. Please don't."

"Stay just like that." His voice was dispassionate. "Look at the ground." With a curiously gentle caress, he drew his hands slowly across her thighs and cupped her buttocks, awkwardly giving them a lingering massage, perhaps imitating affection. "Just stay like that until I'm gone. Give me lots of time."

He stood and walked a short distance to the edge of the shadowy cedars. From the sounds she heard, she figured he was dressing. Then she heard nothing. He must have approached her naked, she thought. He must have felt ridiculously vulnerable. What if she had laughed? Would he have run off, would he have hurt her?

Slowly, Miranda rolled over. She didn't know whether to cry. Her whole frame shivered violently and then became very still. She was confused by the strange diffusion of pain that spread from a sharp centre between her legs through her entire body. She wasn't revolted, and if she was stunned, she conveyed this by acting with deliberation, as if everything were the same. She got up and walked over to the dam, dived cleanly into the dark water, swam to the shallows where she squatted and splashed waves of water against herself. Then she went back to where her clothes were still neatly piled on the grass beside the towel, got dressed, folded the towel, opened it again, shook it out, spread it in the sunlight, stained and ugly, and left it there. She walked out along the race, past the mill, where the green sports car was gone, strode up and over the hill and down into the village, into her house where her mother and sister were watching *Days of Our Lives*, into her room where she changed her underwear and threw her panties into the disposal bag in the bathroom reserved for used sanitary napkins. After a scalding shower, she dressed in a loose shift, went back into the living room, sat beside her sister and mother, and watched the rest of the soap opera, never admitting to her innermost self until now that the incident had happened, or that she might have known who her first sad lover had been.

8

Red Herring

Morgan sat on the edge of the formal pond, arranging his thoughts in a neat rhetorical design as if he were preparing to address disciples in the Athenian agora. Dogs didn't have a vocabulary; they didn't respond to language itself. He was sorting Griffin's notes in his mind, trying to cope with the unaccustomed discipline of reconstructing a formal argument.

A large and purposeful German shepherd loped across the garden, circled the pool, stood for a moment with his forepaws on the elevated wall, then, with the free end of his leash in his mouth, sat directly in front of Morgan and stared at him. The handler had set the dog loose in the yard when he went back to his van and had asked Morgan to keep an eye on him. Morgan's indifference offended the dog, who dropped his leash so that it dragged on the ground as he trotted over to the base of a Japanese maple, cocked a leg, and peed. Then, skirting the lower pond, he came back, stepped lightly up onto the wall, and nudged his reluctant custodian, who was thinking about dogs and hadn't noticed the German shepherd's absence.

Morgan didn't understand dogs. In Cabbagetown they were guards and scavengers. He didn't think of animals defining themselves by their connection with humans. Morgan edged away while the big German shepherd manoeuvred to maintain contact, then gave up and gazed wistfully into the water. The dog leaned forward until his nose touched, withdrew with a sneeze, and leaned forward again, teetering in a very fine balance, threatening to topple into his own reflection.

The end of the German shepherd's leash dangled below the surface, and the dog growled at the fish shimmering in flight. Distracted, Morgan spoke to the dog; inconsiderately, his tone ambiguous. Sensitive by training to verbal nuance, the dog heard only a jumble of words, without the slightest inflection to indicate the required response.

Unable to resolve his confusion, the dog wagged his tail with greater and greater vigour until his entire hindquarters quivered. Then, suddenly bounding away in apparent embarrassment, he tore around the big trees, leaped over shrubs and through compost remains, sent divots of grass flying askew, and careened through the air past Morgan, over the wall of the pond, and into the water.

Morgan smiled and turned away to protect the dog's dignity. The fish would be safe near the bottom.

The dog clawed against the side of the pool. Each time he reached up to drag himself over the stone wall, the compromised ratio of buoyancy to displacement plunged him backward and under. Each time he rose sputtering to the surface, he was closer to drowning and even more bewildered by the man who ignored him.

The handler finally appeared, reached across, grasped the dog by the scruff of the neck, and hauled him over the edge with relative ease despite his size. The dog raced away and shook vigorously, then crept back to sit directly in front of Morgan. He leaned forward and burrowed his damp head deep between Morgan's arm and body, shivering in gratitude and affection.

"You've made a friend for life," the handler said. "He thinks you're his saviour. He could have bloody well drowned."

"No," said Morgan. "I was right here."

"His pecker nearly did him in. Male dogs can't haul themselves over stuff. Like, if they fall through the ice, they often drown when their pecker gets caught on the edge of the ice."

"I didn't know that. I wouldn't have let him drown."

"He likes you," said the handler. "Generally, he doesn't like men."

Morgan decided he was partial to dogs, though his armpit was saturated and smelled like a wet sofa. If he ever got a dog, it would have to be a terrier. They weren't so needy, he had heard. A Scottish terrier. They had interior lives of their own.

The German shepherd, its world restored by the return of his handler, and not yet being given a task, wandered away to explore. His leash was dragging, and he came back so that the handler could unclasp it from his collar. Then he resumed his peregrination, sniffing and peeing, covering unseen markers with his own scent. Periodically, he stopped and stood alert long enough to confirm his handler's location. As a gesture of affection, the handler pretended to ignore the dog, conveying his trust that the dog wouldn't stray beyond the radius of control they had established between them.

"Nice fish," the handler said.

"They're down deep right now. What's your dog's name?"

"Rex."

"Did you think about Prince?"

"We're not supposed to give them a fancy name. It's gotta go with commands. I call him Schnitzel at home with the kids. On duty he's Rex."

"And what does he call himself?" asked Morgan indistinctly, not really wanting to be heard.

"Dog," said the handler.

"What?"

"He calls himself Dog."

Morgan looked up at the man and smiled. "My name's Morgan."

"I'm McGillivery. They sent me up from College Street. Said you wanted us to sniff around. What are we looking for?"

Morgan shrugged.

"I've gotta have something to look for. We can't look for nothing."

"I thought that's what you did."

"I take it you're not the one who put in the request. I'll see what we can come up with."

"Hold on a minute," said Morgan. He walked over to the house and disappeared through the French doors, then returned. "Work gloves are the best I can do. He wasn't the type to leave dirty laundry around. You think you can trace where he went before he died. He was in the pond."

"Out here? I don't know."

McGillivery set Rex to his task, then motioned Morgan to stay still beside him so that their own scent wouldn't interfere. The dog moved methodically, but at times seemed confused, darting back and forth between the trellised portico and the formal pond. McGillivery reassured him. The dog circled, stopped to gaze into the depths at the fish, then walked nose to the ground in a direct line down to the larger opaque pond, to the green water's edge. He looked around, sniffing the air as if he were trying to catch a distinct and elusive odour, then abruptly dropped his head and trotted in a straight line back to the upper pond where he came to rest at his handler's feet.

"That's about it," said McGillivery. "Sorry. It seems likely the victim walked about quite a bit between the house and the fish-pond."

"There are fish in the other one, too."

"And he made at least one foray down to that pond. It looks kind of grim."

"It's just mud. There's a natural spring. It leaches into the ravine."

"There was something down there Rex didn't recognize, something in the water, maybe the fish."

"It's sweet water, from clay."

"He doesn't know clay from kitty litter. Up closer to the house, the scents are untidy. Your victim came out through the back door and puttered around, then disappeared, maybe back to the house. That's about all we can tell you, but I'm pretty sure of that much, anyway."

Morgan admired McGillivery for his aplomb, and Rex for his capacity to recover his dignity through diligence, however unproductive.

Miranda appeared with two coffees in Styrofoam cups and a bag with gourmet sandwiches. "Sorry, McGillivery. I didn't know you were here."

"That's okay. I had lunch on my way up. Rex doesn't eat on duty."

The dog wagged his tail and looked hungry.

"Find anything?" she asked.

"No, ma'am, not much," he answered quite formally. He had a faint Scottish burr.

McGillivery proceeded to describe the final outdoor movements of Robert Griffin in the late afternoon before he was murdered, speaking with more authority to Miranda than he had to Morgan, but with a trace of humility that might have been almost subversive. Listening to him recount the obvious, she was distracted. For Scots, proscribed from their homelands by the English, there was always an air of laconic defiance about deference — as there was irony in the voices of the Irish, who endured the unpleasantries of alien rule through a fine gift of words. Miranda recognized this in McGillivery's voice. It made her feel Irish.

Her family had been in Waterloo County since it first opened for settlement. Some of her earliest forbears were Mennonites who had trekked up from Pennsylvania by Conestoga wagon after the revolutionary defeat, not for loyalty to the Crown but in fear of closing horizons in the new republic, a nation cobbled from wishes and dreams and given to values of enterprise and self-reliance they admired in themselves and feared in others. She was German, as well, from Bavaria, and English from Northumberland and Kent, and family lore had it that there was Mohawk blood in their veins. But she identified most with her Irish progenitors who had arrived out of famine and were thrust into agricultural wealth beyond their imagining in the lush, fertile landscape of Waterloo County, so strange from Connemara it faded out of their memories in only a few generations, but stayed deep in their hearts, that mixture of cool detachment, wild passion, and an inordinate fondness for language. McGillivery's subversive burr made her feel oddly at home.

Being Anglican for the last couple of generations was like flying a flag of convenience, tattered as it was at this point in her life.

"What about inside?" she asked. "Did you take Rex into the house?"

"Why?" asked Morgan.

"I don't know, she said. "Let's take him in."

When they opened the French doors, McGillivery released the dog without giving him a particular scent to pursue. Rex walked to the armchair, then looked back at Morgan. He walked over and sniffed Miranda, and she resisted her impulse to pat him. He seemed to be assimilating their scent, sorting them out from a complex pattern of odours. Then he paced back and forth, testing different scents that were unfamiliar but suggested only the purposeful activities of police investigators going about their business. Nothing spiked, nothing caught his attention, until he sniffed by the sofa where Eleanor Drummond had been sitting. Rex followed her scent to the chair and around and about the room, losing it in the din. He walked to the open door leading to the main floor, went back to the sofa as if he were confirming a suspicion, then walked purposefully upstairs, through the foyer, and up the next flight to the study door, which he pushed open with his nose. Standing very still, he blocked entry into the room, awaiting instructions.

Morgan glanced at the stains on the floor and explained to McGillivery that Eleanor Drummond had been found here in a pool of blood.

On a command from McGillivery, Rex moved one step at a time through the room, surveyed the patterns of scent, careful to avoid the space the body had occupied, and returned to sit at the feet of his handler, pensively waiting. McGillivery snapped his fingers, and the dog turned and trotted back down to the den. Miranda, Morgan, and Rex's handler followed, the detectives expecting a revelation of some sort, but when they caught up to him, the dog was curled on the Kurdish runner, feigning sleep.

"So what's he telling us?" Morgan asked.

"That he's hungry," suggested Miranda. "How did he know where Eleanor Drummond died?"

"He recognizes violence," said McGillivery. "Even weeks later there's a residual smell."

"The lingering presence of evil," said Morgan, assuming with a name like McGillivery that the handler was a Calvinist.

As if on cue, the dog unfurled, rose to his feet, shook himself, and went to the door that led past the bathroom into the nether regions of the house. McGillivery opened it for him. He stopped at the bathroom, entered, sniffed at the drain, gazed uncertainly at the tile walls, then abruptly went out and along to the next door, which stood ajar, and plunged into the dark, subterranean maze of cellars and passageways.

"He'll get lost in there," said Morgan.

Miranda responded by flicking a switch that drowned out the darkness with pools of light. They saw Rex disappear around a corner and caught up with him near the wine cellar, where he seemed for a moment distracted, standing unnaturally still. Then he gathered himself, veered around them, and disappeared back down the long passage leading to the tunnel. Barking, he returned, sniffed Miranda and Morgan, as if sorting out something, then almost slunk back to the wine cellar door. He stared up toward the small window, lowered his head, and began scratching against the stone and dirt floor by the sill.

"He's got excellent taste," Morgan observed. "He smells what they call 'the portion of the gods,' the infinitesimal seepage of great wine through old cork. I think we'll have to sample a few before it's all gone."

Miranda smiled. The wine fell under her jurisdiction, not his.

Rex moved on, abandoning his digging project. His focus shifted to the pump room, but when he got inside he seemed disinterested, as if it wasn't what he had expected.

"It's the noise," said McGillivery. There was an audible hush of electric motors, the soft rush of water surging through enclosed spaces. "It muffles the scents. My God, is all this necessary to run a fish pond?"

"They're koi," said Morgan. "Highly valued. The proof is the expense you see to maintain them."

"What do you think he thought he'd find?" said Miranda, not sure whether the word *thought* was appropriate.

"Rex? Hard to say. He's picking up too much. He can't process it all. He gets bits and pieces, but no overall pattern. He'd show me if he could —"

"Searching for the master narrative," interjected Miranda. "The story of the stories. He's probably getting undisturbed scents down here from generations, a hundred and fifty years or more, everything from trysts between servants to the depravity of children playing games of fear and retribution."

"Normally called hide-and-seek," Morgan said. "You're in a mood."

"Yeah," said Miranda, surprised that it showed. She hadn't had the opportunity to tell him about the previous night's revelations. She was in no hurry; she had a lot to assimilate. "Let's get back into the light. I don't like it down here. It's all too obsessive."

As soon as they re-entered the passageways, Rex starting dashing about again. He went down to the tunnel door and back, then to the wine cellar door, where he lingered briefly, then back to the door into the garage, which he scratched at and abruptly abandoned, then back once more, pushing his way out into the den with the others, striding ahead of them outside into the sunlight.

Rex trotted over to the pool, rested his forepaws on the top of the raised wall, and gazed down at the koi swimming below him quite calmly, having recovered from his intrusion. He cocked his head to one side, quizzical, the observer observed, his work in the cellar already forgotten.

Morgan was puzzling over the way Rex had avoided contaminating the crime scene when they went up to the study. The dog carefully stepped around the specific area where the body had been. Did his handler give him a command, or did he just know? He asked McGillivery, and the man explained he had used the word *steady*, and that was all it took.

"Would it work for me?" asked Morgan.

"What do you mean?"

"If I gave the same command."

"If it made sense. There would have to be something to avoid."

"Okay, here's where Griffin was laid out on the ground. You try it first."

McGillivery moved so the dog would have to cross over the site where the body had been to reach him when he was summoned. On command, after the handler said "Steady," Rex came directly to him, stepping through the phantom corpse as if nothing were there. "There must have been a groundsheet under the dead man, something to obscure the scent."

Morgan insisted they go back to the study, while Miranda stayed by the pool.

When they returned, Morgan explained. "He wouldn't walk across where the body was, and when I tried it, same thing. He refused to cross over. When I asked McGillivery to vary the command from 'Steady' and say 'Rumpelstiltskin' instead, Rex carefully sidestepped the spot and moved to his side. He wasn't about to violate the crime scene."

"Good show," said Miranda.

McGillivery seemed amused. He walked around a bit. "Sorry, folks. We just didn't have a grasp on what you wanted us to find."

As dog and handler disappeared through the walkway and up the steps to street level, Morgan said, "He's an olfactory psychic, you know. He can smell the past. It's not his job to make any sense of it."

"What's this all about?" Miranda asked when she realized he wasn't going to volunteer an explanation for testing Rex or McGillivery — she wasn't sure which.

"What?"

"Don't be coy, Morgan. The business about walking on bodies that aren't there. It's all a bit eerie."

"I was just wondering. It's something I've been reading."

"You've been reading?"

"Griffin's notes. The dog grasped the situation, but the words were irrelevant. He obeyed 'Rumpelstiltskin,' he obeyed me. It wasn't the words. He smelled death. He knew from his training not to intrude."

"And?"

"Griffin was right."

"And?"

"Nothing."

"He's a nice guy," Miranda said, meaning McGillivery. "Nice dog. Why would you name a dog Rex? What about Lassie or Rin Tin Tin? What about Prince?"

"I said that."

"What?"

"Prince. Seventeen percent of American dogs are called Prince. That's thirty-four percent of the males."

"Did you make that up?"

"Nope. Eleven percent are called Rex, six percent are called Rusty. Of the males."

"What's the most popular name for a bitch? Ellen?"

"Six percent. Did you know that forty-seven and a half percent of statistics are bogus. His real name is Schnitzel."

"Who?"

"Rex. That's what they call him at home."

"Schnitzel? I wonder what his registered name is?"

"Schwangau's Baron von Schnitzelgruber. He calls himself Dog."

"How do you know that?"

"We communed. Some dogs have four names. Fish and cats only have three. I took him for a swim in the pool."

"You didn't."

"His idea. And in the process of nearly drowning he told me his name was Dog. That was his final message to the world. Did you know males can't climb over ice ledges or walls? Their penises get caught."

"I didn't know that. I'm lucky. I don't have a penis."

"You're not a dog."

"Dogs, oh. Told you I'm lucky."

They sat on the low retaining wall, and Miranda produced the gourmet sandwiches. The coffee was cold, but the sandwiches, which cost more than dinner for six at McDonald's, were crumpled, with roast beef and bean sprouts and crusty whole-wheat bread and horseradish mustard from a family recipe passed down through millennia.

"I bought the sandwiches at the Robber Barons. As long as we're hanging out in Rosedale, we might as well take advantage." She fished around in her purse, withdrew a wrinkled bag, and announced, "*Petit pain au chocolat* for dessert."

They spread out their lunch on the stone between them, amused by the fish that converged at the surface, begging for crumbs.

"Did you feed them?" she asked.

"Yeah, when I got here."

"I called Mr. Nishimura."

"Who?"

"Your friend from the koi place. He's on his way down."

While they ate, she told him about Jill. She had informed Children's Services but insisted she would take responsibility herself, for the time being, as long as Victoria, the live-in, was there. Jill trusted Victoria. The girl asked about a funeral. She knew there had to be arrangements. She wasn't sure how to do it. She didn't think anyone would come to a funeral. She was on record as Elizabeth Jill Bray. She was born in Toronto. No father listed, no next of kin. Molly Bray was born in a crossroads village up past Elora. Detzler's Landing. A general store, a mill, and a post office at the back of a service station. Miranda had driven by but never stopped in, cutting north from Waterloo County to cottage country to visit friends.

"How on earth do you know these places?" Morgan asked. "I've never heard of Detzler's Landing. Must be on a river, on its own little lake with a name like that. I'm city. I know Canada from one end of Toronto to the other."

Morgan waited for a laugh, and she complied. She had heard it before.

"Old Sunnyside in the west to the Beach down east," he continued. "Everyone calls it the Beaches, but it was always the Beach. North to Steeles Avenue. Yonge Street, the longest street in the world. And to the south the lake — no, the United States. That's where the world was real."

He still had her attention. Now that they were alone she wanted to talk, but needed even more to listen to his familiar words, his voice. She didn't want to talk until she was ready.

"Living here," he said, "it was like being a smudge on a giant balloon, and inside the balloon was the United States of America, and we couldn't get in. We could peer through from the surface, but we couldn't get in. So when I finished university, did I go to the States? No, I went to Europe, and do you know why?"

"Because you couldn't get in without bursting the bubble?"

"I have no idea why. I am not American, but I needed to get away. I am American, and I needed to get away."

"You were reading too much Samuel Beckett."

"They don't know they're inside the bubble-balloon."

"I've never felt very Canadian," she said. "No patriot fervour, no national angst. Nationalism is like a bad dye job. It's probably better if your roots are showing."

"And I felt badly for stretching a metaphor! Let's take a run up to Detzler's Landing tomorrow."

"Okay."

"Let's take the Jag."

"Don't be ridiculous. It's ... okay, let's take the Jag."

"Okay."

"Do you think I'm going grey?"

"Let's see. No, some lovely pale highlights." He tousled her hair.

They ate for a while, quietly, old friends having a picnic. Morgan watched her watching the fish. He felt he had been unfaithful. He wanted to take her in his arms and hold her, he wanted to be "masculine" and protect her, and he knew if he tried she would laugh at the cliché and say he was the one who needed looking after. Then he would laugh and say something about women who nurtured, and they would both sputter into embarrassed silence.

So he said nothing and she, feeling she would love to lean against him in the midday sun, said nothing. She felt strong with him; the revelations of the previous night were gradually integrating into a coherent emotional pattern.

He felt sad, not for what he had done, but for the distance between them, and for the closeness, and for how the two didn't seem to resolve.

As if she were reading his mind, she asked, "Did you go home with Ellen last night."

"Yes," he said.

"Oh."

"Oh?"

"I thought she might —"

"What?"

"Take you home."

"Take me home! What am I — some kind of door prize? I got a ride as far as her place."

"You don't have to tell me about it."

"You asked. What am I supposed to do? Say no, I'll walk?"

"I don't care."

"You don't care what?"

"You can sleep with whoever you want."

"Thank you."

"She's a slut. You want to be careful."

"She's your friend."

"My friend is a slut."

"You ever sleep with her?"

"I'm a woman, for God's sake."

"So?"

"No. If I had, I wouldn't tell you."

"So you might have?"

"No, Morgan. She's aggressively heterosexual."

"And what about you?"

"Not aggressively. You're a jerk."

"I didn't sleep with her. I just went in for a drink."

"I don't care — why not?"

"What? Because."

"Because why?"

"Miranda …"

"I don't care.'

"I didn't."

"Good."

"Well, it's been a relief getting this off my chest — the fact that I didn't sleep with your former best friend."

"She was never my best friend. Adults don't have 'best' friends."

"Former not-best friend."

"Lost your sex drive?"

"No."

"You sure?"

"It's about delayed gratification, Miranda. At my age patience is an aphrodisiac."

"Or an excuse."

He looked at her. Her smile was enigmatic, flirtatious, or derisive. It could go either way. "Miranda …" he said with wary affection. "Miranda …"

"You could do better than her, Morgan. Do you want the rest of your croissant?"

A voice called from the walkway, and a man emerged out of the shadows. He walked toward the pond, his eyes intent on penetrating the surface reflection.

"Hello, it is Mr. Nishimura," he said without looking at either of them. "My goodness, Detective Morgan, you are right. They are nishikigoi, very wonderful." Reluctantly, he turned to Miranda. "I am Mr. Nishimura. We talked on the telephone."

She stood, took his proffered hand, and bowed slightly from the waist. "Thank you for coming, Mr. Nishimura."

He bowed deeply. "It is a most honourable occasion."

She bowed again, wondering how far political correctness had to go.

The man remained upright and grinned. "Eugene Nishimura," he said in a voice cadenced in irony.

She laughed. "Well, Mr. Eugene Nishimura. Do you even speak Japanese? Where are you from?"

"Your Mr. Morgan saw through me immediately yesterday. People who pay great sums for fish want all the trimmings. I'd dress like a geisha if it sold koi."

"And your life history, Mister Nishimura?"

"Toronto, like Detective Morgan. Parents both born in an Alberta internment camp. Keep calling me mister and we'll leave that in the past. My grandparents were from British Columbia, same town, all four of them — Tofino. They fished before the war. On a clear day they imagined they could see their ancestral homeland across the Pacific. My great-grandparents were, or some of them were, from Niigata Province. Thus, I have a genetic link to the koi ponds of Japan. And what about you?"

"Small-town Ontario. Waldron — in Waterloo County." Turning toward the koi, she asked, "What do you think?"

"These are some of the best I've seen. I buy in Japan once a year. I do speak Japanese a little. I learned at Berlitz, and from my wife. I've seldom seen better fish even there. Better, but not a lot better. There's the Doitsu Showa you brought to me, Detective Morgan. In here he doesn't stand out. This is an amazing collection, amazing. He must be one of the smallest. The Budo Goromo is smaller. There's nothing else less than twenty inches. We should do an inventory. Look at that Matsuba — the Gin Matsuba."

He pronounced the *g* hard, as in *go*. Morgan had been saying the *g* as in *gin*, like the drink.

"Which one is that?" asked Miranda.

"The purist might find him vulgar," Nishimura explained, pointing to a fish hovering just below the surface, about two feet long, a deep lacquer red with reticulated scales edged in black. "He's a living gem, a huge oriental pine cone transformed into the finest jewellery. He seems to radiate soft light from inside — a perfect example. My goodness, you have to love these fish. What a collection! Most people specialize in one or two varieties. He's got a gorgeous cross-section, the best of everything. Look at that dragonfish. Look at that Tancho."

Nishimura was ecstatic, as if he had discovered a treasure hidden from the world. "Tancho," he explained to Miranda, "see the red disk on the head? The rest of the fish is white and black. See how crisp the colour is? Asymmetrical but perfectly balanced. It's black with white, not white with black. Except for the red on its head. Look, a perfect blood moon with a bolt of black running down onto the nose. My golly, what am I doing prattling on?"

"Don't stop," said Miranda.

"I think the Tancho Showa is the single most outstanding fish here. That old-style Showa is stunning. It must be pushing three feet. I've never seen such a big koi outside Japan. There was one in England that died at a show — legendary, a new style, more white. There might be a few in the southern states this size —"

He interrupted himself to look around. "See those stanchions in the ground?" He indicated low concrete posts nestled unobtrusively into the landscape near the pond walls. "You wouldn't get fish this size if the pool wasn't heated in winter. He's had someone bring the walls in to make a giant cocoon, and warm water pumped through from the house, maybe a heater to heat the air, no expense spared. If you want me to manage these guys, I'll do it. His winterization people don't know about fish. You know, you can't have fish like this without word getting out unless you're obsessively private. Obsessive compulsive. And rich. Fish people like to compare notes. You should read some of the chat lines on the Net. Fish people are gregarious. This guy's an exception."

"His name was Robert Griffin," said Miranda.

"Never heard of him," said Nishimura with a trace of admiration.

"So what do you think it's all worth?" asked Morgan.

Nishimura shrugged.

"C'mon, Eugene. A hundred thousand?"

"Yeah."

"More?"

"A lot more. I'll do a complete inventory. Look at that Sushui!" He pointed at a striking fish with a dark zipper down its back set against pale blue, and large mirror scales along the sides, with a brilliant orange belly that only showed as it carved the water in slow, complementary arcs in response to another blue fish, also with a flashing red belly, and scales edged in darker gunmetal blue so that its entire back resembled articulated armour.

"The Sushui, swimming with the Asagi?" asked Morgan tentatively. He felt unsure of his authority in the presence of a master. The master deferred. Morgan was inordinately pleased with himself. "They move in response to each other," Morgan said to Miranda. "And look at the Ogans. They're like synchronized swimmers."

"Yamabuki Ogans," Nishimura explained. "Beautiful and bland."

"Identical twins," said Miranda. "Golden reflections of each other."

"I like the way those other two relate — the Asagi and the Sushui," Morgan said.

"Like us," said Miranda.

The hint of a blush rose to Morgan's cheek, and he scowled. She smiled.

"If we really want a true evaluation," Nishimura said, "I'd suggest trying to get Peter Waddington over from England."

"He wrote *Koi Kichi*," said Morgan. "There's a copy inside."

"He knows more about koi than just about anybody."

"I've read some of his diatribes on the Web. Bit of a diamond in the rough."

"Genius has its privileges," said Nishimura. "He's our man."

"Do you know him?" asked Miranda.

"I've seen him at shows, crossed paths with him in Niigata a couple of times," Nishimura said. "The man exudes expertise."

"I thought he was into Kohaku and Sanke," Morgan said.

"There's no koi lover in the world who wouldn't revel in this wonderful collection, for goodness' sake."

"Okay," said Miranda. "Will you try to reach him?"

"Absolutely," said Nishimura, "but it'll cost you big bucks."

"Eugene," said Morgan, "let me show you the set-up inside."

"Sure, but where's the Chagoi? I need to commune with a Chagoi."

"We've saved the best for last," Morgan said. "He's down in the lower pond with some absolutely exquisite Kohaku."

"You're in for a treat," said Miranda. "We figure the real collection is down there. The other's a major distraction, just for show."

"I put the Chagoi in to bring them up for viewing," Morgan said. "These, they're very special Kohaku he keeps hidden from himself."

Eugene Nishimura squatted by the lower pool's edge. "Bentonite clay. They must have trucked in tons of the stuff."

"Around the turn of the last century, late 1800s," said Morgan, "a son and heir built the place next door and put in the fish ponds, the two lower ones. There's another over there. They're probably connected. It's got koi in it, too. The formal pool came later, maybe put in by the last of the line. Would have been for goldfish back then, prize goldfish. There's a pipe running down from the pumphouse ..."

"But they're spring fed!" Nishimura said. "Natural water flow, clay-lined, they'd never freeze over. Ideal conditions." He paused, then stood back. "Call your fish, Detective Morgan. Let's see what we've got."

Miranda glanced at Morgan. How did you call a fish? But limpid eyes in a massive bronze head were already watching them, responding to their voices. Morgan took some feed from his pocket and hunched close to the pond edge. He reached over and let the Chagoi snarfle a mound of feed from his palm. Suddenly, there were Kohaku swarming like a tangle of kites, mouthing the air for food.

The fish in this pond were used to gathering natural nutrients from their forest-garden setting — insect larvae and algae and small creatures that swam through the green haze. So food pellets were a wondrous treat. But only the Chagoi had been conditioned to associate food with human voices, most recently with Morgan's voice.

"There are some beauties there," Morgan said.

"Indeed, Mr. Morgan. There are some very nice fish. Quality nishikigoi. Very collectible."

"But?" asked Miranda.

Nishimura frowned. "These are no better than the fish in the other pond. How many? Two dozen. Perhaps not quite as good. No, not so good."

The trio gazed into the shifting pattern of white and red awash in the opaque green as it slowly resolved into separate shadows and the water closed over until only the Chagoi was left, still grasping at the air with its lips, eyes fixed above the water level on Morgan.

Miranda and Morgan were disappointed by what Nishimura had said. Morgan, especially, felt a little betrayed. They had wanted this to be a treasure trove and a key to their investigation. Neither was excessively bothered that their knowledge of koi was imperfect, but each felt that their forensic skills had been somehow found wanting.

"There was something …" Nishimura seemed hesitant. He had stepped away from the clay edge, but moved closer again. "He's got such a collection. Why these —" He interrupted himself, nodding at the wall and the de Cuchilleros property. "Are the fish in the pond over there the same?"

"I think they can get back and forth," said Morgan. "A diver went in. There's a grate near the bottom. She couldn't feel a current but thought there must be an open flow. It wasn't blocked with silt."

"A grate?"

"She said the gaps were big enough. She could almost get through herself except for the scuba gear."

"Detective Morgan," Nishimura said with unexpected authority, "get me that big net over there, and a tub. And some more food. There's something —"

"What ..." said Miranda, trying not to impose an interrogative tone.

"Something. There's something. Sorry. I don't mean to be inscrutable. I just don't know."

Morgan returned with the net and tub. He handed Nishimura a handful of food pellets. Nishimura tossed a few to the mighty Chagoi, which was still within arm's reach. Suddenly, the undulating red-and-white mass rose into view, and separate fish peeled away, grasping for morsels floating on the surface.

"That one," said Nishimura. "You two wade in here, over here. In you go."

He was serious.

They kicked off their shoes and socks, and Morgan rolled up his pants above the knee. Miranda's slacks were snug and wouldn't roll or bunch up. Quickly, she stripped them off and tossed them onto the ground away from the pond. She looked Morgan directly in the eye. He said nothing.

"Body-by-Victoria," she said, "lavender briefs, microfibre, on sale — all prices in U.S. dollars. Order number CQ 138 something. Matching bra, underwired, super-soft lining for discreet comfort, sale price $15.99, lavender blue, dilly dilly. That should keep you going for a while."

Morgan grinned, blushed. He would like to have taken off his own pants or something silly to even out the vulnerability quotient.

"C'mon, boys and girls," said Nishimura, who seemed to find them puzzling. "In you go. Hold that tub under, like that. I'll bring her over the edge."

"Who?" said Miranda as she and Morgan waded precariously into the shallows. All she could see was a shifting pattern of red and white and soylent green.

Nishimura didn't answer but moved around on nimble feet along the shoreline, swinging the large net deftly, then slipped it into the water. Suddenly, one fish was separated from the rest, calmly allowing itself to be guided over to the tub, over the edge that dipped down below the surface of the water, and into a tranquil holding pattern, surrounded by translucent blue plastic. Nishimura leaned out and took an end from Miranda. She shifted to the side but wouldn't let go. She was a part of this. Gently, they lifted the tub onto the clay bank.

Miranda stood straight. Her feet slid out from under her. She fell backward and disappeared into the green water. Morgan reached for her, but his feet slipped on the wet clay and he disappeared into the green, as well.

The pool was preternaturally calm for a moment, then they both came up sputtering.

Nishimura didn't seem amused, watching as they helped each other to dry land, both of them looking sheepish, not quite laughing, not embarrassed, as if this were illicit fun.

"Well ..." said Morgan, stripping off his shirt and wringing it out. Soggy as it was, he offered it to Miranda to cover herself after she took off her blouse and swung it up in the air and away as if she would never want it again. She accepted Morgan's awkward gallantry.

"Well?" Miranda said, gazing down at their catch. "What have we here?"

Nishimura glanced up at them both, then down at the fish that now seemed opalescent in the shaft of sunlight falling into the tub. "Look!" he said, and didn't say anything more.

The three of them bent over the fish, which seemed oblivious to being observed as it hovered gently so as not to brush against the sides of the tub.

"Look," Nishimura said again.

"What?" asked Miranda, trying not to intrude on whatever Nishimura was experiencing. She was curious, though.

Morgan looked at Nishimura, who remained silent. Reaching across, he squeezed Miranda's shoulder. His damp shirt bled streamlets of water on his hand, and she shuddered from the cold of wet cloth pressing against her skin but shifted her body weight slightly toward him.

"I know this fish," said Nishimura. "I know her."

"Personally?" asked Morgan.

"Yes."

They were stunned.

"You've never seen such white. Just look. It's layers upon layers of the purest white over white over white, like a blessing. The red's perfect, like continents floating on a pure white sea, like perfect wounds on a sacred relic. This fish is a holy thing." At his own pace Nishimura tried to clarify. "It's the Champion of All Champions, the

Supreme Champion of the All-Japan Koi Show two years ago. I saw her there. I know her."

"How?" asked Morgan.

"She was never missing. As far as anyone knows, she's cruising peacefully in a vast clay pond in Niigata, breeding a fortune."

"A fortune?" echoed Miranda.

"The owners were offered four million for her after the show. In U.S. dollars. They turned it down."

"Gosh," said Morgan. "Holy smoke!"

"My goodness," said Miranda, smiling.

"Indeed," said Nishimura. "What a fish!"

9

Carp

The next day Miranda and Morgan had lunch on an open verandah projecting over the Elora Gorge. Below them the river ran silent and deep, cutting through layers of sedimentary rock millions of years in the making. The restaurant itself had been a large mill. Five storeys of fieldstone, with dressed limestone at the corners and around windows and doors, it appeared to be held together by the generous application of cement, not pointed between the stones as in a more formal design but smeared thickly across the walls so the stone pressed through in a rustic patchwork that made Miranda homesick for Waterloo County, for all the old Mennonite and Scottish-built farmhouses and the rare stone barns like the one down from Waldron on the way to Galt.

"It's beautiful here," she said.

They were the only ones eating outside. Cool air rising, lifted by the September breeze pushing through the gorge, carried the scent of the river, sending a shiver through Miranda.

"You want me to get your coat from the car?" Morgan asked.

"I didn't bring a coat, Morgan. Thank you, really. It was a nice thought."

"This is another world. A stone's throw from TO."

"You've travelled through Europe ..."

"When I wasn't much more than a kid. I know. I've lived in London, hung out in Rome. You would love Italy. Siena's the most beautiful city in the world."

"You were in love in Siena?"

"It's possible. I remember sitting in the Campo. It's a huge cobbled catchment for rainwater. It dips to one edge. There's a system of cisterns under the city. I remember sitting at a café, day after day, watching tourists, trying desperately not to be a tourist myself. I don't remember if I was alone or not."

He did; he wasn't. But it seemed inappropriate to mention a woman whose name he couldn't even recall.

"But you've never travelled near home?" she asked.

"When I first joined the force, I'd go to New York for the weekend, Chicago, New Orleans a couple of times, San Francisco. Just to make sure they were there."

"What about north?"

"It's big and empty."

"Absolute nonsense! Have you ever been to Muskoka? It's a ninety-minute drive."

"To see where Rosedale spends the summer? Never had the need."

"Do you know why?"

"Just didn't."

"No! Everyone goes there. It's beautiful. Goldie Hawn has a cottage in Muskoka."

"No kidding, Miranda. Kate Hudson's mother? Kurt Russell's life partner? I'm astonished. Let's drive up this afternoon."

"Go to hell!" She smiled.

Morgan had hated it when they had to deal a couple of times with movie actors. He liked movies. When he was a kid, he sneaked into the big downtown theatres through the fire exits. And when he was a student, he spent more time at films than at pubs. He watched DVDs at home. Movies were life in the perpetual present. He liked that. They were parallel worlds that made sense if only because they had limits. Actors as people, especially celebrities, undermined the illusion. He was fascinated by how people made movies, not how movies made people.

"I'd like to go to Muskoka," he said. "I like Muskoka chairs."

"Also called Adirondack chairs."

"In the Adirondacks. I like Muskoka chairs and I like Muskoka launches, the old-fashioned inboards."

"Where did you see those?"

"Along the Toronto waterfront."

"Fall colours in Muskoka, Morgan! Just imagine walking out of a black-and-white newsreel into a Cinemascope romance with wraparound sound. Let's go together. I used to go with my parents. We'd get up really early and drive to Muskoka and back the same day. Let's get this business over with and we'll take a vacation. Not boy-girl. Just a trip to see colours."

"Next year for sure."

"Next year ..." Her voice dwindled into awkward silence.

They had talked in the car on the way from Toronto. After waiting a day to sort out memories and responses, emotion and judgment, she had poured it all out in a torrent. It was like a confession on the verge of hysteria, but he was neither analyst nor priest, just a friend. At one point she had had to pull over to regain composure, but had insisted on not giving up the wheel. He had listened, and when her account rounded out to completion, he had talked about ordinary things. He had felt it was important to keep up the usual banter, to give her confidence in who she was now.

"You're a really bad driver, Morgan," she now told him.

"What made you say that?"

"If we go to Muskoka, I drive."

"Are you okay?" He gazed through the gaps between the floorboards of the verandah at the river beneath them and looked over at the restored mill made from the stones of the gorge. "You know, being his executor? You don't have to do it."

"I'm not a little girl, Morgan. He can't hurt me now. And maybe a lot of good can come from this. I'll squeeze something out for Molly's daughter ..."

"Jill."

"Don't worry about me. For weal or woe, I'm involved."

He frowned, with a twinkle in his eyes. "This place isn't one of his mills. You don't see any gryphons emblazoned on menus?" Why had he said that? Was it meant to be funny? He might have become morose, interrogating himself, but Miranda drew him out.

"I think the Griffins' mills were smaller," she said straightforwardly. "Except for the ones in the Don Valley. Most of their wealth came from real estate. They kept the country mills for Robert Griffin's amusement — his country adventures. He didn't sell the one at Detzler's Landing until the late 1980s." She paused. "It was him, you know,

Morgan. I'm not sure it really matters if it was him or not. Knowing the enemy is a snare and delusion."

"Sometimes I wonder about you," he said. "'Snare and delusion,' I've heard. 'Weal or woe' — where did you get that?"

"Voices from other times. It's an ancient expression. Check out *Caedmon*. I'm bluffing. My dad used to say it. So did his dad. It means for better or for worse."

"I figured out what it meant. But mostly we don't go around speaking in medieval epithets. Or is that what we do now when we're being evasive?"

"What am I evading? I'm not saying it wasn't him. I'm saying I'm not sure it matters — if it was him or not. Do you want coffee?" She signalled for two coffees.

"The bastard must have been in his forties."

"Does that make it worse?"

"Miranda, for goodness' sake."

"I don't know if it was rape."

"For God's sake!"

"To hell with God. It was sexual. Understand that!"

"Damn! It wasn't your fault. It was rape!"

"Listen, it was the culmination of a summer of testing, flaunting, I don't know, playing with fire. It was after a year of wondering, dreaming dream lovers, a winter of waiting, playing kissy-face with Danny Webster, who turned out to be gay, and then it was summer again and I went out there of my own volition ..."

"You were raped."

"I don't know."

"You were seventeen."

"Just turned eighteen. What's your hang-up on age? My friend Celia got pregnant with her second child when she was eighteen."

"Eighteen is only grown up when you're eighteen.

You were playing with sunlight and shadows. And then it was real, this guy in his forties. He raped you, Miranda."

"I just don't know," she said, looking wistfully into the gorge, shuddering again from the chill air rising.

"That's the point. You blocked it out for twenty years."

"It was traumatic, for weal or woe."

"There's no 'weal,' Miranda, no good side to rape."

"You're a lovely man, Morgan. Someday I'd like to marry you."

"For weal or woe." He smiled. "Miranda, if you don't think it was rape, that's simply not fair to the girl you were." He paused, thinking of her as an eighteen-year-old. She looked like Susan, her dark hair turned auburn. She looked like herself, through a lens softly. "It's not fair to the woman you are. You were foolish perhaps, but Griffin had all the power."

"Guilt, Morgan. The fact that I feel guilty implies responsibility."

"No way! Guilt is how you deal with something. It's not the thing itself."

"Do you want me to admit I'm a victim, that I've suffered? I didn't even remember until Wednesday night."

"Blanking out doesn't make something not happen, Miranda. Anaesthetic doesn't mean the surgery didn't take place, or leave scars."

"It wasn't violent. I didn't get beat up."

"I don't believe you said that, Miranda. The charge of sexual assault has misled us. There's no such thing as non-violent rape."

"It was him, Morgan." She was looking over at the British racing green Jaguar XK 150 parked by the railing at the side of the mill. "That car — for Christ's sake! What are we doing driving that car?"

"Vengeance?" he suggested.

The coffee came. Miranda glanced away from the waitress, who asked if there was anything else she could get them, fussing over them, trying to catch hold of the drama. "No," said Miranda. "Not another fucking thing."

"I'll get you your bill," the waitress said, scurrying back into the mill.

Miranda looked up at Morgan and smiled through tears. "I don't swear, Morgan. I do not swear."

Morgan leaned across to cup her hands in his. "Why don't you cover the bill? It'll make you feel better."

She stared at him with a depth of affection that disturbed them both. "I'll write it off against the old bastard's estate. Let's give the waitress a fifty, no, a hundred-dollar tip. She'll wonder about us for weeks."

"Grab immortality where you can," said Morgan. "However conditional."

Miranda shifted into reverse, started to back up, muttered, "Vengeance is mine," jammed the gears into first, and roared forward to an abrupt halt, bumper to the rail.

"Glad you stopped," Morgan said, gazing out over the precipice ahead.

"Don't move," she declared, leaping from the car. In less than ten minutes she returned, wearing a first-of-the-season ankle-length black shearling coat, tags still fluttering from a sleeve. "Let's go. Detzler's Landing. Let's get outta this 'puke-hole.'"

As they drove down a side road, Morgan said, "*One-Eyed Jacks*."

"Marlon Brando, the only film he directed," she confirmed. "'Scum-sucking pig' — from the same film. That's all I remember."

They drove on in silence until Morgan leaned over and said, "He followed you."

"Where?"

"To university."

"Morgan, you're scaring me."

"Well, how else —"

"I'm not saying you're wrong. I'm saying it's very disturbing to think about that."

"Can you remember him in your other classes besides semiotics?"

"I don't remember him anywhere. He's in the photograph. I don't know whether I remember him now, or the picture, or the corpse."

"Repressed memory syndrome, you know, it isn't straightforward."

"By definition."

"The invented past doesn't just peel away like the husk of a coconut, and then the shell falls open and there's the meat and the juice inside. It's not that simple."

"That's an astonishingly inept analogy, Morgan. I don't really need to go there. How about an orange? There's juicy stuff in nice neat segments. Or stripping back the skin of a banana, and there's that firm and tender shaft rising to the light. Oh, God, I hate Freud. I don't have a syndrome, Morgan. I just needed to forget. It's too easy to give something a label and then expect the symptoms to conform."

"Your coat."

"What?"

"It comes down to your ankles."

"It's supposed to."

"I like it. It's a good coat."

"Damn right."

They drove in silence for a while, then she said, "It's for winter." After a dramatic pause, she intoned, "Now is the winter of our discontent ... made summer ... by ... my new coat."

"'April is the cruelest month, breeding lilacs out of —'"

"Discontent. How through the winter of our discontent do lilacs breed?"

"Doesn't scan," he declared, counting off the iambs against his leg. "Actually, it does."

They lapsed into silence again, pleased with themselves. She nurtured bittersweet recollections of the games she used to play with Danny Webster; he tried to recall the name of his girlfriend in Siena. In another life, they agreed, they would be students of literature. Each remembered more from English classes in high school than anything else on the curriculum.

When they came to an unheralded crossroads hamlet, they found a large pond extending from one quadrant, a dilapidated wooden mill in another, an impoverished-looking general store in another, with a nondescript service station to the side, and in the fourth, an unpainted frame house beside a huge old barn with a corrugated steel roof in bad repair. The barn loomed over the water, completing the circle.

Strategically erected against the near side of the mill was a crimson sign inscribed with gold lettering: DETZLER'S LANDING GRIST MILL, 1820–1988. Below, on a separate line, was the word MUSEUM. To the side was a laboriously carved, gold-enhanced rampant gryphon. In a lower corner: R. OXLEY, PROP. 1997. An attachment fixed to the bottom of the sign gave the times of business: THURSDAY THROUGH SUNDAY, 8:30 TO 4:30, MAY 24 TO OCTOBER 1. ONLY.

"Government grant," said Morgan. "It doesn't look safe."

"They just got enough for the signage," she quipped.

"Want to go in?"

"With great care."

"It's supposed to be open. We'd better check it out to justify parking here."

She had pulled into the three-space parking area in front of an apparently superfluous picket fence. "We could park in the middle of the intersection," she said. "No one would notice. Have you ever seen such a droopy-looking place?"

"Droopy?"

"Droopy. There's not even a stop sign."

"Technically, Miranda, it isn't a four-way intersection. The road between the barn and the mill over the dammed-up part is more like a driveway."

"There's a house in behind. Must be the original farmhouse."

"How do you know?"

"I'm a village girl, Morgan. You wouldn't build a house behind a mill like that, but you might build a mill in front of the house. Anyway, look at the walls. Those casements are a foot and a half deep. I'll bet it's log under the clapboard, a settler's cabin from the first land grants."

"The Indians were here thousands of years before you guys."

"You guys?"

"I'm from the city. Why would anyone settle here, anyway?"

"Rock and swamp and scrub bush," she said. "Land was probably given to demobilized cannon fodder after the War of 1812. Authorities wanted it settled so roads could be forced through to connect the better land all around."

"We burned down Washington."

"What?"

"In 1813 we burned down James Madison's White House," Morgan said.

"The Brits did."

"Dolley Madison had the table set for forty guests. The invading British troops sat down and had dinner, the officers, I imagine, then burned the place to the ground."

"Very British."

"We were the Brits."

"No, the Brits were us. There's a difference."

"We were British."

"I'm Irish. *Quin*, remember?"

"Anglican, with one *n*."

They walked along the dirt lane that crossed the earthen dam between the mill and the pond until it petered out in front of the old house. Turning back, they stopped on the dam. Miranda moved from the reinforced concrete on the pond side to the mill side and looked down into a deep flume that was empty of water except for leakage trickling through a sluiceway of green boulders at the bottom.

"A perfect place for trolls," said Miranda.

"Trolls? I haven't seen trolls since I was a kid."

"Where?"

"In the Toronto ravines. Under the bridges around Spadina. Under the Bloor Street Viaduct. You know, troll places."

"I had them under my bed. You were allowed to play in ravines?"

"Yeah, that's before anyone knew they were dangerous. It was where city kids played if you wanted trees and mud."

"There were trolls living under my bed for one whole winter," she said. "Then I convinced them to move under my sister's bed, and she was too dumb to notice."

"Same room?"

"No, we had separate rooms. I put a whole wheat peanut butter sandwich under her bed to lure them away. They liked her dust bunnies better than mine and never came back, even after she found the sandwich and had a conniption because it was mouldy green. Trolls like green sandwiches, but she threw it out."

"Maybe they moved here," said Morgan, leaning over to peer into the flume, fascinated by the dark reflections of slime-coated walls, reinforcing rods of rusty iron running criss-cross, draped with dried detritus, fractured reflections of a few rotting boards that might have been the remains of a walkway, and by his own diminutive image in water-shard fragments looking eerily like a creature from another world. "Where's Billy Goat Gruff when you need him?"

Miranda had forgotten about "Three Billy Goats Gruff," the Norwegian fairy tale about a trio of goats who overcome a troll. They were an important part of her story, but what she remembered vividly was the presence of trolls under her bed. They had been almost her friends, and sometimes she missed them after they moved in with her sister.

"The secret is unbelief," she said.

"What secret?" asked Morgan, still trying to comprehend the figure in the depths of the flume that moved when he moved but didn't resemble him in the crackling water.

"The secret to trolls. If you say 'Do I believe in

trolls?' I'd have to say no. If you say 'Do you not believe in trolls?' I'd have to say no."

"You have a theory of trolls."

"It isn't about believing at all. It's about knowing. If you know they're there, then you can enjoy them, or frighten yourself with them. We lose that — the ability to know without understanding. That's when childhood ends."

"I see a troll down there," said Morgan. "Come and look. I'll bet there are two if we look carefully enough." He put his arm around her to steady them both so she could lean past and peer into the shimmering darkness.

"Can I help you?" asked a troll.

They both flinched in amazement, nearly tumbling into the flume.

"Can I help you?" asked the voice again through a vertical chink in the side of the mill. "Just a minute. I'll come around. The mill's closed for repairs."

A middle-aged man appeared through a makeshift door. He had a full beard and wore floppy overalls with no shirt, despite early autumn in the air. The stranger wore rubber boots folded over at the tops the way boys once did before running shoes became the universal footwear of childhood. He welcomed his visitors, speaking in a rustic twang that Miranda recognized as pure affectation. The man flaunted a slight Southern drawl as if he had learned to be country by watching reruns of *Petticoat Junction*.

Morgan noticed his teeth. They were crooked but healthy, despite the ragtag beard and stringy hair. He was probably English. Miranda and Morgan both marked the lack of underwear. When the man stood close, they could see down along his hips where the denim gaped away from his body. They kept backing away from him as they talked.

"You must be R. Oxley, Prop.," said Miranda.

He acknowledged he was and in his function as curator seemed not at all interested in their identities. "I don't know anyone called Bray," he said responding to their question. I've researched this town to the roots. There's no Brays, far as I know."

Morgan could always tell when someone distorted grammar intentionally. He saw it sometimes with cops, and men in hardware stores. There ain't no Brays would be trying too hard. There's no Brays was just about right

"You could try asking around," Oxley said, "but I've read everything there is to read 'bout Detzler's Landing. And the township, this part of the county.

"There must be a lot," said Miranda equivocally. Then, with appropriate deference, she asked, "Do you know why it's called Landing?"

"Used t'be river traffic. You can see where the banks of the river were higher, couple of centuries ago, before the invaders moved in. It was Huron country, but they couldn't farm it. It was just for travelling through. They were wiped out, and Algonquins took over, Ojibwa hunters. It was better for hunting. They were followed by Iroquois stragglers up from the Finger Lakes who didn't like life on the reserves. Then Frenchmen came through even before that and established a post here, just a storage shed really. But it was the new settlers who called it Detzler's Landing. Named it after the first mill owner, who changed the flow of the river. A German who fought with Isaac Brock and Tecumseh. He was wounded, an officer on half-pay, the lord here of his own little realm."

"You rebuilding the mill?" Morgan asked.

"Restoring. It's kinda tough. There's parts from every era. It's like archaeology in reverse — trying to work your way through from the past to the present."

"What a lovely project," said Miranda, quite moved by the man's sincerity.

"I don't know about lovely. But it's fun. Daunting, but fun."

"Daunting," said Morgan. "Where are you from?"

"Right here," said Oxley. "Sometimes I sleep in the mill. I've got a cot. I keep out the vandals that way. They don't know when I'm here and when I'm not, not when I park out back."

"You have much trouble?"

"Village kids. You know, nothing better to do. They're not so bad. They're used to me now — getting protective, some of them. When it was a mill, they would never have bothered the place. Then it was empty and they figured it was theirs. Now I'm filling it with history, and I got it just about workin' again. They respect that."

"How many?" Morgan asked. "You make it sound like hordes."

"Heathens at the gates? You'd be surprised. There's a lot of houses and abandoned farms with people living on them."

"Squatters?"

"Old families mostly. They let the farms run down generations ago and they live on in the houses. It's a small pocket of poverty here, surrounded by some of the richest farmland in the country. You'll find more like this over in eastern Ontario, along the edge of the Canadian Shield."

Someone from around Detzler's Landing wouldn't have said Shield, Morgan thought.

"Any fish in there?" Miranda asked, nodding toward the still waters of the pond.

"Carp. Some say walleyes and pike. I've only seen carp. Sometimes one'll get caught in the grid when I'm running the water. D'y'know, this mill powers a turbine combine from water? There's a steam drive, as well. I'll have it working by spring. Are you two cops?"

"Why do you ask?" questioned Miranda.

"Just wondered."

"Did you buy this place from Gryphon Mills?"

"Yeah, Robert Griffin. I never actually met the gentleman. Read where he's dead. Are you here about that?"

"Did you ever meet someone called Eleanor Drummond?" Miranda asked.

"She sold me the place. She handled the paperwork. Is she dead, too?" He observed them warily as if trying to decide whether they somehow held him responsible. Deciding that wasn't the case, he relaxed. "She was a stunning woman — too bad." They hadn't confirmed her death, but he knew. "A very high-class lady." His drawl had fallen away, and the abbreviated sibilance of what Morgan recognized as residual Cockney pulled his vowels askew. "Very high class. You don't find many like her. Sorry, Constable …"

"No offence taken," said Miranda. "It's detective."

"Sorry again, Detective. It's just that Miss Drummond wasn't someone you'd expect to see around here. She wasn't murdered, was she? I suppose she was. You don't die in your prime except from murder or suicide or accidents or disease, I suppose …" He seemed to be reaching for more possibilities to reinforce his litany of premature death.

"She came out to Detzler's Landing then?" asked Miranda, trying not to look down the gaping side of his overalls.

"A couple of times. To show me around. To bring out the papers."

"Did she know anyone in the village?"

"Lord, no! She walked across the dam once, just over to the edge of the old lady's property. For a minute I thought she was about to pay her a visit. You know how someone stands when they're stuck between coming and going? Then she turned back, and so far as I know, she never touched ground in the village except on this property."

"She made quite an impression," said Miranda.

"Yes, she did."

"Did she ever return?"

"Not that I know of."

"Do you think the old woman in the house might answer some questions?"

"She doesn't say much. Taciturn, she is." He savoured the word. "Bit of a recluse. Has her groceries delivered. We got into a fence dispute a couple of years ago. Had to get the fence viewer in. Kids leave her alone on Halloween. I don't quite understand how she's immune, but she is. She's long past her allotted four score and ten."

"Three score," Miranda said.

"She's old," said Oxley.

"Will you buy her property when she dies?" asked Morgan.

"I dunno. It belongs to the Griffin estate. If they'll sell …"

Miranda exchanged glances with Morgan. "We'll see," she said.

"Yeah," said R. Oxley, hitching up his overalls and turning away. "Meanwhile, back to work. Come tour the mill sometime."

Miranda and Morgan walked up the slight incline toward the house. It was on a virtual island since the main flow of the river ran around behind it and over another dam where it fell across a tumble of rocks and converged with the channelled sluice water that flowed out from under the mill.

"I paid for it myself, you know," said Miranda. "The coat ... with my own money."

"Why are you telling me this?"

"I didn't want you to think it was on Griffin's account. I am a woman of means, somewhat modest perhaps, but I can pay my own way."

"I have not the slightest doubt."

They ambled across the grass to the house and stepped up onto the porch.

"It seems deserted," said Morgan, looking at the faded crewelwork hanging lank beyond small panes of glass in the door. They moved to the edge of the porch and gazed beyond the pond to where the river emerged from a channel in the marsh. "Carp and koi," he said, not feeling the need to explain the equation. "Imagine this river teeming with koi."

"They used to shovel them out in the spring for fertilizer."

"Carp?"

"Out of the streams when they were swimming to spawn." Miranda touched his arm. "Do you really think my coat's too big? It was the only one I tried on."

"I like it."

"Good. I like it, too."

They turned back to the door that strangely projected an emptiness inside. As they were about to knock, it swung open.

"I've been observing you," said an elderly woman, not at all what they expected. She was slender, small, bright, absolutely solid on her feet, and smiling. "It's a lovely view. You two seem to be having a very good day."

Thrown off guard, Miranda blurted, "Do you know Molly Bray?"

"Of course, dear. She's my granddaughter. Come in and have some tea. The water's near boiling already."

10

Crayfish, Walleyes, and Pike

"Let me describe her," the old woman said, blowing across the top of her cup. She looked from Morgan to Miranda and back again, then talked into the space between them. Her voice was warm, embracing the past, inviting them to share in her affection, while her eyes moistened with images visible only to her.

"She was an angel and a devil, Molly Bray. It would make your head spin. As a wee girl, she'd march along beside you like nobody's business. She wouldn't hold your hand, mind you, but she'd be close enough you could feel her little body against your leg. Do you know she had her own garden? She wouldn't let me help. She grew a whole garden of radishes one year."

"She lived here with you?" Miranda asked, sipping her tea, trying to be as subtle as possible about straining the loose bits through her teeth.

"Oh, yes, from an infant. She was such a good baby ..."

"Where was her mother?"

"She didn't have a mother. What's your name, dear?"

They had introduced themselves when they came in, but the old woman was busying herself with tea paraphernalia and hadn't paid attention.

"I'm sorry. I'm Miranda Quin. This is David Morgan. We're —"

"She didn't have a mother and she didn't have a father. In those days we looked after our own."

"That wasn't so long ago, Mrs. …?" Morgan asked. The woman had neglected to give them her name, the tea ritual taking precedence over niceties apparently deemed less important.

"Former times. I'm thinking of my parents' day. When you don't have a family of your own, you do that. I'm *Miss* Elizabeth Clarke. I'm an old maid. I'm very pleased to meet you, Mr. Morgan. Would either of you like a dash of hot water?"

"No, thank you," said Miranda and Morgan simultaneously.

"I have my tea mailed to me directly from England. This one's Lapsang Souchong. Do you like it?"

"It has a distinctive flavour," said Miranda.

Morgan, who wasn't so diplomatic, said nothing.

"If you'd prefer, I have some Tippi Assam."

"You buy it in England?" asked Morgan, succumbing to the notion he had to say something on the subject. "Are you English?"

"Yes," said the old woman. "Seven or eight generations back. Depends on whether you follow my mother's side or my father's. I've never been there. No desire to go. It's all Jane Austen and Charles Dickens in my mind, and that's how I like it. And Winston Churchill and Twiggy."

Morgan took a deep breath over his teacup. The odour of hot asphalt gave way to an aroma of damp winter evenings warmed by the embers of an open fire.

He looked around. There was only a space heater, smelling faintly of rancid oil. Maybe Miranda was wrong. This house, a cottage, really, must have been built after the advent of cast-iron stoves.

Elizabeth Clarke watched him as he surveyed the small room. She had lived here all her life and her mother before that, and her people before that. She knew what he was thinking.

"There was a fireplace in the back wall. It was filled in. Caused a dreadful draft. The iron pot-belly was better, but it leaked smoke. Then we replaced it with another made from steel. It's still out back. After that we brought in a modern oil burner. I suppose most heat with electricity now."

"I suppose they do," said Morgan.

He was enchanted by how comfortable she was among the generations that had lived here and died. Strangely, it was a bit like he felt himself in the subterranean depths of the Griffin house. That was something he admired about Europe — how people lived less on the surface of history than in its midst, as if it were a place, not a line of descent. "How did you —" he began to ask.

"Because you're from the city, Mr. Morgan. You expect a fireplace in an old house like this. Now the young lady, she knew better. She'll be from a small town, I imagine."

"Waldron," said Miranda.

"The Griffins had a mill there, too," Elizabeth Clarke said. "Not many log houses over your way. You mostly built with stones from the fields before hauling in brick when the Grand Trunk went through."

That would have been in the 1880s, Morgan observed to himself.

"I'd be happy to let you try several," she said. "You seem like a young man of good taste."

Morgan was disconcerted for a moment, then realized she was talking about tea. "Thank you, no."

"Some other time perhaps."

Miranda was sure the old woman was flirting with her partner. Elizabeth Clarke must have been in her eighties. She had exquisite ankles and crossed them proudly in front of her for Morgan to admire. The old woman kept adjusting her posture, re-crossing her ankles a couple of times. Miranda and Morgan felt comfortable in the embrace of Elizabeth's Clarke's ramshackle home that from the outside had seemed virtually empty. She welcomed the invitation their patience affirmed and continued her narrative.

"In her teens Molly was a magical creature. Bright as a whip, determined. My gracious, she did homework like it was fun. She'd make surprises for me in home economics, cooking and sewing and crafts. She taught herself to knit one winter and made me a sweater better than I could have done, and she brought animals home. She always had a wounded chipmunk around or a frog half-chewed up, or crayfish in my good crystal bowl under her bed. Once she rescued a duck with no skin on its neck. A big snapping turtle got hold of it, and she waded right in there and rapped the turtle smartly with a stick. That duck's neck was as bare as a skinned chicken, but she wrapped it in a rag full of Vaseline and kept it beside her bed. And, can you believe, it lived and went back with the other ducks, only they always made it swim behind. When they walked across the lawn, the ducks all in a line — they did that to take a shortcut from the pond to the marsh — that little duck would bring up the rear. Sometimes it would veer over to where we were sitting on the porch, maybe shucking some corn or peas from the garden, depending on the season, and it would stop right in front of Molly and give her a big quack. Then it would scramble on through the grass to catch up with the others. We never saw them after they flew off south for the winter. Molly never was a problem, you know, with puberty. She just grew up real easy. Not that she wasn't a handful, at times."

"What do you mean?" asked Miranda.

"Well, for instance …" The woman paused, savouring the past, trying to sort out the flavours. "She was feisty. Easy, because I admired her causes. But, oh, she could be determined."

"How so? Tell us about her."

"She would take control of a situation. When she was just little, in late November of grade one, yes, and she walked home from school. Well, that was four miles, and it was bitterly cold. When she didn't get off the school bus over by the mill, I was worried. I phoned around, and the bus driver thought she hadn't been to school that day. Her teacher said of course she had and I'd better notify the police. I called the police and was just going out to the car to search for her when she came walking down the lane — I used to drive then, but now I get my groceries delivered. I told her I was worried sick and the police were looking for her, and she was as calm as could be.

"'The bus driver smokes,' she said. 'He's not supposed to smoke.' 'No, dear,' I said. 'He isn't.' 'Well,' she said, 'he smokes in the bus and it's cold out now, so he drives with his window closed. So I walked home.' Just then the OPP cruiser pulled in past the mill and parked behind my car.

The officer got out and asked if she was the missing girl. 'I'm not missing,' she announced. 'I walked home from school because Mr. Poole smokes on the school bus, and he drinks, too.' 'How on earth do you know that?' I demanded. 'Well, he does,' she said.

"I don't even know if she knew what drinking meant. There was never anything here except cooking sherry. But the policeman talked to the driver and then to the bus operator and Poole was reprimanded and the next school year he was replaced. I was that proud of Molly I didn't scold her for walking home, and I was even more proud when she went out the next day and climbed up into that bus without the slightest fear of recrimination for what she had done, though I imagine Roger Poole scowled as mean as he could. They were a nasty bunch, the Pooles. They've died out now, or all moved away."

"Sounds like an amazing little girl," said Morgan.

"I told you she was feisty. Do you know that in grade eight she took on a child abuser and beat him at his own game?"

"Good grief!" said Miranda. "How did she do that?"

"It was that same family, the Pooles. The old man used to beat up his son, Troy, who was in school with Molly. After Roger Poole stopped driving the school bus — that was his only job — he mostly just sat around the house, and I hear he would get drunk. If he wasn't too drunk to move, he'd beat up the kids, especially young Troy. And his wife, too. She was a sorry case. One day Troy came to school all bruised where no one could see — the teachers are supposed to report when they suspect domestic violence — but the other kids knew by the way he was moving that he was hurt pretty bad."

Miranda grimaced and glanced at Morgan, who was listening intently.

"Molly was twelve years old, and she marched right into the Poole house after school with Troy in tow — he was three inches shorter then. She confronted Roger Poole — it was a village legend for years — and called him a bully and dared him to hit her. Of course, he didn't. He wasn't drunk enough, or he was too drunk, or he had a streak of decency or whatever. Instead he backed off, and she screamed at him so that the closest neighbours all heard. Then she backed him against the wall and yelled that if he ever touched one of his kids again, or his wife for that matter, he would have to deal with her and she would tell the police and say he attacked her and he'd go to jail and he was a despicable bully.

"Well, he never touched those children again, and the next time he hit his wife, she called the police herself. They didn't do anything, but Roger Poole stamped around the village all through the night, wailing about being violated, and in the morning he was gone and nobody ever saw him again, not in Detzler's Landing."

"My goodness," said Miranda, "and you said she grew up easy."

"She certainly understood power," said Morgan.

"She did," said the old woman.

"But not necessarily its consequences," he added.

"No," she agreed. "You know, Troy Poole was never her friend. After that, when they went to high school together, he wouldn't speak to her, and he dropped out and moved away, too. By then he was a foot taller than her, but scared of her because she was tougher than his father."

"Stronger," said Miranda. "Did she learn that from you?"

"I think she came with her character already complete. I raised her from the start. She was magic, you know. A girl I never saw before in my life turned up at the door one day. Nineteen seventy-two. Held out a fresh new baby and said, 'Her name's Molly Bray.' I took hold of the baby, then the girl walked smartly away and I never saw her again. The baby was a little beauty.

"I called old Dr. Howell, and we registered her right off. I don't know what he put down for her parents. Maybe my name — a virgin of fifty. Ha! And his own. He was always interested in me! Might have seemed odd that we named her by her own name, but we did. Doc Howell would have known how to do it. He called in on Molly Bray regularly until two days before he died. I told him he looked rundown. She was too young to remember. Well, I brought her up and was glad of the company."

"Miss Clarke, have you seen her recently?" asked Miranda.

"No, dear. When she was sixteen, she had to go away."

"She had to?"

"I was sad. Oh, I was sad when she went."

"Did you call the police?"

"No, dear. She said goodbye to me, and I'll love you for always. She wanted to go, so that's what she did, and I knew she would be all right."

"Miss Clarke, we're police officers," Miranda said.

"Oh, no, dear. I don't want to hear it. You finish your tea. Would you like a refill? I'll get some more biscuits. No, you'd better go, dear. I'm tired. Thank you so much for visiting. It was nice to meet you, Mr. Morgan. I'll just go into the other room. If you'll see yourselves out ..."

When they were on the porch, Morgan leaned into Miranda and said, "There was no point ..." He let his voice trail off.

Miranda gazed up at him and smiled. For an instant she felt small and secure, then looked away to the mill, annoyed with herself. It had never occurred to her before that Morgan was taller.

They walked across the lawn and along the drive, stopping where it passed over the dam. R. Oxley had opened the sluice gates on the pond side of the road, and water was gurgling underneath them, rising to fill the flume. They could hear the low rumble of antique wood and iron machinery inside the mill gathering force to begin work.

At the car Miranda asked Morgan if he wanted to drive. He shrugged in the negative, and she got behind the wheel. Morgan appreciated the way she had offered — not as if she were submitting to social convention, but just that he might want to give a vintage sports car a try.

They pulled away from the village and within twenty minutes had entered more prosperous terrain. He observed her watching the road, seemingly oblivious to his gaze. She was enjoying the drive, as if Detzler's Landing, like an inversion of Brigadoon, had slipped off into another reality when they left, a place where time and customs conformed to different imperatives than the ones shaping the world everyone else shared. Or maybe, he thought, everyone lived in different worlds that overlapped at the edges, creating the illusion that everyone was in the same place. The only thing to prove Detzler's Landing still existed would be its mark on a map. He took a road map out of the glove compartment and checked. "There is no Detzler's Landing," he told Miranda.

"No," she said. "You're probably right."

"It's not on the map."

"Doo do, do doo, doo doo, do do," she trilled, trying to replicate the sound of *The Twilight Zone* theme, which actually had been a defining moment in North American television long before either of them was old enough to pay much attention to paranormal phenomena. She didn't know the theme for *The X-Files*.

"Seriously, how did you find it?"

"Morgan, I'm a good detective. I phoned CAA." She couldn't remember which one was Scully and which was Mulder in *The X-Files*, but she could see the actors who played the FBI agents clearly on a television screen in her mind. "What did you think of Miss Clarke? She was flirting with you."

"Don't be ridiculous."

"Morgan, she was."

"I take that as a compliment — from both of you. It was curious, insisting that Molly wasn't difficult, then telling stories that would make your hair curl."

"And with pride."

"Yeah. I'd say she loved her foundling daughter."

"Granddaughter. To be age appropriate she designates herself a grandmother."

"But I'm not really sure she understood her. Must have been like nurturing a wild animal until it springs free of affection. The loss leaves you grateful and grasping, resigned and triumphant."

"That's poetic."

"She was a lovely woman."

"Morgan, do you know what I like about you?"

"I'm poetic?"

"You wear baby powder–scented deodorant."

"I do?"

"You smell nice."

"You smell earthy," he said.

"I do not."

"You smell like winter. You always smell like winter."

"That's nice, Morgan. Thank you."

They came to the 401, but instead of crossing over to the Toronto ramp, Miranda veered west toward Waterloo County. Not anticipating the turn, Morgan lurched to the side, recovered, and slouched into the comfortable leather depths of the bucket seat. He looked for an explanation, but she was completely focused on the road ahead.

What difference would it make if he didn't go into headquarters? Alex Rufalo, their superintendent, knew Miranda was off the case. He also knew they were working together as usual. That meant they were relatively autonomous or, at the least, hard to pin down.

Neither said a word during the short ride to Waldron. Being on a monster highway that swayed across the landscape under the burden of eighteen-wheelers spewing fumes as they passed wasn't enough to erase his pleasure in the pastoral experience. The low-slung car rolled solidly along, indifferent to the contours of scenery. Miranda drove with casual confidence, but not fast.

Morgan had never been this far west except in the air. Taking the Waldron exit, Miranda drove down past her mother's house without slowing and didn't indicate to her partner that that was where she had grown up. She drove directly over the hill and parked the green Jaguar at the end of the loading dock under the lee of the corrugated steel walls of the mill. High above, in faded orange, a rampant gryphon lorded over all he surveyed, even though the mill had long since passed into local ownership. This was exactly where she had last seen the same car, parked right here, twenty years earlier.

Miranda got out of the Jaguar, strode up onto the embankment, and plunged into the cloistered canopy over the millrace. Brooding cedars tinged with autumn russet and perforated with a filigree of light cast dappled patterns between them as Morgan raced to catch up with her. When he reached her, he took her arm and she immediately slowed to a walk, almost a stroll, as if they were lovers. They hadn't spoken for almost an hour, but driving into the rolling hills of Waterloo County, Morgan had felt perfectly attuned to her needs, if not privy to her thoughts.

When they broke into the open space of the meadow, they saw the pond water divide in the gentle breeze: one branch flowed over the dam, sliding smoothly, carving down into the spillway, where it broke and re-gathered in the trout pool and cut randomly toward the bridge in the valley beyond; and the other branch flowed to the race, where it took on dimensions of shadow and darkness as it moved between parallels under the cedars on its way to the turbines of the mill.

They both stood astonished. Morgan had never seen such beauty. He had never imagined, in all his reading and limited travels, that there could be such a place. He knew other people were moved by mountains or wilderness, the Sistine Chapel or Stonehenge, Mount Rushmore or the Grand Canyon, the Acropolis, High Arctic archipelagos, or the gardens at Kew. But his mind raced and found no comparisons. For him this was the right combination of nature and the gentle intrusion of human design. For Miranda there was shock, a chilling bewilderment that nothing had changed.

Stepping into the light, she walked to an imagined depression in the grass, knelt, placed her hand on the ground, and ran it slowly over where she would have been spread out so long ago, so recently that it hurt. Morgan came up and stood beside her, resting his hand on her shoulder. He looked over at the dilapidated structure of the old mill, the roof still precariously balanced in sheet metal shards on its tumbledown tower.

Crossing the dam to the mill, Morgan shifted his weight carefully over the thick walk-board. When he got to the mill, he pushed open the door and stepped into a dank maze of shadows and light, crenellations of the sun shining between separated boards of the ancient walls. He pushed against myriad cobwebs, some wheeling in small riots of intricate strategic design, some invisible in the shadows, and choked when they clasped at his face.

Morgan climbed gingerly up the suspended ladder steps into the tower loft and stepped onto the precarious floor, bracing against rafters that swooped ominously over his head. He looked down through the splayed floorboards into a watery shimmer two storeys below beneath gaps in the ground-level floor — still-water seepage, closed off long ago by the earthen embankment when the pond was diverted to the race. Morgan crouched where the wallboard opened and peered toward the dam and down at Miranda, who was lying spread-eagled on top of her coat on the grass, fully clothed but pathetically vulnerable. She was staring up into the sky, not at the tower but into the layers of cloud and open blue.

Morgan's eyes adjusted to the chiaroscuro lattice of shadows and light that surrounded him. Tracing in his imagination where the man must have spent all those hours, he lowered his weight to the floor and found it difficult to breathe.

A hand-forged nail lying on top of an exposed joist caught his eye. He picked it up and toyed with it, imagining other hands holding it, other eyes examining the flanged head where it had been drawn and snipped from red-hot iron two centuries earlier. Morgan had read about nails. He knew the different shapes of pioneer nails, each peculiar to one region or another, declaring its vintage as clearly as if it were labelled. He didn't own antiques, but he loved reading about Canadiana, especially early Ontario furniture with its original paint. He watched the *Antiques Road Show*, both the British and American versions, on late-night reruns.

As he replaced the nail, exactly where he found it, he noticed deliberate marks etched into a wallboard. He brushed the dust away with the side of his hand, blew across what seemed to be letters.

The inscription was brief and enigmatic, like the flourish of a signature that concealed yet expressed identity. The first letter was a capital *M*, like a skull with the top carved away. The next was a *B*, crudely done with the eyes of the letter gouged out. Then there were a linked pair of letters, what seemed like a gaping mouth with a slash to one side, followed by the crooked jaw of a *G*. Leaning to the side, he spied in the shadow of an upright beam other marks scratched into the wood. When his eyes adjusted, the marks became very distinct: *M* period. *Q* period.

Griffin knew her name!

Morgan could taste bile in his throat. How many hours and years did he hide here, watching? Morgan spat into the dust.

"Mary Bingham Carter-Griffin," Miranda explained when he described what he had found after rejoining her. "His mother. He named the semiology institute after her."

"He knew *your* name!"

"So you said. Names aren't that big a mystery in a village. It would be easy to find out from the mill hands. Everyone knows who everyone is — you don't know them, necessarily, but you know who they are."

"That's why I like cities. You know who you know. And who you don't know, you don't know. It's simple. That wanking creep knew it was you he was watching."

"Why does that make it worse? Morgan, there are people in the city, you see them for years, they have your coffee and muffin ready when you get off the subway because you're a regular and you tip them at Christmas. They sell you a paper, a haircut, shoes. They nod to you in the hall, you pat their dog. They work in your office at unknown labours. On the street corner you give them a dollar once a week and miss them when they're gone, maybe in rehab or dead, you don't know. You know these people. You don't know anything about them. We all live in villages. The difference is that in a village like this you know everyone's name. You can be just as lonely."

Miranda wasn't sure why she had added the bit about loneliness. She wasn't certain why being known made her more vulnerable, but it did, at least now, looking back.

"He wasn't just looking," said Morgan, turning her perspective around. "He was watching. There's a difference. He was watching your life."

"Or I was putting it out on display."

"For goodness' sake, Miranda. You said yourself he may have been there for years."

"We used to gather crayfish in jam jars. I wonder if he saw us. Sometimes we didn't come by the mill. You could cut across Mr. Naismith's pasture from the village if the bull wasn't out. He couldn't always know we were here. Celia and me, we'd come out when we were only nine or ten, even younger, and we'd catch crayfish in the shallows."

"What did you do with them?"

"We talked about taking them home to eat, but we let them go. I can work out how old we were by the sequence of gatherings. When we were really small, it was bits of driftwood and pebbles. Then we graduated to crayfish for a couple of summers. Then it was gathering flowers. We'd pick great bunches, and naturally they'd die. We'd pluck water hyacinths and lay them out in the mud like drowned things, and lilies with long, snaky stems. Then we got old enough and we'd come and just admire the flowers, wade out and smell them, and swim by the dam and lie in the sun. We wore bathing suits then. We were modest until we hit puberty. Celia was fully mature at twelve. I think we sunbathed naked after that, except we kept our panties on. I'm not sure why. It seems reckless now to strip down like that, even here, but we kept our underwear on, for periods I suppose, not propriety, and we read romances aloud, graduating year by year from the most romantic drivel with pastel covers to almost Jane Austen. By the time I was reading Jane Austen, Celia was married or close enough to it. Donny was all the romance she could handle, and I preferred Austen in solitude."

She took a deep breath and glanced up at Morgan, who seemed to be listening, seemed to be waiting. Miranda felt under pressure, as if something were expected of her and she wasn't sure what it was. "Perhaps he was our necessary witness," she went on. "Scrunched up in his tower. Dreaming of his dead mother. We had him trapped there, Morgan. We kept him locked away day after day. Rapunzel, a bald-headed wanker. In all our innocence we had the power."

"Not if you didn't know he was there until later."

"But maybe we did. I can't remember. Sometimes there were pigeons, sometimes maybe there weren't any pigeons."

"Pigeons?"

"You know how kids play, as if there's an unseen audience applauding, or being horrified. Kids play to ghosts, before they grow up and lose them."

"They just lose them?"

"You were a kid, too, you know. We lose our familiars when we get big enough to know they can't possibly exist. That's what makes them go away. We stop unbelief."

While she talked she wondered how she had avoided immediately connecting the green sports car in Rosedale with the car parked by the mill. No one in Waldron drove a Jaguar. She would have known. Would she have known it was him in the tower?

"No one would want to stay innocent forever," she said. "But after the Fall, amnesia settles in. We forget what Eden was like."

"No," said Morgan. "We forget the Fall, not the Garden." He paused. "Pre-lapsarian nostalgia," he said, just to see if the words worked, out loud. Then he added, "When we start talking like televangelists, at least one of us is being evasive …"

"Maybe that's what I want."

"We came here to deal with things, Miranda. You brought me here."

"It's still beautiful, isn't it? An interlude from the world."

"A strange sanctuary."

"Strange sanctuary," she repeated, listening to the sounds echo deep in her mind.

"He was probably up there wanking all day."

"Is that anatomically possible?"

"Only if he was really bad at it."

"I imagine it was creepier than that," said Miranda. "I mean, you wouldn't come back day after day through the long hot summer to ejaculate in the shadows."

"I don't know."

"Not for sex. It's about needing to watch to prove you exist. Like taking photographs of Niagara Falls to confirm you're there. Making connections."

"The connection, of course, is illusion. Even for non-voyeurs. An orgasm is the most solitary act in all of creation."

"Speak for yourself, Morgan. He must have loathed us, you know, in direct proportion to how much he despised himself. We're lucky the bodily fluids being spilled weren't blood. Not 'we.' The summer I was eighteen, Celia was getting legitimately laid. I was on my own."

The car, she wondered, had Celia and she gossiped about the Jaguar? It was always there. It had seemed as if it had always been there. If they had known who had owned it, they had known he was older, an outsider, and rich. From another world. They were trespassing technically. It was his property. Perhaps they wouldn't have given it much thought.

"We cooked some of them once — the crayfish. Celia said her friend Russell Livingstone used to roast them on a stick when they didn't catch any trout, and the shiners weren't worth bothering with. Russell was like Celia's brother, but he moved away. It was like he died."

"Did you eat them?"

"No. I don't think so. We let them go. But don't you see? We didn't release them out of kindness. We were cruel. We just didn't know what else to do with them."

"You weren't cruel. You were just kids."

"Innocent?"

"Innocent. In Toronto we used to hunt along the ravines with slingshots and BB guns."

"Did you ever kill anything?"

"Not even close. I had a friend who cut the tail off a road-kill raccoon and we took it to school as a trophy, but everyone knew it was road kill and that we'd get rabies or leprosy. The teacher made us throw it out in the big garbage bin and then wash our hands in boiling water and go home and change."

"In boiling water?"

"Near enough. The teacher was really scared of dead things."

"I can see Molly Bray as a girl catching crayfish," said Miranda, changing the subject. "She's wading in the shallows. You can see her. Scrunch up your eyes and stare into the sun."

Morgan thought perhaps he could, by shielding his eyes from the light.

They sat close together beside the dam, both with their knees drawn up, gazing out over the pond, feeling the soft autumn breeze on their faces.

Morgan envisioned a grown-up Eleanor Drummond, realizing she had never been a child. She was dressed in city clothes, her tailored skirt hiked up and tucked into a black leather belt, her Jimmy Choo boots set neatly on shore. She was wading with slow, deliberate movements through water up to her calves, with a small net in her hand, staring intently through the fractured glare, able to see down among the rocks where her own reflection rippled the sun.

At first it seemed she was just across from them, with the sun at her back, then she was in the shallows by the house where the old woman lived. Every few minutes she would reach down and fastidiously turn over a rock, careful when she straightened not to let water drizzle along her arm into the sleeve of her blouse. She had a crystal bowl in one hand. He couldn't see her pluck crayfish from the bottom. The net was gone, maybe there had been no net, but the crystal bowl was slowly filling with crayfish.

She turned and looked at him, directly away from the sun, so that her face was haloed in light, and yet it wasn't in shadow but softly radiant and he could see her features clearly. Her expression was serene. She bore the look of composure he had seen on the lovely dead face of the figure in the morgue, but she caught his eye and smiled. She gazed into her bowl with satisfaction, then back to the water, peering intently into the shallow depths for her quarry.

The old woman sat on the porch of the farmhouse off to the side, rocking in a painted chair near the railingless edge, watching Eleanor Drummond gradually fill up her bowl with small scrambling creatures.

Miranda saw Molly Bray splashing in the shallows across from them, spraying sunlight into the air. There were no sounds. It was a silent vision, but vivid in every detail. Molly was thirteen, old enough to have abandoned crayfish hunts, still wanting to play, refusing to submit to the maturity her body was taunting her with this summer for the first time, like a promise and threat rolled into one unnerving sensation that wouldn't recede except when she played fiercely, as she was now, at childish games.

She was between her grandmother's house and the mill. She was swinging an old metal grain bucket, scooping up water and swinging it around so that the streamlets of water leaking out the bottom bent through the air in fine splattering rainbows. She would suddenly stop and look down, drive her hand through the surface, and come up with a crayfish caught between pincers of her thumb and forefinger. Then she would wave it around to her grandmother back on the porch, toward the old wooden mill like a talisman, warding off evil so trivial that it was funny.

Miranda felt what the girl felt. She was her emanation, not her likeness or double, but connected as if they were joined in another dimension, two minds not yet born into the world that would drive them apart. Miranda looked through Molly's eyes and thought she could see eyes staring back between the boards by the flume. The mill was rumbling against the silence. The slow, laborious groaning and keening of wooden shafts turning and wooden gears grinding on iron and wood filled her head as she gamboled forward through the shallow water, defiant. *Let him watch.* Her clothes were soaking, her T-shirt and shorts clinging to her supple young body as she stepped up onto the roadway above the dam, squarely in front of the peephole, shaking like a puppy, spraying the air with fine rainbows of mist, turning toward the old house and strutting haughtily home.

"My God, Morgan! He used to watch her!"

They withdrew from their separate reveries, which had converged more than they knew on images of water and innocence: the defiant innocence of a wilful young girl and the illusory innocence of a worldly woman on a break from too much reality.

"What is it we were after, going to Detzler's Landing?" she asked, sliding away so she could address Morgan face to face. "Why did we go there?"

"It seemed like a good idea at the time," he said. "I wanted to get a feeling for who Eleanor Drummond was. You wanted to find Molly Bray. We went to detect. That's what we do. And now we're here. In Waterloo County."

"Detzler's Landing isn't that far away."

"Maybe not from Waldron, but it's a very long way from Toronto. There's a huge leap from Molly Bray to Eleanor Drummond."

"But, Morgan, in Toronto she was both."

"From the girl to the woman, the foundling who grew up in the sticks to the sleek-city woman who tortured them both unto death, there's an abyss …"

"Maybe so. But I'm the bridge! I *am* the bridge."

"You?"

"I know that girl, Morgan. She wasn't like me, but I know her, and I knew Eleanor Drummond. In spite of myself, we connected."

Morgan stared into the depths of reflected water shining in her eyes and then dropped his gaze so she could think out loud

"Look," she said, "I can imagine Molly, from what Miss Clarke described, flaunting her adolescence if she knew he was watching. She did. She would do that."

"How so?" He hadn't meant to speak up.

"It's a matter of power. She's being watched, she watches. He knows she's onto him, but he can't stop. He's obsessive-compulsive, excited by knowing she knows."

She proceeded, forgetting that Griffin peeping through from the mill hadn't been revealed to Morgan, who at the time had been imagining the woman from the city, not the girl. He struggled for a moment and caught up, glancing at the mill tower and back at Miranda, whose features were bathed in the soft light of the late afternoon.

"When they occasionally pass on the road, when she walks by the mill to the store and he's out tinkering, maybe building that absurd picket fence, they're cordial. It's part of the game. He's a balding man in his early fifties. She's a country girl, barely into puberty, a socially nondescript pretty young thing. But from the shadows he sees her as purity incarnate, his own mother restored to primal innocence."

"There's a lot about innocence I don't understand."

"That's probably true, Morgan."

"Where do you fit in?"

"A decade before … and I was older. I mean, she wasn't naive, but she wasn't Lolita. That's male fantasy, that a girl that age understands what she's doing. It makes it exciting. But she doesn't. She feels it, her hormones are burning her up inside, but she doesn't understand. It's imagination and hormones, powerlessness and power ..."

"And neither did you. You didn't understand. You and your friend."

"By that summer we were seventeen, Celia was sleeping with Donny, we weren't kids. Not sleeping. Doing it in Donny's car. There were lots of better places, but sex and back seats of cars were tradition."

"Not where I came from. We didn't have cars."

"No premarital sex?"

"Working parents and living-room floors."

"So he was repeating history. There was a pattern."

"It takes more than two."

"But how likely is it that we were the only ones? It could have been something he did over and over. Sometimes it ended with sex, other times rape. It's a matter of perspective — no, judgment. There's a fine line between. Anyone watched by a predatory voyeur is a victim but doesn't know she's a victim until she submits to his gaze."

"Miranda, you were —"

"No, Morgan, I wasn't." She paused. "How did he poop? That's a long time. Sometimes I stayed most of the day. What did he do?"

"It wouldn't be hard to go five, six hours, but he'd have to pee. He must have peed in a bottle."

"Can you do that — pee in a bottle?"

"Yeah, I can," he said.

"I can't. I tried once, but I wasn't very good. In a tent, in a jar in a tent. I peed my initials in the snow in front of Hart House one night. You could read it, too, but it dribbled down my leg and I got really cold and had to go home."

"You were drunk."

"I was not drunk. I was making a statement."

"About what?"

"I don't know. What is it about when you pee in the snow in the middle of a university campus?"

"He probably had a jar," said Morgan. "Maybe he kept them and his wine cellar is filled with jars of old urine."

"I wrote an entire name in the snow once." She didn't want to return to questions of moral responsibility. "It wasn't my own pee, of course ..."

"Your handwriting's legendary, Miranda."

"Is it? He watched me. I let him, and then we were lovers."

"You weren't lovers."

"I was eighteen."

"A virgin?"

"Yes, I was."

"Well?"

"What? I forgot losing my virginity, Morgan. If time heals, why didn't I forget enough to remember? All these years I never thought about it. Isn't that funny?"

"Time doesn't heal. It creates scar tissue. I remember."

"You weren't there!"

"Losing my own —"

"I don't want to hear about it. God, Morgan!"

"Sorry. I'm not too smart sometimes, but I have good instincts, and I'm sensitive."

"You're relentlessly intelligent, Morgan, with the sensitivity of a watermelon."

"And?"

"The instincts of an aardvark."

"Now that's funny. So what do you think happened?

Why did Molly suddenly leave town?"

Miranda seemed from her benign expression as she faced the breeze drifting over the millpond to be almost passive, sorting things out, following things through. It was difficult, Morgan thought, to connect the dots when they were swarming like gnats or mosquitoes. You didn't want to rush the design; it was all in the perception.

"Did you notice that Detzler's mill closed in 1988?" she suddenly asked. "That was the summer she was sixteen. Griffin left. Oxley bought the abandoned mill nine or ten years later. Yes, well. Then. No. Yes! Yes, they did. They did it! That last summer, that's what happened!

"At sixteen I wasn't a foundling, but I *was* sixteen. You want desperately to know the limits of identity from the outside in … from the immeasurable genetic sea, to know the current that flows through your veins. Know what I mean? So you endlessly analyze your parents, you find them wanting. Maybe they were exchanged at your birth. But she had no parents at all, not even an origin myth, just a girl at the door with a baby, and a self-professed spinster and her old friend who pooled their affection to make a place for her in the world, but it wasn't a place of her own.

"So she turns to Griffin. She'd been pushing and pushing. He was like a great ugly mirror, but she could see herself in the glass. She was exploring her awakening sexuality, maybe skinny-dipping or sunning on the grass between the mill and the house. She loved her old granny, but she needed to know who she was, from the inside out as well as the outside in.

"After summers of playing him, not knowing whether he was walleye or pike, fresh fish or foul, she needed to connect. She walked in on him literally. He was her prince, and he raped her, Morgan. There's a precedent, there's a pattern. He raped her inside the mill, in the shadows, on a cot on the planks over the watercourse, inside the mill. I know he raped her. And then he closed down the mill and left."

"And next?" he asked.

"She was pregnant."

"Pregnant!"

"Pregnant with Elizabeth Jill."

"Named after Elizabeth Clarke."

"Molly Bray went to the city."

"What happened?"

"She tracked him down to his Rosedale mansion. It would have seemed like a mansion to her."

"And?"

"Griffin sent her packing. Maybe he gave her some money. My guess is she spent the next few months on the street learning Toronto."

"How do you figure?"

"There had to be a period of metamorphosis. Where else could she go? I know about metamorphosis, Morgan. I can imagine what she must have endured. You don't just shuck off one identity and unfold your wings to dry in the air. Transformation is traumatic. There had to be time. She didn't just pass from being a girl to being a woman during the course of her pregnancy. She remade herself ..."

"Became her own creation."

"She worked on it."

"No one was looking for her."

"Even if they had been, she was invisible."

"Seven thousand, maybe ten thousand kids on the streets last winter, just in TO."

Morgan took the statistics as a personal affront. When he was a kid in Cabbagetown, he had never seen street people. There was one old guy called Bert Shaver who lived in a cardboard shack in a ravine and did odd jobs for the poor in return for a meal. He never talked except to say thank you. The poor looked after their own, and the rich after theirs. And the government looked after the addicts and the damaged and the defectives in institutions.

"The RCMP figures there are fifty thousand homeless kids in the country," he said, his words taking flight. "There are some wee little kids caught up in porn rings and prostitution, kept out of sight by the worst of the creeps, pervs who get them on booze and drugs, eight-year-old drunks, ten-year-old hookers, kids who can talk their way around lawyers and cops and social workers, and have energy left to roll a john, cut up a derelict, do themselves down with the drugs of their choice."

Sometimes Miranda thought Morgan should have been a professor or a politician, but she realized he was too restless for either. He might have been a preacher, except for the part about God.

"So," she said, "Molly was on the street long enough to know she didn't belong there. She went back to Robert Griffin's place, determined to hold him responsible. She was no butterfly, not the iron butterfly she would become, but she was on her way. That's what I would have done if I were her, which I wasn't … I'm not."

"No, you aren't."

"You saw her, Morgan. That was a woman in control of her life."

"And death."

"So it seems."

"Did she blackmail him? Was it extortion?"

"It's not extortion when he's the father. It's just negotiation."

"You think she could wield that much power? She was sixteen."

"Sixteen can be tough."

"I don't think a few months on the streets, no matter how bad, empowers anyone that much," said Morgan.

"Something did. Maybe something innate. He set her up. There might have been a transition before Wychwood Park, an apartment or condo, and he hired Victoria, or she did, and she became Eleanor Drummond. Without abandoning Molly Bray she brought up Elizabeth Jill to be a very together young woman." She corrected herself. "Girl, she's still a girl."

"We can't even be certain Robert Griffin was the father."

"You can bank on it, Morgan."

11

Shiners

They talked very little on the way back from Waldron. Miranda needed to assimilate her imagined account with the facts. Morgan was uneasy about how her assumptions made her seem vulnerable. There were still the circumstances of a suicide-murder to be resolved. He feared for her if she turned out to be at the centre.

Cutting down from the 401, Miranda asked if he wanted to be dropped off at his place in the Annex. He told her yes if it wasn't out of her way.

"I've never understood why people say that, Morgan. Since I'm going to check in on Jill before I go home, it's considerably out of my way."

"Margot Kidder."

"What?"

"Lois Lane — that's who would play you in the movie. When she was quite a bit younger."

"What movie?"

"Don't you cast yourself in movies?"

"Yes. But I cast myself. I'd play me. Isn't that the point?"

"Sandra Bullock?"

"You just want to wear tights."

"Tights?"

"Lois Lane, Superman, changing in phone booths. Maybe Kate Nelligan."

"If you couldn't be you?"

"Yes."

"Doesn't it sometimes feel like you're watching yourself in a film, like someone else is calling the shots?"

"It's called dissociation, Morgan. Or Calvinism. And who would be you? Gene Hackman, right? All men want to be Denzel Washington or Gene Hackman, no?"

"You might as well be someone you like."

"Aren't you already?" As soon as she spoke, she realized she was offside. As comfortable as he was with himself, that wasn't who he wanted to be. No one really wanted to be himself, or herself, she thought.

She wheeled up in front of his house. There were still a few kids hanging out, playing hopscotch, two girls and a boy skipping rope. In the heart of the city and down-at-heels trendy, the Annex tried its best to be a neighbourhood. "Here we are, Morgan. Home is the hunter."

"You want to come in?"

"Not on your life. No, I've got to check in on Jill. She's too calm."

"It's her Eleanor Drummond side."

"She's pure Molly Bray."

"I hope so for her sake."

"Would you help me put the top up?"

He got out and undid the snaps on the tonneau cover, folded it, and tucked it behind the seats. The car looked black in this light. In the sunlight it was racing green. He hauled the top out of its well, and Miranda reached up and pulled it over and down, clinching it into place.

"Thanks, Morgan," she said through the window. "I'll call you in the morning."

He surprised them both by getting back in the car.

"What is it?" she asked. "Are you okay?"

"I'm okay. Are you?"

"I'm fine. Don't worry about me."

He gazed at her in the ambient light of the city, in the glow of the instrument panel. Dark illuminated circles in the burled walnut exuded a faint violet that caught in the highlights of her eyes.

She reached over and touched his hand. "I'll see you tomorrow."

"Miranda, the girl, Molly Bray, whatever she did, and you're only guessing, she didn't learn anything from you. And neither did Griffin."

She looked startled, as if Morgan had exposed something she hadn't yet confronted herself.

"Whatever happened between you and Griffin, you in no way, no way, empowered him to try it again."

Miranda realized pattern formation was a way of taking the blame on herself, using her own sense of guilt to obscure Griffin's depravity, which she felt was somehow her fault.

Morgan observed her watching him, the violet highlights in her eyes cryptic, as if she were waiting to hear him out before passing judgment, which could go several ways. She could be angry or hurt, or possibly relieved, or resentful for being exposed.

"Listen," he said, "you had similar needs. That doesn't mean you were the same."

At first she thought he meant her and Griffin.

"You talked about the absence of parents catching up on her. Miranda, your father left you just when you hit puberty."

"He died, for goodness' sake."

"At fourteen you held him responsible. No amount of love or anger could bring him back, no amount of crying or wishing changed anything. I know from how little you talk about it how much it hurt you, his leaving. Your mother and sister had each other. Your father left you alone."

The violet in her eyes glistened.

"By the pond ..." He hesitated. "You didn't know you were being watched until that summer when you were seventeen. You didn't know if anyone was there for sure, but the possibility excited you. What was Celia's reaction? She got married. Donny was her way of proving she was normal. Griffin scared her into doing what she was going to do, anyway.

"You went back there on your own. Why? It wasn't about sex. For the first time since your father died your behaviour, Miranda, determined the quality of existence of someone else, an adult, a male. It was no more sexual at first than a teenage girl's love for her father. Intimacy, without any threat of encroachment. You went back again and again. It gave you the sense you could make anything happen.

"Lying there butt-naked, bare-assed in the grass, you were celebrating being Miranda. You were cavorting, disporting, with fate. Robert Griffin was essential to the scene. That he was Robert Griffin was irrelevant, or maybe not. Maybe if you knew he was the mill owner, it was even better. It gave you more power. He was a grown-up, a man, at your mercy, and you were merciless. You were merciless that August challenging death.

"But you were also afraid you were being manipulated by your unseen observer, that it was his desire making you return to play out what must have seemed a charade in a foreign language, afraid that it was your desire to please him. You were merciless, Miranda, merciless in judging yourself, your brand-new sexuality.

"Through the next year you found your kissy-face boyfriend who didn't like sex. Perfect. Daniel Webster kept you safe among words, gave you a context to let your confusion run free.

"And you got older, fall, winter, spring, and nothing was resolved. When you returned the next summer, it was a very deliberate act. You were eighteen, a young woman, you walked by the mill, you knew he would see you, you went back to prove once and for all you were responsible for your own fate. It wasn't sexual that day. It was all about contesting the limits of power, maybe defining the limits of being.

"And he followed you. He was supposed to be your necessary witness. It wasn't meant to be a trial by fire, nor law, but he became judge and executioner. He intruded in the negotiations with yourself. He violated your relationship with your father, what was left of him in your heart. And he brutalized your capacity for being open to love. He raped you, Miranda, and left you bleeding inside, with a great wound, a gap in your life that only began healing in the last few days since the predator died."

"David."

"Yes?"

"I'll call you tomorrow."

"G'night, Miranda."

"G'night, David. See you tomorrow. It's buck-naked, Morgan, not butt-naked. And I wasn't."

"Good night, Miranda."
"Good night."

As he unlocked his front door, Morgan was startled by his reflection hovering within the depths of paint in the evening light, and then reassured. He had given the door fourteen coats of midnight blue, sanding lightly between each coat until the depthless patina gleamed like a Georgian doorway in Dublin. He had done that a dozen years ago, and still approached it like a welcoming friend, whatever his mood, whatever time of day or night he came home.

His house was red brick, a neighbourhood sort of home that had been bought by a contractor and turned into an agglomeration of condos that related to each other like disparate planes in an M.C. Escher drawing. His own place was partly on the second floor but extended via an open-concept stairwell with a wrought-iron staircase up to a third-floor loft. That was his garret bedroom. His kitchen, toward the back of the building, dropped half a storey to accommodate the entryway into another apartment from cantilevered steps up the side of the building over the driveway. He prided himself on not knowing just what fitted where or how many people actually shared the house with him. Not that it mattered. The building was well constructed, the renovations were sound, and his place was sepulchral, unless the shared furnace was running, which sent a hush through the air.

Morgan walked across the living room without turning on the lights. The two-storey window that dominated the front wall, between the foyer and the far-side wall of exposed brick, let in enough city light that he could see his way through the intricacies of modular spaces envisioned by the builder fifteen years ago as urban chic. Two banks of vertical blinds had been installed, but since Morgan first moved in while reconstruction was still going on, neither set had worked. The upper bank stayed permanently closed, which was fine, giving him privacy in his garret loft and a modicum of darkness for sleeping. The lower bank was irreparably open. His neighbours could look in if they wished, just as he could see them, but by urban convention they lived their lives as if neither could observe the other, as if their pre-dawn and evening activities were privy to themselves alone.

He picked up the remote in the darkness and flicked on the television, then without waiting to see what was on went into the bathroom, which doubled as a laundry facility. Shucking his clothes into a basket, he plucked pajamas from a hook on the back of the door, sniffed them, and without showering put them on, splashing a bit of cold water on his face before going out into the hall. He turned abruptly back into the bathroom, clicked on the light, and brushed his teeth. Then he flossed. He always flossed. Even though he hadn't had dinner yet, he flossed to subdue the bacterial detritus of the day.

In the kitchen he whipped up a quick spinach salad from pre-washed leaves and took it with two bagels and a beer back into the living room, where he settled in front of the television. Reaching over, he turned on a table lamp. Morgan always found it depressing to walk past houses at night and see only the light of a television flickering against the ceiling and walls like some sort of primordial campfire. He watched television with the lights on, though he often listened to music in the dark.

When Harry Meets Sally was playing, or was it *When Harry Met Sally*? He couldn't remember, but he recognized the scene immediately. Meg Ryan was just beginning her tumultuous orgasm in the restaurant. Billy Crystal was bemused. Meg was awesomely sexy. Billy was quizzical, unmanned. Meg was frightening, ecstatic. Morgan set his bagels down on the side table.

The most amazing thing about the scene was how erotic it was. There was no other scene to compare, not since Marlene Dietrich snapped her legs apart at the Blue Angel. Sharon Stone was primal, but predatory. And yet Meg Ryan was faking. The whole point was that she was faking. The turn on wasn't the unrestrained and voluptuous display of sex, but the fact that she was in such awesome control.

Morgan sank back into the sofa, clutching his beer in one hand and reaching for a bagel with the other. The salad sat on the table untouched.

He was restless. He turned off the television and climbed to his bedroom as if he were looking for something, sat down on the edge of the bed, then got up and went back down the spiral staircase. Settling on the sofa, he clicked on the TV again and switched to CNN, with the volume so low that he couldn't make out what was being said but could follow parallel stories in the sub-script scrolling across the bottom of the screen.

The bastard had never lost track of her, he thought. That was the part that made his skin crawl. He lived as a reclusive lawyer, he played in his mills, he amassed his fabulous collection of koi. He did what he did with Molly Bray, and with how many other young girls, as well. But all the time he shadowed Miranda.

Perhaps Griffin enrolled in Sandhu's semiology course because he was enthralled with language, and wonder of wonders, Miranda was there, too. An older student wouldn't stand out. They weren't interested in job potential. They took high-interest seminars with high motivation. He might already have sat behind her in lecture theatres, taking anthropology and human geography courses. Maybe he was in the cafeterias, in the library, watching her on dates. Morgan felt enraged as he thought about Griffin haunting Miranda's life, and frightened, to know that she had been oblivious.

That was a big leap, though, from university to the present. She did a tour with the RCMP, and she and he had been hanging together in homicide for over a decade. Had Griffin been watching both of them? It wouldn't be hard from a distance. They had even been in the news every once in a while.

Why, Morgan thought, why name her executor? Griffin lived in her shadow for years, but when he knew someone was going to kill him he came out of the shadows, he touched her, he understood it would bring back the past.

Miranda knew about Molly Bray now. Had Eleanor Drummond known about her?

He switched back to Harry and Sally and turned up the sound. They were getting together at a New Year's party. Billy Crystal wouldn't play him. The comedian was charming, but there was nothing ambivalent about him. The best actors projected menace or suffering, even at their lightest moments. Meg Ryan, no, Miranda wasn't sad and perky. America's fallen sweetheart. Falling, perpetually falling. Miranda was Miranda. That was what he liked about her.

Morgan wondered about Ellen Ravenscroft. Maybe he should give her a call. He knew he wouldn't. Miranda would know if he did. He didn't feel he had to be faithful to Miranda. They lived separate lives, or went through the motions of conducting themselves as if they lived separate lives. It was just that she would know.

He found it easier, at this age, if he tried not to think about sex. During the day, he noticed himself monitoring skirt lengths and panty lines and the contours of sweaters, the peep line of blouses, but he sublimated his visceral responses until evenings, and often by then, now, in his early forties, they dissipated into vague yearnings for company. Not that he wasn't up for it when the necessity arose. It wasn't that he was becoming asexual.

Since moving into his postmodern Victorian condo, Morgan hadn't had many visitors. His former wife, Lucy, had come over once, drunk, and had tried to seduce him. That was when the paint on the door was still tacky, and he hadn't seen or heard from her since. The Bobbsey Twins had once paid a memorable call. That was an episode that overloaded his stock of erotic recollections to the point of short-circuiting the system. It was the best of adventures, but also the worst. He savoured it sometimes in the depths of the night, and he cringed at how absurdly distressing the whole affair had been.

It wasn't an affair.

He sat back, staring into the radiant play of colour emanating from the tube, and remembered.

One was blond with big hair and a strapping physique. The other was slender, with a pixie-punk hairdo of indeterminate hue, mostly mahogany mauve, and suction-cup lips. They were known around police headquarters as the Bobbsey Twins.

He looked over at the front door, relieved to know they wouldn't suddenly appear. At the same time he felt a certain dissolute urgency, hoping they would coalesce out of the images of their indiscretion into another encounter.

There had been a loud rapping on the door. It was evening, the beginning of July, the first real weekend of summer in the city, and the town was alive with festivities marking the First and the Fourth. One holiday marked a revolution, the other was the legislated celebration of an end to tedious negotiations. There were enough Americans living in Toronto, and enough would-be Americans, that parties often extended from one date to the other, especially if they contained a weekend between. It was raining outside, but he had heard street parties only a block or two over in the more bohemian parts of the Annex. Then there was a knock, like a drum roll, on his dark blue door.

That was three, maybe four years ago. Three. He was forty. He opened the door, and a drenching wind hurled weather into the foyer, along with two very young, very wet women.

"Close the door, for goodness' sake," he said.

"Hello, Morgan. May we borrow your dryer?"

"My dryer?" He scrutinized them, trying to place them in a recognizable context.

"You know us. I'm Nancy."

"I'm Anne," said the other, while rainwater streamed from her mauve hair over her pouting full lips. "No last names." She grinned, and her lips quivered. "We're on reception. You've seen us at headquarters on College Street, the big new modern building —"

"I know where it is. I work there, too."

"We know that," said Nancy with the drowned blond hair. "That's why we're here." She looked satisfied, as if she had explained everything that needed explaining.

"You work together?" Morgan blurted out. God knows, he had seen them often enough. He knew they did.

"Mostly," said Anne, smiling hugely. Then she exchanged a knowing look with Nancy. "Sometimes we do. It just depends how things turn out. Can we borrow your dryer?" she asked, enunciating the word *dryer* very clearly as if he might not understand.

"I don't use a dryer," said Morgan.

"Your clothes dryer," said Nancy.

"You've been partying," said Morgan, stating the obvious.

By now his visitors were in the middle of the living room and he had circled around as if to prevent them from going any farther. As they danced about, trying to generate warmth, pools of water sprayed out beneath them.

"Turn your back," said Anne with a sly curl to her swollen lips. "You mustn't watch."

She began to pull her soaking T-shirt over her head. Morgan turned away and stared at the exposed brick wall. He heard wet clothes puddling in piles on the floor. He had no idea what the protocol was, given the circumstances. Suddenly, he realized the lights were on full, and whirled to face them. "For pity sake, the neighbours!"

He didn't know where to look. They were both stark naked. The neighbours across the street must be having a hard time about now, pretending they couldn't see everything. He lunged for the overhead light switch, but when he snapped it off all that happened was the glare in the window was reduced. His table lamps still managed to cast full illumination on the entire scene. If he turned them off, too, it would signal to the entire neighbourhood that an orgy was in progress. He moved into the shadows by the spiral staircase. Maybe the neighbours would think he wasn't home.

"What kind of music you got?" Nancy asked.

She was shaking out her hair in front of the window into the pile of dripping clothes she held in front of her. Anne was ambling around, inspecting the artwork, casual, as if she were at a gallery, wearing a little black dress and over-high pumps. Nancy dropped her clothes onto the hardwood floor beside Anne's, avoiding the thick Gabbeh rug that so far had only been subjected to a few random droplets. She approached the stereo as if it were a potential dance partner, cocking a hip slightly off centre and coming to rest a little too close to Morgan. "Can I put on something?"

"Anything," he said. "Please."

He was flustered as much by the casual familiarity as by their lack of clothes.

"You like Eskimo art?" asked Anne, picking up an intricately carved miniature tableau of whalebone and ivory.

"Inuit art," he said. "In Canada they're Inuit." Pedantry was a way of retrieving composure. "It means 'the people.' Inuit is plural. Inuk is one. Inuuk is two. The ivory is from the tusk of a narwhal. The bone is very delicate. It's very old, from a petrified vertebra."

Anne smiled indulgently, and her lips quivered. "Can we use the dryer? Sorry about the mess."

She scooped up the drenched clothes and followed him into the bathroom. He opened the dryer, but she held out the end of a wad of clothes and stepped backward into the shower.

"Grab tight and we'll wring them out," Anne told him.

Water poured down the front of Morgan's slacks.

"Sorry," Anne said, her full lips swelling into another smile. She stuffed the clothes into the dryer, and he turned it on. Then she took a towel from the neat pile on the shelf over the dryer.

For a moment Morgan thought modesty had finally set in, and he offered another towel for her friend. Anne declined, saying ominously that one would be enough, and walked into the living room where Nancy was dancing with herself to music that was almost inaudible.

Kneeling on the warm dry wool of the Gabbeh, Anne stretched out to draw the puddles of water on the floor together in large, sweeping motions. Morgan couldn't help staring, first at Anne, wondrously slender and smooth as she reached and twisted while she dabbed at the floor, with her bottom cocked upward like a beacon, then at Nancy, moving in a dream world of her own to music he could barely hear, her fulsome young body shaping the air as she moved like a Henry Moore carved out of voluptuous flesh. Giving in, Morgan sat on the bottom step of his wrought-iron staircase, absorbing it all, eyes sliding back and forth from one to the other. Anne walked over to the window, stood fully framed for a moment, gazing out at the street, then bent down once again, bottom in the air, and mopped up the remaining water.

"I'll just throw this in with the clothes," she said when she was finished.

He looked at the towel, dripping and mottled with residual dirt from the floor, which he tried to keep clean. He was a good housekeeper.

When she came back, she said, "Lovely and warm in here. It's been a bugger all day, really hot. We needed the rain. Trouble is, we got soaked to the skin, absolutely drenched. It's been a movable party. We dropped into HQ and picked up your address. We've noticed you, Morgan. Happy Canada Day." She leaned over and gave him a big hug. "Shove over," she said, sitting on the step beside him. "Hey, what's that you're wearing?"

"Clothes."

"So what do you do when we're not here?"

"Um ..."

"You want to smoke dope?"

"No," said Morgan. Then, almost in apology, he added, "I'm okay."

"No, you're not." Anne smiled with her great lips less than a head's breadth away. "Do we make you nervous?"

"No," said Morgan. He didn't want either to protest too much or appear nonchalant.

"I've got some dope," she said, and walked over to her bag in the foyer. As she strode away from him, Morgan could see incised on her bottom, like an erotic abstract, the pattern of the wrought-iron step. He relaxed a little. It made her seem vulnerable. She turned and walked toward him. Full-frontal exposure — he felt imponderably vulnerable.

"Come sit with me on the floor," she said.

She sat cross-legged on the thick Gabbeh, and when he approached, she turned him gently like a marionette so that he settled with his back to her and she drew him down to lie against her lap.

"Comfy?" she asked.

He looked up at her lips. Her breasts came to firm points just above his temple. He couldn't bring them into focus at the same time, and his eyes, bleary from trying to adjust, shifted back to her lips. "Every man's fantasy," he said aloud. But he felt sick. She was twenty. She had the body of a girl.

He could feel her pubic hair against the back of his scalp as she moved about, preparing to light up. He nestled into her, and she seemed to open and press back with her thighs. He felt unnervingly intimate and distant, lying so close but facing away. He watched Nancy, who was still dancing gently, now close to the stereo.

They both watched Nancy. Then Anne placed the crudely rolled joint in his mouth, and he drew in deeply and held. Morgan hadn't smoked since Ibiza, and there he had mostly observed others doing it. He didn't like the taste very much, or the sensation of ingesting effluent into his lungs. It made him feel queasy. She was careful not to drop burning embers onto his face.

After a while, she said, "Take those off. You don't want to burn holes in your clothes."

He flinched, panicked again. She was twenty; he was a forty-year-old detective. He felt like a pervert. Nancy must have heard them, because she came over and knelt beside him. She undid his belt, zipped his fly down, and with knowing hands reached under him and shrugged his slacks down past his buttocks. He was barefoot, so it was easy to tug them away and slip off his underwear. Then she leaned over him so that her pendulous breasts brushed against his face as she reached between his back and Anne's thighs and grasped his jersey, which she hauled up and over his head in a single smooth motion. She stood and looked down, surveying her handiwork. Her breasts were perched high on her rib cage. She was young and they were resilient, with lives of their own.

Damn, they were kids, he thought. But he settled against Anne and savoured his torment like a drowning man clutching a treasure of gold as he plummeted into the depths to a gruesome demise.

Nancy returned to her dancing. Morgan glanced up at Anne, seeing her in parts, her breasts, her collarbone, her slender neck, her full lips, nose, eyes gleaming their separate highlights, tendrils of damp hair, all suspended above him like the discontinuous sections of an Alexander Calder mobile. Her lips were succulent, possibly for her as well — she seemed to suck against them in a kind of perpetually rearranging pout as if she were savouring the taste of her own body. Morgan looked down at himself, surprised to see an erection.

He was aroused through his entire being, ready to burst into an annihilating orgasm that would leave him in a pool of fluids on the floor. Morgan hadn't focused on his penis until then, and now it seemed an absurd appendage, isolated and vulnerable. He half twisted against Anne's lap to see if he had caught her interest down there. She adjusted her weight and pressed her pubic bone against his skull, and he settled back.

Nancy must have tuned her subliminal sensitivities in his direction. She danced over lazily and dropped slowly to his side, examined him without touching, then rose on tiptoe like a dancer and spread her legs over him, languorously descending, holding herself open and tilting him back as she settled firmly with her bottom against his pelvis. Nancy stayed squatting over him like that without moving except for the slight quivering strain of her thighs. She gazed at him eye to eye, and at Anne, smiling fondly, conspiratorially, then back at Morgan, staring deep into his eyes until the incomprehensible stillness that closed around him began to send waves through his entire body and he shuddered, the two young women like sculpture enfolding him in their cunning stillness. In a slow explosion of pure sensation, he exploded inside her, inside both of them, inside himself.

No one moved. They swayed, Nancy's thighs quivered, Anne's lips were moist in the lamplight. Almost on cue, as Morgan struggled between apprehension approaching dread and the pleasures of utter depletion, the dryer bell sounded. Nancy rose over him, draining across his torso, smiling down, standing for a moment, then moved away. Anne smiled with her voluptuous lips and said with affection, "Come on, old man, it's over." She slid gently out from under him, stood, and moved away.

He lay back on the Gabbeh, examining the ceiling of the loft, able to recognize details in the patina of paint on the drywall. He wasn't stoned; he had never been stoned. But he was spent. He felt physically and emotionally and morally spent.

Anne squatted beside him, fully dressed, and kissed him squarely on the lips, sharing her succulence for a long moment, then stood while Nancy, also dressed, leaned over and covered him with his jersey, across his depleted private parts. She knelt by his head and gave him a soft kiss, hardly touching his lips.

"Happy Canada Day," she said.

At the door Anne called back in a low voice, "Happy Fourth of July."

The door swung open and clicked shut, his beautiful door. Morgan lay on the Gabbeh for a long time, contemplating.

12

Shiromuji

The next morning Miranda returned to the house in Wychwood Park, the most coveted residential enclave in Toronto and a fitting place from which Molly Bray could negotiate her life with Eleanor Drummond. Past tense, she reminded herself. What was it about Wychwood Park that made Miranda feel good about her own limited resources, about the complexities of a fractured identity? It wasn't about money but taste. Perhaps it was the absence of fences, how one neatly appointed property flowed into the next and into the common grounds shaped by the contours of the ravine. Maybe it was the huge trees standing at random like the towering remains of a natural-growth forest. Or perhaps it was the houses themselves, all of them reflecting the Edwardian precepts of their common era, but each very different, each having reached the present in its own way. It wasn't about privilege but class.

Wychwood Park nestled in the lee of Casa Loma, the Victorian monstrosity devoted like the Taj Mahal to a beloved wife, in this case one still alive while her memorial was being erected. The woman's husband, as a bankrupt widower, eventually shared quarters in the carriage house with his valet. Miranda loved that such follies existed, but like most Torontonians she had never been inside, though it was kept open by public subscription.

The previous evening, when she arrived to see Jill after dropping off Morgan, the girl was already asleep. It was barely past nine. Miranda had talked with Victoria in the kitchen.

"How's she doing?" Miranda asked.

"She's fine. I think she just wants to sleep more than anything. Sometimes you have to, I suppose."

Miranda liked Victoria. The woman seemed comfortable in the rambling house, moving through its spaces as if it were her own. At the same time she broadcast a subtle disinterest in her artful surroundings. Victoria seemed self-sufficient, and that appealed to Miranda, who suspected self-sufficiency and self-reliance were traits undermined in herself by her admiration for them in others.

Victoria was maternal, but home was a quality she projected more than a place she inhabited. She gave Miranda confidence that Jill was well cared for and loved.

"Have you always been with Molly and Jill?" asked Miranda.

"I was here from day one. I took them in for Mr. Robert Griffin. I used to clean for him. After the baby was born, we searched out this place. Molly thought it was just right, so Mr. Griffin bought it and we moved in. We've been here ever since, for fourteen years. Just over there is where Marshall McLuhan used to live."

A brief look of defiance crossed her face, which immediately softened to forbearance. "I don't know if we can afford to stay. Molly paid the bills. But don't you worry. I'll look after the girl. Molly counted on me."

"You'll be all right, Victoria. This is your home."

"I come from Barbados," she said. "I speak Barbadian with my friends. Lord, you wouldn't understand us. No, you wouldn't. We speak Canadian dialect here."

"Do you know who Eleanor Drummond is?"

"Never heard of her before yesterday, the night when you brought the girl home. Jill asked me about that — did I know Eleanor Drummond? I don't think there are any relatives or otherwise out there, not at all. There's not anyone but me and the girl. Miss Molly never got a Christmas card in her life."

"Tell me about Molly Bray."

"Oh, dear, it's hard to believe she's gone." Victoria lifted her hands to shoulder height and gestured into the depths of the house. "She's everywhere here. She was so young, too young, you know. There's no good age for dying, but there are some worse than others. She was too young to be dying on us." She looked into Miranda's eyes. "She never took something for nothing, nothing that wasn't rightfully hers."

Victoria smiled almost wistfully. "But, boy, oh, boy, if it was hers, she was fierce." She wasn't crying. Her eyes glistened with pride. "Boys," she declared as if there was an argument. "She could be as cool as a breeze from heaven, and hot as the fires of hell." She nodded in affirmation to herself, evidently pleased with her summary description, enjoying the familiarity of her own words. She had clearly said them before. "The hellfire was all inside," she clarified. "She was serene, a lady, out where it counted."

"And you never even heard the name Eleanor Drummond before?"

"No, ma'am, I never. Like I said."

"Was Mr. Griffin a part of your life?"

"Oh, no, ma'am. Molly hated old Robert Griffin. I never thought there was enough of him to make any difference."

"How do you mean?"

"He wasn't much of a human being, one way or another."

"He certainly had an impact on her," said Miranda.

Victoria suddenly became wary.

"All this," said Miranda, indicating their surroundings.

"Don't you believe it. This was Molly Bray's doing. From the time she was sixteen she was who she was. This is what she set out to make for herself."

"Tell me about Jill."

"She's sleeping now, or as good as asleep."

"What's she like?"

"She's family, Miss Quin. Family is family."

"And was Molly Bray family?"

"Well, she was and she wasn't. She was Jill's momma, and Jill is my very own child, like the child of my womb. We loved her no matter what, so I guess we were all family."

Miranda picked up on the phrase "no matter what."

"Was she difficult sometimes?"

"Jill or Molly? Molly wasn't difficult, Detective. Distracted maybe. Sometimes Molly Bray was, like, here and not here."

"Distracted?"

"Like she was following another agenda, you might say. You know, in her head. She was a loving mother. She was my very good friend. Nobody should die so young. Nobody should die if they can help it."

"I'll call in to see Jill in the morning," said Miranda,

getting up and moving through the central hallway toward the panelled vestibule by the front door.

"It's Saturday tomorrow. She'll be here. She went to school today. I wanted her to stay home, but she's headstrong like her mother. She was going, and that was that."

Miranda noticed the rug in the vestibule. It was like one of Morgan's, a Gabbeh, a thick weave from Anatolia done with old-style vegetal dyes. She could hear his voice, expounding. "It's a Gabbeh," she said. "The rug's very beautiful. It fits in perfectly."

"Maybe so. I don't know about Gabbeh. It's the last thing she did, buying that, the last thing to make this house like it is."

Before leaving, Miranda had reached out and given the woman's hand a reassuring squeeze.

"Now don't you fret, Detective, and I won't worry too much myself, just enough. Jill and I, we'll manage fine."

Now, the next morning, at the large front door with a full night's sleep behind her, Miranda felt good about coming back to see the girl. For now Miranda was content with getting to know this strange woman-child who, like herself, was a link between Molly Bray and Eleanor Drummond, and who was virtually, as events were unfolding, Miranda's ward.

Jill came to the door and opened it wide. She welcomed Miranda with a flourish, then turned and walked purposefully toward the kitchen. Miranda followed, thinking the outfit Jill was wearing, prescribed to make young girls feel sexy, made her look as if she were playing dress-up — pretending to be women without quite developing the knack.

"Hello, Victoria," Miranda said when they reached the kitchen. "Good morning."

"Good morning, Lady Detective. We're just having breakfast. Pancakes or French toast?"

"Scrambled eggs," said Jill. "Let's have scrambled eggs and brown toast and coffee."

"You don't drink coffee," said Victoria matter-of-factly. "You can pour Miss Quin a cup. We're having French toast."

After breakfast, Miranda and Jill sat out on the front steps. A few people strolled by, walking dogs, exchanging pleasantries as they passed one another without stopping.

"How are you doing?" Miranda asked.

"I don't like my mom being dead."

Miranda waited.

"She left me. I don't know what I'm supposed to do. I've got to look after Victoria. Do you know that she's got three kids in Barbados? They live with her mother, and she sends them money, but they'd rather live here. She's going to go back some day and be a family again." The girl looked resigned. There was nothing to count on for certain, not in the end.

"Jill, we'll have to talk about your mother's funeral."

"I told you, I don't want a funeral. There's no one but us."

"We could have her cremated and just have the ashes placed in a vault."

"Do they make little vaults just for ashes?"

"I don't know. I'll make the arrangements. Do you want to speak to a minister, or have someone say a few words?"

"Who? About what? That's not my mother at the morgue."

"Because she's Eleanor Drummond?"

"It's Eleanor Drummond's remains, and it's my

mother's remains." She looked up into Miranda's eyes ingenuously. "Will they need two caskets?"

Miranda blanched.

"My mom's gone. I want to forget that she's dead. No funeral, no words over ashes, no fuss. Please, okay?"

"Forgetting's not easy, Jill. And maybe not right."

"I don't want to think about dead!" She took a deep breath. "Not a dead body, a corpse, a cadaver, ashes formerly known as …" Miranda put her arm lightly over the girl's shoulders, but Jill sat upright, untouched. "I just want her to be inside my head. You know what I mean?"

Miranda understood. She remembered when her father died, trying in bed to summon up good memories only, or to avoid him entirely in the dark. She couldn't bear images of absolute stillness, silence, and decomposition.

Thinking about murder victims, Miranda tried to maintain the fine line between clinical disinterest and common humanity, a line occasionally erased by a personal detail, an imaginative leap, and then there was loneliness in the dead of night and fear that was both visceral swarming through her mind.

"That pin you were wearing …" she said to Jill.

"At the morgue?"

"You said your mother gave it to you."

"Why are you asking?"

"It was pretty."

"Yes. She didn't like fish, but she liked the design."

"How did you know what kind it was?"

"A Shiro Utsuri? She told me."

"Jill, did you know Robert Griffin?"

"No."

"Does the name seem familiar?"

"I've heard it. Like, that's where they found my mom. At his place."

"Did you ever go there?"

"I didn't know him. He was an associate of my mother's."

"As Eleanor Drummond?"

"I guess. I'm not sure. Could you take me to where she died? I would like to see where she died."

"I don't think so, Jill. Why?"

"It's just — she was alive, and then she wasn't alive. I need to see where that happened, where she changed from one thing to another like that. Do you know what metamorphosis means?"

"Yes, I do," said Miranda.

"We read stories about metamorphosis in school, stories from Rome a long time ago. And we studied metamorphosis in science. I just want to see where it happened."

"All right. Tell Victoria I'll get you back in a couple of hours. We'll have lunch downtown. Tell her I'll have you back after lunch."

When Miranda pulled into the Rosedale garage, she knew Jill had been at Robert Griffin's before. They were both a little windblown. Jill had insisted they drive with the top down.

Miranda was self-conscious about the Jaguar. She expected Mrs. de Cuchilleros would be watching them from among the ferns in her receiving-room window. As far as the neighbours were concerned, she was a police detective investigating a possible homicide and she was driving the dead man's car. She hadn't returned it the previous night, and somehow that made her feel even more truant.

As they had approached, Miranda saw Jill avert her eyes, keeping the house out of her line of vision, then stare up at it abruptly when they turned down the ramp and descended into the depths. Parked, Miranda smoothed her hair back while Jill resolutely got out of the car as if she were obeying a command. Together they raised the top back up into position, and Miranda locked the doors. She started toward the inside entrance, then realized Jill was already striding back up the ramp. She followed her onto the front steps where the girl was pushing at the door.

"It's locked," said Miranda. "I've got the keys."

Inside, Jill's eyes followed the stairs in the direction of the study where her mother had died, but she walked through the hallway to the side, down the stairs into the den, and stopped at the French doors, waiting for Miranda to catch up, looking out through the portico into the garden. Miranda moved beside her, careful to give her enough distance.

"Jill, tell me about it. Why did you want to come here?"

The girl turned to her and stepped back. "To see what it was like."

"You've been here before?"

"No."

"Jill, you have."

The girl looked angry and hurt. "What do you want from me?"

"Jill?"

"I can be anything you want."

"What do you mean?"

"I could be the daughter she wanted. She would see if she came back. I can be his Shiromuji girl if that's what he wants. I didn't mean for all this to happen. I can be whatever, whatever."

Miranda was stunned by her compliant ferocity. "Did he call you that?" Panic rose in her gut.

The girl didn't answer.

"Did Robert Griffin call you that?"

No answer.

"Did he?"

"Yes."

"Jill ..." A great wave of despair rolled through Miranda from deep inside to the surface, where it was quelled by an icy chill, and for a moment she felt nothing at all. She stood very still. Then her skin seemed on fire. "I was there, too ..." She didn't know if she had said that aloud. Miranda touched the girl, and neither of them burned. She took the girl in her arms.

At first they stood stiffly upright, the girl defiant. Then Jill leaned into Miranda, letting her body weight slump against Miranda, and together they sank to the floor, holding each other on the Kurdish runner, swaying gently in a silent embrace, both of them waiting without apprehension for something to happen.

"Jill," Miranda said after a long time had passed, "I need you to tell me about it."

"You knew him before?" Jill asked in a conspiratorial whisper. "Like before he died?"

"Yes, I did. I was a girl your age ..." She didn't know how to avoid the euphemism. It was more honest than anything she could think of. "When he came into my life."

"Did he hurt you?"

"Yes, I think he did very much. He hurt me more than I understood, perhaps more than I understand even now."

They were sitting now, facing each other on the Kurdish runner, hunched forward like girlfriends.

"Did he hurt you, Jill?"

"He hurt my mother. Did you know she worked for him? She had an office and managed his money. Not the money he had invested — you know about that. It was money he used for buying things and running his life. She looked after him."

"Do you know where her office was?"

"I could find it. It's over a fancy gallery in Yorkville. I was only there once. That's when I discovered she called herself Eleanor —"

"You knew at the morgue! Of course you knew."

"Only after I followed her. I just found out."

"You followed her?"

"We had a really bad fight. She caught me smoking with my friend Alexandria. She said I couldn't see Alexandria for a month, like that was worse than being grounded. The fight was about that, more than about smoking. I mean, she knew I wasn't really a smoker."

"Did she ever smoke?"

"My mother? Are you kidding? She was death on tobacco. She had what I'd call a counter-addictive personality."

"You would?"

"No way she'd give up control, not to a vice, not to a pleasure."

"Where did you come up with 'counter-addictive'?"

"We looked it up, Alexandria and me. We researched our parents."

"Okay. So you had a fight. And you skipped school and followed her to work."

"Yes."

"Why?"

"I was researching, like I said. There was a picture in the paper. I wasn't supposed to see it, so I knew it was important. She threw it out without reading it, so I dug it out of the garbage. There was a picture of her with some guy I'd never heard of."

"Robert Griffin?"

"Yeah. She was in the background, but you could see there was a connection between them. Well, it said she was Eleanor Drummond and she managed the Gryphon Gallery. Surprised much? So I didn't exactly follow her. I just went there. Anyway, he paid a huge amount of money for a paddle with some writing on it."

"Rongorongo, does that sound familiar?"

"Yeah, maybe. So suddenly I discover she has a whole other life."

"To protect you, Jill."

"A life without me. Maybe it was. I think it was. I think she needed to keep me away from him."

"What happened?"

The girl glanced over her shoulder toward the corridor into the bathroom and cellars as if she were expecting someone to appear. Then she looked back at Miranda. "He was my father. Did you know that?"

"Yes, I think I did. When did you find out?"

"When I went to my mom's office ... to Eleanor's Drummond's."

"Are you mad at your mother for being someone else?"

"Yes."

"Is that why you won't let yourself grieve?"

Jill stared at her intently. She seemed relieved to be sharing her secret world and, at the same time, angry that her secrets were being exposed.

"How did he hurt you?" she asked Miranda.

Miranda wanted to keep the focus on Jill.

"The same way he hurt me?" asked the girl, answering her own question. "The same way he hurt my mother. That's why I was born, you know. Because he hurt my mother. I wasn't a love child."

"I'm sure your mother loved you very much," said Miranda, feeling the words hollow in her mouth. It was more complex than love.

"Which mother? Molly Bray was my mother. Eleanor Drummond was my mother. Victoria is my mother. You want to be my mother?"

Miranda flinched. "I want to be your friend."

"Okay," said Jill. "That's reasonable."

Miranda almost laughed. *Reasonable* wasn't a word sufficient to the relationship, but perhaps it would do for now. "Tell me about going to the gallery. This was just a few days ago, right?"

"Yes."

"It's not listed under your mother's name. I put a trace on her name and only came up with Griffin's address here. The gallery was in his name."

"I think the building was in my name, and maybe the business was in his."

"Why do you think that?"

"Because that's what she'd do. Because I went through her files."

"You went through her files! Is that how you found out about Griffin being your father?"

"She wasn't in her office when I went there. She was in a smaller room at the back of the gallery. She didn't see me. I went upstairs. As soon as I opened the door, I knew it was Molly Bray's space, whatever she called herself. You know how everyone has colours? I mean, the decoration wasn't the same as at home, but I could tell from, you know, the arrangement of things, textures and colours, the feel of the place, that it was hers.

"So I snooped. I found letters. Nothing compromising, but they showed an unhealthy connection between them. So he was a mystery. I couldn't figure out who he was.

But I knew from the way his name was in my mother's files that he was my father."

Miranda continued to be amazed by Jill's use of words such as *compromising* and *unhealthy connection* and found herself scrutinizing the girl-woman seated on the carpet in front of her, searching for a sign of childishness to balance the preternatural maturity. But right now Jill seemed composed. "You knew, like there it was, a paternity file?"

"Sometimes a connection that doesn't make sense, makes sense," the girl said.

"Point taken."

"So she didn't come up to her office for a long time. At first I was just doing research, making mental notes to share with Alexandria. But there was more stuff than I wanted. And then my mother came in. She seemed hurt rather than angry … that I had discovered who she really was."

"Jill, she was Molly Bray, you know that."

"Do I? Okay. So you don't get to be my age without wondering about your parents. I think real kids wonder if they were adopted, or maybe exchanged at birth. In my case it was my mother who was exchanged, and at my birth, not hers."

Miranda thought of the same quip passing less poignantly between Morgan and her on their trip to Waterloo County. "And you're not a real kid?" she asked.

Jill ignored her and continued. "I knew, just the way she was upset, that he was my father. Her files were proof positive. She cried. I never saw my mom cry before, and the way she cried, I knew he had hurt her. My father wasn't a nice man. But there she was, running an office or gallery or whatever. She was his partner. Only I wasn't part of the equation. I was off living in a bubble in Wychwood Park."

"She was the one in the bubble, Jill — Eleanor Drummond. When she went home to you and Victoria, that was the real world. She was Molly Bray. That's what was real. You can see it in the furniture, the art, the loving attention to detail and design in your home. You can see it in you, Jill, how you've turned out to be you."

Jill smiled sweetly. Miranda figured the girl wanted to believe her, needed to reconcile with her natural mother.

"Did she know you thought Griffin was your father?" Miranda asked. "Did you rush over here directly from Yorkville?"

She wanted to let the revelations come without being forced, to suppress the urgency welling inside her, generated perhaps from the inextricable connections between herself and this girl. She wanted to know everything.

Miranda recognized the name of the gallery. She had browsed there a few times, trying to look prosperous, not at all sure she was carrying it off. The staff — they could hardly be called clerks — had treated her with unwavering cordiality. But the time she had gone in with Morgan they were almost obsequious. It must have been the way Morgan subverted snobbery, wearing quality clothes as if he dressed in the dark.

Morgan had almost bought a bronze sculpture, then had decided against it, possibly because they were asking the price of a new condo. She didn't remember seeing Eleanor Drummond, but then she would have had no reason to deal with management in the little back room with the Salvador Dali on the wall, or in the office upstairs. If they had met, she would have remembered.

"Do you want to tell me what happened?" she asked Jill.

"Nothing happened." The girl rose from the Gabbeh and started pacing, fingering books on the shelves. Suddenly, she withdrew a fat book and tossed it onto the floor beside Miranda. "Have you read any of these?"

Miranda picked up the book. It was a collection of international short stories. She knew there would be a story by Yukio Mishima. Miranda expected Jill to say the book was her mom's. She opened the volume to the Mishima story and wasn't surprised to find that passages detailing the grisly procedures of seppuku had been underlined in ballpoint. With a different pen someone had put a large exclamation mark beside the brief description of the wife's modest death.

The book felt familiar. Miranda opened it to the flyleaf. "Miranda Quin." Her name leaped out at her. Underneath were the words "Annesley Hall."

Grasping for an explanation, she realized this must have been one of the books she had sold when she moved into her apartment at the end of her first year at university. The bastard had followed her, gone through the bins, bought her old books.

She recalled being deeply disturbed back then that her own reading of Mishima's story, according to her professor, was diametrically opposed to the author's intent, which had acquired awesome authority by his real-life disembowelment. Seeing into Mishima's world from such a different perspective had disrupted her moral equilibrium, far more than the obscenity of his pleasure in the details of death. It was a book she had gladly discarded.

"I read that," said Jill, "about the warrior's wife."

Miranda waited for her to continue. Instead she walked to the corridor exit. Miranda assumed she was going to the bathroom. The girl stopped outside the door, waiting for Miranda. Together they went into the bathroom. Jill slumped onto the shower ledge; Miranda sat squarely on the toilet, curious about the unusual intimacy. Jill stared at the drain in the tile floor.

"I was bleeding. I had a shower, and then because I didn't have a towel I jumped around to get warm, and blood came out, so he gave me a towel and I dried myself off."

"Griffin?"

"My father."

"He brought you down here?"

"I came to the front door in a rage, all confused. I didn't know what I wanted."

"You got the address from your mother's files?"

"I practically ran from the subway, and when he answered the door, he didn't look like my father. I could hardly breathe. He knew who I was. He brought me down to the den. I kind of walked around. He watched me. Neither of us had anything to say. What do you talk about when you first meet your father, like, when you're already grown up?"

Grown up? Miranda at about the same age had lost her own father, and there were parts of her that would never grow up.

"I kept mumbling 'bastard,' over and over, so I guess I did say something. Bastard, bastard." She seemed almost amused. "I didn't know if I meant him or meant me. He asked if I wanted to see his fish."

"His fish!"

"I think I screamed. He brought me into the cellar. He didn't drag me, but he made me walk through the big door."

"Into the old part?"

"Yeah, in through there." She got up and thrust out her trembling hand to Miranda. "Come with me."

They pulled the huge door open and entered what seemed even more than previously like a vast and intricate crypt. Jill's grip was as dry as soot, but her forehead glistened. They walked slowly, purposefully, the girl feeling her way into the past. "Here," she said, stopping in front of the wine cellar.

"Here?" Miranda was puzzled and apprehensive. "It's locked."

The girl reached overhead into the deep shadows of the joists above one of the dangling light bulbs and took down a key. "He didn't care if I saw where he kept it. It didn't make any difference."

When the thick thermal door swung open, revealing on the other side a dented sheet-metal panel, the looming darkness was palpable. Miranda hesitated, then reached for the external light switch, but it flicked against her finger with no effect.

"Here," said Jill, "let me do it. It's tricky."

The girl fiddled with the switch, a loose connection made contact, and an austere vault gaped radiantly behind the shower curtain with the wine cellar motif. Miranda stepped forward, pulled the curtain aside, and gasped with a sharp intake of breath that for a moment wouldn't release so that she felt asphyxiated. The chamber contained no racks of fine wine but, instead, a bed, larger than a cot but not full-size, made up with a pillow, flannel sheets, and a blanket. A wooden chair, a small table, and a stainless-steel bedpan on the floor by the table were also in the room. Two bright lights were recessed into the ceiling. It was a cell.

Miranda turned to look behind her at Jill. The girl was fingering the shower curtain.

"This is the privacy barrier," Jill said. "He didn't care if you ripped it down, but you didn't. It was all you had."

"Jill, what do you mean 'you'? I need you to explain. Were you a prisoner here?"

"Yes."

Horrified, Miranda stared at her. The girl's face was expressionless. They sat side by side on the edge of the bed, then Miranda stood, moved over to the chair, and took a seat facing Jill.

"Is this where he …" She wanted to avoid the brutality of a certain word. "Is this where he …" The word *rape* was hard and trite and ominous. "Is this where he did things … to you?"

"Yes."

"He made you bleed?"

Jill looked into Miranda's eyes. "He fucked me."

Miranda reached out to her, but the girl didn't respond. "He kept you prisoner here?"

"Yes."

"For how long?"

"Until my mother came."

"How long was that?"

"Maybe three days. I slept a lot. I slept when he wasn't here, and I read."

"Did he come back? Did he do it more than once?"

"Yes."

"How many times, Jill?"

"I don't know. Three times, five times? He let me go in and take showers. One time he watched. The next time he left me alone, but I couldn't leave. The exit doors were locked. He had the key, so I came back to my room."

"Here?"

"Yes."

"Jill, did you make the bed like this?"

"Yes."

"Before your mother came?"

"No, after."

"Where was Griffin when she came?"

"He was dead."

"How do you mean?"

"You know, not breathing. Lying very still. Dead."

"Where?"

"In the den."

"In the den?"

"She came and got me out. I tried to shout where the key was through the door. She couldn't hear me, but she knew where it was, and she unlocked the door and got me out."

"And he was in the den and he was dead?"

"He called me Shiromuji. He said it's a kind of fish. He said I wasn't his real daughter. That things didn't work like that. He told me he fucked my mother. I tried to scratch him. He said she was a girl like me, only she was better. She was only a girl. He said he liked her better, but I was okay. He said Shiromuji means you're only okay. I was too young, he said. I wasn't purebred, he said. I said, 'That's because you're my father.' He laughed at me. We both laughed. He called me his Shiromuji girl. I think he liked me. He just didn't want to say it. He didn't know what to say. He didn't have the right words."

"Jill, when you went out into the study, where was he?"

"He was lying on the floor, on the carpet."

"On the carpet that's out there now?"

"No, on the thick one with all the colours."

"The rug at your place by the front door?"

"Yes."

"Why did you take it home?"

"Because … it had blood on it, just little specks, and they came off. But my mom didn't want to leave it, just in case."

"In case what?"

"Well, she killed him."

"She killed him?"

"We couldn't just leave him lying there."

"He didn't die from a blow, Jill, not from bleeding."

"No. He died from sleep apnea, my mother said. Only Molly Bray helped him along. When he died, he slipped off his chair and bumped his head a little. There wasn't much blood, but my mom's fastidious."

"Yes," said Miranda, enjoying the girl's vocabulary in spite of the gravity of their conversation.

"Can you die from sleep apnea?"

"You can," said Miranda. "Especially since he took Valium and wasn't used to it. It would relax his throat muscles. It's possible if he already had problems. Yes, he could die that way."

"Sitting up in his chair?"

"Possibly."

"She said she held a pillow over his face. He didn't struggle or anything. He just, you know, expired."

Miranda thought it was more likely that Griffin had been stretched out on the sofa, possibly with his legs up over one end and his head low on the cushions. If he had truly suffered from apnea, he probably didn't need help dying.

Perhaps Eleanor or Molly — she wasn't sure whether they were separable at that point — just said she had smothered him. Maybe he was dead when she arrived and she hadn't come to find Jill at all. Perhaps when she discovered Jill, she needed to murder a man who had already "expired." She needed to take responsibility for what he had done by co-opting his death as murder.

"Jill, how did your mother know you were here?"

"My cigarettes. There was a package out on the table. He wasn't a smoker. He bought them for me. He let me smoke in the bathroom. I don't really like smoking. It's just to bug my mom. In here it made her seem close, knowing she'd really be, you know, pissed off. Did you ever listen to a Zippo? *Clickety-click-click*. Like a gun. Very Quentin Tarantino."

"You like guns?"

"No. That's why I carry a lighter."

Jill reached for the lighter in her pocket, then realized she had lost it. "I think smoking's dumb really. I'm giving it up."

"For your mother's sake?"

"No, it's just dumb. It wasn't that big a deal between us. But she saw the cigarettes and figured I must be here, since she thought that was what our fight was about. You know, about smoking."

"But it wasn't?"

"No."

"Did she know how much you saw in her files?"

"She knew I discovered who she was. She didn't know I had discovered who I was! She didn't know I knew about *him*."

"Did you and your mother have lots of fights?"

"I think it was because we're the same. It's easier when you're different."

"You know that from your research?" asked Miranda, smiling.

"No, just from life. It's something I've learned. It's harder to be the same than different."

"I'll have to think about that."

"Okay."

"Wasn't your mother worried if you were away for three days?"

"Yes, she was. And no."

"Explain."

"I'd run away before. I lived at a Sally Ann hostel one time for a week."

"What did she think of that?"

"It terrified her, me being on the street. But I wasn't. I wasn't walking the streets, or streetwalking. I was living with the Salvation Army, for God's sake."

"So to speak. She must have been worried sick."

"I guess that was the point. But when I realized how much, I felt bad."

"Bad, as in wicked? Or badly?"

"Both. You like words, just like me and my father. I promised her I'd never do it again. She should have known I wouldn't."

"Jill, your mother might not have killed Robert Griffin."

"I didn't do it. I was locked up in here."

"No, no. It's just that he might have, well, let himself die."

"She said he didn't struggle."

"That's not what I mean."

"She didn't want anyone to know she did it except me. She said the police would find him. They'd think it was suicide, especially if they didn't know we'd been here. She left me with his dead body. I sat beside him on the floor. He didn't seem like my father and yet he did. She came back with the long carpet from the hall upstairs. She said we'd have to hurry. It was almost time for the old woman next door to switch from spying out front to spying from her attic at the back. Before we rolled him up she turned on an air bubbler thing that was on the bar. It's for fish. And she really gently put the tube in his mouth and blew air in until he burped. My mother said she didn't want him sinking out there — polluting and killing the fish.

"So we rolled him sideways in the underpad. My mom said it was top quality, or it wouldn't take his weight, but we didn't need the rug like she'd thought. So we carried him out through the big doors, sort of lifting him over the sill, and then we hauled him over to the pond in broad daylight, holding his weight off the ground so we wouldn't leave marks. Then we slipped him in. One big fish, all brassy and crinkly, came up too close just to watch, and Mr. Griffin, my dad, landed right on top of him. Mom said it would be okay. It would just go to the bottom for a while."

Miranda listened as the gruesome account fell open before her in the strange, dispassionate voice of a young girl talking about her family reunion.

"So then we went home."

"That was it?"

"Well, my mom spread out the carpet from upstairs on the floor, and we took that other one. It's called a Gabbeh. She placed books, big ones with pictures of koi, open on the sofa. She took the Gabbeh and its underpad to the car —"

"And the pillow?"

"The one she killed him with. We took it. She rolled it up in the underpad, which wasn't that smudged from the grass and flagstones, and we threw them into a dumpster on the way home. Oh, yeah, before we left she sent me back in here to clean up this room. That's when I made the bed. And I took the book back out to the den and put it in the bookshelf where it belongs."

"The short-story book? He let you read?"

"Yeah, I told you. Mostly, the lights were on full blast. But I slept a lot, anyway. She was outside already, so I locked the door. Then we went home."

"And you forgot your cigarettes?" Eleanor Drummond must have created the inept smoking business as an excuse to tuck the pack into her purse. She didn't want anybody to know Jill had been there.

"Yeah, I guess I did. And I lost my lighter. Maybe at the morgue. It wasn't for smoking, just a souvenir."

"Of what?"

"Of whatever happened while it was mine."

"Jill, how did your mother know you were in this cell? I don't think a package of cigarettes would be enough. You could have been and gone. They could have belonged to somebody else."

"Well, she did."

"But she didn't come in right away?"

"No, I guess not. It was just some place she checked when she was here."

"Was she surprised?"

"To find me? Shocked, but not surprised. By the time she opened the door, she already knew. I could tell." The girl seemed almost wistful. "Do you think he did that to my mother like he said?"

"I think he did bad things to many people."

"I didn't really have a father, you know. Not if he raped her."

"No, you didn't, not a real father."

"How come you're looking after my interests?"

Miranda smiled at the arcane description of their relationship.

"You didn't know my mother until after my father was dead. If he hurt you, why would you care?"

"Because." Miranda gazed into the girl's troubled eyes, acknowledging the truth of their common experience. She rose and reached out. "Come on, Jill. Let's get you out of here."

"Okay," said the girl, allowing Miranda to take her hand and rising from the edge of the bed. They stood side by side and surveyed the chamber, Miranda with an overwhelming feeling of horror, Jill with unreachable memories and surface indifference.

"Do you think my mother really murdered my father?" she asked as if the thought had just crossed her mind. "Molly Bray, I mean. Not Eleanor Drummond. I didn't really know her."

"I think your mother was involved in Robert Griffin's death, but I don't know that she killed him. We'll have to see."

"Why?"

"Why what?"

"They're both dead."

"We have to know what happened."

"It won't make any difference. She's dead."

"We'll sort everything out."

"I told you what happened."

"Yes."

"So why not leave her alone?" She said this as if it were a test.

Miranda moved toward the door. Jill pulled her back.

"No," said Jill. There was an indefinable urgency in her voice. "Let's just stay for a minute."

They returned to the bed, and Miranda sat down. Jill walked to the shower curtain and stood with her fingers running along its slippery folds, almost leaning into it for support. She looked back at Miranda, who was slumped over on one elbow, anxious, exhausted, wanting to escape, but also feeling patience, compassion, and the desire to protect this girl from the terrors within.

"I don't want it like this," said Jill. There was an edge of hysteria in her voice. "I shouldn't have told you. She wanted me to know. I thought she wanted you to know, too. Please, Miranda, you have the power. Why can't we leave the past in the past? Wouldn't that be best for all of us — to bury the past?"

"I understand," said Miranda. "But even if we could, the law won't let us. There's a lot at stake here, Jill. Two deaths under mysterious circumstances. And a huge estate. You're an heiress, you know. You stand to gain a great deal from all this."

Jill glowered at her from across the room. "All this?" She gazed around, almost cowering within the confines of the cell, despite surface bravado.

"Griffin's estate —"

"I don't want anything!"

"It's not your choice, I'm afraid. I'm sorry, Jill."

"I'm a rich orphan," Jill said with disdain.

"Come sit down, Jill. Let's talk."

"No, I've got to figure this out by myself, Miranda." She spoke her name as a challenge, like a barrier between them. Her eyes flicked furtively about, and the bleak walls seemed proof of her guilt for having been raped, evidence of her shame for being her father's child, a horrific reminder of her burden as the keeper of her mother's secrets. A shadow of defiance and rage crossed her face, giving way to the pallor of quiet despair.

"Miss Quin, I'm sorry. I'm really sorry. My mom didn't want anyone to know about this place, about what he did to us, to all of us. You're the only one who can put it together."

Jill stepped backward through the doorway out into the corridor, drawing the huge door closed behind her, all before Miranda could assimilate what was going on. The girl turned the key in the lock and switched off the overheads.

Miranda was engulfed in a stifling absence of light, too stunned to move. After what might have been only seconds, she saw the small, glowing rectangle in the door disappear, and she gasped in astonishment, like a diver plunging into absolute darkness in the depths of the sea.

13

Ochiba Shigura

Morgan spent Saturday shopping. He called Miranda in the morning, but there was no answer. He dictated a rambling memo, explaining to her voice mail that maybe Eleanor Drummond for some reason had raised the spectre of Griffin's suicide not to conceal murder but to reveal it. Stumbling, he apologized for his incoherence, then added that he would call her again on Monday.

After a brunch of scrambled eggs, back bacon, and toast — he kept the bacon in the freezer and usually allowed himself no more than three slices a week, sometimes four — he got dressed and wandered over to Bloor Street and Avenue Road, refusing to admit to himself that he was going to Yorkville.

But he needed a winter coat.

Morgan thought he might check out the early stock in a few of the Yorkville shops while he was in the area and get an idea of what he was up against. He hadn't bought a coat in almost a decade, and he had no idea of the prices. Morgan was pretty much committed to sheep-skin, probably in natural suede, possibly like something Pierre Trudeau would have worn, down to his ankles, but more likely not, most likely conservative; and double-breasted, to keep out the vicious cold of a Toronto winter. He liked the way natural suede weathered, getting better-looking as it got older.

By the time he went into the first shop in Hazelton Lanes, the complex that marked one end of Yorkville like a flagship forging ahead of the fleet, he had decided exactly what he wanted. The price wasn't outrageous. They didn't have precisely the right fit, but the main bulk of their stock for the coming season wasn't on display. He said he would come back later.

Walking east along Yorkville Avenue itself, he went into a coffee bar where the old Penny Farthing had been, or near where it had been, where Neil Young and Joni Mitchell had once sung for their suppers. Bohemian Yorkville was before his time, but he liked the small-scale quality the area retained, despite haughty pretensions. Some of the galleries were museum-quality, and he had always found them amenable to browsing, even though he seldom bought anything.

Morgan sat by the window, sipping a *cappuccino molto grande*, as it was described in commercial Italian on the blackboard, and watched the world go by. The coffee was made with whole milk. He hadn't asked for skim, which was what Miranda usually did. He had waited to see what they would give him, and had felt guilt-free because it hadn't been his decision.

Leaning back, he withdrew the silver lighter from his pocket that he had picked up with loose change from the table in his foyer. He flicked it a couple of times and stared into the orange-blue flame, marvelling at what a simple instrument it was, and how seductively well it was made. It was chrome, actually, or nickel, not silver. For a moment he was charmed by its unfamiliarity, then remembered having found it at the morgue.

From where he was sitting he could see the play of shadows and light through the windows of a prestige gallery across the side street. In front of the gallery there was a huge rampant bronze, the preternatural abstraction of an animist nightmare. Paradoxically, it cast an aura of excitement over its setting that was strangely appealing.

Morgan remembered the time he and Miranda had wandered into the same gallery and he had threatened to buy an exorbitant sculpture by the same artist as the piece outside, which he had described then as "the preternatural abstraction of an animist nightmare" and was impelled to explain what his words were obscuring.

The artist was from Peterborough. Morgan had noted from a brochure that he was apparently doing well enough to have a perfect studio in the Kawartha Lakes, built with timbers and boards salvaged from ancient buildings and reassembled by Alexander Pope who, as the brochure had affirmed, was an oblique descendant of the poet.

So fulsome was the description of the builder that Morgan recalled wondering whether the brochure was for the artist, whose name he had forgotten, or for Pope. He had suggested to Miranda that maybe they were the same person. The name of the artist was a sly pseudonym. Buyers might not trust themselves purchasing sculpture by someone called Alexander Pope who, as the brochure had declared somewhat defensively, was a tall man skilled at the reconstruction of stone buildings and the reproduction of antique cabinetry, and who also antiqued paint and painted landscapes.

Miranda had allowed herself to be amused by Morgan's meandering discourse on the frangibility of artistic identity only after they had safely left the gallery. In this same coffee house she had let herself laugh and then had slipped into stifled hysterics at the absurdity of Morgan having nearly become a patron of the arts, singular, of one piece of sculpture. He had sat watching her burst with merriment and had marvelled at her display, since she seldom let herself go like that, usually fending off laughter with turns of irony and wit.

Morgan stared at the grotesque beauty of the sculpture in front of the gallery. Slowly, the realization came into his mind that this was a misshapen rendering of a gryphon, the same figure that appeared on the side of the gristmill in Waldron, which marked it as a possession of Miranda's assailant.

He was stunned by the fact that he hadn't made the connection immediately, but he was mollified a little by knowing that the context was so entirely different. He was on a Saturday outing. He was relaxing, enjoying the day.

Miranda gasped, and woke up feeling strangled. She sat upright on the side of the bed, waiting with futility for her eyes to adjust to the darkness. There was a complete and utter absence of light. Her body convulsing with surges of panic, she clutched at her gut, wrapped her arms around her rib cage, and tried to hold enough air in her body to breathe. She lifted her hands to her face and could see nothing. Even when she covered her eyes, it made no difference until she pressed hard into the sockets and saw dazzling red streaks against black.

She was afraid to move, to stand. She had no idea where up was or down. She would fall, she thought, or step off the edge of the world. Images rushed through of being underwater, of being deep below the surface of a raging sea in the dead of night.

Miranda took a deep breath and held it, then slowly released air through pursed lips, then took another and did the same. She did this repeatedly, trying to focus on her training for PADI certification, the diver's course she had taken in the Cayman Islands. She cast herself back to the Caribbean, visualized herself at ten metres, about thirty-three feet, hovering over the sandy bottom, taking her regulator from her mouth, releasing bubbles through pursed lips, recovering her reg, breathing again, filling her mask with water, tilting her head back, blowing out through her nose until the mask was clear. In her mind she took off her scuba gear and laid it on the sand, put it back on, secured the BC vest in place, and made a controlled ascent, absurdly slow, moving to the surface while releasing air in bubbles that rose faster than she did as she watched them expand and transform from spheres into elliptical disks.

When she broached the surface, having expelled more air than she had thought possible, she blew out one last heroic breath, then filled her lungs, inflated the BC, leaned back, tasting the sweetness, and floated near the boat until a gorgeous blond youth, a sun-bleached instructor who applauded her from the rails, helped her aboard and gave her a big innocent hug, apparently oblivious to the suggestive drape of his Speedo.

Her breathing was now under control. She groped behind her for reassurance that the bed was still there. Lying back, she shifted around to stretch out, comforted by the embrace of the softness beneath her. It wasn't like floating; gravity pinned her against the pliable surface of the bed. No, it was like being cradled, or whirled gently against the side of an invisible centrifuge.

As Morgan would say, oh, my goodness!

Now that her breathing was normal, she had to go to the bathroom. Not an apt expression, she thought. She wasn't going anywhere. She needed to pee. She reached down and surprised herself by grasping the side of the bedpan on the first try. She had surveyed the room when she came in. She knew where everything was. As long as she remained calm, the room would stay the same size and everything would be in its appropriate place.

When she was finished, she lay down on the bed again. Her mind danced like an escaped marionette. She was slipping deeper into fear — not from claustrophobia but from disconnection, from an abhorrence of death. She had no idea how long she could last without water. She knew it wasn't as long as people thought. It was dry in here, which made it worse. What kind of wine cellar would be bone-dry? The room had humidity controls — wasn't the point to make it humid? But this wasn't a wine cellar; it was a prison cell, a dungeon, a vault, a crypt, a tomb, a grave — the words rattled through her mind.

Miranda held her arm up to look at her watch. She had a digital at home with a light, but her analogue watch was invisible. She held it against her ear. Nothing. She took the watch off and placed it gently on the floor under the side of the bed. Her Glock and her cell phone were in the car, safely in her bag tucked under the seat. She was off-duty, on compassionate leave.

She pulled the cover over her legs, which were a little damp from her episode with the bedpan. Miranda had no idea how long she had been there. Afraid to sleep because she would lose track of time, she stared up into the darkness, her eyes sore around the edges, smarting from the strain of finding no depth to her vision. She closed them softly, and the room seemed to float away, leaving her suspended in a strange, empty universe, a black hole leaking from inside her own skull.

My goodness! she thought. *What a dilemma!*

That was what Morgan would have said. *My goodness!* He never swore.

She remembered asking him once, over dinner after a gruesome day's work, why he didn't swear.

"Why should I?" he had said.

"Morgan, you know what I mean. I'm not saying you should. It's just refreshingly unusual."

"You use a word like *refreshing* and I'm liable to start. Makes me sound like a room deodorizer. I do know all the words."

"I have no doubt."

"Darlene and Fred used to swear.

"A lot?

"My parents? Like troopers. Maybe I didn't swear the same as I didn't smoke, because they did."

"I like that you don't swear."

"Yeah, well, it's an intentional rejection of male privilege and human conceit."

"Pardon?"

"Obscenity is an expression of male privilege."

"Go on!"

She said this in mild derision, but he took it as an invitation. "Men swear because they're lazy with language and/or because they're bullies — it's a power trip over women who flinch at the words, whether they're present or implied. And, of course, women who don't flinch are simply proving they can be as ignorant."

"Morgan, do you have an opinion?"

"Damn right I do."

That conversation had come back to Miranda virtually intact, perhaps polished a bit, his rhetoric improved in recollection.

They had both been eating wiener schnitzel. It was a mistake, and neither of them had eaten very much. They were sharing a nice German Riesling that Morgan had picked out. She didn't recall the names of the wine or the restaurant, and yet it seemed she remembered, word for word, the entire contents of their discussion and the endearingly pontifical tones with which Morgan had delivered himself of his views.

"Profanity," he told her. "It's not the same as obscenity. It's about fear and conceit."

"As opposed to privilege and conceit?"

"Like spitting in a windstorm, whistling in the dark."

"Which?"

"Both. If you spit upwind, it hits you in the face. Downwind and it's sucked out of your mouth. Either way you're diminished. You've challenged the wind and, paradoxically, you've proved its power. A simple 'goddamn' and you've reaffirmed your sad relationship with an indifferent God."

"My goodness!"

"Whistling in the dark — you asked? A string of profanities is a feeble emulation of Descartes. I swear, therefore I am. Invariably, it's the believer who swears at God, since profanity only works if on some level you know it's profane, and it's only profane if God is real. And if God's real, then maybe you are, too."

"You don't swear because you're an atheist!"

"Yes."

"You're a strange man."

"Thank you."

"Thank *you*, Morgan."

She now heard their words echoing inside her skull, and the chambers of her mind seemed to open in all directions as she fell into deep sleep.

Morgan wandered south along Avenue Road in the late afternoon, passing through what he regarded as home territory. Sauntering by Annesley Hall and Victoria University, down past St. Michael's College, he acknowledged that his roots were right here. The University of Toronto was oddly secluded from its urban setting and yet criss-crossed with busy streets that declared its relevance to the city and world at large. This was where he had stepped outside the boundaries of his upbringing. He had been raised in Cabbagetown during its transition from poor place to rich, but he grew up in a different way between Queen's Park and Bloor Street.

Walking east along College Street, he spied with satisfaction the familiar planes of glass and granite shimmering in the cool autumn sky, but until he was almost at Bay Street, nearly in front of police headquarters, he had no sense of the parts coming together. The entire complex, which took up the better part of a city block, was a building that literally worked — a marvel of materials and design. The rosy pink granite and gunmetal steel that might have been daunting deconstructed with casual elegance as one entered from the street and walked through a welcoming mélange of space sculptured on a human scale. The imposing structure, redolent with power and authority, was still a secure and accessible place for visitors and people who worked there. Morgan regretted that to truly appreciate the whole one would need to clear away the surrounding buildings. The structure must have been breathtaking on the drawing boards.

Morgan strolled past reception and was greeted cheerfully by his rank, detective sergeant, rather than by name. He blushed at being recognized, feeling somehow that the young woman, whose own name he didn't know, was privy to his intimate adventures with the Bobbsey Twins.

The twins and he were history now; they had made choices that weren't his doing. Nancy with the big blond hair had married a cop, was pregnant with her second child, and lived in the depths of Scarborough. Anne had tried modelling, he had heard, but her voluptuous lips had led only to lingerie catalogues of the second order, and she was now a vice squad cop in Vancouver.

Still, whenever a pretty young receptionist smiled at him, Morgan was discomforted by a vague sense of the erotic. He would hurry past with a shy smile, avoiding eye contact, and would feel a tickling sensation of relief when he was safely on the elevator. Sometimes he would flirt with women his own age to prove to himself that he was normal.

Morgan slumped down at his desk and began to wade through the accumulated paperwork. Mostly, he came in when Alex Rufalo, the superintendent, wasn't present. Rufalo tended to work executive hours — long but with weekends free. Others around Morgan, after initial salutations, left him alone.

By early evening he was on top of things. Not finished — "things" were never finished — but they were under control. He reached into a bottom drawer and took out a crumpled linen jacket. Lying under it was his standard-issue 9 mm Glock semi-automatic and a shoulder holster. Despite regulations, he seldom carried his gun. Miranda did more often, but it always seemed to him that homicide was the one detail where guns were redundant. The critical focus was on people who were already dead.

On the way home he stopped in at a bookstore on
Bloor Street and picked up a short-story anthology, along
with a gourmet sandwich and a yogourt shake to go at
a place next door. He was too tired to read, so he ate
in front of the television, watched back-to-back episodes
from the *Law & Order* franchise, and went to bed. He
dreamed sporadically of full lips and police procedures
and judges on high benches, some of them comic and
others quite sinister.

Sunday morning Morgan woke up feeling queasy, as
if he had endured a train ride in a windowless sleeper,
conscious the whole night of the tracks clicking beneath
him. He called Miranda again, but there was no answer,
and hung up before having to deal with her voice mail.

Settling in for a good read, he selectively worked his
way toward the Yukio Mishima story in the middle of the
collection he had bought. The first piece was Ernest Hemingway's "Hills Like White Elephants." He was struck
with how a story about female empowerment could have
been written by an icon of machismo. Perhaps Hemingway had had no idea what he was doing. Maybe that
wasn't at all what he had wanted and that was why the
story was subversively powerful. Then there was a story
by D.H. Lawrence — "The Rocking Horse Winner" —
that blew him away. It was about a kid's pact with the
devil. The boy wins and dies. He read William Faulkner's
"A Rose for Emily" twice. It was the most masterfully
grotesque story he had ever encountered — the horror of
necrophilia and a mouldering corpse not just macabre but
a haunting representation of Faulkner's American South.
Next he read a story by Alice Munro with the disingenuous title "Something I've Been Meaning to Tell You."
Disingenuous was the operative word. The detailed id-
iosyncrasies of a few charming characters in small-town

Ontario gradually resonated with each other to reveal genteel emotional mayhem, suicide, and possibly murder.

While he read "Patriotism," the Mishima story, through his own sensibility, Miranda was always in mind. And Eleanor Drummond. Following the course of the warrior's blade, driven by will through the intricate design of his gut, Morgan felt an overwhelming sense of estrangement. Seppuku meant nothing to him, a horrific gesture; and it was undermined, as Miranda had said, by the quiet devotion of the wife dying without vainglory as if death were a domestic detail.

Morgan felt like a voyeur peering into a world so different from what its author must surely have meant to convey. He closed the book and thought of Miranda living in a parallel world, utterly estranged from her watcher. He thought of Molly. He thought of Eleanor Drummond, the absurd humility of her end, the outrageous conceit. He wanted to phone Miranda again to share his reading, but the more he considered it the more he realized he had nothing to say.

Miranda touched her eyes, trying to affirm that she was awake. A faint hum from the ventilation system accentuated the darkness clenched tightly around her. She was shivering and drew up the blanket. Her mouth was dry, but when she ran her hands over exposed skin it felt clammy. The air was thick and warm. She removed the blanket, not wanting to sweat. She needed to vomit, but she didn't want to lose fluids and fought the spasms in her gut by opening her eyes wide and focusing on an imaginary horizon above her. After a while, the nausea began to subside.

She knew she had to move around or she would strangle on fear. Her mind would take flight. Entropy would set in. She would die. Miranda listened intently until she could hear the walls. The hush in the room reverberated softly in her ears, and she started to reconstruct the dimensions of her cell in her head. She got up carefully and groped for the edge of the table to steady herself, the way one did when blindfolded in a children's game. She kicked the bedpan and heard a splash.

"Damn!" she said out loud, and the sound of the voice startled her.

"Damn, damn, damn!" she repeated. "Miranda calling Earth, can you hear me?"

She felt better. Hearing her own voice was proof she was alive. *I am afraid, therefore I am,* she thought. Her throat was constricted from lack of moisture, and speaking was painful.

"I am afraid, therefore I am," she said aloud.

No one answered, and she fought a feeling of dread emanating from the silence by taking a step away from the table toward the back wall. When she reached it abruptly — it was closer than she had anticipated — she slid her hand along and up to the grillwork where ducts would connect to humidity control and heat. It was absolutely flush with the wall. She tried to force her fingers into the metal grid to get a grip until her fingernails split and she felt blood spurt. Miranda moved away, feeling her blood smear across the rough wall. She edged around to the door. The glass was impervious to blows. She felt dents in the sheet-metal back of the door and wondered if these were marks of Jill's rage at confinement.

Jill had read stories. Griffin had left the lights on even when she slept.

Which would be worse? Miranda wondered. Light was confining: in darkness the end of the world could be glimpsed.

She worked her way back around to her bed, kicking the bedpan again as she sat down. The sound of slopping against the steel made her thirsty. It was dry and warm. She felt moisture leaking through her pores. Her lips were beginning to crack. She lay back, waiting. She didn't know for what, though.

Would Morgan find her? Would Jill relent? Miranda didn't think she would. In the mind of a girl so morally distraught, what surely wasn't a premeditated act wouldn't weigh on her conscience now, at least not enough to offset the respite gained by Miranda's erasure. She winced at the notion of being erased, but she directed resentment only at herself. Jill was the heir to Miranda's fall from grace, a notion Morgan would have vigorously rejected — the implications of fall and of grace. She felt the inevitability of her imprisonment, that it was somehow her own doing.

Eventually, she would be discovered.

Would her corpse be mouldering in the bed, her desiccated remains inseparable from the bedclothes and mattress, or dried into dust? Images of the grotesque and macabre entertained themselves in her brain, stopping her from slipping into a state of calm that scared her more than the taunting illusions of death.

Suddenly, the window in the door flashed with illumination, her cell reverberated with light. Gasping, she struggled to the door, her eyes searing in the dim glow. She couldn't see or hear anything through the thick, narrow window. Miranda banged against the dented sheet metal, but could feel the door thud against the flesh of her hands, feel her efforts dissipate into the depths of its thermal layers. She walked around the room, straightening and tidying. The light suddenly flicked off, and she felt relieved as she stepped carefully through the darkness back to her bed.

That would have been Eugene Nishimura. It must be Sunday afternoon. She hadn't thought to check her watch, which was under the edge of the bed. She leaned over, picked it up, and set it on the table. It was either Sunday or Monday. Surely, she had been here more than twenty-four hours. Her body felt drained and depleted. She had to conserve. She was leaching vital energy and fluids into the air.

The absence of humidity, the warmth, these were conditions that could easily be controlled by a system ostensibly set up for wine. This place was designed as a prison specifically to hold captives. Jill wasn't the first. Those weren't Jill's dents on the back of the door. Miranda hadn't noticed any bruises or abrasions on the girl.

Her mind raced. Griffin had kept other victims locked in here, warm and dry, had let them take showers and use the toilet, or at least empty the bedpan. He could have kept them on hold indefinitely for his personal use. She shuddered. How many rapes had occurred in this room? How many women had died here? She settled into the bed, feeling it rise to her weight, feeling a strange kinship with the girls and women who had preceded her in this terrible place.

Morgan went out for Sunday dinner to a restaurant on Eglinton Avenue. He walked there and worked up an appetite. After a pasta dinner, savouring the pleasant taste of garlic in his mouth, he ambled back along Yonge Street and into Rosedale.

Eugene Nishimura's van was parked in front of the Griffin house, and though it was dark, enough light from Mrs. de Cuchilleros's side windows enabled Morgan to see his way around to the back garden. Nishimura was inside. Morgan saw his head bobbing through the abandoned casement that was all that remained of the outside entry into the pump room.

"You're working late," he said when Nishimura emerged from the house.

Nishimura called out, "Is that you, Detective Morgan? Just a sec. I'll turn on the pond lights."

Suddenly, the most astonishing tableau flashed before Morgan's eyes. He had been trying to make out the shapes of separate fish in the indirect garden lighting. Now a spectacular cube of illumination and colour opened in the ground, the depths of water resonating with absolute clarity.

"What an amazing collection!" said Nishimura. "I moved the grand champ up from the lower pond. Look at her! Have you ever seen red so wonderfully intense? Asymmetrical continents floating in absolute stillness, perfectly balanced. Such harmony! There's a perfect tension between all the parts. She's beautifully healthy. She's a living haiku, a perfect living haiku."

"Speaking of which, what does Ochiba Shigura mean?" Morgan asked. "Isn't it something about autumn leaves and still water?"

"It just means Ochiba Shigura. That's what kind of fish it is."

"Don't the words mean something? Translate it into English."

"It means Ochiba Shigura. That's a beautiful name for a fish."

"Meaning what?"

"I don't know. My Japanese isn't that good."

"It's my favourite. Except for the Chagoi. You've moved it back up, too."

The two men stood mesmerized, staring into the pellucid depths at the fish weaving patterns of colour and

form, lazily ignoring the laws of gravity as they expound-
ed the dimensions of their home in soaring slow motion.

Eventually, Nishimura said, "I've got to get going.
My wife thinks I've got a new mistress."

"A new one?"

Nishimura looked at him with an embarrassed smile.
"I *am* a family man."

"Lovely."

"I fed them earlier. I'll be back tomorrow to clean
the filters."

"I'll walk out with you," said Morgan. "I don't want
to be left in the dark."

Miranda slept fitfully for an indeterminate period of time.
Getting up with excruciating effort, she sat at the table,
propped on her elbows, and fiddled with her watch. She
had no desire to eat, but a craving for water sent burning
cramps through her abdomen. Miranda contemplated
opening one of the small wounds in her fingers and sucking on her own blood, but she was afraid the strain in
processing the rich fluid might deplete more than nour-
ish. She had no stomach at all for drinking urine, which
now smelled sour. She had gone again a couple of times.
Nothing much had come except a few drops and a sensation in her urethra as if she were trying to pee needles.
She hadn't been able to have a bowel movement, but a
heavy urgency hovered painfully in her lower gut.

She decided she needed to think. Despite the miserable depletion of her physical resources, her mind seemed
clear. Thinking would make the time pass, keep her focused. Images of the sun-glowing youth in the Speedo
drifted through her mind. The last thing she felt was sexy.
Her lips seared with pain, and she knew she had to be

smiling. He had been a lovely temptation. Like seeing something sinful on a menu — too many calories, too much money. What if she had splurged? Why not? When she got out of this room, she was going to hop on a plane, fly to Grand Cayman, and find that luxuriously endowed young man. She was going to go scuba diving with him and dance beyond gravity in an erotic undersea ballet. Then she would take him back to her hotel room and do it and do it and do it.

"My goodness!" she said aloud, and this time she was strangely reassured by the resonance of her voice, despite its distortion.

Her throat was so dry that the utterance had nearly strangled her, and the deep fissures opening on her lips had caught at the words as they had emerged from her body. Her voice sounded familiar, but not like herself. She whispered, refusing the silence. "When I get out ... I want ..."

She couldn't think of what she wanted. Miranda tried to redirect her thoughts. She knew she had to exercise her mind or she would lose control. She didn't know what that meant, but it frightened her.

If Griffin had died the way she thought he had, and Eleanor Drummond had only killed him after he was dead, he couldn't have known he was going to die. Miranda's mind seemed separate from her body and was clearly a better place to be.

Two things. Why had Eleanor come to Griffin's house if she wasn't expecting her daughter to be there? Where had she thought Jill was? If Jill had run away before, say, downtown, and hung out with street kids, then her mother must have known she would come back. Eleanor had recognized how headstrong Jill was: bull-headed, determined, and smart the way she had been herself —

a survivor. She had expected Jill to return home in due course after sorting out the revelation of her mother's double life. Eleanor Drummond, or Molly Bray, hadn't known that the issue for Jill was her father's identity, not her mother's deceit.

So Eleanor had come here and found Griffin dying or dead. It hadn't mattered which. Then, for some reason, she had entered the wine cellar, this godforsaken room, and discovered her ravaged daughter. She had looked in here because it was a place she had habitually checked! The last thing she had expected to find was her daughter. She was shocked. Eleanor had murdered the man in her mind — redemption for the suffering of her daughter. She had planned her own murder — atonement for complicity in her daughter's brutalization.

Eleanor had come down here because she had known what this place was! She had investigated this room because she had been a prisoner here herself!

No, she had looked in because she had known there had been other young women. She was checking.

Miranda got up and walked around as if the lights were on. She was adjusting to the darkness, to the walled limitations on her existence, to the limits of perception, of being.

Molly Bray wasn't a psychopathic deviant, nor was Eleanor Drummond. Therefore — Miranda moved toward the idea with steely determination — she was some sort of guardian, policing her Faustian mentor, monitoring his perversion, trying to protect others, to control or subvert his predatory appetite for young women. Was she guilty of collusion? Why hadn't she reported him? Her life, not just her constructed identity as Eleanor Drummond, but her life as Molly Bray with Jill and Victoria in Wychwood Park, the intricate contrivance of her life, would have collapsed without Griffin, had perhaps existed because she had used what she had known. She had sold her soul to protect her life. And with terrible irony she had failed to protect her own daughter.

That vile man had savaged their daughter, his own child. *Oh, my God!* Miranda thought, shuddering. *Oh, my God!*

Morgan woke up Monday with what felt like a hangover. Before he shaved he got on the telephone to Miranda, but she must have already gone out. There was no response on her cell phone. A little troubled by his inability to reach his partner, he showered, shaved, and got dressed.

The Griffin affair was going to break very soon. He had the feeling he got when the disparate details of a case started falling together. But he was wary, uneasy. Murder-suicide in a Rosedale mansion didn't resonate like this without complications. Where the hell was Miranda?

Morgan went out for breakfast. In an attempt to kick-start his body, he ordered a hungry-man platter of sausages, bacon, pancakes, eggs, and toast, which when placed in front of him seemed obscene. He stared into the unnaturally orange fluid in his orange juice glass. Oranges could be too orange, he thought. Sometimes things weren't what they were. Griffin was a deviant, but he was a student of semiology. They weren't mutually exclusive. He had followed Miranda into an academic program. He was already an ineffectual lawyer — not the first. She must have known at some level who he was, his name if not his face.

Was that why she had turned down the scholarship? She had tried to get away as far as possible. That meant joining the RCMP and loving a man, Jason Rodriguez in

Ottawa, who couldn't love her enough. Meanwhile, Griffin stayed on and earned a Ph.D. What a wasted mind, he thought. What a pathetic creep.

Eleanor Drummond. He glanced down at the meal in front of him and pushed it away, retrieving only the toast, which he mouthed, dry, with a bit of coffee to wash it down. She had killed herself. She had wanted them to think she was murdered. She had needed them to think there was an intruder, an interloper in the scene, *deus ex machina*, an operative from outside the narrative. Put that together with Griffin's murder. She had wanted them to think he was murdered, too. She had diverted them long enough to work out her own death. Simple. They were looking for something too complicated. Eleanor/Molly had known they wouldn't see the trees for the forest.

It made sense, yet her motivation defied comprehension. *Why, why, why?* Miranda would be able to shed light on this conundrum if he could ever find her.

Knowing she should be conserving her physical resources but fearing, even more, that stasis invited the onset of death, Miranda paced back and forth in the darkness, not rapidly enough to force a sweat but sufficient to create a modest breeze as she moved. She had stripped to her underwear, keeping that on in morbid anticipation of being found dead, wanting to maintain a certain propriety in front of forensics, whatever her condition of degradation, and in front of Morgan, who always displayed an endearing curiosity about her undergarments. Once at the morgue, pretensions would collapse, of course, particularly after being here a while. Eleanor Drummond was the only corpse she had ever encountered whose beauty seemed enhanced by death. And they had gotten her before she was cold. Miranda hoped she didn't get Ellen Ravenscroft. Anyone but that marauding coquette, her old and dear friend and acquaintance. She figured the cooling air was keeping fluids inside her, though she knew, in fact, from her goose bumps that she was losing water through her skin, which was why she felt a chill.

Sometimes she slept. She was painfully numb, her lips were bleeding, and she had cramps, but she kept moving when she could, occupying her space like a prowling animal rehearsing the limits of its cage. It had to be Monday or even Tuesday by now.

In the absolute darkness, words seemed tangible, as solid as flesh. Eleanor, Molly, Jill, Miranda — she shuffled through names in her mind. Griffin? Had he written her a letter when he knew he was dying? But it was unlikely he had known that, especially if Jill's second-hand diagnosis of sleep apnea was a factor. Could he have caused his own death? Not with enough certainty to write Miranda beforehand.

She could envision the manila envelope. It had been recycled — at least the label had been stuck on where another label had been removed. Lots of people reused envelopes. Millionaires? Maybe. Then, as Miranda studied the postmark in her mind, she thought perhaps it was the cancellation date that was being reused. She saw the deep creases in the envelope and realized it had been stuffed through her mail slot. The postman had a key. He always opened the whole panel of boxes and put the mail in without scrunching it up. Even her Victoria's Secret catalogues, which the postman obviously thumbed through, came out folded but not creased. That meant the envelope had been delivered by someone else.

Miranda lost track of the darkness. Slumping down on the chair, she continued her interior discourse. People didn't send posthumous mail. So who had access to his stationery? Who knew about his souvenir clippings? Who knew about her, could draft a document, witness it, and forge his signature? And then, to be authentic, in her own spidery handwriting label the envelope because she was, after all, his amanuensis, his accomplice and wicked familiar.

Miranda was ecstatic. She would have to discuss this with Morgan. He would like *amanuensis*.

The passageway light suddenly flashed through the door. Pressing close to the glass, she saw a shadow slip by, probably Eugene Nishimura again. She overrode the reluctance of muscles and joints that had begun to seize up as her body shut down, lurched back across the room, and collapsed onto her hands and knees, feeling for the bedpan in the murky gloom. Dumping its contents on the floor, she struggled to her feet and scrambled as fast as she could manage back to the door. She held the bedpan up where she could see the polished steel gleam and aligned it carefully, trying to mirror the light that penetrated her window back into the corridor, tilting the pan gently to make the beam dance. Peering around the bedpan through the glass, she waited for an interminable time. Then she spied a shadow moving across the opposite wall and cast her frail beacon against the stone and brick at eye level. But the shadow disappeared, and the light was suddenly extinguished. Miranda threw the bedpan into the darkness, strode over to her bed, lay back exhausted, and allowed herself for the first time to let tears drain precious fluids from the corners of her eyes.

~ ~ ~

When Morgan arrived back at Robert Griffin's house, Eugene Nishimura was already on the scene. A woman dressed in jeans and a sweater was with him. She introduced herself.

"My name is Ikuko. You are Detective Morgan? I have come to see my husband's mistress. She has many parts, all of them beautiful, like a geisha."

Morgan and Ikuko sat on the limestone parapet, talking and observing the fish, while her husband worked around the pool and inside the house.

"I know that one is best," observed Ikuko, pointing to the champion Kohaku when her husband was in the pump room. She lowered her voice to a whisper: "I like the Ochiba Shigura."

"Me, too," said Morgan. "Do you speak Japanese?"

"Oh, yes, I was born in Kyoto. I am *issei*, a true pioneer. My husband is *yonsei*. Our children are *gosei* when they will be born — old-style Canadian."

"Can you translate Ochiba Shigura?"

"I don't think so."

"Doesn't it mean anything?"

"Not in English."

"In Japanese."

"Yes," she said. "Sometimes it is difficult to translate from one culture to another, Mr. Morgan."

Her husband came out, bringing food that he divided among the three of them. They each leaned over and hand-fed the more confident fish. The Ochiba Shigura came directly to Morgan, trying to shunt aside the Chagoi, which was voraciously mounting his half-closed hand. It gave up and swam to Ikuko where it ate delicately from her open palm tilted almost to water level.

"Eugene," Ikuko announced, "I do not like the Takai Kohaku best. I like the Ochiba Shigura."

~ ~ ~

Miranda sat up suddenly, coming into consciousness in
an upright position. Words tumbled through her mind.
She was in mid-argument, anticipating the next twist
in a convoluted rhetoric. "Thirdly," she muttered with
a throaty rasp into the darkness, "number three, Morgan, is why?" The words sounded less convincing outside her head where they floated hollowly in the thick air
and dissipated into the darkness. "My third point ..."
she continued sub-vocally, trying to recover her composure, knowing illusion was everything in a debate and she
had to seem to be in command of her inner voice. What
were points one and two? "My third point, Morgan ..."
she ventured, a little reassured by the sound of his name
reverberating inside her skull. "Morgan, the tertiary ele-
ment to my deductive argument is —"

She must have passed out from the effort of sitting up,
because when she became aware again she was sprawled
across the bed with her knees on the floor. They were
bruised as if she had fallen in a posture almost of prayer.

Without moving she drifted into a dream where everything was bright and beautiful but nothing was distinct or familiar.

Flung suddenly back into wakefulness, she crawled
onto the bed and stretched out. She had to think. If she
could think through the pain, the pain would leave.

One — it was as though she could see a number
one shaped like a child's giant birthday candle. Eleanor
Drummond had come here to monitor Robert Griffin's
proclivities for nasty behaviour. She was his conscience;
he had none of his own. She needed Jill to see his death as
righteous, to restore innocence to her daughter. Ambiguous! To prove Jill's innocence to herself.

Miranda rehearsed the scenario so that she could explain it to Morgan. Time passed.

Two. The number hovered over her head, crudely formed like a numeral made from a twisted balloon. The letter authorizing her as executor was delivered posthumously. Eleanor must have known she would figure that out and go along with it, anyway! The dead woman had known things about her even she didn't fathom.

Number three must be coming up! Miranda waited for a numeral to appear. A constellation of stars hovered in the middle distance, forming the number. An image of three crosses on Calvary loomed into focus in the guise of a Roman numeral. Threes swarmed her like the aggressive graphics on *Sesame Street*, then faded to black.

Okay, she thought. Eleanor had recognized Miranda when Morgan and she were beside Griffin's body. The woman had already planned to die. She had set up a scene where Griffin might have been reading, then had impulsively, on a morbid whim, walked out to the pond and ended it all. She had seeded obvious notions of suicide in his case, but why? So the police would suspect murder. Later they'd do the same when her body was discovered. Terrible crime, a double homicide. Distasteful perhaps, but not a disgrace. One problem: how could Eleanor guarantee her daughter's inheritance?

And then Jill's mother saw Miranda!

Miranda searched the darkness for numbers, but there were only a few strands of dazzling red surging against the insides of her eyelids.

What if they had driven Griffin to it?

No, Morgan, listen! You can't leave me out of the equation.

And what if Molly's transformation into Eleanor Drummond was the beginning of murder? Perhaps until then he could have justified rape as a response to his victim's desires, the voyeur seduced by his vision. But she had backed him against the wall, the way she had Roger Poole, the man who beat up his kids. Instead of retiring, perhaps into fantasy, Griffin had turned to something more sinister — a metamorphosis of his own. He again had the power. What if she had known that and believed it was her fault?

A brief thought snapped like a whip through her mind. The horror, that summer, was learning she had the capacity to make a man monstrous! That was what she couldn't forgive herself for.

They — Griffin and Eleanor — had sustained each other by mutual hatred, but Eleanor had another life. He had only this dungeon and his beloved koi.

Miranda doubted they were lovers.

He had needed Eleanor's soul. Dried walnuts?

No, Morgan, no. That's your expression, but no. The soul is whatever's inside that gives a human being moral dimension, like air in a balloon. You can't see it, but it's there. Don't give up on souls because you've given up on God.

Griffin had needed Eleanor's soul because he didn't have one. And after he finished with their daughter, he knew Eleanor's soul would be gone, as well, and it would be time to die.

And he did finish with her, with all his victims. Perhaps because of their enfeeblement or their desperate affection. Maybe because they were no longer innocent; no longer incarnations of his virgin mother.

You check, Morgan. I bet she died just before all this started, before his watching got out of hand. You check it for me, okay?

And he had left them in here, turned up the controls. They had died by desiccation, their juices gone, their corpses dried to the bone. This was an execution chamber. How many had died here between Molly and her? Was she the first?

Oh, my God, Morgan, I'm tired!

Miranda could feel the overwhelming rage rising within her, and with bitter irony she realized she no longer had enough strength to sustain it.

Eleanor had wanted them to think they were lovers. That was strategic. Better her daughter was the offspring of a wealthy eccentric and his mistress than sired by a serial killer. Better they were lovers than she was the keeper of his conscience, and a failure at that.

Jill's mother had counted on Miranda being compelled to understand her connection with Griffin. She had sent her daughter to the morgue. She was sure Molly Bray and Eleanor Drummond would merge when Miranda met her daughter. The dead woman had known everything about her. She was a knowledge broker — that was her power, and her downfall.

She was right, Morgan. Jill is my responsibility. I'll look after Molly Bray's daughter as if she were my own.

Morgan tried sporadically through the day to locate Miranda, pacing his initiatives to keep his rising apprehension in check. When she didn't turn up at Robert Griffin's house before Nishimura and Ikuko left, he went inside and used the telephone. His cell phone was back in his kitchen where it usually was when it wasn't with his pager in his desk at headquarters. He called her cell phone, he called her at headquarters. He called her at home and listened to her voice mail greeting.

When Nishimura came to the door, Morgan looked up from where he was comfortably ensconced in the wingback chair and explained he would wait for Miranda here. She had said nothing to suggest she would come to Griffin's, but he didn't know where else to look.

He dozed awkwardly in the chair, wanting, when she walked in, to seem as if he had been thinking with his eyes closed. When he awoke and glanced at his watch, it was mid-afternoon. He called the office again. No one had seen Miranda. Maybe she was sick, they told him. He knew that wasn't it. She would have called him. Morgan thought of trying to call someone in Waldron to see if she had gone up there on family business, but where? He tracked down her sister in Vancouver, and she said they hadn't been in touch, but if Miranda did call she would let him know that he was asking about her. Morgan gave her Griffin's number and said she should phone him collect. He expected no resolution from that quarter, but it amused him to be building up the outstanding balance on Griffin's bill. Miranda would have to deal with it. She would be exasperated but tolerant.

Morgan walked through the corridor and into the labyrinthine crypt under the oldest part of the house, heading directly to the pump room where the door opened easily. He surveyed the elaborate convolutions of pipes and tanks, went over and picked up the rag draped across the tap. He knew what a gusset was and tossed the rag aside.

Striding out to the main passageway again, he turned and stopped at the wine cellar door without noticing there was a key in the lock. He leaned forward to peer through the glass but could see nothing, not even his shadowed reflection. Returning to the main passage, he made his way to the door of the tunnel connected to the de Cuchilleros estate, pushed it open, and stared into the darkness. Another dead end. He returned to his chair.

Morgan was too restless to settle for very long, and after a while he rose, put on his rumpled jacket, though it wasn't cool in the cellars, and picked up a pewter candle holder. Taking the Zippo from his pocket, he lit the candle and went back to the tunnel entrance. There was an imperceptible breeze that made the flame flicker as he entered the darkness. The tunnel took several abrupt turns, and Morgan felt increasingly claustrophobic. Then a turgid movement of air snuffed out the candle, and for a moment he froze. The floor was suddenly a dark abyss, as if he might step off the earth into a terrible void.

The lighter dropped when he took it from his pocket and clattered against the cobbles. As he squatted slowly toward the sound where it had landed, warm wax dripped onto his wrist. In surprise he released his grip on the candle holder and was startled by the resonant thud of pewter on stone as it fell to the floor. Shifting to his knees, he made a sweep through the darkness with his hand and almost immediately brushed against the holder, but the candle was gone. He was amused and annoyed at his fear. His fingers closed around the lighter, and he rose to his feet. His mind, even before a flame leaped into the darkness, summoned an image of Jill at the morgue.

Locating the candle, he relit it, carefully shielded the flame with his cupped hand, and moved forward inside the flickering aura of light until he was confronted by two heavy oak doors, one of which opened with considerable effort onto a stone stairway. At the top of the steps he discovered he was in the de Cuchilleros carriage house, which was attached to the main house and was used as a garage. Descending, he tried the other door, which swung freely as if the hinges had been oiled, and found himself staring out into the widow's back garden.

Morgan was strangely unnerved by his feelings of violation as a trespasser, and he returned through the tunnel. He had been enthralled by the cellars and passageways, but now it all seemed more sinister, perhaps because for a moment the darkness had closed around him like the walls of a grave.

Before going home he went down to police headquarters, did a search of hospital admissions with no result, and finally decided Miranda had gone off on a fling. When he got home, he sat in front of the television, angry at her and worried. If she was touring the Muskoka colours, it was a dumb way to do it, not telling him first. No one at headquarters had showed any concern. Alex Rufalo had pointed out that she was on compassionate leave, so she could do what she wanted.

Morgan fell asleep sprawled across his sofa. When he woke up, the television was flickering grey. He shivered while he stood beside the toilet to pee. Weighed down with the excessive gravity of early morning, he struggled to get up the stairs. After he crawled into bed, he dreamed of autumn leaves falling on still water.

Miranda awakened in bone-wracking pain. She tried to raise herself, but her body was a dead weight. Her mind seemed uncannily lucid, her mental world separate from its violated container, reaching to float free. Her body was holding her back, urging her that it was time perhaps to leave it behind.

I remember the victims, she thought. *I try to remember the victims*.

Miranda had known the names of all fourteen young women who were shot to death at École Polytechnique de Montréal in 1989. But then they began to slip away, and she jumbled first names with last, distorting their identities, and was ashamed. And she was angry that she couldn't forget their killer's name.

She recalled reading about Kitty Genovese who had died in New York in the 1960s while witnesses had looked out their windows and watched her being stabbed, then watched again when her assailant returned a half-hour later and stabbed her some more until she was dead. She remembered Mary Jo Kopechne at Chappaquiddick, Massachusetts, who may have been implicated in her own demise, or maybe not.

She remembered she had never been to Europe.

Envisioning her subterranean prison of stone and plastered brick and old timbers, she summoned images of European timelessness, the walls of medieval towns weaving through cities, and these pictures gave way to visions of utter depravity, the mounds of human corpses she had witnessed with fascinated horror in old newsreels, trying to pick out among the twisted limbs and torsos and gaping misshapen heads whole figures, somehow as if she could restore dignity to a few of them if only she could recognize individuals, not a jumble of parts.

She thought of Safiya Husaini, the woman in Nigeria condemned to be buried to the waist and stoned to death with rocks of a prescribed size because she had submitted to forced sex with an elderly relative. This was her fate under the jurisdiction of *sharia*, proclaimed by some as the fundamental laws of God. Sometimes Miranda felt sorry for God. To her horror she couldn't recall whether or not the execution had been carried out. She didn't know whether Safiya Husaini was alive or dead.

In Ontario *sharia* was accepted as law. Was it? Her eyes burned without tears to wash away pain.

If she walked through a slave market, should she stifle her outrage because it was custom, or tear off the manacles, even of slaves who found comfort in slavery?

Fadime — that was the name of the young Kurdish woman in Sweden who was killed by her father for loving a Swede. Honour killings in Canada. Surely *dishonour*.

A poem by Margaret Atwood came to her in precise, cruel images; there was no beauty in them. The poem was called "Women's Issue," or it should have been, but that was close enough. Nameless women give birth to the men who arrange to have stakes driven between other women's legs and their vaginas sewn up, and to the men who line up for a turn at the same used prostitute, adding their semen to the spilled waste of the world. She couldn't sort out the poem's grisly imagery from her own memories of brutalized women, nameless, blood-drenched, in ditches and bedrooms and cars, and splayed out on stainless-steel trays at the morgue.

When did political correctness become moral compromise? That was her last, pellucid thought, which she associated with burkas, with cultural brutality, with the infinite pain of bearing and not bearing children, with tolerance for death.

Miranda's whole system was shutting down. She could feel her guts shrivel, could identify each organ by its unique tremulations of pain as she did a ghoulish inventory. Her heart beat like a fist clenched over nothing, expanding and contracting in exhaustion; her breath grated against her throat, her lungs were in flames.

Thinking was suddenly unbearable. One minute she was filled with ideas, the next almost vacant. Except she knew something. She knew she had been the victim of a crime, of rape, and of consequences fast approaching closure. Not through her death. Through the revelation of suffering.

She groped with her hands until they found each other over her stomach. Then she let her elbows drop and her forearms settle against the bed by her thighs. She gave a mighty heave and swung herself forward through a muffled scream so that her legs draped over the side, pulling her upright, and a dry sob emerged from deep in her chest. She felt her feet scrape against the floor as she struggled to get them under her weight, and slowly she rose to her full height.

Miranda stood, wavering, getting her bearings. She brought words up through the raw flesh of her throat to whisper into the darkness.

"My name is Miranda Quin!"

Her lips cracked open and bled as she spoke, and her throat seized so that she clutched it with her hands, pressing hard against the pain until she could breathe. She edged her way along the wall between the bed and the door. Stopping, she pressed the fingertips of her right hand against the rough concrete.

In violent movements she ripped skin from her fingers until she felt warm blood flow back over her wrist. She turned and shuffled slowly across to the far wall, which she knew was already streaked with her blood. Steadying herself against the wall with her extended left hand, she began to inscribe with fresh blood, using her right hand. Her message was simple: "I am Miranda Quin."

Her fingers had lost all feeling when she finished, and she felt a strange sense of ease as she sank to the stone floor. After unmeasurable time, she crawled to the bed, hauled herself up onto it, and stretched herself out, reconciled now to her imminent death.

14

Kohaku

Another bright autumn day greeted Morgan as he hurried down the steps of his Victorian postmodern condo. It was cool, almost crisp, anticipating the onset of the interminable stretch from the end of October through early December before winter set in. He resisted calling Miranda at home. When he checked in with headquarters, he only asked as an incidental question if she had been around. On his way to Robert Griffin's house, he picked up two coffees at the Robber Barons.

There was no sign of her. The doors were locked. He sat on the edge of the pool and drank his coffee. He was just finishing hers, as well, when Eugene Nishimura strode down the steps through the walkway and into the dappled sunlight like a man entirely at home in his setting.

"Good morning, Mr. Nishimura."

"Good morning, Detective Morgan. How are my koi doing today?"

"Fine. Our koi are doing just fine."

"Fed them yet?"

"No."

Nishimura walked over and scooped out a small canister of feed from the bin by the door. He sprayed it out across the closest end of the pool, then sat beside Morgan on the retaining wall to watch the flurry of colour as the koi crowded the surface to eat.

"I've heard from my people in Japan. It's Wednesday there now. They've been making discreet inquiries, Mr. Morgan. We weren't sure what we were getting involved in, and I thought it best not to make it seem like a police matter."

"No, of course. And?"

"And there's no report that the Champion of Champions is missing. The breeder was approached. He said, 'Oh, yes, she was in the big pond, the soil was just right —'"

"The soil?"

"That's what they call the combination of clay, natural waters, and the micro-climate that determines the worth of the fish."

"Like Chateau Margaux is valued higher than its neighbour, Chateau D'Issan, and D'Issan is valued higher than the chateau next to that."

"Just so, Detective Morgan," said Nishimura. Drawing the conversation back to the matter at hand, he continued. "Only their skill in choosing what's best from tens of thousands of fingerlings is more important. The owner of this breathtaking Kohaku whose simplicity is infinitely complex, who has the shape of perfection —"

"Mr. Nishimura," said Morgan, "the name of the breeder?"

"His entire business is based on this fish. She is thriving, he assured my informant, in the opaque waters of his largest pond, high in the hills of Niigata. He can't afford to acknowledge otherwise."

"Do you think he knows she's in Toronto?"

"Yes, he does. Otherwise he would have claimed insurance, either that or a national outpouring of sympathy. He knows exactly what's in his ponds. But he doesn't need her anymore."

"He doesn't?"

"Likely the breeder has a fix on her line. With a few generations of her offspring selected, she was no longer essential for his breeding program, so he sold her to someone with no need to broadcast his divine acquisition."

"An ignominious outcome for the Champion of Champions."

"I doubt she cares."

"And you think Robert Griffin bought her legally?"

"More or less. It would be preferable for the breeder's reputation if the koi world assumed she was still in Niigata. Mr. Griffin was the ideal customer because he was discreet to the point of obsession."

Morgan was fascinated by the contradictory notion of keeping a treasure concealed. He tried to connect the compulsive hoarding of beauty with the psyche of a rapacious voyeur.

"I doubt very much that he declared her true worth when she was processed through customs," Nishimura continued. "I would say she came in with some of the lesser Kohaku. He probably brought some of these other prizewinners in the same way."

Humility made Morgan uneasy: these were the Kohaku he and Miranda had proclaimed the best of the lot. "Do you think he was wheeling and dealing?"

"Selling for a profit? No. An unequivocal no. Otherwise I would have heard about him. I know the koi world. I would have known if he had sold even one really good fish. This man had money, so why bother with crime? He was an obsessive, reclusive collector. I mean, this guy was clinical. He was pathological."

"I think you're right, though I'm not sure we'll ever know the full extent of his pathology."

Morgan realized Nishimura had no idea about Griffin's deviant behavior. He knew him only as a dead recluse found floating among fish of astonishing worth. The Japanese koi expert shrugged and asked to be let into the house.

"My partner has the keys," Morgan felt compelled to explain. The house was open. Then he asked as they walked through the French doors, "Have you heard from her, Eugene? I haven't been able to track her down for a couple of days."

"She should be here right now. I told her I'd report back on my clandestine, um, inquiry."

Now that wasn't a word people used in real life, Morgan thought. He realized Nishimura was enjoying his part in a police investigation, especially one that combined murder with koi. *Clandestine* implied furtive. Appropriate perhaps, but it also suggested treachery. He should have said *covert* if he wanted to raise the level of intrigue.

"When did you talk to her?" Morgan asked.

"I don't know. Maybe Saturday morning. I've got to clean out the vortex filters. I'll let you know if she calls. I have my cell phone."

Nishimura walked off toward the cellars, and Morgan settled into in his wingback chair. Why wasn't Miranda carrying her cell phone? The green Jaguar was parked in the garage. Perhaps her phone was in the car.

He walked through the stone passageway past the wine cellar door to the garage. The car was locked. He peered through the windows. From the passenger side he could see a small corner of her handbag protruding from under the driver's seat. The convertible top must have been lowered and then raised again, or she would have stashed it in the well behind her.

Even though he had been looking for the bag, he was disconcerted to find it. She suddenly seemed more vulnerable. He hoped she had her semi-automatic Glock with her, that she hadn't turned it in while on leave, that it wasn't locked in this car. With her wallet and phone! The bag had been there at least since Saturday. Reason struggled against panic, asserting that this was a spare and she was carrying another bag wherever she was.

It struck him that if the convertible top had been down since he had last seen her she would have been in a playful mood and distracted. It had to be Jill Bray. He guessed they had driven around together. Morgan knew Miranda was going over to Wychwood Park on Friday after dropping him off. He wished he had his own cell phone. He could at least call her number and see if hers was inside the car.

Morgan didn't want to break in. That would seem irrationally preemptive, especially when she turned up safe and sound. If she was with the girl, with Jill, she was all right. If she had entered a sanctuary, a refuge of some sort, a secular retreat, or a spa … Maybe it didn't seem necessary to let him know where she was. She was only his work partner and was officially on leave. It worried him that he fretted so much, as if his anxiety might cause bad things to happen.

Walking up the ramp and around the side of the house, he treaded a fine line between petulance and fear as he went back inside and called Molly Bray's number. Victoria answered. He introduced himself and asked if Jill was home for lunch.

"She didn't go to school yesterday or today, Detective," Victoria explained, pleased to have the opportunity to speak to an adult. "I think her momma's death has finally sunk in. She's worse after talking to Miss Quin than before. She mostly just stays in her room, mostly sleeping, I guess. She keeps the door locked. I have a key, but I don't want to disturb her grieving. Sometimes it's better to grieve by yourself, even when you're only fourteen."

"You've seen my partner then?"

"She was here on Friday. And she was here again Saturday morning."

"Saturday?" Morgan knew what Victoria would say next.

"Yes, sir. She and Jill went off together. Miss Bray without a proper jacket — these kids will catch their death of cold — and she came back around three."

"Miranda and Jill?"

"No, sir, just Jill. She said Miss Quin dropped her off up the way, by the gates."

"Could I speak to Jill?"

"I'll see what I can do. I don't think she's talking to nobody right now. She's so distressed."

After what seemed like an interminable delay, a girl's voice whispered, "Hello?"

"Jill?"

"Yes."

"I'm David Morgan. I'm a detective, a friend of Detective Quin. We met —"

"I know. I remember."

"Have you seen Ms. Quin?"

"She said I'm supposed to call her Miranda."

"When was the last time you saw her?"

"Saturday."

"In the afternoon?"

"Yes."

"Where, what time? Can you tell me about it?"

"She came here."

"Did you go to Robert Griffin's house?"

"Where?"

"Your mother's associate. Did you go to his house? That's where I'm calling from."

"Yes." She paused. "Miranda wanted me to see it."

"Why?"

"I don't know. I came home by myself."

"Didn't you tell your housekeeper she dropped you off?"

"Yes."

"Did she?"

"No."

"Jill, how did you get home?"

"I left Miranda downstairs at Mr. Griffin's house, then I walked up to St. Clair and came home by streetcar."

"Why did you tell Victoria you got a ride home?"

"Because she worries."

"Does she always worry?"

"Yes. But more now because she thinks I'm really upset."

"Are you?"

"Yes."

Morgan was thrown. When he met her at the morgue, the girl had seemed eerily strong, her voice modulated with an inflection of constrained hysteria but firmly under control. Now it was faltering despite her attempt to cover by being exceptionally terse. "You left Miranda here?"

"At Mr. Griffin's … yes."

"But I would have thought —"

"We parked the car in the garage. I think she was going to walk home, so I said I would, too. It seemed logical."

"Logical?"

"I left her there. That's the last I saw of her."

"Jill, if you hear from Miranda, will you have her call this number? And I'll give you my number at police headquarters. If you tell them it's very important, they'll know how to reach me."

"Okay. I left her there downstairs."

"Write this down."

"I am."

"Are you okay?"

"Yes."

Morgan got off the phone, suspecting that Jill's staccato responses concealed more than they revealed. For now his concern was Miranda, but Jill's obvious pain resonated with the anguish of the girl he knew Miranda had been, the young woman Miranda had kept like a prisoner locked deep in some darkness inside.

From his perspective slouched in the wingback chair, Morgan surveyed the beautifully modulated subversions in the antique Kurdish runner. The woman who had tied these knots had challenged death with modest flourishes. Within the rigid parameters of tradition she had affixed an elusive signature, writing in symbols only she could remember. This rough rug, in Morgan's eyes, was as exquisite as all the formal carpets he had ever seen.

Disturbing his reverie, Eugene Nishimura emerged through the corridor, carrying a bucket of sludge. "Too mucky to go down the drain," he explained as he ambled across the Kurdish runner. Morgan flinched. "It's from the skimmer pump filter." He walked out. Nothing had slopped over.

By the time Nishimura returned, having dumped the muck over the embankment into the ravine, Morgan had rolled up the runner and placed it behind the sofa.

Nishimura strolled through without speaking, leaving a spoor of mud bits behind him.

Reseating himself, Morgan spied at eye level another of Griffin's notes. It was barely visible, poking out from the top of a book. A little reluctantly he got up, retrieved the note, and sat down again. This one was written as if it were part of a larger narrative: "I write so beautifully it breaks my heart, rereading what I have written and knowing that no one will decipher my words. Writing and reading are utterly separable. Rongorongo is a code. It conveys messages in the absence of meaning."

Very enigmatic, thought Morgan. One of the messages of Rongorongo might be that a rich and reclusive degenerate could bury whole lives in a basement hideaway. More followed: "If critics are incapable of grasping what I do, it is not their fault but my own for being out of their reach. They cannot comprehend what they miss."

Morgan telephoned the Robarts Library at the University of Toronto. There were no records of a book ever being published under the name Robert Griffin. They asked for a title; there might be something under a pseudonym. Then it suddenly came to Morgan that the notes meant nothing. He hung up abruptly.

Griffin had fantasized that he was the author of esoteric works beyond comprehension. Meanwhile he had written little missives about language and the nature of being. He had imagined a parallel universe made only of language where as a creature of words he might leap out of this world and come into his own over there.

The wretched old bugger hadn't even been real to himself.

Morgan glanced over at the polished surface of the Rongorongo tablet. The hieroglyphs aslant to the light appeared as nothing more than random incisions. The curiously cavalier lodgement beside a cluster of walking sticks seemed somehow appropriate now.

He recalled from reading the Bible as a child, and from studying scripture in university, that he had always felt the real reason humans were driven from Eden was for naming the world. Language preceded knowledge of good and evil; words separated people from primal innocence.

He wished he could talk to Miranda.

In Miranda's notion of unbelief, anything was possible. Perhaps even a God still in his garden beyond the limits of language.

He needed to talk to her. She would tell him he was being pompous or immature, or bring him to earth with speculation on where he was wrong. Where in the world was she?

The telephone exploded into sound, and he leaped to his feet, then realized it was on the table beside him. Grasping the receiver, he sank back into the chair. "Miranda, where are you?"

"Morgan, is that you?"

"Miranda ..." he repeated, this time unsure.

"It's Ellen Ravenscroft."

"Sorry. I'm expecting a call from Miranda."

"Hasn't she turned up yet?"

"No"

"I'm sure she's okay, Morgan. She's a very resourceful lady."

"Yeah, she is."

"Headquarters relayed my call. They said you're at Griffin's."

"Yeah, waiting for Miranda."

"I've got an interesting bit of news."

"About Robert Griffin or about Eleanor Drummond? You haven't released them?"

"Of course not. Miranda's responsible for their funerals. Morgan, something crossed my strange little mind, so we pushed through some DNA tests."

"The bit Miranda sent on from the drain? Was it blood?"

"It was blood, but no, it's being processed. DNA from the bodies —"

"Eleanor Drummond is really Molly Bray."

"Morgan, Griffin and Eleanor Drummond —"

"They're both imposters?"

"No. But they're related."

"To each other?"

"He's her father."

"Whose father?"

"Robert Griffin is Eleanor Drummond's father."

"She's his daughter?"

"It works either way."

"Molly Bray, Eleanor Drummond, the woman who presented herself as Griffin's mistress, she's the man's daughter?"

"You've got it."

"I knew she had something on him. I was sure of it."

"Morgan?"

"I knew it. When Molly became Eleanor, there had to be something to account for the radical shift in power."

"Morgan, I have no idea what you're talking about."

"Sixteen years old, pregnant, Molly Bray searches the provincial records at Queen's Park. She wants to find out about herself. She finds her birth registration papers. Elizabeth Clarke told us she was listed as the mother, and her doctor friend wrote himself in as the father. Okay, but Molly would have known that was unlikely. She called her grandmother, and the woman was in her fifties when Molly was born.

"So then Molly would have researched her own name. I don't think she would have found any Brays in the Detzler's Landing area, but she was a very savvy young woman. She would have traced the name in other villages where Griffin owned mills. She would have found Brays living in one of them. And I'm betting there was an Eleanor Drummond in the Bray's family tree. So she figures Griffin is her own father as well as the father of her unborn baby. And she confronts him with the good news."

So Miranda wasn't the first, Morgan thought. Strange relief.

"I'm still trying to figure out where Detzler's Landing is, Morgan! You're talking about things I know nothing about, and it's scary. It's beginning to make a certain amount of sense, though. Not a lot, but I'm assuming she was pregnant with Jill, the girl waiting for her at the morgue. But why would she think to check out other mill locations?"

"I'm getting ahead of myself."

"Then back up a bit."

"Molly must have found information in township records, through the public library computer system, about the house where she grew up. She would have discovered it belonged to Robert Griffin. You with me?"

"Did it?"

"Yes."

"I'm with you."

"Elizabeth Clarke lived there rent free."

"And she is?"

"A lovely old woman who drinks tea that tastes like pavement. It's imported from England."

"Lapsang Suchong."

"We know Griffin bought her house in 1972, the year Molly was born. It was Elizabeth's ancestral home.

But she didn't work and she was on her own. Maybe the doctor helped her out, but when Griffin offered to buy and to let her live there free for the duration of her life, she would have jumped at the chance. In turn she looked after the baby. That was the deal."

"And Molly figured out the arrangement?"

"More so than her grandmother. Elizabeth Clarke may never have known that Griffin was the child's father. She didn't want to know. The baby was a godsend to a lonely woman."

"Not all single women are heartbroken if a baby doesn't turn up on their doorstep, Morgan."

"No, but some might be. Let's say she had a tragic love affair with the old guy, Dr. Howell. Maybe he married the wrong person, knocked up his housekeeper, and did the right thing. Then Molly became a bond between them. Genetics superseded by love. She was their child, as the certificates say. But she wasn't. When Molly left, Elizabeth knew she had never really been hers."

"That's a very sad story."

"Molly needed something more than a real-estate deal to explain the connection between Griffin and Elizabeth. She must have guessed she was the link between them. Her own name was a good place to start. That was the only thing she had from her natural mother. She had to find a Bray girl who would have been at a vulnerable age and within Griffin's reach."

"So he could seduce her?"

"Griffin didn't seduce. He raped."

"He raped the mother and he raped the daughter, and he made them both pregnant. That's quite despicable."

"It makes you want to weep for what happens in the world," Morgan said. "And it makes you enraged."

"I wonder what happened to the original mother. Do you think her name was Eleanor?"

"Probably. And her own mother's maiden name was likely Drummond. There's a strange continuity here between mothers and daughters, some related by blood, some by affection, and it's not over yet. I'd say Eleanor Bray, Molly's mother, moved on, with her past tucked away in remission. She's out there somewhere living her life. She would have checked out Elizabeth Clarke — maybe old Dr. Howell made the actual arrangements. He might even have been involved in forcing Griffin to buy the old house. Sixteen years later I don't imagine Molly much cared about tracking down her birth mother. She had no reason to be sentimental. And fourteen years after that she hoped the spiral of sex and death would collapse when she passed on responsibility for Jill to Miranda."

"Oh, my goodness, love. It's a funny old world. It's always about sex and death, at least from this perspective."

"From the morgue?"

"Story of my life. Sex and death. More of the latter, I'm afraid."

There was a long pause.

"What made you suspect he was her father?" he asked.

"Coroner's intuition. They were lying there side by side. I don't know. Him, nondescript. Her, lovely even in death. But there was something ... They had similar feet, long fingers, eye teeth the same, you know, an accumulation of details."

There was another long pause. Morgan didn't want to break the connection.

"So," Ellen said at last, "confronted with the fact that he was Molly's father, as well as being the father of her unborn child, Griffin had no choice but to look after her. It all came down to negotiating the details. And she became his mistress …"

"I doubt it."

"And the murder-suicide, suicide-murder — all this, Morgan, doesn't explain that."

"No, there's a huge gap between motive and intent. The intention? Well, she was confident we'd discover Jill's parentage. So, to ensure that Jill was recognized as Griffin's heir, to protect her daughter's interests, and at the same time to keep Jill from finding out that her father was also her mother's father, she counted on us to be just good enough at our jobs to reveal and obscure as directed, from beyond the grave. Motivation? Why start the ball rolling? It's a mystery."

"Gap? It's more like a yawning abyss! The woman killed herself in the most horrendous way, Morgan. To endure such appalling pain, to put herself through that, there had to be something unthinkably worse that she was trying to obscure."

"Yeah," said Morgan. "There's more to the story. Where the hell is Miranda?"

"I gotta go. My clients are getting impatient. You take care now. She'll turn up one way or another. She always does."

Morgan sank deeper into the cushions of the wing-back chair, aching from Miranda's absence, wanting to toss these latest revelations and speculations around with her to see if she could sort them out, take them farther. His anxiety was becoming more focused, and curiously, as he worried about her, he needed her warmth to assuage his fears. Caught up in anxiety, he was hardly aware of where he was, and virtually went limp at the sudden sound of a voice out of nowhere.

"Well, don't we look cozy."

It wasn't the utterance of a fiend or mischievous sprite but merely Mrs. de Cuchilleros speaking from an alarmingly unexpected position behind him.

"Hello, Detective Morgan! I thought you were outside."

"No," he said without looking around. "I'm not." He needed a moment to construct in his mind what was happening. "Please come around where I can see you," he finally said, remaining seated in the chair.

"Yes, certainly," she responded cheerfully. "I would be happy to. I knew you were here somewhere. I wanted to speak to you."

"How did you get in, Mrs. de Cuchilleros?"

"Through the tunnel, dear. Come along, Dolores. Dolores came with me, of course. I wouldn't come alone."

Morgan was nearly as disconcerted when the maid came into view and stood beside Mrs. de Cuchilleros, who had made herself comfortable on the sofa. He felt foolish. He hadn't conceived of the passage between houses as going both ways.

"It's not the easiest route," he suggested.

"Oh, but it is, and here we are."

"Do you often do this?"

"No. Not since my husband died. One time Mr. De Cuchilleros thought there might be burglars. Mr. Griffin was away, of course."

"You must have been compelled to examine the place thoroughly."

"Oh, yes, we went through the entire house."

I'm sure you did, he thought. "Did you have a weapon?"

"Good grief, no. Just a flashlight. The late Mr. de Cuchilleros was a very accomplished boxer."

"Boxer?"

"When he was a youth."

"Good thing you didn't run into a burglar."

"Oh, yes, it would have been very unpleasant. My husband was a strong man even at seventy. He had an excellent physique. He lifted dumbbells every morning of our married life."

"Mrs. de Cuchilleros, could you explain why you're here? This is a crime scene."

"We're not going to contaminate anything, dear."

"That's not the point."

"The Chinese boy is walking about like he owns the place."

"Mr. Nishimura is a man, and he's Japanese. He's a Canadian of very long standing, he's an authority in his field, and he belongs here by invitation of the police and the executor of the deceased."

"Well, I wanted to speak to you personally."

"Perhaps we should go outside," said Morgan as he rose to his feet and shepherded the two women through the French doors.

"It's chilly out here," Mrs. de Cuchilleros said.

Dolores looked at her sympathetically but didn't offer her cardigan, seeming to know the gesture would be wasted. Since Morgan didn't offer his own jacket, the old woman braced her shoulders and marched over to the pool where her neighbour's body had been floating when she discovered it from her aerie next door. She waited for her maid and Morgan to catch up, then made a declaration. "Dolores and I cleaned out the leaves."

"You what!" Morgan was annoyed both at her presumption and at the triviality of her announcement.

"Dolores and I cleaned out the leaves."

"You came here?"

"Early this morning, and we raked the leaves off the

top of his pond." She paused for dramatic effect, then pointed at the green pond. "That one." Ominously, she added, "It looks like mine ... on the surface."

"You've done this before?" asked Morgan, irritated by the way she was trying to position herself in a drama with pregnant pauses and curious inflections.

"I've only been here ... once ... since poor Mr. Griffin was found dead in his fish pond."

"They're all fish ponds."

"Oh, no. I would say the two greenish ponds are ponds with fish in them and this one, where he was floating, that's a fish pond."

"Fair enough," Morgan said, appreciating the distinction. "Did you come here through the house?"

"Yes, but we didn't disturb anything. He had more leaves on his pond than we ever have in ours. It's the trees, you know, and the wind. So I could see his needed caring for and I wanted to be neighbourly."

"You did?"

"Yes, I did. Dolores came over with me and we skimmed all the leaves, but a few were waterlogged, and when Dolores tried to scoop them up, they sank. That's when we discovered it."

"Discovered what?"

"The discrepancy."

"Mrs. de Cuchilleros, what are you talking about?"

"Be patient, Detective. Dolores's net went down so deep in the water she reached the end of the long handle and could just scrape the bottom."

"And?"

"And nothing. You see, that's the point!"

He didn't see, and nodded a solemn invitation for the comic relief to proceed.

"Well, we went home and had our morning tea.

But then I began thinking. I asked Dolores if the pond froze around the edges last winter. Our pond, I'm talking about. It seems to come closer to freezing each year. Didn't I ask you that, Dolores? And what did you say?"

"It seems to come closer to freezing each year," the maid said.

"Mrs. de Cuchilleros —"

"Detective, you're in such a hurry. I told Dolores we had to get a long pole. So we went out into the carriage house and found a long bamboo pole. And just as I suspected, our pond wasn't as deep! That's why it's been freezing up."

"Mrs. de Cuchilleros, where is this going?"

She smiled.

The old woman had read Agatha Christie, Morgan thought. She knew how these things worked. Pacing was as important as the details being revealed.

"Detective Morgan, the bottom of our pond is lumpy. The bottom of Mr. Griffin's pond is smooth."

Morgan was uneasy. He cocked an eye quizzically and waited for an unpleasant denouement.

"So there we are, Detective, prodding away with the pole, but it broke. We couldn't get hold of anything. Then a few bits of plastic floated up."

"From the lumpy bottom?"

"That's how we would describe it, isn't it, Dolores? Our pond, not Mr. Griffin's."

The maid nodded ambiguously. Dolores appeared to be more and more reticent as the story unfolded, as if she might avoid some grotesque revelation through affected indifference.

"Dolores," Morgan pressed, "what do you think is down there in your pond, in the de Cuchilleros pond?"

"I don't know, sir."

"I'll tell you what's down there," said Mrs. de Cuchilleros.

"All right. What do you think is down there?"

"Dead bodies."

Morgan had been afraid she would say that. He looked at the Filipino maid for confirmation and grimaced when she receded into inscrutability. In contrast Mrs. de Cuchilleros seemed to rise more and more with each passing moment to the role fate had cast upon her as central protagonist in a drama of unimaginable proportions. A small facet of Morgan's mind clung to the serio-comic performance, even as a suffocating fear rose inside him for what lay ahead, a dread that must inevitably connect with Miranda's disappearance.

Mrs. de Cuchilleros smiled solemnly, the way people did at funerals, and lowered her voice to a whisper as if she feared being overheard by the dead. "I felt down there with a rake — we taped a garden rake onto the handle of a hoe — and I could feel things. They felt slippery and mucky. We stirred up a lot of clay. There are bodies covered in silt and clay and wrapped in plastic. I didn't want to puncture anything, so I let the rake slide around, but I could feel them. I don't know whether they're cut up into pieces or not. It's hard to tell with a rake."

Morgan grasped for alternative explanations, but nothing took hold. Details and patterns careened through his brain in slow motion as if he were in a car spinning out of control and a part of his mind was poised off to the side, waiting to see how everything turned out.

Griffin had forced himself on Miranda. Before that, on Molly's mother, and after, on Molly, his own daughter. This history alone, foreshortened by the intensity of the moment, seemed proof of the man's rapacious depravity. A whole range of ghastly scenarios radiated out

from the probability that Robert Griffin was responsible
for multiple murders and that Eleanor Drummond had
known about his homicidal proclivities.

Molly Bray had become part of her assailant's world.
She had brought up her daughter with Griffin's resources
and assumed strange authority in his life. Was her control not only through using the sordid particulars of her
birth like a weapon, but in knowing he was a serial killer, knowledge that would implicate her in his crimes? If
power corrupted, wielding power over evil might corrupt
absolutely.

Morgan was intrigued, as his ideas coalesced, that
he had immediately accepted the explanation offered by
Mrs. de Cuchilleros for the unnatural contours at the
bottom of her pond. There was a ghastly inevitability
to the revelation of profligate death. The bodies, he was
sure, were there.

And Miranda was part of the equation, an inextricable and vital link between Molly and her mother, between Molly and her daughter. Among the convoluted
relations revealed about daughters and fathers, the release
of Miranda's suppressed memories was strategic. Molly,
playing with death like a puppeteer, had died with the conviction that Miranda would fiercely protect Jill's interests.

Morgan turned directly to face Mrs. de Cuchilleros.
"We'll drain the ponds. We can do yours from over here.
I believe they connect."

"Oh, my goodness!" she gasped. "Really?"

She was stunned, faced with the sudden possibility
that what she imagined was real. It was as if she had
been anticipating the relief of being scolded and sent
home. Morgan's response had thrown her into giddy
confusion. She grasped Dolores by the arm, obviously
wanting to withdraw.

"My goodness is right," said Morgan. "You've been a great help."

Mrs. de Cuchilleros seemed to have suddenly aged, and Dolores glanced furtively around like an anxious tourist yearning for something familiar.

"You should leave now and make sure the door in the tunnel isn't locked. The police will need to get back and forth. And please unlatch your gate so we have access from the street."

"I don't know what we've got ourselves into, Dolores. Come along now. It was very nice talking to you, Detective Morgan."

He grimaced at the woman's genteel formality as the old woman took her accomplice by the arm to steady herself. Leaning precariously forward, they made their way to the French doors and disappeared into Griffin's den.

Mrs. de Cuchilleros's closing words drifted back to him. "I believe we both need a nice cup of Tippi Assam."

Morgan forced his way through the undergrowth outside the pump room and rapped on the glass of the low window to summon Eugene Nishimura. Then he went back to the formal pool and watched the fish weaving colours in the transparent depths. When Nishimura appeared, they both gazed into the water as Morgan explained the situation, looking up at each other several times to confirm the horror of their expectations.

They discussed how best to drain the slime-green water. The simplest thing, Nishimura suggested, was to pump it over the bank from Griffin's pond. Assuming they were connected, that would empty the de Cuchilleros pond with the least disturbance. They would have to check both ponds, anyway, smooth bottom or not. Nishimura had a portable two-inch pump in his van that could keep ahead of the natural seepage.

Eugene Nishimura got started on that while Morgan went in to call headquarters. He explained to Alex Rufalo that he thought he had multiple human remains and asked the superintendent to notify the coroner's office.

After he got off the phone, he walked through the tunnel and out into the de Cuchilleros garden. The water level in the widow's pond was already beginning to recede. He called over the wall to Nishimura but couldn't be heard above the sputtering of the pump's gasoline engine. Shrugging, he went back to Griffin's place to check that Nishimura was removing the fish, which he was, transferring them to the formal pool.

Morgan returned to watch the water drop slowly down the clay edges of the de Cuchilleros pond. He splashed the water periodically with a rake to make sure the fish swam through to the Griffin side. Turning, he saw Mrs. de Cuchilleros and Dolores, side by side in the dining-room window, each of them holding a bone china cup of Tippi Assam. He waved and they waved back.

By the time a lump at the bottom of the pool emerged into open air, the place was swarming with police personnel, a forensic team, an emergency unit from the fire department, and a squad of coroner's people, including Ellen Ravenscroft, to whom he nodded without speaking.

Everyone watched in horror as the water receded and the extent of the atrocities became apparent. At first it looked like a series of clay drumlins rising from the depths, the long thin deposits of silt from a glacial retreat. As glistening contours of limbs and torsos and heads took shape, Morgan grieved. He mourned because no one had missed these girls and women enough to resolve the circumstances of their disappearances.

Just as he had immediately accepted that Robert Griffin was a serial killer, Morgan knew with certainty that the man's victims were female. How many had gone missing each year from the streets, how many would have leaped at a ride in a sleek convertible, driven by a man getting on in age who would easily be satisfied and undoubtedly generous? He might just want to bring them home to talk.

Someone turned a hose on the pile with a gentle spray. Morgan's assumption that they were female was confirmed as body after body separated in the wash from the mass, each of them wrapped naked with plastic sheeting and duct tape, in various stages of dilapidation. Their flesh seemed shrivelled to the bone despite the water. Decay had been arrested and the effects of putrefaction had been controlled by the clay silt that shrouded each body in layers stirred up by the fish, season by season over years, and by the coldness of the water and its continuous flow through the soil, leaching through the embankment into the ravine.

Morgan felt an overwhelming loneliness. It should never have happened this way to these human beings, most of whom were known only to God. He was drawn, he wanted to hold them, and he was repelled by what they revealed of human depravity and the human condition. Morgan gazed away, up into the foliage of the silver maples, then down into the gaping hole. His eyes were dry, his mouth was dry. He could taste his own blood.

On impulse he looked around and saw that Mrs. de Cuchilleros and Dolores were absent from the window, but striding toward him from the direction of the door below the carriage house was the young woman he had last seen at the morgue. Before he could stop her she was at his side. He tried to steer her away from the hellish scene, but she was focused on him. Her eyes were raw and her expression was resolute. She had clearly been coping with demons of her own.

"Jill, for goodness' sake, you shouldn't be here!" he declared.

"I need you to come with me, Mr. Morgan."

"Jill, I can't. Wait for me over at Griffin's. Tell them I said it's okay. You should be at home."

She pulled on his arm. "Please, you have to come."

She wasn't a young woman; she was a terrified child.

When he resisted, she turned and peered into the gaping hole at the tangle of bodies, and emitted an involuntary moan of pure anguish. Morgan gazed down at her, confused by her unflinching refusal to look away and by the incomprehensible pain she seemed almost to share with the dead. He put his arm around her, intending to guide her back up the lawn.

Abruptly, she took the lead and drew him toward the door leading into the tunnel. He stopped at the darkness and indicated the scene behind them. "Did you know about this?" he asked.

"I knew there were others."

"Others?"

She pulled away from him. "Mr. Morgan, you must come with me. Now."

Jill wheeled about, striding ahead of him through the tunnel. When they emerged in the den, instead of taking the bypass that led directly into the bowels of the labyrinth, he expected she would lead him to the garden. But she turned and entered the corridor and went past the big door that was slightly ajar from Nishimura's comings and goings. She walked past the bathroom, with Morgan two paces behind, so that he had to step back when she swung open the second big door and plunged into the gloom.

Unexpectedly, she veered to the right. They hurried past several side passages and stopped at the wine cellar.

The key was in the lock where she had left it. She turned the key and pulled back on the massive door. Morgan helped her, then stepped around her into the rank darkness as she fiddled with the switch. There was a snapping sound, and the room suddenly flared into light. He squinted at the filthy rumple of sheets on the bed. With horror he realized what he was looking at. He lunged forward, stopped, pulled the sheets gingerly aside, and gazed down at Miranda's tortured body.

Morgan dropped to his knees beside her, reaching tentatively to touch her forehead, which felt clammy and colder than the air. He raised her against his chest and cradled her carefully like a broken thing, examining the fissures of dried blood extending from her mouth in grisly contrast to her taunt and sallow skin. Morgan breathed deeply against her, trying to quell the rising panic, trying to breathe for her, too, as if his own vitality could be passed between them.

"Is she okay?" Jill's voice was tremulous.

There was an interminable silence. Morgan shuddered, holding Miranda close. He leaned down so that his cheek pressed against hers.

"Is she alive?"

Morgan looked up at the girl without pulling away. His eyes glistened. He lowered his gaze, then closed his eyes. Tears appeared at the corners, gathered, slid down his cheeks. He rocked her gently, and a humming dissonance emerged from his lips. The sound of his involuntary keening startled him. Returning his attention to Jill, he said in a low voice, "Get water. A doctor. Ask for Ellen Ravenscroft."

"Where?" Jill asked, confused.

"Out where the bodies are. She's over there. Hurry, Jill."

The girl disappeared, and Morgan shifted his grasp on Miranda, lowering her weight back to the bed. Then, still kneeling, he placed one hand on her head and lightly mussed her hair while with the back of his other hand, tentatively, as if afraid he could damage her, he stroked her cheek.

She had to be alive. He knew she was alive despite the room being permeated with the presence of death. Morgan focused wholly on her. She needed his strength; she was strong. He thought of how close he had been over the past few days, relaxed in the den, standing casually outside the door, looking in, seeing nothing.

Morgan spoke softly to her. He thought of how he had let her down, not searching, not finding her, not acting on his concern. He had failed her. Morgan concentrated only on her, urging her to respond, to rise from the depths of her suffering and be with him again. Her skin clung to her skull, her torn lips were an untended wound. He leaned down and placed his own lips on hers and remained like that, breathing her air, breathing for her. Then, from deep within her body, a sound slowly rose to her mouth.

"Morgan … you're smothering me."

"Oh, my God, Miranda, my God!"

He pulled back. Her eyes opened in the shadows of his body, but as he twisted away to see her, they were battered by the light. She squinted, the lids of her eyes wavering heavily, then she opened them wide.

"Oh, my God!" he repeated.

Her voice scraped against her bloodied mouth. "Morgan …"

Jill came rushing through the door, a mug of water

in her hand. "The doctor's on her way. She's coming. Is Miranda all right? Miranda! Did she speak?"

Jill knelt beside them. Morgan reached to take the mug, but Jill held it away, refusing to release it. Leaning over him, she poured a few drops between Miranda's lips. Miranda struggled to find the girl's eyes, and then the corners of her own eyes crinkled. Her lips made a gesture, but they were crusted and she painfully whispered, "Jill ... I'm smiling."

"I know," said Jill. She tried to smile back, to fight away tears.

Morgan picked up on the intimations of a complex narrative between girl and woman that their nearly wordless exchange brought to some kind of resolution. He recognized Jill was responsible for Miranda's entombment, but whatever had traumatized the girl to such an extreme had been, through Miranda's ordeal, transformed into a shared experience that bound them together. *All in good time,* he thought. *It will make sense all in good time.*

He cradled Miranda while Jill poured her another few drops, knowing instinctively not to give her too much. Miranda coughed dryly, choking, then nodded for more. Jill tilted the mug, and Miranda drank a full mouthful, then fell back into Morgan's arms.

In a voice that seemed to tear at her throat, cracking open her wounded lips so that droplets of fresh blood glistened in the bright light, she murmured, "I was dreaming —"

"For God's sake, don't talk," Morgan cautioned.

"Underwater dreams ..." She took a long, shallow breath, exhaled slowly, releasing all the air from her lungs, then inhaled again, her head lolling back as she tried to bring him into focus. "Will you ... with me?"

"What?"

"Under ... water," she said with throaty deliberation, then breathed deeply through her nose and relaxed, pleased with her effort.

He grinned and rocked her gently against his body.

From the corridor they heard Ellen Ravenscroft calling, "Morgan, are you here? My God, this is a terrible place! Where are you?"

He called back, and they heard her continue to mutter as she approached. "What the hell's going on? I've got bodies out there. This place is a bloody crypt, Morgan. I've got work to do. It's bad enough —" From the door she spotted Miranda. "Oh, my God, Miranda! What happened? What's going on?" Then her voice took on sudden authority. "Morgan, let the poor woman lie back so she can breathe. Here, girl, give me the water!"

Jill and Morgan backed away, but only a little. Ellen quietly examined Miranda, who didn't try to speak at first. After a while, Miranda rasped, "Bedside manners ... appalling."

"I'm used to more passive clients. What do you expect?"

"Sorry," said Miranda. "I'm ... I'm not dead."

"That's all right, love. You were close enough."

There was silence. Ellen explored Miranda's entire body, not healing from the laying on of hands but drawing life from within. It was a form of magic, Morgan thought. A form of love.

"You'll pull through," said Ellen at last. "You need fluids, my love, and lots of affection." She turned to Jill. "Girl, go and —"

"Her name's Jill," said Morgan.

"My name is Jill," the girl echoed.

"Sorry, love. I didn't know you were a friend of the family. Go and find the emergency unit. They look like firemen. Tell them Dr. Ravenscroft needs a saline drip pronto. Tell them I've got a live one." Ellen leaned over Miranda, and Morgan knelt beside her. "How the hell did this happen, Morgan? Where the hell were you? Your partner was near enough dead we'll have to cancel the wake."

"Not funny," whispered Miranda.

"Coroner humour, my love."

Miranda gagged and coughed what sounded like a prolonged death rattle, and her eyes rolled back into her skull. She closed her eyes, then opened them with a mischievous glint. "Cop humour," she said.

Morgan stepped back. Miranda searched for him, and as Ellen bantered, she reached out, drawing him closer, her hand trembling from the effort. He took her hand in both of his.

"I did it myself," she said in an unexpectedly strong voice. "I locked myself in. It wasn't your fault, Morgan."

"Well, you left the key in the door, love," said Ellen. "That's a hard one to figure."

"Don't try," Miranda said, pausing to swallow against the pain in her throat. "Morgan, you got me through this …"

"Where there's lust there's life," quipped Ellen.

Miranda lay back, too exhausted to respond. Morgan felt emotionally depleted.

"Sorry, Morgan," Ellen said. "It was dumb scolding you. Nerves. I'm not used to life *and* death, just death. She's going to pull through."

"Damn right," murmured Miranda without opening her eyes.

Jill returned with a medic, who was carrying equipment for the saline drip. He went about setting up the stand while Ellen inserted an IV needle into Miranda's forearm. The medic didn't ask what was going on. When he was finished, he exchanged glances with Ellen to see if she needed anything else, then left without speaking a word.

"Taciturn fellow, but very efficient," Ellen said.

Once she hooked up the drip and regulated the flow, she pulled the chair close beside the bed and arranged Miranda's hands over her breast, gently resting her own hand over Miranda's. She sent Jill for more water and at intervals poured small amounts through Miranda's lips, which had become swollen, restoring their elasticity and relieving the discomfort a little.

As the deathly pallor of her complexion slowly receded, Miranda imagined she could feel the entire inventory of her internal organs rearranging themselves, one by one, for further use.

After hooking up a second bag of intravenous solution, Ellen said to Morgan, "I've slowed down the drip. I've got to get back out there. It's a miserable scene. Give her a couple of more litres. I'll be back with the talkative guy in a bit, and we'll get her to a hospital. But she's coming around. Everything seems to be functioning. I don't often see this in my line of work — the coming-around part."

She turned to Miranda. "Bye-bye, love." Then she looked at Jill. "Thanks, Jill, for your help. We brought her back, didn't we?" As she went through the door, she said to Morgan, "I think you'd be a great partner, Morgan. I really do." She paused for dramatic effect. "Did you hear that, Miranda? You've got a great partner."

Miranda muttered something inaudible.

Morgan and Jill stood side by side, watching droplets of saline solution gather and flow through the tubes. Miranda appeared to drift into a peaceful slumber.

Reaching into his pocket, Morgan retrieved the Zippo and handed it to Jill. She took it gingerly as if it were hot. Then, with a practised motion, she flicked it open and spun the flint wheel into life. A blue-and-orange flame hovered about the wind shield, and she let the fire burn until her fingers were seared. Snapping it closed with a single click, she handed it back to Morgan.

"I don't want it," she whispered.

He smiled and slipped it into his pocket, flinching as he felt the hot metal against his thigh. They turned again to watch Miranda as the life flowed back through her veins.

In the solitude of their vigil the man and the girl were engaged in shifting moral paradigms. Morgan's sense of responsibility was being subsumed by his relief that Miranda was okay. But still he felt grinding anxiety, perhaps for the women who had died.

Jill was thrilled by Miranda's survival. Guilt faded rapidly, abandoned like remnants of a chrysalis after the release of a butterfly into the world. She felt curiously beautiful and free.

They looked away from the plastic tubes at each other, both a little embarrassed by the closeness they felt through Miranda.

As if roused by their awkwardness, Miranda spoke without opening her eyes. The painful constriction in her throat had eased enough from the intravenous that her words were clearer. "Morgan's going scuba diving with me," she announced. She exhaled and inhaled in long, deliberate breaths, then appeared to drift off again into sleep.

Morgan surveyed the room. He was appalled at the depravity — to devise such a place was beyond comprehension. Jill tugged on his shoulder. He turned and for the first time focused on the letters scrawled in swathes of dried blood on the wall. Silently, Jill mouthed the words over and over: "I am Miranda Quin."

Miranda opened her eyes, squinting and blinking against the light. She tried to sit up but fell back and settled deeper against the mattress. Morgan reached for the emptied mug from the table and poured the last few drops between her lips.

"Thank you for finding me, Morgan. I knew you would."

"Jill found you. She brought me here."

"You both found me then."

Miranda felt the fluids flow through her body, filling the empty dry places, displacing the pain. She could almost talk normally, and raised her head enough to peer at herself. "My God, Morgan, I stink."

"Nice underwear," he said. "Victoria's Secret?"

Her lips broke into a crooked smile. She looked from him to Jill and back again. "There's a house I want to show you." She licked blood from her lips. The blood and saliva were soothing. "The house where I grew up. I want to show you both."

"Don't talk," said Morgan.

"Jill," Miranda said.

The girl came closer and knelt beside her, leaning into Morgan for support. "Miranda?"

"Jill, there's someone we want you to meet."

The girl seemed puzzled.

"You have a grandmother. She'll want to know all about you."

"I have a grandmother?"

"You were named after her …"

"Go on," Jill urged.

"Elizabeth Clarke — she's your great-grandmother, really, and she's a lovely old lady." Miranda settled back into Morgan's embrace, and reaching out, took hold of the girl's hand. "You have a family, Jill. That's a promise." She glanced up at her partner. "Everything okay, Morgan?"

"Everything's okay."

"For goodness' sake!"

"Yeah, for goodness' sake."

March / 2013

One of the cutest
Books I've ever read